THE BEAST LORD

JULIETTE CROSS

For Kevin, my beloved

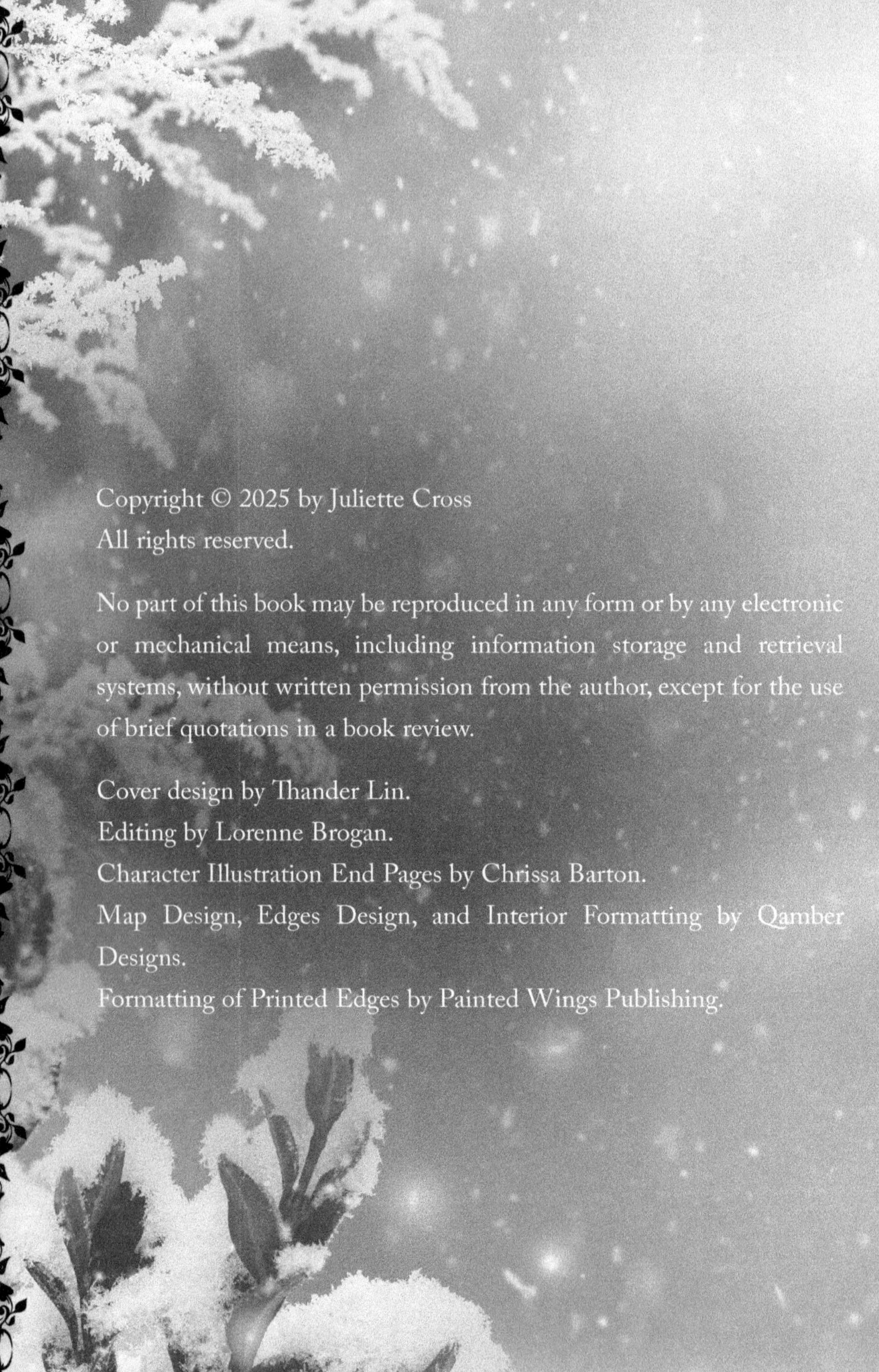

ACKNOWLEDGMENTS

I would like to thank my lovely readers for their compassionate
encouragement and support. Your devotion means
the world to me.

SOLGAVIA MOUNTAINS
Solzkin's Heart
MEERLAND
Vanglosa
LAKE MOREEN
PELLASIAN PLAINS
BLUEVALE RIVER
Valla Lokkyr

WYKEN WOODS
Láveen Orla
Ghasta Vale
THE SISTERS
BORDERLANDS
Nævhail Glen
JÔHL TUNDRA
NORTHGALL

THE MYTH OF THE EARTH DEMON

Once, there was a young female wood fae who was kind and beloved by everyone. When she was suddenly struck by a horrible sickness, everyone in her village was distressed by her misfortune. But none more than her beloved husband Kamzel who loved her more than life itself. He was helpless with despair at her wasting away with illness. He summoned all the healers, and even a sorceress to help him, but still his wife withered and faded day by day.

One evening, when he could not bear the sound of her dying breaths a moment longer, he fled into the deep woods and flung himself to the ground beneath the stars. He begged the gods, any god, to help him save his dear wife.

Suddenly, a large figure shrouded in an ebony cloak appeared from the shadows and loomed over Kamzel, his red eyes piercing.

"Did you summon me, faeling?" His voice boomed.

"I b-begged for anyone to hear my prayers, great one."

"You are fortunate that I, Näkt, heard your pleas. For I am the most powerful of my brothers and sisters."

Kamzel thanked him profusely, for it was known that the God of Night truly was one of the greatest and most superior of the gods.

"What would you give for the life of your wife?" he asked.

"Anything, my lord," answered Kamzel foolishly.

"Then bring me the babe of a dryad. If you do so, then I will heal your wife, and you will live long years together until you both are gray and old."

Kamzel hesitated as he lifted his gaze up to the looming god, his face hidden beneath a mantle.

"What will you do with the child?" Kamzel asked in a shaking voice.

To which the god answered, "If it saves your wife, does it matter?" The god then vanished, leaving the husband with dark thoughts and darker desires.

A dryad was a creature of the light, like himself. However, they were touched with special magick by Elska, the Goddess of the Wood, and were given long life. They rarely gave birth for the gods did not like long-living creatures to be bountiful as well. The price for their near immortality was to reproduce very rarely.

Furthermore, it was known that taking a babe from a dryad or naiad meant death. The child could not survive without the magick of their mother coursing through them as a swaddling. Could he murder one of his own to save his beloved wife?

Kamzel hurried home, distraught, and knelt at the bed of his beloved. She tossed and turned, drenched in the sweat of her sickness, calling out his name in hoarse whispers. He slept at her side, falling into a nightmare where his lovely wife was devoured by death, her ghost chasing him with banshee screams.

When he woke, he knew what he must do, though his heart shrank from it. He crept out into the forest, using his skills as a woodsman to find a coven of dryads in a sycamore grove. It was known that they often nested in the giant, knotted trees amongst the thick foliage of leaves. He did indeed hear the creaky cry of an infant and took the child, replacing it with a wooden figure he had carved to trick the mother until he escaped the forest.

He did not think as he took the mewling bundle, its spindly, twig-like fingers reaching out of the swaddling. But Kamzel thought only of his beloved wife and ran until the child mewled no longer, until its body was still in his arms and he set the still bundle on the very spot where he'd met Näkt the night before.

"Here is the sacrifice!" he yelled, crying tears of shame for what he' had done.

The dark god appeared, bellowing with laughter as he snatched up the bundle and then swallowed it whole. His aura of power shivered around him, magnifying with the pure blood of the magick-rich babe.

"How could you do that!" screamed Kamzel. "He was just a wee child."

"I believe it was a girl," corrected the dark figure. "And you were the one who killed her by bringing her to me."

"I did not know you were such a cruel, heartless god," cried Kamzel, weeping for what the god had done, for what *he* had done.

"That is because I am not Näkt." He tossed back his hood, revealing his six-horned head, jagged fangs, and cruel, monstrous face. A face that Kamzel could hardly look upon. The figure was not Näkt at all, but the trickster earth demon Dagdal, the sinister, outcast son of the god Vix.

"Dagdal," whispered Kamzel.

"Thank you for the meal, faeling. The bright lights always taste sweetest."

Kamzel fled from his evil presence instantly. Dagdal's echoing laughter chased him as he tried to escape his wicked sin.

Unable to live with the shame and guilt, Kamzel fled to the Temple of Vix and confessed his transgression against the light fae.

It is not known what happened to Kamzel after that. Some say that the gods forgave him and he lived a long life, childless, but happy with his wife. Others say that his wife died because of his sin, and he killed himself with the grief of it. Some say that his wife lived, but the dryads found and killed Kamzel in his bed next to her. For everyone knows that the dryads are vengeful creatures.

But one legend that rings true in both light and dark fae lore is that the mighty god Vix heard Kamzel's confession. Furious, he dragged his son Dagdal deep, deep into the mountains and bound him there, held in place by a god's spell so that he would menace the fae creatures of the world no longer. Since he bore the touch of immortality from his father, he would remain chained in his cold, dark prison for eternity.

Some say that Dagdal cried out to his father and swore he would be free again one day. And that when he was, he would eat all the bright lights in the world until there was nothing left but darkness…and death.

This has been the story told to the light fae children for many ages. Mothers would warn their misbehaving faelings, "Be good or Dagdal will get you and eat you." The story has kept naughty children obedient for centuries. And though this frightening and sad story has been told throughout time, no one gave much thought to whether or not it was true.

CHAPTER 1

Jessamine

"Colder than a witch's tit, I tell ya," groused the old wraith fae as he guzzled the warm, spiked cider I'd set in front of him. He was a trapper, for certain, judging by the string of pelts he'd dragged into the tavern with him, not trusting any criminals about to leave them outside with his horse and cart. His two horns curled back out of his head, the tips coated with ice, as were the tips of his pointed ears.

Laughing, I added, "Good thing you avoided the worst of the weather. Haldek's made a hearty venison stew."

The wraith fae set his tankard down with a loud belch. "Pardon. Been in the woods too long. Needed that, I did." He leaned toward me conspiratorially. "Bring me a bowl filled to the very top and there's an extra coin in it for ya." He gave me a wink.

I glanced over my shoulder to where Haldek was waiting on a table in the corner then whispered to the trapper, "I'll cut your slice of bread a bit bigger, too, eh?"

"Thatta girl," he chuckled, lifting his tankard again. Before he took another sip, he eyed me carefully. "What's a pretty fae girl like you doing in these parts?"

I couldn't count the number of times curious customers had asked me that. The Borderlands housed all kinds of fae—dark and light alike—but never had I seen one of my own kind so far from the Nemian Sea. That was exactly why I'd chosen it. It was a rough line of territory separating the Lumerian lands of the light fae from Northgall where the dark fae lived. It was made up of randomly situated inns, taverns, and a few mills, where any and all fae traveled and did business.

"I want to see all parts of the world. I'm just here to make a bit of money then I'll be traveling on soon enough."

It was somewhat the truth. I'd been here for months, but I was biding my time and saving my coin before I had to find another small village where I could hide.

"An adventurer, are you?" He grinned, revealing his long canines. "Like me, I'd say. You speak demon tongue pretty good for a foreigner."

Smiling, I replied with pride, "I studied many languages with my tutor."

I always thought my magickal gift to speak to naiads in their language had made it easier to learn other tongues. The dark fae language commonly called demon tongue had come to me almost as naturally as my native language, high fae.

"An educated girl, too."

He raised a clawed finger, his gray skin pale from the cold, then he reached over to the bench at his side where his pile of furs sat. He pulled out a narrow, white pelt and handed it to me.

"How about you take this for your extra efforts on my behalf?"

I took the small but very fine, silky pelt. "Oh, I couldn't. That's worth far more than good service." I gave him a smile and handed it back.

"You take it, girl. It would make a fine pair of gloves for those little hands of yours." He frowned as he stared at my hands. "Just be mindful you measure for your, uh…" He gestured toward my webbed fingers.

"Thank you." I smiled at him. "It's very generous of you."

The color filled his cheeks, his skin darkening to a deeper gray. He was blushing.

"Well, it's not often I can get a pretty girl to smile like that at me. Besides," his voice turned serious, "the elkmine otter's hide is as soft as the fur. Touch it and see."

I flipped the pelt over and ran my fingertips over the underside of the hide. "Wow, you're right."

"Hmph," he grunted with confidence. "Trust me. Those will keep your dainty fingers warm, girl." He gave me another wink. "The gods have been good. I got me a good prize of them. I can go home and rest till summer now."

"Let me get that warm stew for you then." I tucked the otter pelt into my apron pocket. "You'll need it for the trek home, I imagine."

"Aye. Not too far to go, but far enough."

I hurried back through the small tavern, which was quieter than usual with very few customers out in this kind of weather. Haldek was in the kitchen when I entered, ladling stew into two bowls for the table he was serving.

"The old trapper always makes a stop here before returning home," he told me as I stepped up to pour my customer's bowl.

"Does he?" I asked.

Haldek was a wraith fae as well, with four black horns instead of two curling out of his head. He was a brawny male, which served him well being a tavern-keeper in the Borderlands. I'd seen him break up a fight between two shadow fae once with barely any effort at all. And he'd been more than kind to me, never asking why I'd come here or why I'd decided to be so far from my own kind. For that, I respected him most of all.

"Aye," he said, setting his bowls on wooden plates with thick slices of buttered, brown bread. "But he's come a bit early. The snow must have cut his trapping off too soon."

I dipped the ladle into the bubbling pot of stew hanging over the fire spit. "He's had a good run, it seems, even if he was cut short."

"Good for the old one," he added as he carried out his platters of food.

After I set the brimming bowl of stew on the platter, I cut two thick slices of the brown bread, and then a wedge of sharp cheese to put on the side plate with extra pats of butter. That old trapper needed sustenance if he was heading back out in this weather. The snows had come early.

I carried his meal to the table. He grunted with appreciation as I set the bowl and each plate in front of him.

"Now that's what I call a feast." He dug in hungrily.

Smiling, I asked, "Can I get anything else for you right now?"

He heaved back and tapped his tankard. "I'm afraid I'll have to bother you for another of these, soon as you can."

"No trouble at all." I took his tankard and headed back into the kitchen.

Haldek kept his regular barrels of ale and mead behind the bar in the dining hall, but his special cider had to be heated over the fire. After pouring another tankard for the trapper in the kitchen, I pushed the door open back into the dining hall, completely oblivious until it was too late.

"Nay," Haldek was saying to the four moon fae males in the doorway with blue and golden fae wings, all of them large and armored with swords and fur cloaks. But most specifically, all of them wearing the sapphire and silver colors of Mevian royalty, their lord's regalia. "None of that kind here."

I was frozen in the doorway, fear sinking its claws into my gut.

"We were told someone of this description—" The moon fae male who was speaking suddenly stopped when the one beside him slapped his shoulder and pointed to where I stood.

Haldek snapped his head to me, his eyes fierce. "Run!"

I dropped the tankard and spun, looking back over my shoulder to see the old trapper shoot out his walking stick and trip one of the warriors while Haldek wrestled with the others, shoving two back against the wall.

Where fear had frozen me a moment before, it now jarred me into a full run, panic spurring me on. I flew through the kitchen, around the chopping table, through the larder, and out the back door into the snowy night. Without a thought, I fled north, determined to go as far into dark fae territory as I could. I should've left months ago. I should have known they'd find me here in the Borderlands.

The dark swallowed me, the snow falling lightly now. The half-moon far above peered through the clouds, casting a pale glow on the white-covered forest floor.

"Help me," I begged the moon goddess Lumera, running faster into the woods.

Though I'd not worshipped her much in the past, she was a light fae deity. Surely, she'd have mercy on me.

My feet quickly began to numb. Though I always wore the boots Haldek had given me, made of thick deer hide, the freezing cold was seeping through. Still, I ran fast and hard, my breaths puffing out in white mist. I'd rather die in the cold than be caught and taken to Mevia.

In the far distance, I heard one of the moon fae calling, "Jessamine! You can't run forever!"

"Like hell I can't," I muttered and ran faster, snapping branches as I delved deeper into the forest where the trees grew closer together.

Before long, my feet and legs were stiff and frozen, my limbs moving automatically to take me farther away. My face stung, the tip of my nose and ears pierced with the sharp pain of cold. I couldn't feel my fingers or hands. But still, I ran.

The clouds covered the moon, darkening the forest, enveloping me in an ethereal haze. For a moment, I couldn't tell if it was the moonlight fading or if I was dying. My shoulder clipped the trunk of a tree, knocking me to the ground.

I gasped in pain, panting, my lungs stinging as I gulped down air before pushing myself back up and trudged on. My energy waned. I hadn't summoned my magick to help me see, too afraid the light would guide my enemies closer, but it seemed my body acted on instinct, more determined to save my life than I was.

Heat suffused my body as the magick ignited my blood, my skin glowing with pearlescent light. As my mind grew fuzzy, I determined that if they caught me, I could at least try to use my magick to subdue them. To kill them. But they'd have been warned about me, about what I could do, and I'd not escape all four moon fae males.

The radiance of my skin shined bright, magick pouring heat through my blood, so that I could still find my way through the forest without running into a tree again, or over a ravine. While the bitter cold beat against me, my limbs frozen to the bone, the warmth radiating outward from my chest put me into a drowsy state.

Somewhere behind me, I could hear the moon fae calling my name and saying nonsense, like they wouldn't hurt me. My mind drifted back to another time when I had run deep into the woods.

"Jessamine!" My brother called for me.

I remained crouched behind the fallen tree, nestled among the twiggy branches, determined to never go home again.

"Jessamine," Draydyn called again, closer, as he crunched over fallen leaves. "I know you're here, sister. Please come out."

"No!" I yelled, pouting where I still hid.

He chuckled and sat upon the log, his grass-green hair shining brighter than usual among the golden and red autumn foliage.

"Come out, Jessa. You know I'm your friend."

I stood up, fuming, tears streaking my cheeks. I was only twelve, but I was already terrified of my future fate. "It doesn't matter if you are. You can't stop Father."

He sighed and gestured for me to sit next to him on the log. Stepping through the fallen limbs, I climbed over the log and sat beside him, both of us facing the wide meadow, yellow instead of green at this time of year. From here, I couldn't see the sea on the other side of our castle, its spiky turrets pointing toward the sky, but I could still smell the salty air. The scent gave me comfort as I sat quietly next to Draydyn.

He wrapped a comforting arm around my shoulder. "We all have our duty to our kingdom, Jessa."

I sniffed and wiped my face with the lily-embroidered white sleeve of my day gown. Nurse would be angry that I'd gotten it dirty.

"You mean to our father," I snapped angrily.

Draydyn sighed and hugged me closer. "He only does what he thinks is best for us. And for our kingdom."

"Like sell Ada to that awful lord from Hellamir? He is a disgusting oaf. And he only wants Ada because of her magick."

My brother remained quiet for a moment. "Ada is a gifted willoden. Lord Cardyn is the highest lord in Hellamir, which is a port town. A very important one for the trade-waters. Ada will help him by controlling the waters and keep his merchants and fishermen safe. He's also very rich."

"Yes, I'm sure Father will enjoy the gold he pays for Ada," I spat angrily.

"That's not what I meant." He squeezed my shoulder again. "He will keep Ada well-protected and give her a good life. He has also shown nothing but kindness, no matter how big of an oaf he is."

"But," I whined, "he's so ugly. And she's so beautiful. How could she possibly want to go with him?"

Draydyn laughed. "From what I've seen during these past few weeks of their courtship, he has won her with his gentle and kind ways. Ada may not mind his ugliness, because his heart is good."

I thought about that for a moment. "If Ada is happy, then I am happy for her." Then I snapped my head to look up at him. "But I never want to be sold off to a man like that."

My brother looked down, his expression sympathetic, "We all have our roles, little Jessa. You have the gift of a nendovir."

I had another gift, but I was still keeping it a secret. It frightened me.

"That would come in handy for any lord of land near lakes or the sea," Draydyn added.

"Why? So I can tame the naiads for him? So he can build on their riverbanks and eat all their fish?"

Draydyn chuckled again. He did that often with me. "You only think of the worst when your temper is hot. By having the gift to speak to naiads, you could be their ambassador, bringing peace between the fae who live near their watery homes. That is a positive gift and would be an asset to any lord near the seas."

"I'm not doing it," I told him emphatically, "but I'd rather live near the seas. Or a lake would suffice."

"I know it's hard for you to understand," he said, "and I know Father is harsh sometimes. You are right when you said he didn't give Ada a choice. He rarely asks our opinions."

"Never, you mean."

He hugged me closer. "Don't worry, Jessa. I won't ever let him marry you to someone you don't like. I will always protect you."

I snapped out of the memory, colder than I was before. Draydyn had lied, not that he'd meant to. When he died last year in the war against the wraith fae, Father decided it was time I was put to use. Me and my gift as a syrenskyn, which I was unable to keep secret as a grown woman, was auctioned to the highest bidder. And the bidder who came calling had very specific plans for me. I ran away from home the next day.

I stumbled into a small clearing, the snow thick on the ground. My toe caught on a branch hidden beneath the snow and I fell sideways, knocking my head.

The woods were quiet. Fat, downy flakes drifted down from the gray sky, falling on my cheek. But I couldn't move anymore. Nothing but stillness and silence. No one called my name. No sounds of boots in the snow or wings in the air behind me. Just the barely-there whisper of snow falling to the forest floor.

Sleep began to take me once more. But this time, I wondered if it might be death instead that was freezing my limbs and hazing my mind. For some reason, I wasn't afraid at all.

As I blinked slowly, staring into the dark, a chilling, deep growl vibrated in the air. Two silvery eyes appeared, shining from the abyss, watching me. I smiled, for all I could think was that the eyes of death were quite beautiful.

CHAPTER 2

Redvyr

here did that bloody wolf get off to?

WHe often took to the woods when we came out here on our own, but he always returned when the meat was on the spit. The boar I'd killed a few days ago was all but gone, the last of the loin sizzling over the fire now.

"If you want any dinner, Wolf, you'd best get your ass home," I grumbled toward the crackling fire.

Not that this was home. We were leagues east of Vanglosa. My own tradition of leaving the clan for a solo hunt before we moved to our winter camp had always given me some inner peace, time to be on my own without the daily trials of the clan. Time to reflect on the clan's needs and how I could best serve them.

This short respite alone each year always grounded me in my duties and my role as lord of Vanglosa. But it also gave me time to reflect on the past. That was the hard part, but something

I needed to do. I couldn't ever forget where I'd come from, or *who* I'd come from.

Usually, this retreat gave me a sense of serenity that I craved. For some reason, this hunt hadn't. If anything, I felt restless, an itch under my skin. But I had no idea why. I flicked my tail in frustration, an unknowing I didn't like. Perhaps that was why Wolf had run off, sensing my restlessness and needing to be away from me. I didn't blame him.

Slicing a chunk of the pork from the spit over the fire, I chewed the juicy meat, beginning to grow slightly concerned that Wolf wasn't back yet. He'd been gone much longer than usual, and I had been sure he wouldn't stray from his dinner for too long.

There was another emotion I hadn't experienced before this year which seemed to weigh on me more than ever. Loneliness. And yet, I still wasn't yearning to return to my clan, to my people, to my warriors and friends. Perhaps it was for the best that I did. Sometimes the deep woods weren't good for the mind.

The rhythmic lope of Wolf's tracks in the snow drew my attention away from the fire and toward the shadows beyond. My beast fae senses allowed me to see well into the gloom, his ebony figure, darker than the shadows, trotting closer. But he had some sort of red cloak draped over his back.

Tossing the meat aside, I stood and rounded the fire, hands on hips. "What in all the devils are you wearing, Wolf?" I called to my approaching hound.

He loped closer, the firelight giving me a better look at whatever the hell he was carrying. I suddenly realized it wasn't a cloak, but a female. Once he'd entered the circle of light, the giant hound casting a wide shadow on the forest floor, he knelt and shimmied until the female rolled onto her back, her berry-red hair spilling around her head.

Wolf then sat on his haunches, wagging his tail, tongue lolling out of his open mouth happily. Like he'd brought me some sort of prize. For a moment, all I could do was stare down at the light fae female. I'd never seen that color of hair on any creature before. Of course, I stayed away from the light fae as much as I could. But no wood fae ever looked like that.

Her skin was nearly as pale as the snow beneath her. Her hand twitched, which dragged my attention to the webbing between her fingers.

"Fucking hells, Wolf. You've dragged a skald fae into our camp. Where the hell did you go?"

He whined and nuzzled her head. She made no movement at all though I could hear her pulse beating in her veins, her heartbeat sluggish but there.

"Well, what am I supposed to do with her?" I snapped at him. "She's a damn light fae." I pointed to the woods. "Go take her back to wherever you found her."

Wolf barked in that disobedient way of his and remained firmly by her side. As a Meer-wolf, he was a great mountain of a beast, standing as tall as a Pellasian stallion. *When* he was standing. Right now, he remained where he was, tail wagging, looming next to the small female at his side like her personal guard.

"Damned dog," I muttered, finally squatting down over her to get a better look.

Her slow heartrate wasn't a good sign.

"I'm not a fucking healer either, you bloody beast. What do you expect me to do?"

Her skin wasn't simply as pale as snow, but it appeared just as soft. I'd probably gouge her with a claw trying to help her and then she'd bleed to death, and it would be my fault. Then her people from Morodon nearby would blame me and attack my clan.

I growled. Wolf growled back.

"Shut up. I'm thinking."

Wolf then huffed and crouched down over her, biting her sleeve between his teeth and trying to drag her toward our tent.

"For fuck's sake, stop it." I stood and waved him off. "You'll tear her sleeve." Bending next to her, I scooped my arms beneath her legs and neck. "You didn't pick a smart one, I can tell you that. Some stupid fae girl wandering the woods without a cloak."

Lifting her against me, I stood and inhaled a deep whiff of her. Gods be damned, it stunned me still for a moment. Her scent was a salty sweetness completely unfamiliar to me, and yet, it drew me in. I wanted to press my nose into her unusually red hair and suck in a deep breath of her.

Tossing that feeble thought aside, I tromped away from the fire and through the tent flap. I kept blue coal burning in the tent, since it gave off no smoke and a good bit of heat. The blue glow was soothing as well in the night. Though all beast fae preferred keeping warm by an open fire, the blue coal mined by the wraith fae was an efficient source of heat inside our tents. We used it when we had it available.

It was comfortable and warm. I set the girl on top of my furs and then stood again, staring down in wonder. Wolf sat beside me, wagging his tail and staring up at me expectantly.

"If you think to be rewarded for dragging an injured light fae female into my camp, you are sorely mistaken."

Wolf licked her hand and nuzzled it, whining. I knelt next to the furs and lifted her delicate hand into mine. The contrast between her kind and mine was remarkably clear when I held her small, fair hand in my much larger, calloused one.

"She's cold."

Wolf yipped, and I swear the beast rolled his eyes at me.

"Yes, I know she is. I'm just stating it aloud. You don't have to get such an attitude. She was obviously caught out in the storm somehow. She's no beast fae so she can't regulate her body temperature the way we can. I'm assuming, anyway. I know nothing about the skald fae."

I pressed her hand between my palms and gently rubbed to get the circulation going again. Then I did the same to her other one. When I pressed my palm to her forehead, she was slightly feverish, despite her body feeling so cold.

Moving the pads of my fingers to the base of her neck, I felt around to determine if her pulse was as slow as I'd thought. Then I lifted my water satchel and poured some into my palm. I poured a few drops into her mouth.

Suddenly, her eyes opened—green as gems—and her skin brightened with the glow of the moon. Without warning, she gasped and a shock of magick jolted up my arm. I leaped back off the furs with a cry and stood over her, staring at my hand. When I looked back down, her eyes were closed again and her skin was its normal color. If you can call bloodless a normal color.

"She shocked me," I told Wolf. "You've brought a damn harpy to our camp, Wolf. And now she's using her witchy magick on me just for trying to help her."

Wolf simply licked her hand.

"Of course, she isn't stinging you with her magick," I grumbled. "Why don't you heal her then?"

Wolf sat on his haunches again, staring up at me with that ridiculous, superior stare of his.

"Stop it," I told him. "Yes, I know the law. But that law refers to creatures of dark fae."

He didn't make a sound, still staring.

We were too far from camp for me to fetch a healer. And she couldn't travel until her fever broke. It could make her worse. The best I could do was get her sustenance to fight it off.

"Fucking fine!" I lifted one of the extra furs at the foot of the bed and slung it over the witch, making sure not to touch her this time, lest she zap me with her wicked magick.

"I will help her, Wolf. Are you happy now?" I snapped. "But only because our law demands it. And if she kills us both in our sleep with her witchcraft," I turned at the tent flap and pointed a finger at him, "I'll hunt you down through all eleven hells to kill you again."

He hopped onto my bed and draped his body alongside hers before resting his chin on her legs. He dwarfed her. I suppose I wouldn't have to worry about anything harming her while I was gone.

I grunted with irritation. "Maybe she'll awaken again and have a heart attack with a monstrous hound slobbering all over her," I told him as I left.

Once outside the tent, I tromped over to where I'd left my belt and short sword, the black blade given to me as a gift from the wraith king in exchange for a favor. I'd wondered then when Gollaya Verbane had strolled into camp with the moon fae princess at his side, claiming her as his mate, whether he'd gone mad. It was unnatural for a dark fae to take a light fae to his bed for more than a night's pleasure. To take one for a mate was simply against nature.

I huffed out a breath of misty air as I strapped on my belt and the short sword. Yes, it was true that my own second, Bezaliel, had taken a wood fae as his wife. And while I respected and trusted Bezaliel as I would a brother, I always thought him a little addled in the head for doing such a thing. The light fae were not like us. And their women who had magick were witches.

Proof enough was that skald fae wench who just pierced me with her powers when all I was doing was trying to determine if her heart was about to stop beating.

With my belt fastened and my blade hanging at my hip, I stepped toward the game trail where I'd had luck a few days ago. "Far be it from me to be the first chief to break the Vanglosa oath."

I heaved a sigh, knowing that female was a stranger in need. And even though she was an evil, red-haired witch, our law demanded that I help her.

Stomping into the darkness, I snorted. "I assume boar meat won't be sufficient for a high and mighty light fae."

I'd need a deer, I suppose. Or does she require swans or some other sort of exotic animal? Not that I'd kill a swan, but who knows with these fae that live so far south near the Nemian Sea. I had no idea what they ate. And yet, Wolf acts like I'm the fool for even asking questions.

Maybe she'd gone into the woods to end her life or something. For who would come out here without even the thinnest of cloaks to protect oneself? Especially a frail light fae. And here we were, thwarting her plans to meet death on her own terms.

Well, if that's the case, she can put a curse on Wolf for it. It's his damn fault.

Aggravated, I wished I could turn back the clock to when I was sitting pleasantly by my fire without the welfare of a skald fae witch on my hands. But the gods always loved to play games with me, especially ones that tormented me by stirring up my emotions. I hated to deal with anything that required depth of emotion. I'd rather rely on my animal instincts, that kept decisions straightforward and clear. Feelings muddled everything and made us do stupid things.

Like tromp into the woods to kill a deer to revive a nearly-dead skald fae who didn't belong here in the first place.

"Fucking hells, Wolf," I cursed my beast one last time before I marched away from the trail to hunt the witch some bloody dinner. If I was lucky, she'd die before I got back. Then she wouldn't be my problem anymore. That was the best I could hope for.

CHAPTER 3
Jessamine

I awoke to feeling warm. Too warm. Blinking my eyes open, I pushed off the covers. No, not covers. Furs. At first, I thought I'd been captured and was imprisoned in the Mevian guards' tent. But then I saw the horse-sized, black Meer-wolf spread out on the bed of furs next to me. No moon fae kept a Meer-wolf for a pet. They were companions of only one kind—the beast fae.

Carefully pushing to a sitting position, not wanting the wolf to attack, I vaguely recalled waking from a fever and seeing a giant dark fae—bigger than any I'd ever laid eyes on in my life—with his hand at my throat. Then I remembered I'd electrocuted him. My magick had defended me in my weakness.

Had I killed him?

Surely, this wolf would've killed me if I'd murdered his master. So he was somewhere nearby.

The wolf with silver eyes wagged his tail then stood and trotted outside of the tent. I breathed out a sigh of relief. The wolf was frightening, even if he didn't appear to want to harm me.

Taking a look around, I was in a rather tall and large tent. This bed of furs was also over-sized. I suppose both must be to fit the size of the creature who lived here.

Gods above. Was I now captive of that monster?

Pushing out of the bed, I stood and wobbled on my feet. I still had all of my clothes on, thank the gods. Even my apron. I tucked my hand into the pocket, finding the elkmine otter pelt still there. I sniffed at the sting of tears wanting to spill over, remembering the kindness of the old wraith fae. And especially of Haldek. He'd helped me escape. If I made my way back to Haldek's tavern, he would give me supplies to flee farther into dark fae territory. I was certain of it. Unless the Mevian guards were waiting and watching his tavern for my return.

I had to try. I needed to sneak out of here and make my way back through the woods. Taking one of the furs—a soft gray one—from the bed, I wrapped it around my shoulders, pulling it tight around my neck. Then I tip-toed toward the opening of the tent.

Peering through the flap, I didn't see the wolf or the beast. Only the flickering of a campfire. I slipped through and carefully stepped toward the dark woods—not exactly thrilled about setting off back into the cold.

"Where do you think you're going?" came a deep, gravelly voice behind me.

Heart pounding, I turned to see the beast fae male standing in the halo of firelight opposite me, his arms bloody with one clawed hand holding half of a deer carcass over one shoulder.

He was bare-chested, wearing pants made of a dark hide. Demon runes decorated his upper chest, curling across his pectorals in swirls and slashes with smaller runes inked by his gods across his forehead. Four massive black horns with a thick ridge of bone spiraled out of his head, slightly curling over his skull. One of his long, pointed ears twitched as he scowled at me with bright, golden eyes. And his tail, also long, covered with the same fine pelt that seemed to cover his skin and tufted slightly at the tip, flicked behind him with agitation.

My pulse sped faster. He was more terrifying than I remembered in that blink when I woke from my fever. If I ran, he could take two pounces and tackle me down without any effort.

"Seems your fever broke," he grumbled then marched toward the fire, heaving the haunch of bloody deer off of his back.

With his free hand, he gripped the wooden handle of the long spike hanging over the fire between two tripods. And with hardly any effort at all, he stabbed the spike straight through the deer carcass then set it back over the fire. He walked a few paces away from the fire and dipped his hands into the snow, lifting a handful of it and rubbing it along his bloody arms.

He was cleaning himself this way?

I stared in absolute wonder at this barbaric creature as he took a rag hanging from a branch and dried his hands, only half the blood gone from his limbs.

He sat on a stump that had obviously been cut and rolled to the fire, the perfect width and height for him. Even sitting, he was intimidatingly…large. I couldn't quite catch my breath. His wolf plopped down next to him and stared at me, just as his master did now.

The beast fae's scowl deepened as he regarded me. "Are you mute, woman? Or did you lose the use of your tongue when you ran off into the snow to kill yourself?"

It was my turn to frown. "I wasn't trying to kill myself," I snapped.

"Ah, she does have a tongue, Wolf."

That drew my attention to the regal hound at his side. I'd heard that beast fae rode their Meer-wolf hounds. This was a colossus of an animal. He'd have to be, to carry this beast fae.

"Never seen one before?" he asked, watching me staring.

"A wraith fae once brought a Meer-wolf pup into the tavern," I said softly. "He'd found him abandoned. He was big, his head past my waist, even for a baby."

"Meer-wolves don't abandon their pups," he stated with some superiority. "Likely, the mother died defending it from another predator."

"So they all reach his size?" I gestured toward the black hound.

He scoffed, his long canines showing when he sort of sneered. "No. None get to be Wolf's size. He's a king of his kind."

"What's his name?" I asked, still standing on the perimeter of the firelight.

"I've said his name already. Wolf."

"You named your wolf, Wolf?"

He leaned down, one elbow on a knee as he reached for a log and tossed it into the fire, the flames licking up to the meat. My stomach turned.

"What else should I call him?"

"I don't know. Perhaps Näkt for the god of night?"

Stepping closer, I sat upon the ground since there was no other log or stump for another person. He was alone here.

"Or perhaps King since you said so yourself, he is a king of his kind."

The wolf rounded the fire and stretched out at my side. I froze for a moment, but then he licked the back of my hand before resting his head on his paws. Hesitantly, I brushed a hand along the back of his neck.

"He is gentle for being such a giant."

The hound huffed and nuzzled closer to me.

The dark fae male snorted with disgust. "Traitor beast." He then reached to the ground and lifted a water satchel before tossing it to me. I caught it in my lap.

"You've broken the fever, but you need water. Drink."

Grateful, I twisted off the cap and drank greedily. Then drank some more. The water was cool and welcome on my parched throat.

"Not sure how you broke that fever so fast," he added. "Is it your witchcraft?"

I arched a brow at him. "If you mean my magick, then possibly so. My kind rarely stays sick. Water is its own kind of magick for skald fae."

It was true that water itself was a magickal healing property for skald fae. Especially those in my family with a deeper connection to water. If I hadn't fallen unconscious in the snow running from the Mevian guards then I'd have used my magick to transform the snow into a healing cocoon in the icy cold. But I'd been in a panicked run for my life. I'd had no time to stop and think, too afraid they'd catch me if I did.

"Hmph. Witchcraft," he grumbled.

Suddenly, the beast fae pulled a black blade the length of my entire arm from a sheath at his belt. I flinched but kept still as he knelt closer to the fire.

"I'm not going to kill you, female."

He sliced a piece of the meat from the deer haunch and placed it on the rag he'd used earlier to wipe his hands. Then he sliced another before carrying it around the fire and handing it to me. I blinked up at him, still in awe of his size, but I took the offering and set it in my lap.

He sliced himself a giant chunk and sat on his stool, taking a bite. I didn't miss that his canines were longer than any I'd seen before. He was an incredibly impressive beast fae. He was an incredibly impressive beast fae, in that he could kill me with one swipe of his claws. I stared down at the roasted meat in my lap, my stomach souring.

"Eat. You need food to warm your body on the inside and fight the cold."

I blinked at him. "I…can't eat this."

"Why not?" He gave me that same scrutinizing look like he thought I might be addled in the head.

"I don't eat meat."

He stared with open confusion. "What do you mean you don't eat meat?"

"Just what I said. I don't eat it."

"Everyone eats meat."

It was my turn to scoff. "Perhaps on this side of the world. But I don't. Nor do I eat fish. It is not our way."

"How do you live then?" He seemed completely perplexed.

I laughed. "There are other things to eat in the world besides meat."

"Like what?"

"Bread, cheese, vegetables."

He curled his lip up into a snarl, revealing those awfully sharp fangs. "You can't live on that."

"Obviously, I can live on that." I gestured toward myself, the fur I'd been wearing over my shoulder slipping to my waist. "I'm sitting here, quite alive."

His gaze dipped to my body. I was aware that I had a robust figure which attracted males. While my sisters were willowy and elegant, I'd been built differently. It was part of my allure as a syrenskyn. Another gift from the gods which only attracted the wrong sort of attention. Like now.

"You look like you eat meat," he said.

Rolling my eyes, I snapped, "Don't be vulgar." Refusing to let fear take hold, I set the sliced venison before the wolf who instantly ate my portion. I stood, pulling the fur with me and wrapping it around myself. "So, am I a prisoner now?"

He frowned. "What would I do with you?" Then he ate the giant piece of meat still in his hand. I couldn't help but notice his forked tongue when he licked the juice from his lips. He was more of a monster than any creature I'd met in my travels and my time hiding away in the Borderlands.

"You're free to go." He gestured toward the woods.

So, he didn't have nefarious plans for me after all. That was good. I looked off into the cold night, not relishing leaving the warmth of this fire, even if I had to share it with this ornery beast fae.

My relief vanished when he asked, "What were you running from?" He shifted off the stump and knelt with one knee beside the fire and sliced off more meat, sliding his golden gaze to mine. "Or should I say *who* were you running from?"

It was useless to pretend he hadn't figured me out. He may look like a beast, but he was cunning enough.

"Someone I didn't want to find me," I answered.

He chuckled. "I gathered that much, female."

Wolf chewed the last of the meat and stood at my side facing his master. The beast fae kept his focus on me.

"You stole something?"

"No," I snapped.

"Killed someone?"

"No!" I cried louder.

"Then what did you do?"

"I ran away from home. That is all."

He arched a brow at me, taking his seat again and continuing to eat. "Do you mean to tell me that skald fae came chasing you all the way from Morodon through the Borderlands and into Meerland, deep, dark fae territory?" He shook his head, disbelieving.

"They weren't from Morodon. They were from somewhere else." I didn't want to confess too much to him. What if he was some sort of mercenary and decided to turn me in for ransom?

"Why are you so important?" he asked, his deep voice a silky rumble. It was a disturbingly lovely sound. He was trying to coax me into telling him the truth with a gentler tone.

"It's not your business."

"No. But here you are, all alone in Meerland. If you go marching off into those woods on your own, there are plenty of other monsters who will find you before those you're running from." He shook his head. "You don't want the monsters of these woods catching you."

I gulped hard, knowing he was right. While I'd rarely left the safety of Haldek's tavern, I heard plenty enough about the predatory animals who roamed the wilds of Meerland and the foothills of the Solgavia Mountains. And my syrenskyn magick wouldn't work on monsters. Not that kind.

Returning to the fire, I sat back down. "Perhaps, if you wouldn't mind, I could stay here until morning. Then you could point me to the nearest village. Other than the Borderlands."

"The nearest village is mine," he said. "And it's the only one within leagues. It's a two-day trek."

"Oh." I was surprised. "You don't live out here?" I gestured toward the tent.

His frown returned as he leaned forward, elbows on his knees. "Why would I live out here in the middle of nowhere?"

I bit my tongue before responding with *because it looks like you do*. He was still half bloody from carrying the deer carcass on his back, and half-clothed like a wild barbarian. This environment suited him well.

"Would you mind leading me to your village? If I could stay for just a little while until…"

He examined me with those eyes the same color as the firelight. "Until the ones chasing you have given up and gone home."

I gave a stiff nod.

He grumbled something under his breath that I couldn't hear.

"I can work in the local tavern or inn. I'm a good worker."

"We don't have taverns or inns in my village. We're a beast fae clan."

He was obviously put out by my request, but I had few options. "What is the village nearest yours?"

"Belladum. A week at least. And only *if* you had a mount, which you don't. Unless you go back to the Borderlands."

"No. I can't go back there."

They'd be waiting and watching for me at Haldek's. They'd likely have staked out all of the inns and taverns along the Borderlands.

He sat straight again and heaved a frustrated sigh, his breath coming out in a cloud of white mist. "Fine," he snapped. "I suppose I have to take you." He muttered something about an oath. "You can sleep in the tent. I'll stay out here since I'm forced to."

"No, you can sleep in your tent. I'm fine right here and—"

"What? Freeze to death when the fire goes out? Then what would they say?"

"What would who say?" I asked.

"My clan," he snapped before barking more orders. "Just go on inside and sleep. You may think you've recovered but you're still pale as the moon. You need rest. And we leave at dawn."

Then he tossed the chunk of meat he'd been eating to Wolf and tromped angrily back into the woods. To do what, I had no idea. He was obviously upset about having to cart me to his village.

I had no other choice but to put up with him. I couldn't take a chance on my own out here or travel a week or more by myself to Belladum. Plus, I was in dark fae territory. Whereas the light and dark fae often mixed in the small settlements along the Borderlands, that wasn't always the case in the dark fae towns and cities of the north.

While King Goll married a light fae princess, there was still a great deal of animosity brewing between the light and dark fae. Perhaps even more so now. That was the reason I'd been running from the moon fae male I was supposed to marry. Because he had intentions to make war on all dark fae. And I wanted no part of his rebellion.

Heaving a sigh, I made my way back inside the tent, noting that Wolf followed me. I curled up in the furs again, the giant hound at my feet. I stared at the tent wall, determining it was made of deer hides sewn together and wondering what I'd gotten myself into.

But before long, my mind and body were too exhausted to fight. I drifted off to the heavy breaths of the wolf sleeping beside me.

CHAPTER 4

Redvyr

"My name is Jessamine," said the woman riding my wolf while I walked ahead.

Wolf was plenty strong enough to carry us both, but he also had the bundle of hides that I used for my tent and bed strapped behind her.

Besides, I didn't want to be so close to her. She was a witch, and though she might appear normal in the daylight, I hadn't forgotten how she'd used her magick to sting me last night. She'd been unconscious, yes, but still, there was wickedness hiding behind that pretty face. I was sure of it. After all, she was running from someone. If she was innocent, she'd have told me who she was running from and why. Females could be conniving, and I'd rather not get too close to this one that wasn't even of my own kind.

"Did you hear me?" she asked.

"Yes, yes. Your name is Jessamine. Noted."

"Someone is awfully grouchy. Even more so than last night."

"I didn't sleep last night because I had to keep watch for whoever is chasing you. Though you refuse to tell me who they are, they might've tracked you to my camp, so I wasn't going to let my guard down. Meaning, I didn't sleep. So yes, I'm in a shitty mood."

"Oh," she said in that simple way of hers. "Sorry."

Somehow, her apology prickled me more.

"What's your name?" she finally asked as we picked our way along a snow-covered path near a brook.

The brook was frozen along the edges but the water bubbled around the stones where it was rocky. This path would lead to a cave that I often used on my hunting expeditions.

"Redvyr," I answered.

"Redvyr," she repeated. "That sounds rather regal."

I didn't bother telling her that's because it was. It was a name for beast fae royalty. Which is what I was.

"Tell me about the beast fae."

I hesitated, unsure how much truth to give her. "What do you know of us?"

"I know that you're descended from one of the sons of Vix, a great, dark fae god. And I know you are the most—" she paused, which drew my attention to her face.

Her cheeks were pink. She was blushing over something.

"The most what?"

"Instinctual," she finally said, "of the dark fae."

"Animalistic was the word you were looking for. And you'd be right."

"Animal senses, you mean?"

"That, yes. Unnatural strength as well."

"That is your magick?" she asked, genuinely curious.

She must not know much at all about our kind. All fae had some sort of magick. Except the beast fae.

"It is said that we had magick once as well. A gift of speaking to the forests, the trees and plants that live there. Dryads once protected our kind, too. We also had a gift for taming the wilder beasts of the woods."

"Animals like Wolf? You seem to still have that gift."

"No. Monsters like bargas, nightvyrms, the great cats of the Solgavia Mountains. Dragons."

"Wow. What happened? You lost this gift?"

I glanced at her over my shoulder. There was no mocking expression on her face.

"You've never heard about the curse of the beast fae?"

She shook her head. Her bright red hair was in a long braid over one shoulder, the breeze blowing a loose strand across her cheek. I tried not to get distracted by watching it lift in the breeze. But it was difficult.

Facing forward, I headed away from the brook through a natural archway made of vines and trees overhanging the narrow path. During spring, this area would be richly green and thick with vegetation. The sound of sprites flying through the branches above and birds singing would fill the forest. Winter had come early, blanketing these woods with snow. I imagine my clan would be frustrated I'd stayed on the hunt so long. We'd need to break camp and move from Vanglosa as soon as I retuned.

"Will you tell me about this curse?" Jessamine's voice broke into my thoughts.

It wasn't an easy story to tell, but something compelled me to tell her anyway.

"Legend says that long ago one of our ancestors, whose name was Kaladyn, was chief of his clan and the greatest beast lord among all the clans. By greatest, I mean that his clan was the largest and most prosperous. He had several wives and dozens of children, but he still wasn't satisfied."

"Do beast fae all have more than one wife?" she interrupted.

"No. It was a custom of long ago." I slowed as we came to a rocky outcropping that gave a view of the ravine and brook winding through the woods.

"Oh, wow."

Wolf stopped at my side as we surveyed the land below.

"It's so beautiful here," she whispered.

If she thought this was lovely, she would be shocked to see our winter camp. Not that she would be seeing it. But I liked that look of surprise and wonder on her pale face.

"Are you feeling better since last night?" I asked, wondering if her pallid complexion meant she was still unwell.

She turned her leaf-green gaze to me. "I feel fine." She shrugged. "Perhaps a little hungry."

Frowning at that, I realized she would have to go without food for another full day. We'd have to camp again tonight.

"If you'd eat meat, you wouldn't be hungry," I informed her sharply.

She smirked. "True. But I'd probably vomit it up if I did."

I rolled my eyes. "There are no berries in the woods this time of year. You'll have to wait until we reach my village."

"I'll be fine. So tell me about this chief Kaladyn."

Stepping back onto the trail that wound on a slight incline, I continued with the story.

"Though Kaladyn had many wives, none were his mate. He—"

"What do you mean none were his mate?" she asked. "You said he had many children with them. Obviously, they mated."

I forgot that light fae don't mate the way we do.

"For beast fae, there is a perfect match for each of our kind."

"How do you know who is the perfect match?"

The truth of it would certainly terrify this woman, so I gave her the less graphic explanation.

"The gods guide us and show us. So Kaladyn believed himself greater than all other beast fae. He believed that he was meant to have a special mate touched by the gods. There was a queen of the dryads who lived in the nearby woodlands."

"This is not going to end well," she mumbled.

I grunted in agreement, then went on.

"Suffice it to say, the queen rebuffed his advances. So he took her forcibly. This was a crime, of course, and a great sin against the gods since they beget the dryads. What he didn't realize was that this queen was the daughter of Elska, the Goddess of the Wood, herself. When Elska discovered what had happened to her daughter, she appeared at the center of his clan's village. Kaladyn fell onto his knees and begged forgiveness but Elska would hear none of it. With a touch to his head, he became more beastly in appearance." Glancing back, her attention was riveted on me. I flicked my tail. "We didn't have tails then. Nor did we look quite like this." I gestured toward my face. "We were called the beast fae for our affinity and power to connect with the wild animals of the world."

Of all the dark fae, we were the ones who actually looked more like monsters. But that was only after Kaladyn's curse.

"Elska claimed, 'From this moment onward, your magick is stripped from you and all of your kind. You will keep only the beastly parts of your nature. And within you, chief, I am planting my rage. It will live there always and for your kinsmen to come, reminding you of the peace you stole from my daughter. You will forever be plagued by my fury as a constant reminder of what you've stolen.'"

Jessamine remained quiet behind me as we made our way closer to the place we would be stopping at for the night.

"Is that true?" she finally asked.

"It is what has been told." I didn't admit that I was certain it was true because of my own affliction. Whenever I fell into a rage, there was nothing for me to do but leave, go deep into the woods until it had subsided.

"That's so sad," she added.

"Why? Because I am so ugly to look upon?" I grinned over my shoulder.

Her cheeks flushed pink. "*No.* That's not what I mean."

I laughed. "Witch, you don't have to lie to me. I know I'm a brute. And Kaladyn may have cursed the beast fae, but we are a peaceful people. Whatever sins of our forefather, we have a good life now even if we are small in numbers."

"Why are you small in numbers?"

That was more painful to admit, something I wasn't willing to confess. During Kaladyn's time, ages ago, the beast fae were plentiful and many. Now, there are very few clans. Our females rarely conceive. It was one reason I couldn't fault my second Bezaliel when he brought his light fae female Tessa to our village. Beyond being his mate, she conceived quickly and gave him a healthy son.

"Our population is diminished from what it once was," was all I told her. "We cherish every new life in our clan as precious."

We rounded the corner where the mouth of the cave overlooked a view of the vast valley below. Another reason I liked to camp here was that I could see far and wide with the cave at my back. It was a well-protected encampment. Now that I was carting around this female with enemies hunting her, enemies she refused to confess to me, I needed this kind of fortress to watch for any attack.

Wolf automatically stopped at the cave, knowing my routine well enough.

"We'll stay here tonight," I told her as I untied the bundle of hides stacked on Wolf's haunches.

I heard her slide down off Wolf's back as I unrolled the bundle inside the rounded mouth of the cave.

"You don't think a barga lives in there, do you?" she asked, her voice quivering as she peered wide-eyed into the semi-darkness of the mouth.

Grinning, I pulled the gray fur out and spread it next to the other unrolled hides before straightening.

"Aye. A barga lived here once." I pointed at the gray fur. "But I took care of him. He won't be back."

Wide-eyed, she stepped closer and stared down at the fur she'd worn for warmth last night. "That was from a barga?"

"You don't have to whisper. He can't hear you." I smirked.

She gulped hard and pressed a delicate, webbed hand to her chest. "I didn't realize you hunted…giant bears."

Arching a brow, I asked, "Do you not think me capable of killing such a monster?"

Her gaze roamed up and down my frame, her throat working again to swallow. I stiffened beneath her perusal, tilting my chin higher, blood heating at the quiet admiration in her gaze.

"I do not doubt you are capable," she said sincerely, blinking and blushing as she looked away.

Grunting, I marched past her, disliking how much it pleased me to hear her admit that. "I'll gather kindling. We'll need a fire. I'm out of blue coal."

I'd packed plenty enough of the heat source for a regular solo hunt, but I'd stayed away longer than normal this time. I hadn't known why I'd stayed. That restlessness again, or perhaps something more.

"I can help." Her light footfalls followed me outside.

"Stay close to me," I ordered. "It may seem quiet and peaceful, but there are always dangers in these woods. Some you can't easily see or hear until it's too late."

"I understand," she said, trailing close behind me as we ventured into the woods, trying to find anything dry to burn.

For a light fae, she seemed to have sense enough in her head. Having heard that most fae of her kind were foolish and ignorant, especially when it came to the woodlands, that surprised me. She surprised me.

I wondered again what she might have done to make her want to flee her homeland. There wasn't anything that could make me leave Vanglosa, not even the sins or curse of my own father. It had actually made me stronger, overcoming the reputation he left behind, and more determined than ever to become the best lord of our clan that had ever lived.

So what crime had this female committed to make her run so far away she found herself in foreign lands, at the mercy of the Northgall winter bearing down on us, and in the hands of…me?

CHAPTER 5

Jessamine

I couldn't sleep. Wolf had slipped off into the night after we'd found enough kindling and wood to keep the fire going. Redvyr said that he often left at night. The last time he did, he'd come home with me draped over his back.

Redvyr added, "I hope he doesn't drag any more helpless females into camp. One is enough."

I wasn't annoyed by his description of me being *helpless*. Throughout our brief acquaintance, I realized that grouchy was his normal temperament. Besides, he was right. I *was* helpless. I couldn't make it out here alone. I needed him.

Funny though, I hadn't remembered climbing onto a wild Meer-wolf the night before. I'd fallen unconscious with those silver eyes watching me. He'd somehow managed to scoop me up, or I'd subconsciously climbed on and clung to him. Either way, the wolf had saved my life. As had Redvyr.

He slept now across the fire from me on his bed of furs. In sleep, his expression softened, his prominent brow smooth rather than pinched into a scowl, his mouth relaxed instead of sneering or mocking. He didn't seem so ferocious as he did in the light of day.

My full bladder prodded me to empty it. Since I had no food, I'd filled my belly with water. Redvyr promised there would be plenty for me to eat once we reached his village tomorrow.

When I'd asked if I'd be allowed to stay in his village for a while, he didn't answer me. He'd walked away without a word. If I wasn't permitted to stay, I worried about where I would go next. The Mevian lord looking for his runaway bride now knew I was in Northgall territory. Would he continue to seek me out?

"Your magick is exactly what I need, princess." He gripped my *arm tight, leaning in close. The only sound other than his grating voice was the bees buzzing in our floral garden. "And you'll do exactly as your lord and master tells you."*

I willed the memory to disappear, refusing to think about that day before I left the only home I'd ever known. A home that had given me shelter and food, but not love and affection. Most of all, not the protection or care I deserved. Not after Draydyn died, anyway.

My bladder reminded me again that I must relieve myself. Quietly, I shoved out of the furs and lifted one of the lone branches of kindling before lighting the tip as a torch.

Earlier, when Redvyr demanded we find kindling, I was sure it was a lost cause since snow covered nearly every inch of the forest. What I hadn't realized was that Redvyr was an extremely powerful fae male, stronger than I'd imagined. He found a fallen tree, a blanket of snow covering it. With what seemed like little effort, he picked it up and flipped it over.

Beneath it and on the underside, there were plenty of broken, dried branches and some we were able to crack off of the trunk itself. I'd watched him break off a branch as thick as my thigh with such ease, all I could do was stare until he'd asked if I planned to actually help him gather the kindling or simply stand there and watch him do it alone.

He was such an ornery beast, I thought as I tip-toed to the mouth of the cave and peered out. The woodlands were so quiet, but I believed him when he said there were monsters who lived out there unseen. Though it would be rather embarrassing, for I knew his heightened sense of smell would tell him that I urinated right outside the cave, I wasn't going to be stupid and go any further.

Picking my way to the left of the cave opening, I leaned my makeshift torch against the outer wall of the cave. Grabbing hold of a thin tree branch from an elm growing alongside the cave, I held it for balance and pulled up my skirt with the other.

Before I could manage to relieve myself, something wrapped around my wrist. I gasped and instantly grabbed my torch, thrusting it toward whatever was holding me. The creature holding me then grabbed my other wrist, pulling me up until my feet left the ground.

With the torch still gripped in one fist, I stared in fearful awe at the creature. It was a dryad stag, a big one. His antlers, at least sixteen points, jutted out of his leafy head, his face and body an ashen green. His eyes were full black except for pin-points of red at their centers.

What I'd thought was an elm tree was in fact this frighteningly large dryad which had been semi-attached to the outer cave wall.

"A skald fae beauty," he garbled with a creaking voice, his mouth a black pit. "Far from the waters of home."

"Please," I begged, willing my magick to come to life. "Let me go."

My skin glowed with vibrant energy, bright markings of light glittering along my arms. The creature observed me with interest, those black eyes haunting and so very wrong.

"Great stag," I said with magick in my voice, melodious and echoing. "You must put me down. You must let me go."

While he did appear mesmerized by my voice and the ethereal glow of my skin, he wasn't truly hearing me. My magick wasn't working on him. Blue claws sprouted from my fingertips. My fangs sharpened inside my mouth. When he lifted me close so that he could peer at my face and into my eyes, I managed to barely scrape one nail upon his bark-covered shoulder.

He grunted but otherwise seemed unaffected by the poison I passed to him. He wasn't simply fae. He was god-touched. An ancient one. His massive size and crown of antlers on his head told me so. I couldn't get my hands free to penetrate his leathery, leafy skin with my poisonous claws. And there was certainly something terribly wrong with him.

Now that my face was so close to his, I noted black webbing underneath the pale green of his skin. A vibration of dark power radiated from the creature.

"Mighty ancient one," my voice echoed with the power given to me by my Goddess Nemia. It also shook with the fear welling up inside me. "You will not harm me. You will let me go."

For a moment, he seemed to be falling into my trance, his black eyes widening with awe and wonder as my skin glowed beneath my dress.

"You are more than a mouthful," he croaked and grinned, revealing rows of sharp, black teeth, leaning his antlered head forward. "So bright. So sweet."

He was going to eat me?

Panic took hold. I kicked out with my legs, pummeling his body with my booted feet. He grunted but held me firm.

Suddenly, there was a fierce roar and we were thrown sideways. The dryad let me go and I tumbled to the ground. Snaps and snarls and the cracking of branches was all I heard. I could barely make out the muscular figure of Redvyr wrestling with the long-limbed dryad.

They rolled toward the mouth of the cave into the halo of firelight. Redvyr snarled and opened his mouth on the dryad's throat. A shrieking cry pierced the night followed by silence as the beast fae ripped the dryad's head from its body with his mouth.

The beast fae stood, lifting the severed head by the antlers. With a great roar, he threw the head into the ravine far below. The crash of it landing in the brush was all that could be heard before he bent and broke the limbs from its body, tossing them over the cliff as well.

He was in a frenzy of fury, roaring as he cracked and ripped the dryad into pieces.

"Redvyr," I called, approaching hesitantly.

He didn't hear me, still breaking the body of the stag dryad like he might come back to life and challenge the beast fae.

"Redvyr!" I cried louder.

He snapped his head with a ferocious growl in my direction, his teeth dripping green blood.

"He's gone," I said, raising my hands in a disarming gesture.

Redvyr continued to growl as he crouched over what was left of the dryad, a look of feral wildness in his eyes, shining bright as the sun. His muscles were bunched, ready to pounce.

"Easy," I soothed, intuitively knowing he couldn't come out of this frenzy so quickly. "You've killed him. There is no threat."

His lip curled up at my approach, further revealing his long, sharpened canines. He was indeed a fierce monster, but I knew he wouldn't hurt me. Something compelled me to ease his temper, his rage. After all, he'd fallen into this state to save me. Yet again, he had saved me.

"It's alright," I said softly, drawing so close now, I could smell the wild, masculine scent of him.

His tail lashed back and forth, his pointed ears laid back, a posture of aggression. If I was smart, I would simply cower in the cave and hide under my barga fur. But I couldn't. Somehow, I knew he needed me.

"I'm safe now," I assured him. "We're both safe. The threat is gone." Reaching out a hand toward his shoulder, fingers trembling, I added, "You've killed him."

Crouched low, his shoulder was chest-high to me. When my fingertips touched the tight muscles of his shoulder, he snarled again, but he didn't move. My own poisonous claws and fangs had retreated, but there was still a faint glow to my skin, which he was staring at keenly.

"Thank you for saving me," I said in a soothing voice, caressing his shoulder.

He huffed a breath, his growl rumbling more into a purr rather than that menacing vibration that warned me he might bite my hand off from a moment before.

"I'm alright now. He's gone," I assured him again.

Redvyr dropped his head between his shoulders, still crouching over the body and making that deep purring sound as I swept my palm up his shoulder to the base of his neck and back down.

"See. All is well."

He breathed great gulps of air until finally his breathing evened out and he was no longer snarling or purring or making any sound at all. When he lifted his head, his feral expression softened back into the beast fae I'd journeyed with all day. He stood to his full height, my hand falling away.

He turned his face toward the darkness, his face tight with anger though not the wild rage from before.

"Are you alright?"

"Go inside," he said curtly.

I flinched. "I have to…relieve myself first."

For now, my body was nearly aching with the need. Having nearly been killed had only worsened my situation.

"Do it now. Not out of my sight." His voice was dark and cold.

I didn't argue. I shuffled to the edge of the cave, making sure he didn't watch me directly. He didn't, keeping his gaze over the ravine.

Once I'd taken care of myself, I stood and hurried past him to my pallet of furs. When I'd curled up under the safety and warmth of my makeshift bed, I turned my face to the opening of the cave.

Redvyr settled with his back to the cave wall, his body blocking the entrance.

"Do you need a fur to keep warm?" I asked.

"Go to sleep, witch," he told me, the coldness still in his voice.

"There was something wrong with that dryad," I told him. "Dryads don't attack and eat other fae. Or is that something they do here in Northgall?"

He didn't answer my question but he did turn his face to me. In the dying embers, I saw that the rage was truly gone, though his eyes still shined with an unnatural luster.

"Go to sleep," he said more gently than before, then turned his head back to keep watch.

I wasn't quite sure why he was so angry. Perhaps it was normal for beast fae to launch into a savage madness in battle. My body still trembled from the entire encounter, though by some innate knowing, I wasn't afraid of him.

My eyes blinking heavily, I fell asleep watching my guardian, his gaze on the dangers in the darkness that I couldn't see.

CHAPTER 6

Jessamine

As we walked side by side into his village, Wolf behind us, I realized I'd pictured it completely wrong. When he said there were no taverns or inns, I believed that meant they were simply a private community made of residential houses only. There were no houses at all. At least, not ones like in my home Morodon, where white stone buildings covered the seaside city. Or even the Borderlands, where Haldek's tavern was made of wood and stone.

This village was lined with tents, similar to the one Redvyr camped in, though many were bigger and certainly well-made. The beast fae gathered along the path that we followed through the village, greeting Redvyr while staring at me. Their expressions ranged from curious to unwelcoming.

One rather fierce-looking beast fae walked directly up the path toward us, his hard expression cracking as he smiled at

Redvyr. He stopped us in the path and held out an arm to Redvyr who then clasped his, their forearms aligned.

"Good to have you back, Lord Redvyr," said the newcomer.

I started and looked up at Redvyr. I knew beast fae used the title of lord for their kings. He was the king of this clan?

"Good to be back, Bezaliel."

Three other warriors stalked up the path directly toward Redvyr, gathering around and greeting him. They all wore similar clothes—hide vests and trousers or skirts. One of them wore his hair in a long braid down his back. Their casual manner told me they were close to the beast lord.

"It seems your hunt was fruitful." Bezaliel glanced at me with a sly grin.

Bezaliel was almost equal in size to Redvyr, though not quite. His bare chest was exposed beneath a vest of red-brown hide. Runes swirled over his muscles, and his four black horns curled out of his head in a magnificent sweep. He was an impressive beast fae.

"Wolf dragged her into my camp half frozen two nights ago."

"Did he?" Bezaliel actually grinned at the giant wolf standing behind us.

"She has a request that we need to put forth to the council."

"Aren't you going to introduce us?" asked one of the leaner beast fae with a handsome face.

"Leifkyn," Redvyr addressed him then pointed to the other two, "Dayn and Brohm, this is Jessamine."

The three newcomers gave me a slight bow of the head in greeting.

"Pleasure to meet you."

Bezaliel sobered, then nodded. "I'll gather the council members at the kella'mir. In the meantime, she looks like she could use some tending to."

Redvyr turned to look at me, frowning. "She was attacked last night by a dryad."

"A dryad?" he asked.

"He had the black madness," Redvyr added in a low voice.

"But in a dryad?" Bezaliel asked.

"We'll talk more later. The game was also scarce this year, but there is a buck of red deer packed on Wolf."

"I'll see to it."

"Hi." I interrupted and thrust out my hand for him to shake since Redvyr hadn't properly introduced us yet. "I'm Jessamine."

Bezaliel took my hand in his rough, large one. "It is a pleasure, Jessamine. I am Bezaliel, chief warrior to Redvyr of the Vanglosa clan. It seems you've had an adventure."

"She'll be in my tent until the council is ready," added Redvyr.

"I'll send Tessa."

Redvyr grunted in agreement then marched ahead. "Follow me, Jessamine."

Ignoring the stares of the other beast fae who watched with open wonder as we passed, I followed him until we came to a giant tent at the end of the path. Once inside, he marched to a large woven basket and pulled a pair of black hide trousers from inside as well as a leather vest. For a moment, I thought he was going to change in front of me, my heart picking up speed suddenly.

Redvyr quirked a brow at me. "Afraid of something?"

"No," I snapped.

His mouth ticked up in amusement. "Stay here. Bezaliel's mate will be here shortly and will tend to the scratches on your face and neck."

I touched the tender skin on the side of my neck, having forgotten that I'd been scratched in the tumble to the ground with the dryad.

"What is the black madness? What was wrong with that dryad?"

He didn't answer me and marched for the door.

"Where are you going?"

"To bathe in the stream. I'm a bit soiled if you hadn't noticed."

Between his hunt of the deer and his killing of the dryad, his trousers and body were indeed soiled. He looked every inch the wild beast fae. But he was the king of this clan. How interesting.

There was little in the room other than his very large bed of furs. Several hand-woven baskets lined one tent wall, and each basket was made of a pale weave with a darker thread woven into intricate patterns—leaves, a great tree, and a wolf. There was beauty and art here.

I walked to the left where a tufted cushion backed against the tent and a rug, also woven with delicate patterns of ivy spread out beneath a low table. There was enough pillowed seating for many. He must have others dine with him here. I wondered for a moment if he had a special female amongst his people.

The tent flap opened and in stepped…a light fae female. A wood fae. I blinked in surprise as she walked toward me, smiling, a basket on her arm. She wore a dress of red-deer hide and a baby was snuggled in a cloth sling across her chest.

"Hello. It's Jessamine, isn't it? I'm Tessa, Bezaliel's mate."

"Yes." I stared as she stopped in front of me, her dark hair braided down her back, her tiny, pointed ears exposed and tipped pink from the cold.

"You're a wood fae, aren't you?"

"Yes." She laughed. "Come and sit." She gestured toward the lounge area.

I sat on one of the cushions and she settled beside me, setting down her basket. "First, you must eat something. I passed Redvyr coming in, and he told me you don't eat meat or fish. Or rather, he grumbled it."

"He does tend to grumble a lot," I admitted.

She laughed. "He does. But I have bread and cheese here." She set something wrapped in muslin aside. "Salted fish. I'll save that for myself later." She then unwrapped a thick round of pale bread and soft, white cheese. "Here you are."

I didn't hesitate, falling into the meal heartily. "Thank you so much," I said between chews.

"You're welcome. I have some salve as well that may help with those scratches."

Her baby squirmed and mewled. "Quiet now, Saralyn. This is my daughter," she said to me, pulling wide the sling so I could peek at the sleepy-eyed little girl with long lashes and hazel eyes. Her skin was much fairer than the beast fae, but her hair was dark, two nubs of horns showing on her head.

"She is lovely," I admitted.

"She is a handful," laughed Tessa. "Here, this paste will help you heal quickly and numb any pain."

I let her dab the paste of salve onto my cheek and neck, while I continued to eat. I hadn't realized how hungry I was. The bread was crusty on the outside, soft on the inside. The cheese was salty and creamy.

"Delicious," I muttered as I shoved the last bite of cheese into my mouth.

"We keep some mountain goats for the cheese. But we can't harvest our grain this far north. It simply doesn't grow well here.

We trade with southerners for it." She put the salve away and wiped her hands, her baby now sleeping soundly against her chest. "We are able to grow some delicious vegetables here though. I'll ask Shearah to make you a hearty soup. She runs the hearth guild."

"That would be lovely. Thank you." I wiped my mouth on the rag that the bread had been wrapped in. "You have guilds here?"

"Oh, yes. We have one for each area of need in our community. Each clan member learns what they are most skilled in and what brings them the most joy. Then they join their guild of choice."

This surprised me. "Everyone decides on their own? Your clan leader doesn't appoint them?"

"Lord Redvyr?" She laughed. "No, he wouldn't want anything to do with that. How would he know what guides another's heart?"

I could hardly fathom what she was telling me.

"We have a ceremony of celebration, of course," she added, noting my confusion, "when someone reaches an expert status in their guild."

In Morodon, my father would often speak to the heads of the masonry guilds and such to make decisions on what new temple or bridge or palatial villa to build next. We had guilds for artisans and merchants for villagers to be appointed to in order to learn a trade. But it was *always* my father who would assign guild appointments. The good appointments often depended on the family's loyalty and tribute to the crown.

"It's unusual to hear that your clan have a choice in the matter. That's not how it's done where I'm from."

She smiled sympathetically. "I don't come from a village that supports one another either if that makes you feel any better." She rubbed a hand along her daughter's back over the sling. "I've found that we live in harmony for the most part here in Vanglosa."

"For the most part?" I asked.

"Beast fae are emotional fae, so there is the occasional disruption."

"Like a foreign fae invading their camp?"

She laughed. "Well, when I did, it certainly stirred things up for a while." She pressed a kiss to her babe's head. "But they came around eventually."

Handing the salve back to her, I said, "I can help Shearah. I learned to cook a few things when I worked at a tavern in the Borderlands."

It was far more than was ever taught to me at home in Morodon. It wasn't proper for a princess to cook. Or learn anything of good use.

She stared at me curiously. "You lived in the Borderlands? That's so far from the skald fae."

I nodded. "Yes." But I didn't add more, wanting to keep my reasons secret for a little longer. I had a feeling I'd need to confess more than I wanted to in order for this council to allow me to stay, but I wasn't ready to divulge that yet. "And how did you come here?"

"That's a rather wild story, actually." She pulled a leather canteen from her basket and handed it to me. "My father was a tavern-keeper for our clan of wood fae. We used to live in the Myrkovir Forest, but our lord led us farther northwest when the war between the wraith fae and the moon fae threatened us."

"Your lord led you away from your home during the war?" That seemed risky, and also cowardly.

"Our lord wanted to avoid the fighting altogether," she sighed. "Eventually, he abandoned us, and our clan dwindled. Some of the stronger ones left on their own to either return to Myrkovir or find some other place that was safer to live. You see, we lived in Northgall territory, close to the Borderlands. Then my father became ill, and I knew if he died, my sister and I would be completely alone. So I went into the woods at night, sure I could find the herbs to cure him, to break the fever. I've always been good with herbs and healing. But that night, I met Bezaliel in the woods."

She blushed, and I knew at once that the encounter must have been a special one.

"I have been with his clan ever since."

Confused, I asked, "And your sister? Is she here too?"

"No. She has found her own way. She lives in Gadlizel with her shadow fae priest."

"What?" I was completely dumbfounded. "I'm sorry if I appear ignorant. But I've never heard of a light fae living with a beast fae mate, nor a shadow fae priest."

I'd seen a few shadow fae priests come and go at Haldek's tavern. I wondered if her sister was with one of them.

"There are many new things happening in our world," she admitted. "Some good. Some not." She frowned for a moment then smiled again. "With King Gollaya making Princess Una his queen, we are living in a new world indeed."

I stiffened at the sound of the wraith king's name. The last time I'd heard it spoken was an unpleasant memory. The buzzing of bees and cloying scent of the Mevian lord's perfume wafted over my memory.

"Indeed," I admitted.

She placed a hand on mine. "I am glad you're here. Though it seems you may be in some trouble yourself, don't worry. The Vanglosa clan will protect you. I'm sure of it."

The tent flap slapped open and Redvyr stepped inside. I gasped at his appearance. His dark hair hung in damp waves around his face, his fine black leather vest stitched with a white wolf on each side. I couldn't seem to catch my breath.

His feral frown in place, he snapped in his usual gruff tone, "The council is ready. I will bring you to the kella'mir."

Standing, I asked, "What is kella'mir?"

"Come," he demanded and exited the tent.

I rolled my eyes at his curt attitude.

Tessa smiled and took my arm in hers. "Kella'mir is a place and an event. It is the center of the village beneath the sacred tree, where all important ceremonies and councils are heard and celebrated. Such as when I bound myself to Bezaliel."

"Or when they banish a skald fae into the wilderness," I couldn't help but say.

Tessa laughed and guided me outside. There was no one on the path this time, and I was sure I knew why. They were all waiting for me at this kella'mir.

"They won't abandon you to the wilderness," she said. "Unless you deserve it."

I swallowed the lump in my throat. If they knew I was a syrenskyn, they would surely decide it was better to get rid of me quickly. I was a danger. Though I'd only hurt one person intentionally, and under threat of beatings, I would never hurt anyone in this clan. Still, my former betrothed wouldn't stop sending his men to hunt for me. Of that, I was sure.

"Do not worry," she said, hugging me closer as we walked on. "You'll be fine."

She turned us on a path among a row of tents that were built differently. These had open walls for ventilation with furnaces and anvils for blacksmithing, and burning ovens for cooking and drying hides. Up ahead, there was a massive oak tree, its heavy branches reaching down like arms to crown and embrace the raised dais. Upon the dais, at its center in front of the wide trunk, Redvyr sat on a wooden seat, a throne I suppose. Surrounding him was a line of both male and female beast fae sitting upon stools in a semi-circle.

Tessa stopped in front of the dais and gestured for me to go up the steps, giving me a reassuring smile before she joined her mate off to the side. The hard expressions on the council's faces and on Redvyr's gave me no encouragement. The sound of buzzing wings drew my attention to a sprite with a vibrant blue body and round, black eyes that perched on a lower branch of the oak tree. She must be friendly to the clan, for no one seemed bothered by her presence.

Gulping down my fear, I raised my chin and walked up the steps, ready to plead for my safety—for my protection. I was willing to beg if that's what it took. My own father had already sold me off to a murdering, vengeful psychopath, and now his hunters were closing in. I would do anything to avoid falling into his hands.

If the only outcome for my escape was into the arms of death, then I would go. But in truth, I was too fond of life. I didn't want to die, even if I was 'blessed' with this awful gift from the gods. So I readied myself to say whatever would be necessary to help me stay hidden with the beast fae of Vanglosa.

CHAPTER 7

Redvyr

Jessamine marched up the steps with a hard set to her chin, courage and defiance glittering in her green eyes. I could not help but admire her, knowing she was in a vulnerable situation. Wolf left my side and sat beside her, his head level with hers. She smiled and brushed a hand along his shoulder before facing forward again.

I'd told the council what little I knew of her when they assembled. The only fact I knew for certain was that she was running from an enemy, one she hadn't admitted to me. But now, if she wanted our help, she'd have to confess more truth than she had been willing to give me in the woods when I found her.

"State your name," said Wyzel, the senior elder of our council. Her gray hair was braided in neat, tiny plaits around her four horns.

"Jessamine."

"You must have a surname," added Bowden, a beast fae male descended from a line of healers.

Jessamine's eyes widened slightly, and I heard the speeding of her pulse before she answered.

"I am Jessamine Glenmyr."

I stiffened, noting a murmur among the elders. But it was Wyzel who asked the obvious question.

"You are related to the royal family of Morodon?"

Jessamine clenched her jaw before finally answering. "I am the youngest daughter of Darian Glenmyr, King of Morodon."

I scoffed, leaning forward in my chair, elbows on knees. "You did not tell me this," I accused.

"You did not ask," she answered curtly.

"What we need to know now," began Wyzel, "is why you are running. And from whom. If you are defying your father's wishes, we could start a war with Morodon by allowing you to remain with us."

The defiance slipped from her expression, replaced with a touch of fear. An instant growl vibrated up my throat. I didn't like seeing that on her face. Wyzel arched a questioning brow at me, but I kept my gaze on the light fae female.

"We are a peaceful people," added Bowden gently. "We live apart from other fae by choice, preferring not to embroil ourselves with the politics and wars of others. Tell us, Jessamine. Why are you hiding from your own people?"

She clasped her webbed hands tightly together in front of her and exhaled a heavy breath. "It is true that I am defying my father."

Some of the clan whispered at her admittance, but they quieted quickly when she went on.

"But please understand that my father has sold me to an evil man who wishes to use my…my magick to hurt others."

"*Sold* you?" I growled, gripping the arm of my chair with force.

Her gaze met mine. "In marriage, Lord Redvyr."

"To. *Whom.*" I realized my beastly rage was filling me up, my voice feral, my tail twitching, at this new confession, but I couldn't swallow it down now if I tried.

"His name is Lord Gael of the royal House of Ryleen. He is the high lord of Mevia."

"What magick do you possess?" asked Wyzel calmly while my blood boiled inside my veins.

Jessamine blinked nervously, her voice shaking slightly as she said, "I am a willoden. I can control water. I am also a nendovir. I have the ability to speak to and befriend naiads."

More murmurs broke out among the people. Even Wyzel's gray brows lifted in surprise. "This is a unique gift, to be a nendovir. Naiads are a fierce, unfriendly creature to the fae. How would your mate want you to use this gift for evil?"

"He is not her mate," I bit out angrily with more force than I intended, fury still pouring through my veins. Holding her gaze, I demanded, "You have not bound yourself to this Lord Gael, have you?"

She shook her head. "I have not. I ran away from my home when he made it known that I was to be a tool for violence."

"What violence do you speak of?" asked Lorelyn, the youngest on our council.

Her gentle, calm voice must have given Jessamine some reassurance to say what she was obviously holding back. I'm sure my gruff manners weren't helping, but I also couldn't control the hot fury needing an outlet from my body. I couldn't temper my reaction to hearing that Jessamine was being forced to marry an evil man. What kind of father would do that to his daughter?

"I have another gift," she said, clearing her voice. "It is a rare one. But I prefer not to speak of it." Her face flushed pink with emotion.

When the stag dryad had attacked Jessamine, I'd been in a haze of rage, but I'd noticed her skin glowing as bright as moonlight. It faded after the attack was over, after I'd killed and ripped the dryad to shreds. I'd been consumed by my own thoughts of destroying the creature that had dared to hurt her. I'd thought her luminescent skin was part of her witchy magick of course, but I didn't know what kind. And while she was withholding some crucial information from the council, I didn't want to expose her secret, even if I still didn't understand it.

Perhaps, it wasn't very powerful magick. It hadn't worked on the stag, but that didn't surprise me. He was infected with this disease that had begun to spread to many creatures in Northgall. Perhaps this disease makes them immune to magick or simply stronger against it.

Not long ago, we'd seen a small pack of Meer-wolves with the same infection when they attacked the wraith king's camp near Belladum. And there had been whispers of other creatures behaving strangely. I wondered if that had anything to do with the fact there was little game to be found on my hunt.

"She could be a threat to our clan," said councilman Vedgar, bringing my attention back to the present. "She refuses to tell us, even after she admitted she can do violence upon others with this *magick* of hers."

"If she'd wanted to harm us, she could've killed our own lord out there in the woods all alone," reasoned Wyzel.

"I would not harm anyone in your clan. I can promise you that. Lord Gael wanted me to use my gift on his enemies. I cannot—I will not use my magick to harm others." She paused, swallowing hard. "I simply need a place to hide from Lord Gael's men. They are the ones who are hunting me. I was living and working in the Borderlands, but they found me and chased me into the woods." She gestured toward Wolf who sat loyally at her side, like her own personal guard. "This Meer-wolf found me when I'd nearly died from the cold. Then," she gestured toward me, "Lord Redvyr sheltered me from the cold and brought me safely here."

Wyzel nodded with approval. "It is our way, Jessamine. We have learned this from the Meer-wolves who we revere. Meer-wolves are a fierce pack creature. They will protect their own with their lives. Once, long ago, one of our ancestors was injured in the wild, his leg broken. He would have died if it weren't for the Meer-wolf who took him into his pack, brought him meat to cook on the fire, and nursed him to health."

Jessamine listened attentively, her expressive eyes wide with wonder and curiosity.

"Because of this, it has been our tradition and our sacred promise to be fiercely loyal like the wolves, to protect like the wolves, and to show compassion to strangers as they once did for us. We revere the wolf, because we see ourselves in them. Lord Redvyr honored our sacred oath in helping you and bringing you here, as he should."

"Oh," she said, lowering her gaze, seeming disappointed for some reason.

"She is still in danger," I stated firmly. "To honor our law, we must continue to protect her from the Mevian guards. And this Lord *Gael*." My voice rumbled dark and deep; its timbre rough.

My inner beast wanted to lash out and strike something dead. Bite something hard.

Wyzel turned her gaze to Lorelyn. "Can you see the way forward for us regarding Jessamine? Is it safe for her, and for us, to keep her among our clan?"

Lorelyn stood, hands clasped before her. "I can read the runes, but only with a drop of her blood."

Jessamine turned to me in confusion.

"Lorelyn is a world seer," I explained. "For our clan and the beast fae."

She nodded and took a step forward, holding out her hand without fear. "You may use my blood."

I wasn't sure if she had experience with seers. There were three kinds. Soul seers who foretold the destinies of an individual. Kings typically had a soul seer on hand, but I never did. There were god seers who were quite rare. They channeled the will of the gods. Then there were world seers, the most common kind. They prophesied the fates of fae kind. Lorelyn was born with this gift to guide the beast fae. Her premonitions had helped us numerous times.

Lorelyn removed a small blade from her belt, but suddenly I was on my feet. It wasn't that I didn't trust Lorelyn, but something inside me rebelled at the thought of her cutting Jessamine.

"She is my responsibility," I told Lorelyn as I unsheathed my dagger.

The young seer dipped her dark head, while I gently gripped Jessamine's wrist. I flicked my gaze to hers. "It won't hurt."

"I'm not afraid," she replied instantly.

I couldn't help but smile at her courage. While it was true that I would cause as little pain as possible, she'd been all but dragged to our clan's home where my people weren't exactly greeting her with open arms. She couldn't know for certain that we didn't intend her harm, and for some reason, she trusted me.

With the tip of my blade, I pressed gently into the fleshy part of her palm until a pinprick of blood pooled there. I then returned to my chair.

Lorelyn walked to stand in front of Jessamine. "It is best that we sit."

Lorelyn lowered to the wooden stage and crossed her legs. Jessamine joined her, still holding out her palm. Lorelyn held the light fae's upturned hand in her own, and with her forefinger she swiped the tiny spot of blood in five different directions.

Everyone remained silent while a ripple of magick hummed in the air, radiating from Lorelyn. She was the only one in our clan who held gods-given magick. And that was assuredly because she wasn't pure beast fae. Her grandmother had been a wraith fae. Though she showed no outward ancestry other than her four smooth, elegant horns—not patterned with the thick ridged spirals like ours—she appeared only as a beast fae female.

"Hmm," said Lorelyn, her eyes closed and her head bent over their hands, "the winter holds danger." Her voice echoed with the vibration of magick. "But not because of the light fae female. On the contrary, her presence will bring about…a salvation."

Lorelyn opened her eyes, glowing bright with the ethereal energy flowing through her. She curled Jessamine's fingers into her own palm and looked up at the council. At Wyzel.

"I do not simply recommend that we offer Jessamine protection for her own sake. But for ours as well."

"Can you see any more?" asked Bowden. "Any details?"

"Is it from these Mevian guards that she saves us?" interjected Wyzel.

"No." Lorelyn shook her head. "She is not the cause of the trouble I foresee. Her blood will not show me more. Only that we need her as much as she needs us. Perhaps more so."

I frowned at this premonition. Lorelyn was never wrong, but how could this light fae save us from an unseen danger? Me and my warriors could outfight any monsters, feral or otherwise, in the foothills of the Solgavia Mountains.

Wyzel turned her gaze to me. "Then it is decided, in my opinion. But the council always casts a vote. Heeding Lorelyn's vision, Jessamine will come with us to our winter camp. When we return to Vanglosa after the winter, surely the threat of these Mevians will be gone from our lands. She can journey and seek shelter with some of her own kind then."

My tail twitched, my body restless, agitated.

"Does the council concur with my decree?" asked Wyzel.

"Aye," said Bowden.

"Aye," added Lorelyn.

The others followed suit then I added, "Aye" last, since the lord of the clan must also agree with the council on any decisions.

"Then this kella'mir has concluded," declared Wyzel, standing from her stool with her walking stick in one hand, the beads of glass and silver in her braids clacking together as she moved. "I suggest you assist her with some warmer clothing, Lord Redvyr. That won't be satisfactory for our journey to Ghasta Vale."

I merely nodded as the council stood and ambled toward the steps, each taking a moment to shake Jessamine's hand. Even the older and more distrustful of those outside our clan took a moment to greet her properly. The clan dispersed, slowly meandering away to their work for the day.

I stood and met her at the center of the dais where she had remained, wide-eyed but seemingly relieved.

"Thank you," she said. "For helping me in the woods. Even if it was only to fulfill your clan's oath."

"I always honor my oaths."

"And I owe you more thanks for supporting me here. For voting to shelter me a bit longer."

She seemed suddenly shy, her voice brittle in a way I didn't like. She didn't sound like the willful woman I'd met in the woods and had traveled with these past two days.

"Why do you sound like that?" I demanded.

"Like what?"

"Defeated. Weak."

She scoffed. "Perhaps because I had to admit a shameful secret to your entire clan."

"Well, I don't like it. Get that sound out of your voice."

"You can't tell me what to feel and how to *sound*, whether you're the king of this clan or not, *Lord Redvyr*," she snapped.

"That's better."

She rolled her eyes, muttering, "Insufferable, idiotic male."

I smiled.

"Will you just bring me to someone who will help me with the clothing I need?"

"Right this way."

I led her down the steps and through the village toward Sorka's work tent. Everyone stared as we passed, but Jessamine kept her gaze forward, seemingly undisturbed. I liked that. She may be a light fae but there was obvious strength in her.

"Why didn't you tell me about the Mevian guards?" I asked as we rounded a corner toward where Sorka worked.

"I didn't want to."

"You just told the council. The entire village."

"Because I had no choice. If I didn't tell the truth, they wouldn't agree to help me."

"I helped you."

"Because of your oath or whatever." She exhaled a heavy sigh. "Don't worry. After winter, they will certainly be gone from these parts. Then I can find another place. Somewhere."

I grunted, not liking that same sadness leaking back into her voice.

Sorka's workers were scraping the hides clean of flesh that were stretched taut on wooden frames next to her work tent. The females glanced toward Jessamine curiously but kept scraping their combs over the hide.

Leading her through the open flap of Sorka's tent, I saw her in the back assisting her young daughter who stitched the lining of a skirt with the wool fabric we'd gotten in Hellamir on our last trade visit.

"Sorka," I called to the tall female who led the tailoring guild for our clan.

She looked up, her hair plaited neatly around her dainty horns and down her back. She smiled, at both me and Jessamine.

"I heard you'd be coming to me with our new guest."

"You did not attend the kella'mir?" I asked.

The clan wasn't required to attend and witness council meetings, but I assumed every beast fae in camp would be there today. It was rare to have strangers in the village, especially light fae.

"There is too much work to be done before we leave for Ghasta Vale. Besides," she smiled, nodding to other females pretending to be working on their tailoring while obviously staring at us, "my gossipmongers keep me informed."

One of them hissed in protest. Velga, I believe, in the corner.

Sorka's young daughter, only thirteen if I recalled correctly, was at her side tugging on her mother's white-hide skirt. There were no animals with white hides, but Sorka was a talented tailor. She'd devised ways to dye the hides without compromising the strength of the material.

"Introduce me," young Beska whispered loudly.

"I haven't been introduced myself, Bes."

"I apologize," I added. "Jessamine, this is Sorka. She is the guildmaster of tailoring for all of the clan. And this is her daughter, Beska."

"It's a pleasure to meet you," said Jessamine.

"For us as well," said Sorka sincerely, examining her dress. "Your clothing is made well, though it isn't sufficient for winter here in Northgall."

"That's what I've been told." Jessamine pulled out a white pelt from a pocket in her apron tied at her waist. "Would you be able to help me create gloves from this?"

"Oh, my." Sorka took it and ran her long fingers over the silky pelt. "This is very fine indeed. An elkmine otter pelt. Those are rare."

"Where did you get it?" I asked.

"An old wraith fae trapper gave it to me, right before I left the Borderlands."

"You mean ran away, don't you?" Velga insinuated, barely glancing up from her embroidery work.

"Yes," agreed Jessamine. "The trapper actually tripped one of the guards for me." She smiled, and it made me proud that she seemed stronger in spirit since the kella'mir, despite her circumstances.

"I can make the gloves, Mama," said Bes. "If you would allow me to."

Sorka smiled at her daughter. "Bes is very skillful. She can do the work for you."

"I don't know how to repay you," said Jessamine.

Sorka frowned. "We do not pay each other for work in the clan. We all work and give in some way to keep the clan fed and sheltered."

"I suppose I must find a way to do my part as well."

The females in the corner whispered and giggled together, but I gave them a sharp look that silenced them quickly enough.

"Please supply her with what she needs," I said, changing the subject, my gut sour from the tension in the room.

Jessamine wasn't a member of our clan and she wouldn't be staying beyond winter, so she wouldn't be expected to take on a role here. If she did, that would give her permanence among the clan. That was why the females laughed, mocking Jessamine for thinking she had a place here. And though she was merely a guest, I wouldn't have her be ridiculed for wanting to help.

"Yes, Lord Redvyr. You may go."

I frowned, wondering why I was being dismissed. Then Sorka clarified. "I will need to get her measurements, then she will try on some dresses to see which one fits."

Heat crawled up my chest and neck as I imagined Jessamine disrobing. I turned and called over my shoulder. "Bes, bring her to my tent when you are done."

"Yes, my lord."

Then I was gone, needing some fresh air and to see Bezaliel. We needed to plan to move the camp.

CHAPTER 8

Jessamine

Sorka dismissed all of the beast fae females who had been embroidering and stitching a great many garments when I'd arrived.

"I think some privacy is needed," she said to me when they left.

"I appreciate that."

It was obvious the other females didn't like my presence. And while I understood them mistrusting a stranger, a light fae at that, I wished they didn't dislike me so much.

"May I stay, Mama?" asked the sweet-faced girl with two horns curling prettily out of her chestnut hair.

"No, my sweet."

"Oh, please, please—"

"I don't mind," I interjected. "Bes will need to get measurements for my hands to make my gloves."

"Yes, she's right, Mama," she said, her orange eyes wide and pleading, brown freckles dappling her nose.

"Alright then." Sorka gestured for me to follow her to a wooden frame where many garments were hung on pegs. "I may have something that fits your height, but I believe we will have to make adjustments to the bodice."

She wasn't being impolite. I'd already noted that the beast fae females were built taller and more delicate-boned than the males of the clan. They were slim, while I was a more full-figured female.

"Let's see. This one may be just the right length. I added a fur trim to the rounded neckline for extra warmth."

At home in Morodon, I had dressed in fine silks with detailed embroidery of water lilies and sea creatures. The weather was temperate, so we never needed to dress for warmth. By the time I got to the Borderlands, I'd already traded my finer gown for a practical one. I acquired a few more in the same simple, homespun style with a working woman's bodice, changing my chemise daily and washing my few dresses twice a week

But this was something I never imagined wearing. The entire dress was made of a soft hide dyed a pale green, with the inside wool lining being a deeper shade of green. There was the softest brown and white fur lining the scooped neck all the way around. More fur trim ringed the wrists of the long sleeves. The dress was one piece, but the skirt was sewn in different panels than the top.

"I just finished this one a few days ago. I'm very proud of it."

"You should be. How did you get the hide this color?"

"The leaves of the elderberry tree are ground into a paste and when added with deer tallow, it not only dyes the fabric, but softens the hide further." She pointed to the fur. "This here is from a mountain hare. I am able to gather all of my resources in the spring and summer. Then I spend autumn and winter sewing and embroidering, teaching the others in the guild who work here."

She began to loosen the laces at the back of the gown. I wasn't shy, so I undressed quickly, untying my apron first then undoing the lacings of my bodice. After setting those on a worktable, I slipped my dress over my head, noting that Bes was staring at me.

"Beska, don't be rude."

The pretty girl quickly ducked her head and looked at the floor.

"It's okay," I laughed. "I imagine you've never seen a skald fae before."

She lifted her head and shook it. "You don't have horns. And your skin is so white. Your hair as red as a summer plum. And your hands are weird with the skin in between your fingers."

"Bes! Do not say such things. She may think us rather strange as well, but she isn't pointing it out."

I smiled at Sorka then held out my hands for Bes.

"You can look at them if you want. The skin there is very soft but tough."

"Why do you have it?" she asked.

"Some say it is part of our heritage from our ancestor, the sea goddess Nemia. We have it on our toes too. It does help us to swim. I am a very fast swimmer," I bragged with a wink.

Bes's eyes widened. "I don't know how to swim. Would you teach me?"

"Sweetheart, you know very well we cannot swim in the winter," chided her mother.

"But in the summer, she can teach me. When we return to Vanglosa."

Sorka and I shared a knowing look. I would be gone by summer.

"It will fit better without your undergarment," Sorka suggested, nodding to the chemise I still wore.

After I pulled it off over my head, now naked except for my boots, Sorka held the dress open for me lower to the ground.

"You can step into it and I'll tie the lacings at the back. We'll see if I need to adjust it.

I slipped into the dress, sighing at the luxurious feel of the lining against my skin. "Your wool is so soft. It's not rough at all."

"Thank you. We take great care to create fabrics that are durable yet comfortable."

Yet again, I had to chastise myself. Though I'd never given much thought to the beast fae who lived so far away from Morodon, when I'd been found by Redvyr, I wondered about this clan of his. When I saw that they lived in tents, I assumed they might live without any luxuries at all. I was wrong. Here I was standing in perhaps the most beautiful, well-made gown I'd ever worn. There was even a delicate stitching of ivy along the neckline, enhancing the beauty of the design.

"I don't think there will need to be any adjustments at all," she said as she tied the lacings in the back. "Does it feel too tight?"

"No. It's snug, but very comfortable." I gazed down at it, noting that my bosom pushed up a bit at the rounded neck, but no more than it did in the bodice I wore before. "It's so beautiful."

When I turned to look at Sorka, Bes gasped.

"It is so pretty on you. Mama, it's like you made it for her."

"Indeed." Sorka smiled. "It seems Ivenzel guided my hand for you, Jessamine."

Smoothing my hands over my hips, I asked, "Who is Ivenzel?"

"She is our goddess of the hearth. A dark fae goddess. You have not heard of her?"

I shook my head. "I'm afraid my father only allowed us to be taught about the gods of the sea and waters. He was very strict and made sure our tutors kept to a limited study of only our part of the world."

Sorka's lips thinned as she gave me a sympathetic look. "I see. Well, while you are here, I am happy to teach you anything you'd like to know."

"I can't thank you enough," I told her sincerely. "You've been more than kind and welcoming."

"Lord Redvyr would be upset if I wasn't," she said. "But I am happy to make you feel at home while you are here. Let's get your hands measured for the gloves, and I'd like to measure your feet as well. Those boots appear well-made, but they are likely not lined properly for warmth."

"You are right. I thought my toes were going to fall off when I…when Wolf first found me."

I sat on a stool, liking the way the ankle-length dress hugged my body, the lining making me feel warm and snug. Yet it wasn't constricting, the skirt draping out for movement. My dress I'd bought in the Borderlands wasn't nearly as comfortable.

"I'll need to hold onto my old clothes for the end of winter," I said while shoving off my boots and the thin stockings beneath.

"Of course. I'll have them washed and set aside for you."

"Here, Bes. I know you'll want a good look at my weird toes," I teased.

"They're not terribly weird," she said while gawking at my webbed feet, a blush coloring her cheeks.

Sorka and I laughed at Bes trying so hard not to look absolutely shocked.

"Where is this winter camp?" I asked. "Ghasta Vale?"

"A few days northwest of here, closer to the foothills of the Solgavia Mountains."

"I don't understand why you'd go farther north for winter."

Sorka smiled. "Ghasta Vale is a special place. It is a deep valley between two high-peaked mountains. The valley is protected from the winds and most of the snows. There is a wide stream that provides fish, and the plains provide game. In these lowlands of Vanglosa, the snows can become very deep. But in Ghasta Vale, it is a kind of sanctuary."

"It is warm there?" I asked, somewhat confused.

"Oh, no." She laughed as Bes used a long carved flat stick with markings on it to measure my feet. "But it is warmer there than here. And much less snow in the Vale." She noted the length of my foot then Bes measured my hands and fingers. "Besides, it is tradition. We are a nomadic people, and we thrive on the movement of the clan with the seasons."

"Oh, Jessamine," exclaimed Bes. "Wait till you see where the clans gather at the end of winter. It is a great celebration at Johl Tundra, and it is so beautiful there!"

"I'm not sure I'll be with you for that celebration," I told her honestly. "I'm not sure how long the council or Lord Redvyr will allow me to stay."

We all fell silent for a moment while Sorka stood and gathered my old gown and bodice. "Bes will let you know when we have your gloves and boots ready."

"I appreciate that." I folded up my chemise to carry with me, wanting to keep it to sleep in. Though I wasn't sure where I'd be sleeping yet.

"And here you are. You must also have a warm cloak." She pulled out a fur cloak with a hood, all in silvery gray, looking exactly like the fur I'd slept on Redvyr's camp.

"Is this from a barga?"

Sorka wrapped it around my shoulders and tied the clasp at my throat. "Yes. Redvyr and the warriors hunt at least one each spring when they come out of their caves." She stepped back and examined me with a satisfied nod. "It is tradition."

I smiled. "The beast fae are fond of their traditions."

"We live by them."

I looked down at the dress and cloak and sighed. "Thank you, Sorka."

She laughed. "I can't believe that. A Morodon princess? You've likely been dressed in the finest gowns coin can buy."

I couldn't explain that while yes, they may have been elaborate and lovely, they weren't created with such care for both beauty and warmth, a garment that nurtured while showcasing the finest craftsmanship.

"Trust me, Sorka. You have magick of your own."

The woman's bronzed cheeks darkened with a blush. "You are kind to say so." She heaved a sigh, looking out toward the tent flap. "I imagine my seamstresses are tired of waiting. Bes, you take Jessamine back to Lord Redvyr. I am not sure where you'll be housed."

"Me neither," I told her. "Well, Bes, will you show me the way?"

The young girl beamed. "Gladly." Then she took my hand—my webbed hand—and led me out of the tent to find Lord Redvyr. Wolf was there, waiting for me.

"Come on, Wolf," I called to him, though there was no need. He trotted alongside us, tongue lolling like he was happy to accompany us.

My heart twisted sweetly at Bes's kindness and friendly gesture at holding my hand. I glanced down at the dear girl proudly leading me through the camp and realized I had an instant affection for her. And Sorka. Wolf, too. And dare I admit, even Lord Redvyr.

Lifting my chin proudly, I followed Bes's lead, rather excitedly anticipating the clan king's expression when he saw me in this dress.

CHAPTER 9

Redvyr

"We'll set up camp at the lower part of the Vale." I pointed to the map, showing Bezaliel where I intended.

"We'll be farther from the game."

I shrugged. "We'll be closer to the fishing at the stream."

"Fishing." Brohm sneered.

"It is easier to come by and more sustainable," I added.

"True," agreed Bezaliel. "When do we leave?"

"The camp should begin breaking down tomorrow. Brohm, you'll lead them to the Vale. You and I," I told Bezaliel, "will take Leifkyn and Dayn to Hellamir for grain and barley."

"And Tessa, of course," he added.

"Of course," I agreed. "She is our best liaison."

"And you once said she would become a burden to our clan." Bezaliel grinned as he folded the map on the table and handed it to Brohm.

"That was when you first brought her here," I argued. "I came around."

"And here you are, bringing another light fae beauty into the clan."

My body stiffened while he and Brohm grinned at each other.

"I did not bring her here," I argued. "Wolf brought her and now I'm stuck with her. The council has made their decision."

"Which you heartily agreed with when they suggested she stay with us through winter."

"It is our oath as beast fae to help strangers in need."

"Indeed," agreed Brohm, still grinning. "Especially pretty ones."

"Just what are you two getting at?" I demanded, arms crossed.

"You fancy her." Bezaliel shrugged. "It's not a sin. She's quite fair."

"Very fair," agreed Brohm.

A growl vibrated up my chest, and I realized it wasn't because of their teasing but because I didn't like them noticing how *fair* Jessamine was.

"Lord Redvyr?" Bes's soft voice drifted through the tent flap before she pushed inside the council's tent where I often met with my men. "We've been looking for you everywhere."

Jessamine followed Bes inside, and my entire body locked tight at the sight of her. Dressed in a gown and fur-trimmed cloak made for a beast fae female, one that highlighted her alluring figure, I could do nothing but stare. When I noticed that the other two males were doing the same, I snapped to them both.

"You two may go and prepare as I told you."

"Yes, Lord Redvyr." Bezaliel was practically laughing as he exited the tent with Brohm following.

"I will go and work on your gloves now," Bes told Jessamine. "I don't work as quickly as Mama, but I promise to make them beautiful."

"Thank you, Bes. I know you will."

Then we were alone, and I was still struggling to breathe. She turned to face me, arching a brow at my silence.

"You don't approve?" She glanced down at herself.

"Why do you ask that?"

"Because you're scowling again."

"I have other things on my mind."

"Like what?"

"Like moving my clan to the winter camp when there's a sickness infecting creatures across our land."

"The dryad." She pursed her brow. "So he *was* sick. I sensed it. And his eyes had black threads spreading from the pupil. His skin, there was a dark webbing crawling underneath as well. Is it the Parviana plague?"

I'd heard of this disease that had begun with the moon fae and had spread far and wide. The wraith king's wife was on a mission to cure all of those who'd been infected. But what had taken root in that dryad stag wasn't this light fae virus that stole one's magick.

"No," I told her. "That sickness isn't what is spreading here in the north."

"You've seen it before then?"

"Not long ago, there was an attack by a small pack of Meer-wolves. These hounds were maddened, in a rage to kill. That is not normal for Meer-wolves. They never attack our kind blindly. Only in self-defense do they kill fae kind."

She stepped forward, bringing her sweet scent closer. I stiffened again, not liking my reaction to her at all.

"There was a strange madness in his eyes. And his words," she added.

"What did he say to you?" I hadn't heard what he'd said.

When I'd sensed her in danger, my sole intent was to tear the threat to pieces. And so I had.

"I believe he intended to…eat me."

"Dryads do not eat meat of any kind," was all I could say. "Especially another fae creature."

"I know," she agreed. "That's why it shocked me."

While I wanted to pretend she must be wrong, I believed her. This wasn't the first creature that had been infected with this kind of dark madness.

"There have been strange whispers that come from those living in the mountains."

"Do you know the cause?"

"No." That was what troubled me the most. "So what is this gift you have that you refused to confess to the council?"

Her posture straightened, her chin taking on a defensive tilt. I couldn't help but smile. "I have already said I do not wish to tell. That includes to you."

"If you are a part of this clan, then I am now your lord. You are beholden to tell me."

She didn't respond, clamping her jaw tight.

"You do not like to speak of your magick," I teased.

"I do not."

"You were trying to use it on the dryad, weren't you?"

Her gaze snapped up to mine. She seemed about to pretend that she hadn't tried, to lie to me. But then she answered, "It didn't work on him. Not for long."

"Dryads are god-touched," I informed her. "They are able to resist fae magick more than others. They are also not entirely like us, their minds more linked with the earth and nature than the fae world."

"I am aware," she stated with some superiority. "But I wasn't going to simply lay down and die."

"Of course not. I was there. I didn't let you die."

She went silent again, her expression unreadable, her green eyes glittering.

"This man your father sold you into marriage to. What was his name again?" I remembered his name. It was imprinted in my brain. For if ever I laid eyes on him, I planned to rip his head from his body. Still, I asked for his name, not wanting her to know how absolutely intently I had memorized every word she said at the kella'mir.

"Lord Gael."

There was disdain in her voice when she said it. Good.

"Who did he want you to harm for him?"

She gulped nervously. "I am afraid to tell you."

I stepped closer, basking in her sweet scent now, and crossed my arms. "Why?"

"What if you tell him? And he becomes angry because my family wishes him dead? Then he might target me to get back at them."

"Do I know this male?" My voice had dropped, my tail twitching behind me.

"Everyone does." She dropped her gaze.

"You will tell me, Jessamine. As I have promised to protect you from these Mevians, I will do the same from anyone else who would wish you harm while you are with my clan. Besides, I would not tell this secret. But I am the lord of this clan, and I must have all of the information in order to protect them as well."

"You promise you will not share this information?" She met my gaze again, a plea in her worried eyes.

"Of course. Who is it?"

She blew out a shaky breath. "He wanted me to kill the wraith king. King Gollaya Verbane."

If she'd slapped me, I wouldn't have been more stunned. "Goll?"

She blinked nervously. "Do you know him well?"

I scoffed. "Yes. He is the wraith king. I am a beast fae lord. Of course I know him well. How does this magick of yours work exactly? How would you get close enough to kill a warrior like Goll?"

"I am not telling you," she snapped, her voice rising. "Besides, it doesn't matter. As soon as Lord Gael professed what he intended for me to do for him, I left him in my family's garden. Then I packed my bags and fled that night."

I stared, openly fascinated. "Did this Lord Gael promise nothing in return for you agreeing to murder the King of Northgall."

She turned away, wringing her hands. "He did. He promised me a castle of my own near the Nemian Sea. A staff so that I could live independently of him. That I'd only have to do my wifely duty to bear him an heir then I could live my own life freely."

My frame locked up again, a rumble of disapproval vibrating in my chest, an itch to seek out this *Lord* Gael. But I managed to keep calm, stating evenly, "Instead, you chose a life as an outcast from your own family, a life on the run."

She was royalty, and yet she'd been working in a tavern, living like a commoner to earn her daily bread and shelter. It was rather shocking to discover.

"What else could I do?" She scoffed, turning back to face me. "I wasn't going to actually attempt to kill the wraith king."

"No. You wouldn't have been successful, anyway."

"My magick is very powerful," she stated with confidence.

"I'm sure that it is. Even though you won't tell me what this gift from the gods is."

"Are you laughing at me?"

I was indeed smiling. "Only at the thought of you getting anywhere near King Goll and thinking you could do him any harm." I mused for a moment, wondering why she was so secretive about this gift of hers. Following my instinct, I asked, "Does this gift of yours involve seduction?"

Her eyes widened, but she didn't say a word. I chuckled. "If that is so, then you needn't worry. You'd never have gotten near King Goll. He would never be alone with any woman but his queen."

She blinked, her brow pinching. "I've been told that wraith kings often have many women. Concubines."

"Wraith kings of the past like his father, yes. But not this one. He'd have suspected something of you if you tried."

She frowned, her gaze wandering over my chest before it lifted to my eyes again.

"And what of beast fae? Do you have concubines?"

Uncrossing my arms, I stepped close to her, lifting a strand of her magnificently red hair. "Why, Jessamine. Are you interested in applying for the job?"

"Of course not," she snapped, though she did not back up or knock my hand away. "I merely would like to know what kind of clan I'm being protected by. What kind of lord is in charge."

Letting the strand fall from my claw, I brushed two of my knuckles up the column of her slender throat, an intimate gesture I couldn't stop myself from doing.

"I am a beast fae lord, female. I enjoy the taste of cunt on my tongue and the feel of my cock in a tight sheath as much as any male."

The green of her eyes was swallowed by black as her pupils dilated, her heart rate speeding up, her breath coming quicker from her partly open mouth. A mouth I longed to taste and fill, I suddenly realized with shock.

"You are very…blunt."

"Beast fae don't play with words like the fae in your father's court. Being direct is the most efficient way of communicating." I was mesmerized by the slope of her cheeks, the seeming softness of her skin, the brightness of her eyes. "So I will tell you directly that I do not collect a harem. Females become angry and jealous. I only take one at a time."

I let my knuckles slide to the base of her throat then along her shoulder to the fur-lined edge of her gown.

"I like the way this dress looks on you," I admitted, biting my tongue before I told her I'd rather see what it looked like on the floor of my tent.

She finally stepped away, breaking our contact, dropping her gaze to the ground. "W-will you put me to work in the camp?" she asked, voice quivering. "I would like to be of some use to the clan."

My entire body was hard, my sole being entranced, and she hadn't used one drop of her magick on me. I was afraid that if she did, she could overpower me too easily.

I couldn't allow myself to be weakened by anyone, least of all a skald fae female. Clearing my throat, I stepped around her, trying to knock myself out of the stupor she put me in without even trying.

"You are correct. You must be of use while you're here. Follow me."

I marched out of the tent. Already, many of the work and residential shelters were being taken down.

"We leave today?" she asked, hurrying to keep up with me.

"Tomorrow." I slowed my gait, leading her to Tessa and Bezaliel's sleeping tent which was near my own. "You can help Tessa breakdown her family shelter. With the babe, this is more difficult for her, though she will refuse to admit it."

Bezaliel's woman was a stubborn female. As if to prove my point, I found her with Saralyn strapped to her back, leaning over and digging out one of the corner spikes of her shelter by herself. The bundles of bed furs and storage baskets were already bound and stacked outside of the shelter.

"Tessa," I called.

She stood and wiped the back of her hand across a sweaty brow.

"I've brought you help."

The sprite that doted on Tessa and the babe fluttered around her and settled on Tessa's left shoulder.

"Hallizel, this is our new friend Jessamine," Tessa told the sprite.

I tensed at Tessa calling her our *friend*, but I suppose if we were protecting her, that is what she was. She certainly wasn't a clan member.

The blue-winged sprite flitted toward us and hovered in front of Jessamine. "Hello, new friend. You have bright colors. You look like a sprite."

Jessamine laughed, the sound making my belly twist. "I suppose I do. But I am a skald fae."

"I have never met one of those before." Hallizel had followed our clan around since I was a boy. It didn't surprise me that she'd never met a skald fae.

"It's a pleasure to meet you." Jessamine extended her hand.

Hallizel tapped her finger as a greeting then returned to Tessa, landing on the sleeping bundle on her back.

"Thank you for the help, Jessamine" said Tessa. "I can certainly use it."

Jessamine walked toward her, not giving me even a parting glance. "I am glad to be of use."

"It seems you've been to visit Sorka. That dress is beautiful on you."

"Thank you."

Then they set to work, digging out the corner spikes, forgetting about me. That was good. This is what Jessamine needed. Some purpose in the clan while she was here, whilst keeping out of my sight. Not because I didn't enjoy her being in my sight, but because it brought me entirely too much pleasure.

Forcing myself to turn away, I set out to break down my own tent and get ready to leave tomorrow.

CHAPTER 10
Jessamine

"When you finish eating, I'll bring you to Sorka. She can watch out for you on the journey to Ghasta Vale."

Swallowing my last bite of soft bread covered in berry butter—I'd eaten half a loaf by myself already—I stood and brushed the crumbs away.

"What do you mean?" I asked Tessa who lifted the rolled and tied fur she'd used to sleep on. "You're going as well, aren't you?"

I'd slept on my own fur in Redvyr's tent at his command with Wolf stretched out at my side. Redvyr had said that I was his responsibility, so I must sleep near him. I'd actually fallen asleep before he'd returned from making plans with his warriors for the move, so I didn't have to worry about any awkwardness. And he was already gone when I woke up this morning, so I came to help Tessa.

"To Ghasta Vale? Of course, we all are. But I'm not heading straight there," she answered, carrying her fur to their brown

Meer-wolf named Mishka. "I'll be traveling with Bezaliel, Lord Redvyr, and a few others to Hellamir first."

Wolf nudged my hip. He'd been following me around since I woke up. I patted him on his shoulder.

"Why are you going to Hellamir?"

"We must trade for grains and such." She finished tightening the strap, then straightened and smiled at me. "Otherwise we can't bake that delicious bread you devoured this morning."

"I see."

"Don't worry. We'll only be gone a few days then we'll meet you at the Vale."

"I wasn't aware that the light fae traded with dark fae there."

"Oh, they don't all trade with us. That's why I go. I can go into town and let our contact know we've arrived. Then he meets the others in the woods nearby. We have a routine."

Everyone in the camp was doing their final preparations, and Redvyr wasn't far away with Bezaliel and a few other warriors I didn't know.

"I'd like to go with you," I admitted.

While Sorka and her daughter were kind, it was obvious that many of the rest of the clan didn't like me or want me there. I wouldn't feel comfortable traveling for days with them.

"That will be up to Lord Redvyr."

Of course, it would. I turned and marched across the camp where I saw him gathered with other beast fae males, Wolf trotting alongside me.

His gaze caught on me before I was halfway to him, one of the other males gesturing and talking on until he realized Redvyr might not be listening. I shouldn't like the way he was looking at me.

Just like I shouldn't have liked the way he'd made me feel when he admitted his own needs so vulgarly to me yesterday afternoon. In that moment of time where he traced his knuckles along my throat, his voice velvety deep, speaking of cunts and cocks as if it were nothing, I thought he'd broken my brain.

In Morodon, or at least in the palace where I was raised, no one spoke of their own bodies or desires in such a way. My mother and governesses taught me and my siblings to be demure and modest and chaste. Both of my parents ensured that their daughters were always the perfect pictures of royal innocence and purity.

When my body began to form deeper curves and larger breasts than my sisters, my mother had frowned at me, as if it were my fault my body was becoming too feminine for her liking.

And when we discovered that I was a syrenskyn, she'd muttered, "I should have known. Your body has always been too curvaceous. Too buxom."

I'd been taught that my body was bad, that my beauty was distasteful, and that my ability as a syrenskyn was an embarrassment to the family. My father had made it clear that that was why I was being married off to Lord Gael who lived far away from Morodon, and the Nemian Sea, and the rest of the family. I was a shameful secret that they wanted to get rid of.

So I took care of it myself. I disappeared and found myself a place where for the first time, no one seemed to give a damn what I looked like or that I didn't look the way I *ought* to. The Borderlands were full of fae kind from across the kingdoms. And while I'd certainly had men look at me with lust in their eyes, it wasn't the same way Redvyr looked at me, the way he was watching me now.

Desire was there, yes, but something more. If I didn't know him better, I would call it admiration. But I'd done nothing for him to admire. I'd fled into the woods and nearly frozen to death, then I fell into his lap and became his responsibility. Then I'd nearly gotten myself killed by a maddened dryad stag and was now his burden for the rest of winter.

Still, that golden gaze flared brighter as I drew nearer, and it gave me more confidence for what I was about to demand.

The talking stopped altogether, the four males watching as I came to a stop in front of Lord Redvyr. I knew Bezaliel. The other two males were two of the three I'd met on my first day in the clan's camp—Leifkyn and Dayn. Both were well-built like their chief, though not as big as Redvyr. One had red eyes with lighter bronzed skin. The other had piercing orange eyes, the tip of one of his four horns chipped. He wore his long hair in a leather tie down his back.

"Good morning, Jessamine," Redvyr greeted me casually, and yet it sent a tingling thrill down my spine.

"Morning. I would like to go with you all to Hellamir."

One of his dark brows rose. "It is best that you travel on with the clan to the Vale."

"I could help Tessa with the babe, and I could go into the town with her."

We were both light fae and could blend with the townsfolk with ease.

"It would be safer as well for her to have another pair of eyes with her," I added.

"Hellamir is a safe village," said Bezaliel, his brow furrowed into a frown. "Otherwise I would not let her go."

"When was the last time you traded in Hellamir?" I asked pointedly.

Redvyr scowled at me now. "Early spring."

"Before King Gollaya joined with Queen Una as monarchs over Northgall and Lumeria." I scoffed. "You must understand that not all of the light fae cities and towns in Lumeria are happy about this merge.”

“Of course they aren’t.” His tail twitched behind him. “But Tessa is a wood fae. There will be no trouble for her.”

“Look, I know I don’t know much about the ways here in Meerland,” I said to all of them, “but I’ve traveled all the way across Lumeria from Morodon and have been to many cities and villages in between. Trust me when I tell you that the war might be over, but many of the light fae are hostile and volatile. The target of their anger isn’t always the enemy, there is a great deal of unrest and violence within the lands.”

Redvyr turned to look over his shoulder at his men. “Leave us.”

I could tell that I’d upset Bezaliel, but they must know that the war had changed things. I readied myself to be chastised for raising such fears. What I wasn’t ready for was Redvyr’s angry concern when he wrapped a hand around my upper arm.

“Who hurt you?” he demanded to know.

“What?”

“On your travels,” he pointed out coolly, “who hurt you?”

“Oh.” I hadn’t thought he would read into it. And now I couldn’t think of a reason not tell him. “It was nothing.”

“I’ll be the judge of that.” He dipped his head lower toward mine, golden gaze fierce. “Tell me when and where and who.”

Blinking quickly at the rush of memory, I told him. “It was in a small village on the edge of the Myrkovir Forest called Wyngolsen. I’d been running for a few days. Anyway, I found an inn that seemed safe.” I huffed a laugh. “But I was still dressed in a gown of my own. And I carried a purse attached to my belt. There were a few men in the tavern I was worried about, so I bolted the door and put a chair beneath the knob for protection.”

"But they got in anyway." Redvyr's voice was low and menacing, though I knew it wasn't for me.

"One of them did. Came through the second story window somehow. I awoke to him taking the pouch sitting on my bedside. I should've just let him take it, but I was terrified. Without that money, I had nothing and no way to continue on. So I jumped out of bed and fought the brute."

I touched my cheek where he'd slapped me across the face, remembering the sharp pain. It had stunned me. No one had ever hit me before, least of all a grown male twice my size.

"What did he do to you?" Redvyr's timbre had gone soft, gentler, though there was a touch of steel beneath it, as if he knew he needed to be calm if I was going to tell the rest.

"I was sleeping in my shift, and apparently he changed his mind about just taking the money and running. He attacked me on the bed, but my brother, Draydyn, he'd taught me the best way to get away from a man. I kneed him hard between the legs."

"I like your brother."

I nodded, smiling at the bittersweet memory of him.

"It worked and gave me enough time to grab my dress, my purse and run from the room. The innkeeper and his wife heard the noise and found me in the hall. Thankfully, the innkeeper's wife took pity on me. She sat with me in her parlor with a hot pot of tea until the sun came up."

"Did they catch the bastard who did this?"

"He got away. The innkeeper found a wood fae male I could trust to hire and protect me until I reached the next town. I became wiser after that. Before I left, I bought a dress from the innkeeper and gave her my gown. That way, I didn't stand out as much."

He snorted and eased his hand down to my elbow before releasing me. "That is not possible. You could wear a grain sack, and still, you'd draw the attention of every male near you."

He gulped hard and looked away, frowning.

"Let me go with you to Hellamir," I begged him.

"Now that you've told me there is danger in the towns, it would be best if you went with the clan."

"I'm aware of these dangers. It will be better for Tessa if she has me with her."

"I know you've become quick friends with Tessa, but Sorka and Bes are fond of you. They'd keep you company until we return."

That wasn't why I wanted to go with them, and after telling him that story, I realized the true reason was one I didn't want to admit. Not even to myself.

"It's not that."

"Then what is it?"

I snapped my head away. A group of females sauntered by, giggling when they saw me. One of them was Velga, her sneer telling me exactly what she thought of me. Then I felt Redvyr's claw beneath my chin, guiding me to face him again.

"Tell me, Jessamine."

"Is Velga one of your lovers?"

Changing the subject was always the best way of evading something I didn't want to discuss.

His expression turned amused. "What?"

"Velga. The pretty one who obviously hates me. Is she one of your lovers?"

He chuckled, and I had never wanted to punch a beast fae in the face so much until that moment.

"No. She is not."

"Has she ever been?" I demanded to know.

He shook his head, grinning, his male ego proudly on display in his smug expression. "Though she may have made it known once or twice that she wanted to be."

"Oh." I stared at the group of females as they disappeared among the other clan members packing their belongings. "She doesn't like me."

"No, she doesn't. You are a beautiful female and have been in my company alone in the woods. And I have spent a great deal of time with you since we returned to camp."

"She believes *we* are lovers?" I couldn't help the surprise in my voice.

"Most likely. Or that we will be."

"Well, that's just ridiculous." I forced a laugh up my throat, catching his gaze.

While he continued to smile, he wasn't laughing. Not at all.

"Velga is not the reason you don't want to travel with the clan. You are too fearless for that."

He was right.

"Now that you've tried to distract me from my cause, tell me why you don't want to go with them to the Vale."

Lifting my chin higher, proving that I was indeed fearless, I admitted, "Because I feel safer when I'm with you."

He went silent. His smile slipped entirely. A chilly wind gusted by, blowing a lock of my hair across my face. He gave a soft grunt and pushed the stray hair away.

"Go get your bed bundle you slept on last night. You're coming with me."

CHAPTER 11

Jessamine

Hellamir was not far from Vanglosa. It was the only light fae town on this side of the Bluevale River, the main divide between Northgall and Lumeria. The Borderlands divided the light and dark fae territories, even though both kingdoms were now ruled as one by King Gollaya and his new queen.

Though we had a light fae queen and a dark fae king, that did not unite faekind. Hellamir might have some open-minded merchants willing to trade and do business with the beast clan, but the giant, horned fae would not be welcome in the town.

That, along with the fact that I actually did feel safer with Redvyr, was a big reason I'd wanted to go with them. Tessa would also be safer if I was with her. But now, having traveled half a day on the back of Wolf with Redvyr's broad chest and thick thighs pressing against me, I was rethinking my choices.

Before we'd left the rest of the clan who set out in the opposite direction, Sorka came to me with new boots. I hadn't understood why the leather was so long at first. The top of the boots reached my lower thighs. Then Sorka pointed out that I would need to loosen the side-slit laces of my dress to ride Wolf. The boots covered my skin for warmth when the slits were open, riding high for comfort.

I'd been uncharacteristically silent on this journey to Hellamir, my gaze dropping to Redvyr's leather-clad thighs pressed against mine. The temperatures had plummeted, snow dusting the trees and the trail, and yet I was sweating.

Redvyr and I had ridden mostly in silence, while our companions spoke easily in hushed tones to one another. Bezaliel and Tessa rode behind us, their daughter cradled between them. The sprite Hallizel who seemed enraptured by Saralyn, never too far from her, was buzzing through the branches over our heads. Occasionally, she would zip down and ride upon their wolf Mishka's head. The wolf didn't seem to mind.

The other two warriors—Dayn and Leifkyn—took up the rear. They were both tall and lean but well-muscled with the same feline-shaped orange eyes. Leifkyn wore his long hair in a braided tail, while Dayn let his hang loosely which reached well past his shoulders. From what I could tell, they seemed to be close friends, whispering and laughing to one another almost the entire time.

Every once in a while, I'd hear the two warriors or Tessa and Bezaliel behind us laugh about something. But Redvyr and I hadn't spoken much at all.

I jumped when he finally did speak, asking me, "Why didn't you use your magick against the man who attacked you?"

Back to the conversation of the day before. And that was an excellent question.

"I don't know. I panicked and was terrified and just reacted, using what self-defense my brother had taught me."

I didn't think of it until later, that I must prepare myself to be ready to use my magick at a moment's notice, to summon the syrenskyn whenever I needed it.

"If your brother is so protective of you, why did he not convince your father not to marry you off to the Mevian *lord*?" He said the last word with utter disdain.

"He couldn't."

"Why? He is afraid of your father?"

"No. He always stood up to him when he was alive. But my brother is dead."

His fingers at my waist tensed. "When?"

"Last year. Though my father tried to prevent it, Draydyn set out with a small army to fight in the Northgall wars against King Xakiel's men."

King Xakiel had been King Gollaya's father before him. Xakiel was brutal in his attacks on innocent towns and villages.

"Draydyn had heard of the things Xakiel's army was doing to the wood fae of Myrkovir Forest. He could not stand by and do nothing. And he died for his efforts."

We wound our way out of the woods, and the sun setting over the rooftops of Hellamir came into view in the distance. Redvyr remained quiet for a while before commenting again.

"Death is part of life. Though it is difficult when it visits us, it is best to grieve then accept it. The gods know best."

I smiled. Most people tell me they are sorry for my loss, that my brother died too young, and it should never have happened. But not this beast fae. He gave me the harder words I needed to hear. That he was taken from me for a divine purpose I couldn't understand.

"You believe in the gods?" I asked with some surprise.

"Aye. I do."

"Which ones?"

"Vix, of course," he answered with assurance. "He is the mighty one, the forefather of all dark fae."

"Who else?" I asked.

"Solzkin, the sun god, for he helps with our crops in summer. Gozriel, Vix's watcher. An omen from Gozriel can warn us of danger. Then there's Ivenzel, the goddess of the hearth."

"Sorka mentioned her."

"Yes. She keeps the home and children safe. We also revere Elska."

"The Goddess of the Wood? But she's a light fae goddess."

"You do not own the gods," he chastised.

I looked over my shoulder to find a mocking expression on his face.

"No. But I am surprised that you would worship her all the same."

"We live off the land and the woods and the food it provides. Elska provides all of this for us."

"Hmm." I faced forward again, noting that Redvyr steered Wolf toward a copse of trees between us and Hellamir.

"Quiet now," he rumbled, his hands at my waist tightening. "There could be wood fae from Hellamir up ahead."

Our entire party was silent as we slipped through the evening shadows and entered the small woodland outside of Hellamir. We had rested along the way more than I thought necessary, but now I realized it was so that we might arrive when the shadows were heavy and we could move covertly.

There was no sound but the wind gusting through the bare trees, their limbs rattling together above us. Wolf seemed to move with purpose now, trotting through the trees, going deeper into the woods until a small cabin appeared ahead. It seemed well-made but abandoned, sticks and tree limbs piled across the thatched roof.

Wolf stopped outside and Redvyr dismounted. Without warning, he reached up and gripped me by the waist, hauling me down in front of him. I wobbled, having been on the hound's back for hours, grabbing hold of Redvyr's forearms for balance.

"You got your feet now?" Redvyr asked in a low voice, a teasing smile at the corner of his mouth.

"I'm fine." I pushed out of his arms and turned to cinch the laces of my boots and close the slits of my skirt that had given me the freedom to ride Wolf.

The others had dismounted as well, and Leifkyn, the one who wore his hair in a long tail down his back, entered the cabin with his blade drawn. Bezaliel now cradled his daughter to his chest while Tessa tightened the lacings of her cloak at her throat, lifting the hood to cover her head.

"All clear," said Leifkyn, exiting the cabin.

"Maybe I should go with them," said Bezaliel, staring at his wife.

Redvyr grunted in that disagreeing way of his. "Unless you plan to cut off your horns and your tail, then that won't be happening."

Bezaliel looked at me. "What Jessamine said has me worried. Perhaps it isn't safe."

Tessa put a hand on his shoulder. "I'll be fine. Plus, I have Jessamine with me this time. She has magick we can use if we need to."

My stomach rolled over. I had never actually used my magick to defend myself. Not successfully, anyway. The dryad stag was the first time I'd actually tried.

That first time I'd shocked Redvyr had happened subconsciously. I didn't remember doing it on purpose. Those instances aside, my magick *was* strong, and I was more confident now than when I'd left Morodon.

Redvyr stared at me, his golden eyes glittering brighter now that night was settling in, like a predator's does in the darkness when watching its prey.

"Yes," he said evenly. "She will use her magick to protect the both of them if she must. Won't you, witch?"

"Of course, I will," I assured them.

He gave a satisfied nod. "Wolf will follow you through the woods, which opens up on the east side of the town. Tessa knows the way to our trader."

I glanced back at Dayn who was unloading the many furs packed on his wolf for trading, hauling them into the cabin. Leifkyn was carrying the finely crafted short swords and blades made of black steel that would also be used for the trade.

"We'll be fine," said Tessa in a jovial voice, placing a kiss on her babe's head then pecking the lips of Bezaliel.

Hallizel flew from out of the darkness above us and landed on Bezaliel's shoulder.

Tessa smiled and turned to offer her arm to me. "It's good to have a partner this time. The sooner we fetch Flaxon, the sooner we can return."

I took her arm, and we headed back the way we'd come. I'd only taken a few steps when Redvyr called, "Wait."

We stopped and turned as he ate up the space between us in a few long strides, holding something in his hand. When he held out both of his hands, he pulled a wicked-looking curved dagger from its sheath before sliding it back home.

"Take this, Jessamine. I know that Tessa has a blade, but it's better that you both are armed."

I took the dagger, the blade having some weight as I tucked it into my belt beneath my cloak.

"You don't trust my magick, Lord Redvyr?"

"It's always better to be over-prepared rather than not prepared enough."

I nodded. "Thank you."

Then Tessa and I continued on together. I glanced over my shoulder to find Redvyr still watching me with his predatory gaze. He didn't say a word as we hurried back to the main path of the woods, Wolf shadowing our steps.

Once we were nearly out of the treeline, Tessa whispered, "I really am glad to have you with me. I didn't tell Bezaliel, but the last time we came, on the summer solstice, I could tell there was unrest in the town. Lots of strangers, too."

"How do you know they were strangers?" I asked.

"Well, Hellamir is a wood fae town, but there were several moon fae here from the capital city of Issos and most were in royal armor. Soldiers from Issos."

"Why were they here?"

"It seemed they were refueling for the next battle. Our merchant, Flaxon, was glad to see us. He said he was afraid the army was going to acquire his grain without paying for it. They'd already done as much to a few other merchants in town, and he knew that at least he would get paid by trading with us."

"But Issos is a rich city. They should have had plenty of coin."

"All I know is that the men in charge of the moon fae warriors weren't honorable men. I learned years ago that the light fae might always claim to be the righteous ones, but there are just as many criminals and evil men masquerading as good fae on their side as there are in the dark fae lands."

"You don't have to convince me. I know that well enough."

My father was one of them.

"Though I know the dark fae aren't welcome," I added, "I'm still surprised Bezaliel and the others don't simply come into town to do their business."

We stopped at the treeline, and I turned to Wolf, scratching under his chin. "Stay here, Wolf. We won't be long."

He whined but obediently sat and watched us go.

"I can tell you why they don't," Tessa continued as we crossed an open field, night having fallen over us. "Before I came, they actually did. A group of wood fae males didn't like them in the town and had told them to leave, but they continued to come into town for trade every season. Then Flaxon told Redvyr he would have to stop trading. The males who didn't like them coming had threatened Flaxon and his family."

"That's terrible."

"I know," she agreed. "Not long after, I joined the clan. When I discovered their predicament that first winter, because they were low on grain, I suggested that I be their liaison. I could go freely as a wood fae and fetch Flaxon. So that's what we've been doing this past year. I've never been afraid, except for that last time."

The lights of the town grew brighter as we approached, the talking and laughing from the streets growing louder with each step.

"Flaxon lives next door to his mill near the river. We can take the side streets behind the town square to his house without getting noticed."

"Lead the way."

I followed her as we headed into town from the east side. The dirt road became cobblestones, the sights and smells of a bustling town almost foreign to me after spending so long in the Borderlands, which was nothing more than a few taverns and inns spread out along the route.

An older man pushed open a tavern door, revealing a savory aroma and a room where a dozen or more locals enjoyed a meal and jugs of ale. The clip-clop of a horse pulling a squeaky cart rounded the corner at the end of this side street we walked upon. The crying of a baby from an upstairs open window pulled mine and Tessa's gazes upward before the mother shushed and spoke softly to the babe, both going quiet.

"Watch out." Tessa tugged me around a pile of horse manure in the street.

"Thanks," I muttered.

The doors to the taverns were open, the crowds inside boisterous and loud. But we kept to the shadows as best we could. For a small town, there were many people coming and going, all of them paying us no mind.

I supposed that would be normal for a river port town. People came and went by the Bluevale River to the harbor from all over. But I only saw wood fae milling about the streets and a few moon fae here and there. The moon fae were easy to spot, with wings protruding from their backs. None of them looked to be Issosian solders.

"This way," whispered Tessa, pointing to a torch-lit alley beside a shop that was now closed.

As we hurried down the alley, the shouting of a crowd grew louder. When we came upon the first intersection of the lane, Tessa pulled me to a stop, peering around the corner.

"What is it?" I whispered.

"I don't know. That's the town square. Something is going on."

I peered around the corner with her. There were several torches, and the back of a crowd faced the center where a moon fae with auburn hair was waving for everyone to be silent.

"Hear me, good fae of Hellamir." The voices quieted. "Evil pervades across our lands." The moon fae gestured toward the north. "Even now, the daughter of our great King Connall of Issos has been forced to fornicate with the demon king and beget his child."

"She saved us!" a woman shouted from the front. "Princess Una saved us all!"

"Indeed, she did," he agreed. "But in doing so, she has sullied her bloodline. More than that, she has encouraged the dark fae of the north to take what they want."

Silence fell across the crowd, the speaker captivating them with his fearmongering.

"Have you not heard what is happening in other northern provinces and to farmers on their homesteads? Women and children have gone missing! Taken by these demons for their carnal appetites."

Protests rose amongst the throng. Then one brawny wood fae male shouted, "Then why hasn't it happened here? We live closer to the northern border than any of the other light fae."

The speaker smiled, sending a chill down my spine. "Excellent question. And that is why you are all here tonight." He pointed to his left. "Because that witch living in the glen just across the river has the power to tell us the gods' secrets."

We couldn't see who he pointed to because the building was in the way. I edged down the alley, closer to the back of the crowd, Tessa clutching my cloak but following right behind me.

"She is a god seer!" he shouted. "She knows the gods' will. She could help us, but she *refuses*! She will not tell us what we need to know to save our kind. To save her own kind!"

Over the crowd, she finally came into view. A dark-haired moon fae, skin pale as milk, midnight blue wings at her back, staring coolly out into the crowd. She was bound to a stake at the center of the stage, raised up on a stone slab, kindling at her feet.

"They're going to burn her," I whispered, my voice shaking with fury.

"She has magick that could help us find those who are being taken and kill our enemies. But she refuses even the royal Lord Gael of Mevia."

Then *he* stepped forward. I hadn't seen him because my sole attention was on the petite moon fae, standing glassy-eyed and facing the crowd. My betrothed and would-be captor marched to the center of the stage next to the speaker, who was obviously one of his lackeys. My heart was in my throat, my pulse speeding frantically at the sight of him.

"We don't want your witch burnings!" a woman in the crowd shouted.

Lord Gael held up a gloved hand, the one with all five of his fingers, instantly silencing the crowd. He was formidable in appearance, especially whilst wearing the fine clothes of a nobleman. His long black hair shone in the torchlight, his iridescent blue wings tall and strong at his back. But it was the menacing sharpness of his expression that silenced the people.

"It is an inevitability," he said in a low voice that somehow echoed across the entire square. "Light fae who do not use their magick to aid their own kind are nothing more than witches to be burned."

My blood chilled as I shrank further into the shadows. Tessa didn't say a word, but she sensed my uneasiness, pulling me closer to her. I tugged on my hood and pulled it forward to be sure it covered my face.

"If light fae refuse to help us in our cause to rid this land of the menace of demonkind, then they must be put down. They cannot be used by the enemy, like the former princess of Issos, Una Harstone, has been."

I noted he refused to call her *Queen* Una, the title she deserved and how everyone I came across in the Borderlands referred to her. While I hadn't met many fae during my time there, word spread amongst the dark and light fae in the area of how she had somehow discovered a cure for the deadly plague that had spread across Lumeria.

But no one shouted or called out now. No one defended her name. Lord Gael marched along the edge of the stage, his heavy boots thumping, his regal cloak whipping behind him.

"Do you want your own children to be stolen in the night? Do you want your women to be abducted and violated and used to produce demon children?" His voice rose. "Disloyalty from those with magick means the death of more light fae. I will not allow it. Soon, we will rid this land of *all* demonkind."

"You know him," whispered Tessa, close to my ear.

I nodded and shrank back further. "He is the one my father betrothed me to."

Her arm came around my waist and she pulled me tight against her. "They can't see us. Don't worry."

The auburn-haired speaker stepped forward and shouted, "And then, we will have a new king!" He raised Gael's arm into the air. "One who fights for the light fae of Lumeria!"

The crowd erupted in cheers, those few who had spoken out now silenced by the others who chanted.

"Lumeria! Lumeria! Lumeria!"

"We can't let them burn her," I murmured, turning to Tessa.

Her expression tense, she seemed to think for a moment before nodding. "Follow me."

We rushed back down the lane to the central alleyway we had used to cross behind the town square. Tessa and I hurried down the full length of the narrow street, which opened out onto another lane a block from the square, where the chanting continued.

"Here," she whispered, taking one of the torches from the sconces in the stone wall.

I took it, then she grabbed another and whisper-yelled, "*Hurry*."

"What are we going to do?" I asked, following her quickly away from the townspeople down a quiet street of shops, all dark and closed.

"Fight fire with fire," she answered, stopping at the first shop, a bakery, and throwing the torch on the thatched roof. "Throw yours!"

I did, watching the flames lick and ignite the hay roofing quickly. We dodged around the building along the backside of the stage that faced the square and crawled under the wooden platform into the shadows beneath.

Tessa cupped her hands around her mouth and in a loud voice shouted, "Fire! Fire! Get water!"

Suddenly, the mob started screaming, boots and footsteps pounding across the wooden stage above us and the pavement of the square. Others began to shout, "Fire!"

"Stay here," said Tessa before she crawled out of our hiding space.

I obeyed, too terrified that if I showed myself, Gael would see me. Then take me.

Tessa peeked her head up and peered over the stage. Apparently, seeing no threat, she hurried up the stairs out of sight. I listened to the people dashing to put out the fire, running farther away, most likely to a well or simply to safety. Then someone came hurrying back down the steps. I froze, until I saw Tessa gesturing for me to follow.

"Let's go!"

Right behind her was the female who had been bound on stage to be burned at the stake. She still appeared calm and serene, despite the fact she had nearly been executed in the most heinous, painful way.

I hurried after them as Tessa led us back down another alleyway and farther away from the shouting townspeople. We came out near the port, the moon sparkling on the Bluevale River, the sounds of the boats at the dock gently rocking in the water.

The moon fae pulled Tessa to a stop. We both turned to her.

"Thank you," she said, her black hair framing her pale face, her dark blue wings sagging at her back. "If you ever need a favor from a seer, come and find me. My name is Aelwyn. I'll be heading back to my home now."

"Where is that?" asked Tessa.

"Nævhail Glen."

"They'll come for you again," I told her.

"They'll never find me," she said with assurance, then she turned and flew up into the dark sky shrouded in smoke.

"We have to hurry now, too," said Tessa.

"We are still going to Flaxon?" I asked, following her along the river's edge.

"Yes, we have to."

Rushing along the path that led to the mill, I couldn't stop glancing over my shoulder, certain that Gael could somehow sense I was here. That he would catch me this time and drag me to Mevia to do all the nightmarish things he had planned for me.

CHAPTER 12
Redvyr

"They've been gone too long," Bezaliel said for the second time.

"I know." We walked through the woods to the edge of the treeline.

We'd left Leifkyn and Dayn to guard our goods and the babe, both of us too impatient to stay put. Normally, we waited at the cabin for Flaxon, to keep from being seen by any travelers heading through these woods toward Hellamir. But neither of us could keep still when it was obvious something must have happened to delay them.

"I should've gone." Bezaliel was angry. Of course he was.

"You know that was impossible. We might as well have not come at all."

"If something's happened to Tessa," he growled, "I'll burn the whole fucking town to the ground."

I'd already had similar thoughts, chastising myself for allowing Jessamine to leave my sight. It was my job to protect her, and yet I'd let her go with Tessa. I worried now that the ones who'd been chasing her through Northgall had decided to backtrack from the Borderlands and rest in Hellamir.

Wolf huffed a low bark up ahead near the treeline. I sniffed, a strong scent on the wind, then I picked up my pace as we neared the edge of the woods. Bezaliel followed quickly behind me.

"It looks like someone else has beaten us to it."

Across the open field, several rooftops were engulfed in flames. The shouts of panicked townspeople echoed toward us.

"We're going in to get them," he said, stopping at my side.

Suddenly, Wolf took off running across the field.

"I don't think it will be necessary."

Though I could barely see the two silhouettes making their way across the field, I could smell that sea-lily scent of Jessamine. We both bolted across the meadow after Wolf. The women hurried toward us. Tessa leaped into her mate's arms. I gripped Jessamine's shoulders, noting her eyes were rounded with fear.

"Are you hurt?" I demanded to know.

"No," she replied, though something had obviously shaken her.

"What the fuck happened?" asked Bezaliel, finally putting Tessa back on the ground.

"There were moon fae there," said Tessa. "They were making a speech in the town square. About to burn a moon fae woman at the stake."

"What?" I snapped. "What had she done?"

"Nothing." Jessamine's voice was cold, angry. "She had magick they wanted and she refused to use it to help them hurt the dark fae."

"So I started a fire," said Tessa, "and we saved her."

"That wasn't following protocol," Bezaliel said tightly. "You're supposed to move unseen without being noticed."

"We weren't noticed," she replied haughtily. "And we saved a female fae from being burned to death."

"Where is she?" I asked.

"She said she was returning to her home in Nævhail Glen," said Jessamine. "Then she turned away from the fires, walked into the night and disappeared."

"Literally disappeared," added Tessa. "She seemed to vanish altogether."

Bezaliel huffed but stroked a hand down her back affectionately. "Who exactly were these moon fae wanting her to hurt? And why?"

"They plan to kill King Gollaya," Jessamine added, a quiver in her voice now. Though whether it was fury or fear that put it there, I wasn't certain. "Then they plan to kill all of the dark fae."

I watched her, all of us quiet, letting that threat sink in.

"They want to crown a new leader, a new king of Northgall and Lumeria."

"What bloody bastard do they plan to make their king?" I realized I still had hold of Jessamine, but I couldn't let her go yet, my own fear that she'd been in danger still humming through my veins.

She paused and licked her lips. "Lord Gael of Mevia." She held my gaze, her voice dropping to a whisper. "He is there."

I let her go and took a step back, my hands curling into fists as I gazed across the field at Hellamir. The fire dimmed on the rooftops of the town. But not inside me. A blazing desire to fury unlike any I'd ever known flared bright. I wanted to kill.

"He is there," I repeated to myself, taking another step toward Hellamir. Then another.

As if my body weren't my own, I strode on, slowly but with intention.

"Where are you going?" called Bezaliel.

But I didn't respond. The satisfying thought of wrapping my hands around this high lord's throat was becoming increasingly necessary. I wanted his blood on my hands. I wanted him dead at my feet. I wish I could say it was because he threatened the dark fae king and all of our kind, but it wasn't that at all. It was the fact that he'd once threatened Jessamine, that he'd planned to use and abuse her for his own selfish gain. I could remove that threat from this world here and now.

"Stop." Bezaliel halted my steps, standing in front of me, both hands on my shoulders.

A growl reverberated from deep in my belly. That was my only response.

"You can't go into that town and kill a moon fae," he told me, knowing exactly what had been on my mind.

"Get out of my way," I commanded.

"No. Let's say you find and kill this Lord Gael. What do you think will happen then? Even if you kill all of his guards and make it back out alive, others will witness this. Then there will be a headhunt across the land for all beast fae to find you. You'll put not only our clan in danger, but every beast fae clan."

"I won't be seen."

"No." Bezaliel shook his head, digging his claws into my shoulders, a warning. "I can't let you do this. You can't risk it. Risk *us*."

My entire body locked up, muscles bulging, ready to fight my chief, when a small hand touched the skin of my wrist, holding it.

"Redvyr," Jessamine whispered.

My gaze darted to hers, my breathing heavy, the need to let my inner beast kill and maim desperately urgent now.

She eased in front of me, nudging Bezaliel who stepped out of the way. She wrapped her dainty fingers around my other wrist, my hands still balled into fists.

"You can't kill him right now. He is surrounded by too many light fae." She placed one hand on my sternum, on my bare chest.

It wasn't her words, but her touch that calmed the beast within me. The monster that lived inside, who wanted nothing but blood and carnage, had never retreated until he got what he wanted. But this soft beauty, with her soothing voice and compassionate eyes, quelled the fury, sending the monster back into his cage with a gentle touch.

My breathing slowed. And there it was again. For a second time, this skald fae female had entranced me, pushing my animal rage away. My fury cooled while I held her gaze and luxuriated in her soft caress on my skin. She brushed one thumb back and forth along the swift pulse at my wrist, her other thumb brushing my chest.

The first time she'd done this, I had felt confusion and shame. How could a light fae do what none of my own kind has ever been able to do? How did she so swiftly calm the beast? And this time, she'd done it *before* I'd drawn blood from my target. This had never happened. I didn't understand how or why the gods would put someone like her in my life to do the one thing no other could. Someone who was not my mate and never would belong in my clan. It was maddening.

Trapped in her emerald gaze, I forced myself to look away, wishing I hadn't. For Bezaliel watched me with complete shock, his eyes wide with wonder and confusion. It grated me that he'd seen my weakness to her. I realized then that I'd do anything for this woman, and she wasn't even mine. She could never be mine.

"There's Flaxon," said Tessa, pointing across the field.

Not far along the road from Hellamir was Flaxon in his cart.

"Good," I snapped, stepping away from Jessamine. "Let's get to the cabin so we can trade and get out of here as soon as possible."

I stormed away back along the path into the woodlands, noting that Wolf took his place at Jessamine's side. Good. She had my hound to protect her. I could keep my distance and fulfill my oath of protection. I walked faster.

Bezaliel caught up to my side. "Redvyr," was all he said in a grave voice.

"I know. There's no need to say anything."

"But I think there is."

"What?" I snapped. "That the gods like to play games with me? This, we already know."

He scoffed. "I think the gods have given you a gift. This female."

I looked at him in disbelief. "You *are* mad. She isn't beast fae."

"Neither is Tessa. And yet she is mine. The gods have declared it."

I laughed with derision. "The gods would not give her to me."

"Why would you say that? Because of your father? His sins do not fall upon your head."

"But they do, Bezaliel. I have the same feral rage. My mother couldn't quell it, and it led to her death."

"She wasn't his mate, Red. You know this. That was one of your father's sins. He took a female to bed and beget his heir with one who wasn't given to him by the gods."

It was true. But that was why I'd felt the gods hated me so much. A child born of a beast fae pair unsanctioned by the gods was often considered cursed. My father had lied to his clan to keep my mother in his possession. I was a product of my father's selfishness and lust and greed, so why would the gods show me any favor?

"Are you hearing me?" my friend asked in a hushed whisper, though we moved farther ahead of the females and Wolf.

"I hear you. So the gods have deemed me worthy of a light fae witch to ease my rage for a while. It will be that much more painful when she returns to her own kind."

"By the gods, you're an idiot."

I snapped my head to him. "What have I done now?"

"They've given her to you because she is *yours*, Redvyr. She is your mate."

I came to a complete stop and faced him. Even in the dark, we could see each other clearly because of our heightened senses. The females were making their way slowly along the path, chatting softly. I could still smell the sweet-and-salty scent of her.

"Vix would never give someone like her to me, Bezaliel."

"Why not? What's wrong with her?"

"Nothing." I huffed. "Absolutely nothing. She is beautiful and kind. And powerful. And perfect. That's why the gods wouldn't give her to me."

I wasn't worthy of someone like Jessamine. A sickly feeling swirled in my gut. Bezaliel didn't understand what it was like to have your father's sins follow you like a never-ending shadow, a constant reminder that I must pay for his sins. This was why I always tried my damnedest to be the best clan leader, the best protector I could.

Bezaliel smirked and arched a brow. "There is one way to test that theory."

"Fuck off." I shoved him on the shoulder and marched on, ready to get this trade done so we could get back to the clan.

Bezaliel strode after me, laughing to himself, the bastard. "I was proposing that you actually *fuck* her."

"Vix's blood," I cursed under my breath. "It won't be happening."

"When you discover that I'm right, I want an apology."

"You'll be waiting for that apology until you're wandering the afterlife."

Another laugh echoed to me. "We shall see.

CHAPTER 13

Jessamine

Flaxon had given us bags of ground wheat, barley grains, and some dried beans. He'd also given Tessa a small bag of herbs she said had great healing properties. She'd had trouble growing them in Vanglosa.

"The beans are great in stews. You'll like them." She rode her wolf, Mishka, while Saralyn slept in her pouch on Tessa's chest. The sprite was curled into a ball upon the babe's head.

I rode upon Wolf beside her, remembering how Haldek had taught me to cook stew and bake bread when I'd worked at his tavern. Though I never ate the ones with meat, I'd also learned to make a hearty mushroom and root vegetable soup for myself. I thought the beans and barley might make it even better. It was strange that cooking, something I was forbidden to learn back at the palace in Morodon, had become a comforting chore when I worked for Haldek. I'd even kept a book of recipes, which was still sitting on my desk back in the Borderlands.

I contemplated how I might contribute to the clan as we traveled north toward Ghasta Vale, thinking I might offer my services as a cook. Anything to keep my mind off the brooding giant beast fae lord tromping along at the head of our party. Now that the wolves were laden with our goods as well as me, Tessa, and her babe, the men walked in front and behind us.

We passed Lake Moreen, seeming to give it a wide berth for some reason. I'd heard the trappers speak of it in Haldek's tavern, how plentiful the fish were in the spring. Right now, it was a white sheet of ice, dark at the center where the ice thinned. Reaching out with my magick, I sensed no naiads here, but I'd bet they returned here in the warmth of summer. I imagined it was beautiful then.

Redvyr had been doing his utmost to ignore me since we'd returned from Hellamir last night. I must have offended or embarrassed him when I'd tried to calm him down, to keep him from storming into Hellamir and killing Lord Gael. Not that I'd regret him killing the lord who I'd been betrothed to by my father, but I certainly didn't want Redvyr to be captured in doing so. Or worse, becoming injured or killed.

Though I wanted to ask him if he was angry with me for interfering, we'd had no time alone. And I wouldn't embarrass him further by interrogating him in front of his men. Besides, there was nothing I could do for having offended him in whatever way that I had.

We finally entered a forest that was thick with snow-laden evergreens. Even this far south of the mountain range, there were large boulders littering the woods. We'd come upon one of these clearings with a few large boulders when Redvyr came to a stop.

"We'll stop here for the night," he called back.

He unloaded one of the wolves with Dayn, hauling off saddlebags of grain from their backs. Then they piled them near a wide boulder. It would be the perfect spot to make camp because we could sleep with the rockface at our backs, able to watch for attackers or predators.

I'd learned to look for the most defensible places to sleep since I'd run away from home, especially after my incident with the robber in that inn. I was much wiser than I'd been when I left home as a naïve royal.

Bezaliel helped his wife and daughter down from the back of Mishka. "You and Jessamine can take Saralyn to wash at the pool."

"I remember. *Làveen Orla*," she whispered in a teasing way, her accent thickening as the words should be said in demon tongue.

Bezaliel grinned. "I can't join you this time."

Tessa glanced over at me as I slid off of Wolf, adding louder, "I'm sure Jessamine would enjoy a quick bath much as I would."

"I would."

"I have some toweling here we can use."

"Be quick," warned Bezaliel. "It won't be long before the sun sets."

"Don't worry," Tessa laughed. "It will be too cold to enjoy. We'll make quick work of washing."

The three of us, with Hallizel fluttering above, wound our way past the others. I couldn't help but observe Redvyr, hoping he might acknowledge my existence if even with a small glance. But he continued unloading, never looking our way, as if he didn't even know we were there.

My heart squeezed with disappointment. I'd thought we'd become somewhat friends. But apparently, I'd overstepped my bounds when I persuaded him from heading off into Hellamir and getting himself killed.

That was fine if he didn't want to talk to me. At least I could do something special for my actual friend Tessa and her little one Saralyn. I tapped into my magick, a small touch, letting it warm my blood without summoning it forward just yet.

"The water will be freezing," she said as we drew closer to the gurgling sound of the brook.

"No, it won't."

She frowned over at me. "What do you mean?"

Grinning, I said, "I'm a willoden. One of the gifts of magick I was born with."

"A water wielder? How can that help us?"

"Wait and see," I promised her with a smile.

Once we passed through the brush and stepped up to the narrow stream, I looked around, trying to find the right place.

"Come over here." I led her to a spot where the stream widened into a small pool before it narrowed again, rushing over river rocks and seeming to disappear into the earth, though I could hear the trickle of water falling down a crevasse.

I untied the lacings of the slits in my dress so that I could hike up my skirt and kneel. I didn't want to get my dress dirty, and I wasn't ready to take it off yet in the cold, but I needed to touch the water.

Dipping my hand into the frigid pool, I waved my hand back and forth beneath the surface, the slight current pressing against my palm and webbed fingers. Closing my eyes, I summoned the cooler depths inside me where the willoden magick slept.

"*Keskavalla,*" I whispered in the naiad tongue. "*Septimius orkavalla. Shelliastalyn, preela. Preela ves.*"

I wasn't sure why, but the waters always responded when I spoke the naiad language, the same one I used when communicating with naiads.

My hands began to glow moon-white, tiny luminescent dot markings appearing on the back of my hand. Tessa gasped, but I kept my focus, still waving my hand gently in the stream, speaking to the water itself.

All at once, the water bubbled, the numbness in my fingers fading as the temperature rose, heat billowing up from the pool.

"Gods above." Tessa laughed and knelt beside me, dipping her hand in the water. "It's warm. Almost hot, even. How did you do that?"

"I'm a willoden. It doesn't always work. The waters can refuse to do as we ask." I shrugged. "But I've never had much trouble really."

I wasn't bragging. It was true. While my sisters had difficulty when they were coming into their powers as willodens, I never did. The waters always granted my wishes.

"What language were you speaking?" asked Tessa, having set Saralyn on the bank and quickly beginning to undress.

"It's an old tongue that naiads speak."

When Tessa was naked, she began to unwrap little Saralyn. I hesitated, for I knew what I would look like beneath my dress. I was actually shocked that Tessa wasn't openly staring at my face and neck where the markings glowed on my face. I could feel the radiating heat and hum of magick that appeared whenever my syrenskyn powers rose to the surface.

Though it was true, I held the power of a willoden, I couldn't summon that magick without also calling on my syrenskyn powers. For me, they were tied together.

"Oh, heavens and hells!" called Tessa, laughing as she carried Saralyn into the water. "This is a paradise, Jessamine. You are *truly* blessed by the gods."

She swirled in the waist-deep water, dipping Saralyn in. The baby cooed and gurgled happily. Hallizel tittered and fluttered above the water, dipping her talons in as well. I smiled, having never seen my gift give anyone joy before.

"Warmy, warmy!" shouted Hallizel.

"Come on in, Jessa. Don't be shy!"

My heart tripped at hearing her call me Jessa. Only my dear brother Draydyn had ever called me by that nickname. I swallowed hard at the endearment and began to slide the dress off. I then unlaced my boots and waited for Tessa to remark on the strange glow of my skin and the pattern of dots decorating my arms and legs, swirling around my breasts and belly.

When I looked up at her, she was pressing kisses to Saralyn's wet cheeks. She then cradled her in one arm and dipped her head back into the warm water, dribbling water with her hands over her hair and tiny nubs of horns. I exhaled a relieved breath as I met them in the deeper part of the pool.

"You don't have to be embarrassed about your body," she told me.

I glanced down, seeing the magick of the syrenskyn glowing bright on my voluptuous curves, the body of a sinful seductress as I was constantly told by my mother.

"I've been taught to be embarrassed by it," I found myself admitting.

Tessa glared at me angrily, but I knew that look was for those who'd taught me to be ashamed. "Whoever did that is an imbecile and a rotten asshole."

I laughed, having not heard those sorts of words come out of Tessa's mouth before.

"You are utterly gorgeous, Jessa. Even the pretty glowing dots all over you. Is that because you're a nendovir?"

I wanted to tell her the truth, but I still feared becoming a pariah among the clan. Tessa had been nothing but kind to me, but that didn't mean she wouldn't warn her mate that I had the ability to kill anyone at will if I wanted to. So I lied.

"Thank you. Yes." Though my claws had come out, I hid them in the water. My fangs had descended but I ducked my head and hid those as well.

I wouldn't explain to her what my true purpose was. What this ethereal glow was meant to do— entrap men so that I might kill them.

"The language you spoke was lovely," said Tessa, seeming to know I wanted to change the subject. "What were you saying?"

"It's a sort of request or plea to the water, asking her to be transform for us and nourish our cold bodies with warmth."

"Well, this is a gift beyond my imagining." She paused. "How long will it last? Can the men enjoy it after us?"

I nodded. "I think so. I can ask the water when we are done."

"What a magnificent kind of magick, Jessa. You should be so delighted the gods gave you such a gift."

I smiled and nodded, turning to dip my head back and wash my hair. But I'd simply wanted to end this conversation. To not have to talk about this anymore.

My family had never expressed pride or admiration for my magick. It didn't matter that my sisters were also willodens. It was my secret skill as a syrenskyn that made me an outcast in my own home—to everyone but my brother. Even servants shook with fear around me and avoided me. I wasn't afforded the custom of most royal princesses—a servant to help me bathe or dress, like I'd suddenly decide to kill them out of sport or something.

Perhaps it was for the better. It taught me to be more independent, to learn to do things for myself. It was one of the reasons I had the courage to flee that awful place, to try and find a life of my own.

I'd been taught since the first moment my skin glowed and I revealed the syrenskyn markings to my mother that my magick was meant for only one purpose—to seduce and kill men. At that moment, I had become a weapon. And while my father had no enemies in Morodon, other light fae certainly did. He knew it would gain him a hefty marriage price in exchange for me.

Indeed, it had. Apparently, Lord Gael was a wealthy man, and he'd given my father chests of gold and jewels to gain ownership of me in marriage. I was sure that my father had cursed me every moment of every day since I'd ran away from home months ago. And honestly, I didn't care. He'd never loved me. Not like he'd loved Draydyn. Only his son was worth his time and effort. Daughters were merely bargaining chips for gaining wealth.

That was why my fear began to escalate when Draydyn died. Draydyn was the only one who protected me. When he was gone, I knew my days were numbered. And I was right.

"I'm heading back now," Tessa called as she stepped out of the water and onto the bank, using the absorbent blanket to dry herself and Saralyn. "I'll need to get Saralyn close to the fire to dry off fully. Don't be too long."

"I won't," I said, wading to the farther bank, enjoying the warm rush of water on my skin.

Tessa redressed, slipping her cloak and hood on and wrapping Saralyn in her bundle. "I'm leaving you this blanket to dry off."

"I'll be along soon," I assured her as she set off with Hallizel flying above them.

I needed a moment to myself. A sort of grief had taken root in my chest and I couldn't pluck it out. It wasn't that I'd lost my family when I left Morodon—it was that I never really had one in the first place. Only my brother. And when he was gone, I had no one.

Here, in this clan, I could see the beautiful bond of family. How it was supposed to be. And though they'd allowed me to stay—for now—I didn't belong here either.

"She thought this a gift," I murmured to myself on a sigh, staring down at my arm, half in and half out of the water, glowing bright, the luminescent markings pulsing with magick.

"It is certainly a gift," said a wispy voice.

I jumped, peering into the reeds that grew on this side of the bank. Two bright green, luminous eyes—like the first leaves of spring—stared back at me from just above the water's surface.

"Who are you?" I asked, lowering my body into the water, as if shielding my nakedness would help.

Fluidly, the naiad glided out of the reeds. Her ears had three points rather than one, shaped like the fins of a fish. Her butterfly-blue hair cascaded in long strands, streaming through the water. Her body was a mesh of vibrant blues and greens, glowing with luminescent light beneath the surface of the pool. It did not escape me that her skin bore similar markings as mine. I'd seen them on others before, but it always shocked me to see that I shared this with naiads.

"I am Zella."

"I am Jessamine," I said hesitantly. I knew that naiads could be hostile, though this one seemed rather friendly.

She nodded as she circled me to one side then swam in a semicircle to the other, a fluid silky glide through the water as she observed me.

"I have met ocean naiads," I told her, "but never a river naiad."

The ones I had spoken to, that my father coerced me to converse with on a regular basis, were aggressive creatures in the Nemian Sea. He would charge his guards to take me out once a week to a tiny island off our shores where the naiads were known to sunbathe. He would demand that I speak with them in order gain their trust. I never did.

While they did speak to me, it was mostly to curse me as a land-walker who had the nerve to try to be their friend. One of the males had threatened to kill me if I continued to invade their island home, which they'd declared was theirs when I had told them it was within my father's realm of Morodon. So, I had spoken to naiads many times, but they all hated me because I was the daughter of the tyrant king in the palace next to the Nemian Sea.

"That is strange. You speak our language so well. You are a pretty syrenskyn, Jessamine."

My name echoed strangely when she said it. She finally came to a stop in the water before me. I focused on not panicking, remembering how that dryad stag had attacked me when dryads were seemingly aloof, nonviolent creatures. I wondered if she had the madness that he did.

"Thank you," I told her.

She stood, revealing that she was taller than me, but thin and willowy. There were gills on the sides of her neck as well. Purple water lilies clung to her hair and draped down one arm. I wasn't sure if they were for decoration or growing from her own body.

"You are a beautiful naiad," I admitted.

Her laughter tinkled like bells. Then she sobered quickly, angling her head as she asked, "Why would you not think being a syrenskyn is a gift?"

I stared down at myself and lifted my clawed hands from the water. "I am a creature made to kill, am I not?"

"You are," she agreed easily. "But you are also a creature made to love. A syrenskyn is given the best of a naiad's magick. To both kill *and* to love. And to love is so lovely."

She twirled in the water, her lilies glowing as if sharing her own bioluminescent light. They must be touched by her magick.

Morodon scholars believed that the syrenskyn magick came from the naiads who lived in the deep oceans, whose markings glowed with biolumescence even in broad daylight. Of course, in the conversations I'd had with some of these naiads at my father's insistence, none had ever confirmed if this was true though I'd asked many times. I'd wanted to know what my magick was for, if its only purpose was to kill. If I was created only to harm others. And here was this young river naiad telling me so easily what I'd always yearned to know.

"I don't understand." I flicked my tongue over a fang. "These," I pointed to them, "and these," I raised my hands, curling my clawed fingers, "are for killing."

Her green brow pinched with confusion as she lowered herself back into the water and began to swim again, the steam rising in her wake.

"That is a lie, pretty syrenskyn. The claws are for your enemy." She pointed one of her webbed fingers at my hands as I lowered them back into the water. "But your bite is for your lover."

I scoffed at that. "What are you talking about? The venom in my bite would kill them."

Even now, I tasted the sweet, sticky substance dripping from one fang. It didn't harm me, because it was made from my own body, my magick.

"Whoever told you this is a liar," she said, her voice echoing over the water with ethereal energy. "It is not venom in your bite, silly. It is a pleasure toxin. Your lovers will die at your feet with pleasure." She grinned salaciously. "The venom is in your claws. That," her eyes flared an eerie green, "is for your enemy. To wield both is the best kind of magick. To the have the power to take life and to give pleasure."

She twirled in a circle again, the lilies in her hair floating on the surface of the water, while I stared, stupefied. Did she mean they'd actually die? Was this some kind of naiad trick? They were cunning creatures who liked to play with humans. But she seemed…sincere.

"You have the power to vanquish enemies." She swam closer, stopping within inches of me, staring with those otherworldly eyes. "And you can intoxicate a lover," she whispered, grinning and revealing her pointy, sharp teeth. "He will *never* leave you when you bite him."

She flipped backwards in the water, diving beneath the surface. Her luminescent glow faded as she swam toward the reeds.

"Where are you going?" I called, straightening out of the water, which lapped at my waist. "I have more questions!"

"Never," was her echoing reply, no sign of her at all now.

I realized she was repeating the fact that my lover would never leave me. Did that mean I could force another's will, hypnotize him so he had no choice but to stay with me? That sounded completely awful. I would simply never bite anyone. That would solve that problem. So being a syrenskyn was a curse. To kill or force a male to love me. How could that be a gift?

"You have many secrets, princess."

I startled and sank down to my neck, turning toward the deep, velvety voice at my back. Redvyr stood in the shadows, arms crossed, leaning back against a tree.

"How long have you been there?" I asked.

"What were you saying to her?" he replied with a question.

"Nothing important." I lowered until the pool's surface rippled against my chin, suddenly aware of how naked I was.

"Do you often speak to naiads?" he asked, his stance casual while his gaze was intensely focused on me.

"Rarely, actually," I answered, my voice shaking.

"You can turn icy water into a steaming bath then? That is another gift of yours?"

"I am a willoden. We can do many things with water. Changing the temperature is the most simple of a willoden's charms."

"Simple." He huffed and uncrossed his arms, striding to the edge of the pool. He lowered to a crouch, never releasing my gaze. "Your magick is anything but simple, Jessamine."

He finally looked away, up at the night sky where the stars were beginning to come out. The sun was gone, but there was still a few golden rays gilding his horns, his sharp jaw and square chin in silvery light. His features were harsh, but I wondered how I ever thought him a monster. I found myself mesmerized by the fierceness of his face, knowing what intelligence and passion he kept hidden away from the world.

"You can speak to fae creatures in an ancient tongue of their own, command water to obey you at will, transform your body into..."

He returned his gaze to me, my heart pounding furiously in my chest. "Into what?" I asked, terrified to know the answer, that it might be something my own family might call me—seductress, temptress, harlot.

"The most beautiful female I've ever seen."

It was nearly dark now, and the water distorted my figure beneath the surface. Still, I was aware he was drinking his fill of me with that feral gaze. And yet, I didn't feel the same shame or disgust when other men had stared at me. When my parents had made it apparent my body was formed and created by the gods for sin and for death.

"What does the word syrenskyn mean? I heard you and the naiad both say it several times."

For the first time in my life, I wanted to own the name given to my kind. I wanted to see Redvyr's reaction, to see if he would look at me with disgust the way others did in Morodon. The way my own family did.

"That is what I am." Boldly, I lifted out of the water to my shoulders, not wanting to appear ashamed, even though a part of me was. "That is what they call a skald fae who has the ability to entrance an enemy with her body, lure them close, and then kill them with a swipe of her venomous claws." I lifted a hand out of the water, showing him that my nails had transformed into long, dark green talons that curled at the tips—claws.

His expression tightened with what appeared to be pain rather than disgust. I didn't understand this reaction.

"You don't need the glow of a syrenskyn to lure in anyone, Jessamine. You could entrance any creature with one look of those eyes of yours."

He held my gaze, his own predatory gold eyes glinting in the dark. I could do nothing but stare, wondering at his subdued response to knowing he had welcomed a killer into his clan. Finally, he stood and glanced up at the moon.

"Come. There are more than friendly naiads in these woods. Much less welcoming creatures. I don't want you going anywhere alone."

I didn't question him. I knew the farther north we went, the wilder the lands were, and this was not my native land. It was his. But I wasn't about to get out of this water with him watching me.

"Will you turn around, please?"

His smug smile returned. The one that sent a thrilling shiver along my skin and made me feel overwhelmed. But he turned away as I asked, facing the tree he'd been leaning against.

Slowly, I stepped out onto the bank and quickly dried off with the toweling blanket Tessa left for me. Then I hurriedly slid on the dress.

"What does *Làveen Orla* mean? It is demon tongue, isn't it?"

He turned his head slightly toward my voice.

"Don't turn around! I'm not finished." My fingers moved quickly to lace up the bodice.

He chuckled. "*Làveen Orla* is the name Bezaliel and Tessa gave this pond. It means Lover's Pool."

My fingers paused on the lacings. Tessa and Bezaliel had obviously enjoyed that pond together. And now imagining this place as an intimate one for lovers with Redvyr so close, his broad back to me, his tail twitching slowly back and forth, sent an astonishing sensation through my body. Heated arousal.

I wrapped my cloak around my shoulders and walked around him, needing some space, but I heard him—felt him—following close behind.

Before we made it off the trail and into the clearing where a fire burned with a radiant glow, he caught my arm, his fingers encircling and touching on the opposite side, then he gently turned me to face him.

I didn't ask him why or what he wanted. Nor did I jerk away or tell him he shouldn't put his hands on me. Rather, I sank into his space, staring up into his wild eyes so fixed upon mine, marveling at how my pulse quickened with excitement. Not fear.

"I will not tell anyone about your gift of being a syrenskyn," he said gravely. "You do not need to be afraid that I will expose this secret you want to keep."

My gaze wandered over his hardened expression, my hand wrapping around his bicep. A rumble in his chest told me he liked my hand on him. I should step away. I should keep our communications and interactions cordial. Aloof. But there was no mistaking the forbidden desire burning a flame inside me.

So I leaned my body closer, inches from his. He stiffened. I lifted my chin higher, pretending to get closer so he could hear me.

"Thank you, Lord Redvyr. But I did not fear that you would. I do not feel fear of any kind when it comes to you."

I turned and walked into the pool of firelight, knowing damn well that I lied. There was a small fear growing in my heart. That when it came time, it was going to hurt very deeply to say goodbye to Lord Redvyr.

CHAPTER 14

Redvyr

The gods hated me. That was the only explanation. I stared at the red-haired beauty across the campfire, her face soft and sweet in sleep. When she was awake, her defiance and wickedly alluring eyes had my body hard and my temper at a feverish pitch.

I'd purposely set my furs on the opposite side of the campfire to keep her at a distance. This burning desire was becoming a monster I couldn't tame.

Then there was what my chief and closest friend had said. I looked over at Bezaliel, a giant lump in the furs next to his female and child. Of all the fucking things for him to say to me, that she was meant to be mine by the gods. That she was my mate, and that I should take her to my bed to find out.

Fucking bastard. Now that was all I could think about. For a beast fae, there was only one way to know if a lover was your gods-given mate. And though I longed to bury my cock inside her, that wasn't an option. I had a feeling that if I did, I'd never let her go back to her own kind, whether she wanted to stay or not.

A few of the clan accepted her, but they all knew it was a temporary situation. Many didn't want her with us at all, she was too much of an outsider. It wasn't like she was a wraith or shadow fae, a dark fae who needed our help. She was a princess skald fae from a kingdom far away.

Her brow pinched in her sleep. Her hand twitched.

The council deemed she would go at the end of winter. If I took her for a lover, I wouldn't let her go. I would defy the council. But worse than that. It would lead to my ruin in so many ways.

First, it would prevent me from finding my own mate. It would also make me more like my father, keeping a woman who didn't belong to me. I knew that led to heartache, not just for myself but for the entire clan. I refused to repeat the wrongs of my father, to repeat a tragic history that has damned my family name. The only reason I was chief was because I'd beat all opponents, and I'd pledged that I would never be my father, that I would not disappoint the clan but help it to rise above my father's failings.

Only over time had I proven that pledge true. And here I was, staring at this sorceress across the fire who seduced me even in her sleep.

She twitched again, this time crying out. She was having a nightmare. I contemplated whether to wake her, but considering I slept without wearing any clothes, I wasn't about to do that. It would only be more of a nightmare for her, I imagined.

Suddenly, she gasped and jolted awake, sitting up and breathing quickly. I didn't say a word, hoping she'd simply lay back down and go to sleep. She turned her head and found me. Blinking awake, she shimmied out of her bedroll, wearing that ungodly thin gown she called a chemise. Picking up her furs, she walked around the campfire, stepping softly over Leifkyn who didn't move a muscle.

Without even looking at me, she unrolled her furs next to mine. Though the embers were merely red coals, I could see her body far too well beneath the thin material of her nightgown. Not that my cock needed any encouragement. He'd been at attention from the moment I saw her swimming in that pool, for fuck's sake.

She wiggled into her furs, facing me, but closed her eyes and sighed. I considered asking her what she was doing, why she needed to move herself so close to me, but then she'd likely become angry and snap at me with a hundred questions, the worst being, *why don't you want me near you.* I wasn't about to start lying to the woman, and telling her the truth would be madness.

Heaving a sigh of my own, I spoke in a low voice. "What did you dream of?"

Her lips pursed, her eyes opening to slits, finding mine in the dark. "That I was that fae on trial in Hellamir," she whispered. "That I was being burned at the stake before a cheering crowd."

My entire body tensed at the thought and at the fear shaking her voice. "It was a dream. Nothing more."

"For me, yes. But he's done it before. I know he has." She sniffed, curling farther into her furs. "And he'll do it again."

I rolled to my back, staring up at the stars. I couldn't look at her. "You are speaking of Gael." I was no longer going to give him the title of *lord.* There was nothing noble about this light fae prick of Mevia.

"Yes." Her voice was so small. It stirred my anger.

"How do you know this?"

"I just do. I can't explain how."

"Part of your witchcraft?" I turned my head to see her reaction.

She tilted her head up, frowning, until she caught my smile. "It's not funny."

"Why isn't it?"

"Because that moon fae from Nævhail Glen was targeted as a witch. Any female who holds rare or unusual magick is deemed a witch by some imbecile in charge."

Her defiance and strength were back. I hummed in approval.

"But beast fae have no magick. So any female with magick is a witch in my eyes."

She stared at me then arched a brow. "Are you teasing me?"

"Yes."

She huffed and rolled to her back, a small smile curling her pretty mouth.

"You're an idiot."

I couldn't stop from laughing. "Please tell me why."

"If that were the truth, then Lorelyn, your seer, would be considered a witch."

"Who says we don't consider her one? My question," I stopped her before she could snap at me again, keeping my gaze on the glittering stars, "is why you believe the word witch, or witchcraft, is something terrible. Perhaps, we revere it."

She was quiet, but she shifted her body. She was staring at me again, likely wondering if I was teasing her again or telling the truth.

"Do you?" she asked softly.

Rolling to my side to face her, I shifted up onto my elbow and forearm. "Do I what?"

"Do you revere magick?" She leaned up on her elbow, mirroring me. The line of her delicate neck was utterly beguiling, drawing my gaze.

"Of course I do."

She went silent again.

"Does that surprise you?" I asked.

"Yes. But I'm glad to hear it. I thought it would make you sad."

"Because I have none?" I smirked. "I have never had, it so there is no loss to feel when it comes to magick. I am content living my life without what the other fae have."

She pushed up, sitting straight, her face closer to mine, a serious expression tightening her face. "You do have magick though, Redvyr. It may not be the same kind that I have or even the other dark fae. But I see it, in the way you lead your people, the way you treat them, protect them. And in the way you treat strangers."

"I was not kind to you," I reminded her, my heart galloping faster at her praise.

"You were, actually. You could've left me in the snow and moved on. But you killed that poor deer and tried to feed me." She laughed, and my heart falling further into the wonder that was Jessamine.

"All my efforts were for nothing."

"Not for nothing." She reached over and put her hand on mine which rested on the edge of my furs. "You have been far kinder to me than," her voice broke, and she shook it off with another light laugh, "than my own family. Than most nobility I've known, who were born and bred to be civil and compassionate. You've shown more care for me than anyone I've ever met."

Gods in the heavens and all of the hells, save me from this torment.

She removed her hand and laid back down, tucking herself under the furs again. I couldn't respond to her little speech. Either she was still delirious from her dream, maybe even half-crazed because all she'd eaten was cheese and bread and jam since I found her, or…

Or she was telling the truth, and that is what she sincerely thought of me.

"You best get some sleep," I commanded gruffly, needing to be rid of all these damned, soft feelings. "We have one more day of travel to Ghasta Vale. Then we'll be hosting a visit from King Goll."

"What?" she nearly shrieked.

"*Quiet.* You'll wake the others."

"Why will we be getting a visit from King Goll?" she whisper-yelled.

"Because of the threat Gael has made public in Hellamir. He's rallying men in his favor to start a rebellion. Or rather, he has already started one. King Goll is the king of Lumeria now as well as Northgall. He needs to know."

"How soon will he come, do you think?"

"I sent Hallizel to his castle, Windolek, after supper. He could be here in a day or two. It depends if that sprite goes directly to Windolek or if she gets distracted along her way."

"Goddess above, I'll never get any sleep now."

"Looking forward to meeting the wraith king, princess?"

"*No.* I've heard he's terrible and violent. And he was the one I was supposed to…"

The mere thought of her approaching Goll with her syrenskyn glow, naked and luminescent, had a growl rumbling from my belly up my throat.

"Don't worry. He's no more terrible or violent than I am."

She huffed a laugh and snuggled deeper in her furs, muffling, "Goodnight, Red."

I smiled. She must've heard Bezaliel call me that earlier. "Sleep well, Jessa."

She sighed contentedly and drifted off much sooner than I'd thought she would. As for me, I lay awake staring at the stars, wondering why the gods would bestow this challenge on me. Having her near me was torture, but the thought of her leaving me was a worse agony. One I already knew I couldn't bear.

It must've been near dawn before I finally fell asleep.

CHAPTER 15

Jessamine

By the time I'd dragged myself out of a heavy sleep this morning, it was to find our entire party nearly packed and ready to leave. I'd been a little embarrassed that I'd slept so long, quickly dressing then rolling my bed fur into a bundle and tying it with the leather sashes the way Tessa had taught me.

When I'd carried the bundle to Wolf where Leifkyn was cinching the saddlebags, he said, "Good morning, princess. So glad you decided to wake and join us."

At first, I'd thought he was digging into me for being a lazy good-for-nothing. When he laughed and nudged me in jest, I'd felt a weight drop off my chest. It was the first time that a man of the clan, besides Bezaliel, had spoken to me as a friend would.

Apparently, this had encouraged his friend Dayn to be more friendly as well. Since we'd set out this morning, all of us on foot except Tessa and Saralyn who rode upon Mishka, the two serious friends—or whom I'd thought were serious—had been regaling me with humorous tales of their clan, many of which featured their ornery king.

Redvyr hadn't said anything to me at all. While Leifkyn and Dayn walked on either side of me, he kept toward the front, leading us, not even glancing back. Bezaliel walked alongside Mishka, talking quietly to Tessa. I couldn't tell if Redvyr was grumpy about something in particular or if this was always his 'on the trail' demeanor. He watched the woods as we trekked across a wide, open field.

Snow drifted down lightly in small flakes, the temperature dropping as we moved out of the woods and the wind gusted more fiercely across the plain we crossed.

I'd pulled on my hood, tugging my cloak tightly around my shoulders and wrapping my hands in the folds as we walked. I'd noticed Tessa had bundled herself and the baby up warmly as well. But the males strode on without even a cloak or long-sleeves. It was maddening how well-adapted they were to this climate.

"That was when our lord there," Dayn said drawing me back to the present while he gestured toward Redvyr, "told the wood fae trespasser that if he didn't head south and head fast, that we were going to skin him and roast him for dinner."

"What?" I exclaimed. "He didn't!"

I stared at the broad back of Redvyr, seemingly unaffected like he didn't even hear us. He must have heard, of course. He was only a few strides ahead of us, and that fae male had the most heightened senses of anyone I'd ever met.

"He did," laughed Leifkyn. "The poor man believed him. He took off running back toward the Borderlands. Never saw him again."

"I guess not," I laughed. "I'll bet he—"

"Quiet," snapped Redvyr, coming to a halt, his gaze on the sky.

Dayn and Leifkyn instantly drew their swords, corralling me between them, their faces turned toward the sky as well. I heard nothing, but apparently, they did. Bezaliel had drawn his blade too. Mishka had lowered to the ground, all of the wolves growling. Wolf stood at my back, his rumbling snarl fierce. But it was Redvyr now in front of me, tail lashing. His black claws extended, his muscles flexed and bulged, ready to fight, that had my attention.

In all my life, I'd never had this sort of protection. Least of all in my own home in Morodon. That was what struck me the hardest as a whooshing sound from above, high in the gray clouds, drew my gaze to the skies as well.

The snow swirled in great loops as a behemoth of a beast, a black-scaled dragon, descended out of the clouds. I gasped, backing away on instinct, my shoulders nudging Wolf's chest. The dragon landed on the white-covered meadow in front of us, shaking the ground. That was when I saw there was a rider upon its back.

Redvyr relaxed, standing straight and tall. The others resheathed their swords, obviously deeming this dragon rider no threat. He was a wraith fae, his deep gray skin, four smooth horns and black armor familiar to me because some wraith fae warriors in similar garb had traveled and stopped in Haldek's tavern on occasion.

This wasn't simply a warrior, though. I knew who this was. I'd never seen him, but everyone in all the kingdoms knew there was only one dragon rider in the realms. King Gollaya Verbane. His dragon lowered until its belly hit the ground.

As the wraith fae dismounted and strode toward us with purpose, I shrank further into Wolf, wishing I could disappear. The dragon's silvery blue eyes mirrored its owner's, both of them assessing our party with keen scrutiny. The wraith fae stopped several feet away from Redvyr, his long, silky black hair blowing in the wind.

I was surprised to see that the gods had blessed him with a regal, handsome face. He wasn't as tall or as broad as Redvyr. I hadn't met anyone who was. But magick—intense power—radiated from him. It was known that he was a zephilim—a formidable fire-wielder. He didn't need to be the biggest or strongest among other warriors. With a single word, his gods-given magick could decimate us all.

And yet, Redvyr seemed somehow relaxed in his presence, though I noticed that he had moved to stand directly in front of me, blocking me from the approaching wraith king.

A tinkling laugh and fluttering of wings drew my attention over my shoulder to Tessa, where Hallizel flew in circles around Saralyn's head. The babe giggled, her playmate having returned from her errand.

"Redvyr," said King Goll, his deep voice a rasp on the wind. "I received your message."

"Goll." Redvyr nodded in greeting, his tail still lashing slowly. "I didn't expect you so soon."

I couldn't see him with Redvyr blocking my view, so I shifted to the side to peer over his shoulder.

"Your sprite said, 'Lord Gael has started a rebellion and is burning witches.' That was all. Of course I came."

"How did you find us?" asked Redvyr.

"Drak scented you on our way to Ghasta Vale."

The dragon snorted and turned his head toward the wraith king. His brow furrowed, his gaze flicking beyond Redvyr to me and his eyes widening in surprise.

"Well, well," he crooned more softly. "This is not a beast fae from your clan. Aren't you going to introduce me?"

Redvyr stepped slightly to the side, and I eased forward. "Goll, this is Jessamine. She is under our protection."

The wraith king reached out a clawed hand, a rather civil gesture from the man I was told was a murderous, debauched king who abducted Princess Una of Issos, now Queen of Northgall. I reached out my hand and shook his. His gaze flicked down.

"You are a skald fae. So far from home?"

"Yes, my lord," I answered courteously with a curtsy and bow of the head, as I was taught to greet all nobility. Especially royalty.

When I straightened, it was to find King Goll smiling and Redvyr scowling.

"You can let go of her hand now," muttered Redvyr.

King Goll dropped my hand and crossed his arms, seemingly amused as his gaze flicked from me to Redvyr and then back again.

"And who are you protecting this pretty skald fae from?" the king asked.

Redvyr glared at him for a moment before answering. "The same man who has started this rebellion in Mevia, which apparently has now spread to Hellamir."

King Goll sobered. "Gael?"

"Yes," Redvyr snarled.

A slight pressure on my booted ankle drew my attention downward. Redvyr had wrapped his tail around it.

"Why is that, Jessamine?" King Goll asked me, his watchful gaze missing nothing, in particular Redvyr's possessive grip on my ankle.

"My father betrothed me to him," I said, my voice shaking. "Upon meeting Lord Gael when he came to court in Morodon, he told me what would be required of me in a marriage with him." I dropped my gaze to the snowy ground at our feet, unable to look him in the eye when I confessed, "To kill the King of Northgall. You, my lord."

I had expected anger, rage even. Or a furious silence. Instead, King Goll laughed.

"I knew he'd send assassins at some point. But his own wife?"

"They are *not* bound in marriage," Redvyr clarified, a note of danger in his timbre. "She is not his wife."

"Jessamine, who is your family? For I know this Lord Gael, and he would not ally himself in marriage to just anyone."

I cleared my throat. "I am Jessamine Glenmyr, daughter of King Darian of Morodon."

His silver-blue eyes flared. "So the king of Morodon has allied himself with Gael against me."

I should've felt remorse or shame for outing my own father, but he had never been the kind of father, or king, that inspired my loyalty. Or my love.

"Yes, my lord."

"And now he is burning seers with magick who refuse to help him?" He turned to Redvyr.

"She and Tessa witnessed it in Hellamir. We were there just two days ago when it happened. They were able to free the seer before she was executed."

"Good." King Goll sighed, glancing back at his dragon, whose silvery eyes scanned the meadow and woods beyond as snow piled in drifts on his snout and along his spiked tail. "Jessamine. You are most welcome to return to Windolek with me. I can protect you there, and it would please my wife to have some female company."

"*No,*" Redvyr snapped before I could even reply. "She is *my* responsibility. She is ours to protect."

King Goll smiled, his fangs showing. "I see."

"Might I have a word with you in private?" Redvyr's tail slid from around my leg as he stormed away toward the dragon.

The wraith king gave me a slight bow. "It was a pleasure to meet you, Jessamine. You are in good hands here."

He gave a respectful nod to the other beast fae and turned to meet Redvyr, who had stopped within biting distance of the dragon. I found it amazing that he wasn't terrified of the creature. The dragon may have allowed King Goll to ride him but he didn't appear tame in any way, his predatory gaze fierce as he scanned the distant woods.

I watched Redvyr speak to King Goll in hushed, but harsh tones. The king seemed just as grave as they spoke back and forth.

"I'm surprised Lord Redvyr didn't claw the king with his suggestion to take Jessamine," said Leifkyn behind me in a low voice, but not so low I couldn't hear.

"King Goll was taunting him. Lord Redvyr knows it."

"But why?"

Dayn snorted. "That is always the way between these two."

I turned to Leifkyn. "Why would Lord Redvyr claw the king for offering to take me off your hands? He denied the request before I could even give my answer."

Though I had no intentions whatsoever of leaving, unless Redvyr wanted me to go, I was a little shocked.

Dayn and Leifkyn shared a knowing look.

"What? You're not going to give me any kind of answer?"

"Why don't you ask him?" Leifkyn nodded over my shoulder.

Redvyr was marching back toward us while King Goll climbed up his dragon's arm to the saddle on his back.

"Let's move," Redvyr growled, not even sparing me a glance as he walked past me and back onto the path we'd been traveling.

With a chortling call, the black dragon beat its wings and lifted off into the sky. I could do nothing but stare. What a magnificent creature.

Wolf nudged me, so I fell back in line, marching on toward the winter camp, hoping we'd arrive soon. With the snow, I longed for the warmth of a tent over my head. The temperatures seemed to drop further as we continued, perhaps not simply because of the snow, but from the cold beast lord leading our way.

CHAPTER 16

Redvyr

"This will do." I didn't like that we were surrounded by woods in this small clearing, no defense at our backs. But it was nearly dark already. "We should reach Ghasta Vale before midday tomorrow."

With that, the men started unloading the wolves of their burdens. Bezaliel helped Tessa and the baby down from Mishka, and Jessamine walked toward the trees. I instantly followed.

"Where do you think you're going?" I asked when she stopped to pick up a fallen branch.

"We will need kindling for a fire. I want to be useful."

She walked on. I followed.

"Female, you should know by now that it is dangerous in these wilds. You can't walk off anywhere by yourself."

"Then come with me, my lord." She smiled at me over her shoulder, a provocative look in her gem-green gaze. My knees went weak.

Of course, I followed, picking up branches in her wake, that sea-flower scent luring me closer.

"I noticed," she said casually, "that you don't use King Goll's title when you speak to him. Isn't he your king?"

"He is King of Northgall, yes. But I am the lord of Meerland. I don't call him king because he doesn't rule here, and because Goll needs to stay humble."

Meerland was a specific territory of wildlands in Northgall where only beast fae lived.

She laughed, sending my heart rate racing. "Doesn't he find that disrespectful?"

"Probably. But we understand each other well enough."

We were quiet as we collected the kindling, a pestering thought bothering me.

"Did you want to go with him? To his castle at Windolek?"

"No."

"But you did think him pretty, I wager." I couldn't keep my mouth shut. Some masochistic part of myself needed to know what she thought of him.

"How could I not? I have eyes." Her tone was teasing.

I dropped my kindling. She spun and faced me, her eyes wide but daring.

"Tell me what you liked about him," I demanded, corralling closer.

She walked backward, her bundle of kindling held in both arms. "His face is very pleasing."

"What else?"

Her back hit the thick trunk of a birch tree. "His eyes are a beautiful blue with a ring of gold circling the center."

"Drop the kindling, Jessamine." My voice deepened to a raspy whisper as I loomed over her now.

She tossed it aside, flattening her palms against the trunk beside her hips.

"What else?" I demanded.

"His horns are smooth and glossy," she said breathily, her chest rising and falling quickly, the green of her eyes swallowed by black.

A need beyond my control burned hot and fierce inside my chest, a need to claim her as mine. Even though I knew that was impossible, I was reeling, falling, catapulting into a pit beyond desire or desperation. It was like a will outside my own guided me, demanding to let her know that she belonged to me even if it was only for now.

I planted my hands on the trunk on either side of her head, her scent ensnaring my senses beyond reason. "Are my horns too rough for you, princess?"

Slowly, she lifted a hand. I curled my head downward, bringing my face closer to hers, our breaths mingling. She traced her fingers along one of my horns. I had no sensation there, but still, it pulled a groan from me when she touched me with such reverence.

"I like the roughness of them." Her eyes were so wide, searching, seeking, and full of desire, her fingers curling tightly around one horn, her feline gaze sliding back to mine. "I like the roughness of you."

"That is good to hear, princess," I purred softly, leaning closer to her pale throat. Grazing my nose along her silky skin, I begged, "Let me taste you, Jessamine."

I gripped her waist with one hand, careful not to curl my claws into her dress and flesh. I wanted to tear her clothes off and mount her right here on the fucking forest floor. The thought was a maddening temptation.

"Yes," she answered so softly I might not have heard her if I wasn't a beast fae.

Growling, I opened my mouth on her delicate throat, careful not to bite, sucking and licking my way down to the curve of her shoulder.

"Fucking hells, female." My cock grew hard as stone the instant I tasted her, my mouth watering for more. So much more.

She kept one grip on my horn, her other hand clutching my bicep, her blunt nails digging into my skin. I got even harder. A new scent wafted in the air, her arousal. I was undone. Sinking to my knees, I gripped her hips and inhaled the sweet, musky scent of her, wanting to drown in this insane desire that gripped me with an iron fist.

Before I realized what I was doing, I had loosened the lacings of the slits in her dress and was pushing up her skirt. Her arousal was intoxicating, wetness glistening between her plump, pale thighs and on her thatch of hair as vibrant as the color on her head. Without thinking, I opened my mouth on her mound, drinking her in on a groan.

"Ah," she made a little cry, thrusting her hips forward.

"Mmmm," I hummed, laving her slit with my forked tongue, teasing her swollen nub.

"Goddess help me," she gasped, gripping another horn with her free hand.

Sitting on my heels, I spread my knees and held her steady, needing to drink the sweetness of her fully.

"Lean back and lift this leg." I helped her to bend her leg over my shoulder, which opened her even more to me.

Purring, I whispered, "Good girl, just like that." Then I was licking and tasting, going mad with ecstasy.

She mewled and moaned, circling her hips, grinding her cunt against my mouth. It was beyond the most heavenly thing I'd ever experienced.

Jerking open the lacings of my trousers, I pulled out my cock, squeezing it on a long stroke.

"Oh," she whispered.

I pulled back to look up at her while she still held my horns for balance, something obscenely satisfying in it. She stared down where I gripped my cock, her eyes heavy and pupils dilated with desire, her mouth fallen open.

My voice hoarse and gruff, I told her while stroking myself, "You look as if you've never seen a male's cock."

"I haven't," she murmured softly.

My hand froze mid-stroke. I let that information penetrate through the thick haze of lust and sink in, growling at the satisfaction of it. Hot yearning and a deep ache took hold of me.

With her thigh over one of my shoulders, her cunt spread for me, I slid my hand at her waist up to her breast and squeezed, pinching the tip between my thumb and forefinger.

"Ah!" she cried, her luscious mouth falling open as she watched me, her skin beginning to glow, taking on the luminescent colors of the syrenskyn. Her magick responded to desire.

I encircled my fingers around her knee at my shoulder to keep her there and leaned forward to suck her sweet cunt. Within seconds, she was writhing and grinding herself on my mouth. I hummed with pleasure at how quickly she was coming undone for me, flicking her nub with my tongue and sucking, tugging gently on it, while stroking my cock harder and faster.

"Oh, gods," she groaned, her skin radiating brighter, her body thrusting harder against my mouth, one of my fangs catching on her cunt lips. Rather than jerk in pain, she pulled on my horns, guiding my face closer before she began to scream with an orgasm. I slid my tongue inside her, relishing the tightening of her cunt as she climaxed.

My reward was a flood of her juices which I drank, licking up every drop. I purred with contentment at her wild release. When the throbbing subsided and her breathing eased, I sat back, my cock painfully hard and erect.

She panted softly, staring down between my legs. Without a word, I stood before her. "Slide to your knees for me, Jessamine," I told her bluntly, needing to fill that sweet mouth.

If she'd never seen a male's cock, then she'd definitely never done this before. I was too far gone to wonder if this might be scary for her in some way. Desire was a white-hot flame licking up my spine. And I needed to empty my seed inside of her, specifically *her*.

I wasn't ready—nor was she—to fuck her. I wasn't sure if she was even ready for this, but the heat and eagerness in her gaze and my own desperate yearning overrode any sense I had left.

Even though Bezaliel had tempted me with the thought, I'd convinced myself that fucking her wasn't a wise move, no matter how badly I wanted it. But I could have this. I could sink into her mouth and let her suck me.

"On your knees for me, princess," I coaxed softly.

She eased down until her knees hit the snowy ground. I grunted approval at her eagerness to comply. Her mouth quirked in a small smile but vanished just as quickly.

"What do I do?" she asked, an anxiousness in her eyes as she still came down from the high of her orgasm.

"Just open your mouth and let me in. You don't have to do anything else."

She gripped my bare hips and opened her mouth, her eyes drifting up to mine.

Vix's blood. I was going to be sent to the lowest level of the hells for this, I was sure of it. And I simply did not give a fucking damn.

Cradling the back of her nape gently, I whispered, "Yes, tilt your head up so I can see those eyes."

She did, holding my gaze as I slid the reddened tip of my cock into her mouth. I clenched my other fist into her loose hair, my knuckles pressed against the back of her skull. I pumped inside a little farther, letting her get used to the sensation.

"So good, sweetheart," I crooned. "You're doing so good."

She whimpered then suctioned her lips, her cheeks hollowing. The sight of her sent me spiraling closer to coming. She was so fucking beautiful.

"Gods, yes. Just like that," I praised her, fucking her mouth a little deeper, tapping the back of her throat. "Feels so fucking good. Your mouth will be the death of me."

I pumped inside her once, twice, then I couldn't hold on any longer. With a deep groan, I spent some of my come inside her mouth then pulled myself free, ejaculating onto her up-turned throat.

"Swallow that down for me," I told her, a possessive need gripping me in an iron fist.

She closed her mouth and swallowed as I finished pumping onto her neck and upper breasts. When I was done, my chest heaving, I stared at the mess I'd made of her, knowing I had crossed a line that I couldn't return from.

I was doomed, for I knew now that I would take her to my bed. I didn't care if it jeopardized my clan in any way. All I knew was the deep-seated desire I had for this woman which had grown into a monster of its own. The question was, would this monster ruin me, possibly kill me in the end, like it had my father? And did I even care if it meant I could have Jessamine?

"Here," I quickly laced my trousers and helped her to stand. Her skin had dimmed to its normal hue, the brighter gleam of her magick fading.

She lifted the hem of her cloak to clean the mess on her throat and the top of her breasts.

I took the cloak from her. "Tilt your head back."

She did, and I wiped her clean, though I couldn't help but rub a drop of my come into her skin with my thumb at her collarbone. I wanted my scent all over her, so even my men knew not to touch her. The thought of another male touching her made me feral. I knew then and there I was completely lost to reason. I now understood the danger of maddening obsession, of how my father had lost his mind and taken my mother when he should not. And yet, even recognizing how quickly I'd fallen, I couldn't turn back. It was far too late.

Once she was clean, I finally met her gaze, hoping I wouldn't find regret there. I didn't, though there seemed to be disappointment.

"I apologize if I pushed you too much."

"You didn't. I wanted to do it." She frowned. "Though I didn't know what I was doing, really."

"You knew well enough, I promise."

She nodded, her brow still pinched.

"What's wrong?"

Now she wouldn't meet my gaze.

"Are you embarrassed by being intimate with me?"

"No."

I lifted her chin so she would look me in the eye. "Then what is it?"

"You didn't kiss me." She shrugged. "I'd like to know what that's like."

My heart squeezed painfully. *She wanted me to kiss her?*

"You've never kissed a male before? I can hardly believe it."

She cleared her throat nervously. "My parents, in particular my father, made sure everyone—including any interested suitors— knew that my kiss could result in their death."

"Why?"

"My fangs. He told them they are venomous. But they're not." She frowned again, seeming to want to say more. "They're gone now. See."

She smiled brightly, revealing a row of even, straight-edged teeth.

I chuckled. "I'm not afraid of your fangs. I don't mind a little biting."

Her already flushed cheeks darkened to a deeper blush.

"Come here," I urged gently, slipping my hand beneath her hair to the nape of her neck.

I wrapped my other hand around the back of her waist and lifted her onto her toes, pressing her body against mine as I curled down to her. With more gentleness than I normally used, I brushed my lips against her full mouth, before teasing her lips wider and pressing deeper.

She combed her fingers into my hair and pulled me to her, pressing her lush body against me, her tongue playing against mine. I groaned, my cock hardening again at her softness, this intimacy I hadn't imagined could be so beguiling.

Humming with approval, I slid my tongue along hers, reveling in the sweetest sensation I'd ever known—Jessamine in my arms, her scent, her body, her essence cocooning me in ecstasy.

I broke the kiss and pressed my forehead to hers. "You *will* be the death of me, sweet Jessamine."

She laughed, joy in her eyes, because she thought I was jesting. All I could think of was my father, his mistake of taking a female who wasn't his mate into his clan, and how it had destroyed him and my mother, eventually killing them both.

I cast those thoughts aside as I smiled down at her, holding her close for a moment longer, relishing this feeling, for I knew there was no path forward that didn't end with her beside me—in my bed, in my life, bearing my children. If it led to my death, that was fine with me.

Let the gods do what they will. Jessamine was mine.

CHAPTER 17

Jessamine

I did not miss the knowing looks from the other males or the teasing smile from Tessa once we returned to the camp. While the others debated what King Goll would do to squash this rebellion, I kept myself busy by holding Saralyn and playing with the sweet, bright-eyed babe.

Of course, all I could think about was my encounter with Redvyr in the woods. I'd pleasured myself alone many times, but it had never felt like that. So absolutely overwhelming.

And his kiss…

My mind drifted, new desire unfurling in my belly. I was surprised by Redvyr's aggressive intimacy. I knew he was attracted to me, but I didn't realize he would act on his craving like that, in the middle of the woods against a tree. It was the most wonderful experience of my life.

When I glanced at Redvyr, it was to find his steady, golden gaze on me. He'd stretched out atop his bed of furs, leaning his weight on his forearms, pretending to listen to the others chatter about King Goll. But his attention was on me. And by the gods, I reveled in it.

I wanted his eyes on me, his hands, his body. I wanted his mind on me, too. I wanted him to be as twisted on the inside as I was. His unshakeable stare didn't tell me whether he felt as wildly desperate as I did, but it warmed me through.

Saralyn cooed and tugged on a lock of my hair. I smiled down at her in my lap while she wrapped her tiny fingers around one of mine. I admired the pretty babe, wondering if I might have a daughter like her one day—with golden or green eyes.

The thought shocked me, that I was considering such a thing. And yet, I'd never felt this enchanted by a male before. I'd been infatuated with some, but I'd never felt like this. It was a deep longing that felt like madness and exhilaration and unquenchable need all at once. If Redvyr and I were alone, I would already be crawling into his lap.

My parents would be disgusted with me, that I was falling for a dark fae, and a beast fae at that. But I didn't care what they thought. I didn't care what anyone thought, except him.

I caught his ever-watchful gaze again across the fire.

"Here, I'll take her now. It's time to feed her," said Tessa, lifting Saralyn from my arms.

Tessa settled beside Bezaliel and lowered the strap of her dress, shifting Saralyn to her breast. Dayn had come back from the woods with two hares which the group roasted and shared along with the last of the bread and cheese. I'd eaten very little of the latter, my thoughts too full of something else. Someone else.

"I hope Shearah has one of her stews cooking when we arrive tomorrow," Dayn said.

"All you have to do is flirt with her and she'll make whatever you want," teased Leifkyn.

Dayn grinned while he unrolled his bedroll. "Don't be jealous. I'll share with you."

"You'll share Shearah?" Leifkyn sat on a tree stump he'd dragged over to the campfire. "That's generous of you."

"The stew, you oaf." Dayn shoved Leifkyn off the stump with a boot to his chest. "Don't even fucking think about touching Shearah."

Leifkyn laughed. "I thought you said it wasn't serious?"

"Just keep your hands to yourself. Or I'll cut them off."

Bezaliel laughed along with Leifkyn. Redvyr smiled but his attention was still on me. After a brief inner debate, I decided to do what I wanted and not worry about what the others might think. Standing, I lifted my fur bedroll and stepped past Tessa and Bezaliel. Then I spread out my fur directly next to Redvyr and slid inside it, scooting closer to him with my back to his front. Without hesitating, he curled his hand and arm around my waist and pulled me tight against him.

Silence fell around the campfire, Leifkyn and Dayn smiling at each other. But no one said a word. Sighing in contentment, I closed my eyes and drifted instantly to sleep, comforted by the weight of Redvyr's arm at my waist and his body at my back. For the first time since my brother died, I felt safe.

"I wonder if Tylok's wife is cooking something good today," said Dayn as we followed the path downhill toward a small valley and clearing in the woods below.

We were winding through hillier countryside and woodlands toward Ghasta Vale.

"You are constantly thinking about your stomach," complained Leifkyn.

"I wouldn't mind some of Farla's meat pies myself," added Bezaliel.

"Mmm, me too." Tessa walked behind her husband with Saralyn strapped to her back.

This trek downhill with knotty roots growing across the trail was much safer on foot than on wolfback.

"Who is Tylok?" I asked, walking directly behind Redvyr.

"He's a shadow fae who lives in that valley with his wife and children."

"Why doesn't he live in Gadlizel?" I asked, knowing all shadow fae lived in their great city high in the Solgavia Mountains.

"Tylok is a bit of a renegade," Redvyr answered. "He was one of their priest warriors, but he fell for a wood fae female in the Borderlands. His king commanded him to give her up or be exiled." Redvyr looked over his shoulder, catching my gaze. "He chose exile."

"That's so sad."

"It's rather romantic, if you ask me," said Tessa. "Of course, I'm a light fae who fell for a beast fae, so I can understand."

"I didn't threaten to exile Bezaliel when he brought you home," growled Redvyr.

"You couldn't," said Bezaliel. "She was my mate."

There were a few grunts of agreement amongst the group as the land began to level. In the valley below, there was no cabin anywhere that I could see among the sparse trees. There was a giant, black oak tree at the center of the valley, its trunk as thick as twelve beast fae standing side by side.

"Bezaliel," I asked, "how did you know Tessa was your mate?"

Leifkyn and Dayn chuckled then swallowed their laughter when Redvyr shot them a glare. Tessa blushed as she stepped beside me on the flatter ground. "I'll tell you later."

I remembered that Redvyr had avoided this topic once before when I asked, but my curiosity about Tylok got the better of me as we walked across the small clearing.

"Where do they live?"

Redvyr waited for me to move alongside him and pointed to the great oak tree. "There."

I stared as we drew closer, seeing steps carved into the trunk, winding upward into the sheltering branches. Though the branches were covered in snow, I could see the walls of a home nestled high in the boughs.

"How do you know Tylok?" I looked up at Redvyr walking beside me, Wolf on my other side. "He's a shadow fae, you said."

"We met him on our trek this way when he first moved into the valley with his wife, Farla. He had some leatherwork to trade for some of our grain. Since then, we've stopped here each winter to give them a sack or two of our haul from Hellamir. It keeps him and his wife and children going for a while, since they rarely travel down to the Borderlands for provisions. They prefer to stay here in the valley."

"That's very kind of you," I noted softly.

His beautiful eyes slid my way, but it was the quirk of his mouth that held me captive. We were lost in each other for a moment when Wolf suddenly chuffed and stopped walking. Redvyr instantly pushed me behind him, and the other wolves had frozen too, all growling.

"Do you smell that?" Bezaliel whispered.

"Yes." Redvyr's voice had dropped deep, his hands and his hands flexed at his sides.

"I don't hear anyone," added Dayn.

"Bezaliel and Leifkyn, stay with the females."

Hallizel fluttered out of Tessa's hood, the closest place near to the baby. "I will go too." She flitted off up into the branches of the tree.

Redvyr and Dayn strode stealthily toward the steps carved into the trunk and began to climb, circling upward until they disappeared into the house.

I waited, still and quiet, terrified of what they sensed that I could not. "What do they smell?" I asked Bezaliel.

"Blood. And something else…that doesn't belong here."

A whistle echoed from above.

"It's all clear," said Bezaliel.

Then Hallizel zipped down straight to us. "Lord Redvyr says keep Tessa and Jessamine down here."

We closed the distance to the trunk, the wolves flanking us. I stared up but saw nothing at all except the floorboards of Tylok's home up in the branches.

"I'll stay with them," said Leifkyn.

Bezaliel clapped his hand on his shoulder and hurried up the winding stairs, taking two at a time.

Dayn's expression was dark and grave as he peered back the way we'd come from the woods, sniffing the air.

"What is it?" I asked.

"I don't know. It's an unfamiliar scent. An unpleasant one at that."

"A barga or something?" Tessa circled around the huge trunk of the tree, Hallizel fluttering next to her.

"No."

I circled around to the other side, marveling at the craftsmanship of the staircase. A shadow fae wouldn't need stairs since he had wings, but his wood fae wife would. He took great care in carving and smoothing them for her. There was even a decorative ivy design swirling along the trunk of the tree, something to make Farla smile.

Footsteps announced that the others were coming back down. I continued around the tree, noting an iron hanger that held an unlit lantern.

"What did you find?" Dayn asked.

"Tylok's head," Redvyr answered, his voice rough with emotion. "But not his family."

"No!" shouted Tessa.

"What happened to them?" I asked in shock. "His children are missing?"

"And Farla," said Dayn.

Wolf rounded the trunk, but rather than coming to me, he trotted on into the small field behind it. There was something in the long grass where he stopped. He looked over at me, whining. I followed, approaching cautiously. When I realized what I was looking at, I gasped. One wing was torn, or cut, from his body, the other obviously broken, his head missing.

"I've found Tylok," I called back to the others, my voice quivering.

Redvyr was suddenly beside me, setting me gently away from the corpse of their friend. The others rushed over as well.

"What is this?" Bezaliel hissed with disgust, looking at Redvyr who was crouched over Tylok, observing his injuries. "Have you ever seen anything like this?"

Mishka and the other wolves approached, planting themselves in a circle around us, facing outward. They were watching for the enemy.

"A barga would've dragged him into the woods to eat him," Leifkyn noted. "And this isn't nightvyrm territory."

I'd heard of the giant serpents who lived in the Solgavia Mountains, but I was glad to know they didn't venture this far.

"Where are Farla and the children?" Tessa hauled Saralyn off her back and clutched her close in her arms, as if she might get snatched away too. "Was there any sign of them, that they might be injured by whatever this was?"

"No sign of them at all." Redvyr stood, scowling. "Only a struggle."

Tessa blinked away tears, turning toward their home in the tree.

Bezaliel sidled closer to Redvyr. "Could it be Meer-wolves? Like the infected ones who attacked once before?"

I stepped closer. "What attack before?"

Redvyr's expression hardened, his tail flitting back and forth behind him. "Several months ago, King Goll encamped farther south from here, but still in beast fae territory. His camp was attacked by three wolves who were sick in some way."

I scoffed. "In what way? You're making it sound so cryptic."

"That's because we'd never seen it before." Redvyr caught my gaze and held it. "But I've seen it since."

I swallowed. "The dryad stag."

He nodded.

"I don't think it's wolves," said Leifkyn, crouching in the snow where a tuft of grass stuck up, holding something he'd lifted out of the scuffed-up powder.

Redvyr marched over to him. "What did you find?"

Leifkyn dropped something long and spindly in Redvyr's hand. "Tylok must've sliced it off in the fight. But what the hell kind of creature is that from?"

I stepped closer and peered at what Redvyr held. "Gods below," I whispered. "What is that?"

"A finger," answered Dayn, staring at it with disgust.

I arched a brow at him. "Obviously. But from what?"

The skin was dark grayish-green, the digit extraordinarily long and thin, the pointed black claw razor-sharp and curled. Black blood oozed out. Dark fae bled blue. I'd seen more than one get a busted lip or come in with an injury from the road when I worked at Haldek's. But it wasn't this sickly color.

Redvyr growled at the severed finger of this unknown creature, this killer, in his hand. "There was more than one of them."

"How do you know?" I asked.

"I can smell the scent of this one here around Tylok's body, but there is a different scent up there in his home."

"Redvyr, we should"—Bezaliel started then suddenly whirled around, unsheathing his sword.

The others did the same, instantly surrounding Tessa and I in a defensive stance, the wolves crouched and growling. Redvyr had me pressed behind him, a claw at my waist. I didn't have to wait long to discover what had alerted them.

Three shadow fae swooped almost silently out of the clouds, but the beast fae had heard them well enough, already prepared to fight. Redvyr straightened as they drew closer, loosening his grip on my waist.

They all wore silver, gold, and black armor, completely covering their bodies from neck to booted foot. Extending from their backs were the dragon-like wings of all shadow fae. That was where the similarities between the three males ended.

My gaze drew instantly to the one who set foot in the snow first, the others landing behind him. His black wings with a sheen of dark red arched higher than the others. His golden hair was braided in thin plaits along his temples. The effect, with his sun-blond hair falling past his shoulders, revealing the beautiful, sharp features of his face, was stunning. His eyes were an otherworldly—almost unsettling—orange, scanning all of us and the body on the ground in the snow.

The second shadow fae had a blade drawn, his scowl focused on our party since they hadn't sheathed their swords. His brown hair was loosely tied in a knot on his head, his yellow eyes glaring at all of us.

The third was—I recognized him. Stepping around Redvyr to stand beside him, I stared at the shadow fae priest who'd come into Haldek's tavern for a meal with a light fae female not too long ago.

"Murgha," I murmured to myself, "that was her name."

The priest snapped his attention to me. His face and black, silky hair were perfection, but his crimson eyes were unsettling as they examined me. Just like the first time I'd met him.

"Whatever happened to her?" I asked the priest.

"Bezaliel," whispered Tessa behind me, "that's my sister's mate."

"Murgha is your sister?" I asked Tessa over my shoulder.

"Yes. You've met her?"

"That can wait," said Bezaliel sharply, moving to stand beside his lord.

For a moment, silence fell again as the two parties examined one another. I realized I had spoken out of turn. Redvyr should speak first. And if I wasn't mistaken, the higher-ranking noble of the shadow fae party was the golden-haired male with wide gold bands at the base of his four horns. He was of royal blood.

"Prince Torvyn," said Redvyr. "A little far south for you, isn't it?"

"Greetings, Lord Redvyr. Unfortunately, it is. You know Vallon here, and this is Vaygar."

Redvyr introduced his men then Tessa. Finally, with a hand at my lower back, he said, "This is Jessamine."

He didn't explain why I was there, and they didn't ask. Then Redvyr began first.

"What brings you so far from Gadlizel?"

Prince Torvyn pointed at Redvyr's closed hand that was fisted at his side. "That."

Redvyr opened his hand, showing them what he held in his palm. "You know what creature this is?"

"We've been hunting them down from our mountains," said Vallon, Murgha's mate. "We didn't think they'd come this far south."

"Tell me what they are, Vallon."

I recognized the command in Redvyr's voice. His temper was brewing hotter. Vallon stepped forward and plucked the severed finger from his hand.

"Tylok's family is gone," Vallon commented as he examined the grotesque digit before tossing it back in the snow.

"Yes," growled Redvyr. "Now tell me what you know before I have to beat it out of you."

Vallon scoffed lightly, gazing at Tylok's home in the giant oak tree. "I'm sorry for Tylok." He turned back towards his fellow shadow fae. "I'm even sorrier for his female and two children."

"Fine, fine," snapped Leifkyn, the only one with a shorter temper than Redvyr. "Tell us what the fuck did this."

"Grimlocks," said the prince, his expression grave.

"Grimlocks are a myth," I said, dragging the prince's attention to me.

"I'm afraid not, my lady."

"What are they?" asked Dayn.

"A foul creature." Prince Torvyn addressed Redvyr. "They are pieces of different fae twisted into one, beget by black magick. But not just anyone could create them. It would need to be a god."

"Or a demi-god," added Vallon.

"How do you know this is what they are?" asked Redvyr.

"Murgha," said Vallon, his voice softening. "She's a seer." He held Tessa's gaze. "A good one."

Tessa smiled. "I knew she had the gift, though I feared for her. It comes with nightmares."

"That is for certain." Vallon faced Redvyr. "We also know these are grimlocks because our scholars have records of a time these creatures crept through our forests and woodlands once before."

"Tell them all," commanded Prince Torvyn solemnly. "They need to know, now that the creatures have crossed into their lands."

"A millennium ago, the god/sun god Solzkin and a shadow fae female had a son, a dark fae sorcerer. He was an abomination — not because of his birth, but because of his obsession with killing and death. He used the magick he'd inherited from his father and blood magick to create murderous monsters—the grimlocks. An army of them to do his bidding."

"Like wights," interrupted Redvyr. "The armies of dead that wraith fae can summon."

"Similar," interjected the prince, his voice hard and somber. "But unlike the wights, which are mindless bones called up from the graves, grimlocks are sentient creatures of the darkest kind."

"What do they look like?" asked Tessa, her voice shaky.

"They are part dryad, part dark fae, with moon fae wings. They look more like foul sprites except they are as any fae." Prince Torvyn turned his gaze on me. "Easily big enough to carry off a female and her children."

"But what do they want with them?" I asked.

"We don't know," replied Vallon. "What's worse is that we don't know who has brought these creatures back into existence. According to our scholars, they all died with their master, the sorcerer, long ago."

"But something has brought them back." Redvyr crossed his arms. "Or someone."

Prince Torvyn met his gaze with steely resolve. "That's not all. Before the grimlocks came out of the mountains, there were signs of some kind of sickness, an infection that causes madness."

Vallon glanced at the prince when he didn't go on, adding, "We have seen it in some of the animals." He paused. "And faekind."

I turned and placed a hand on Redvyr's forearm. "The dryad stag who attacked me."

Redvyr nodded. "We have seen this sickness as well."

"Do you know where this sickness came from?" Bezaliel had his arm around Tessa's shoulders while she held their infant daughter against her chest.

"No," said the prince, "but the scent of the grimlocks is similar to those touched with the mad disease. One thing is for certain, the grimlocks serve someone else, and that is who we must find."

"For now," Vaygar spoke for the first time, "I'll settle with finding and killing the grimlocks." He stepped closer to Vallon. "We should build a pyre for Tylok."

"We will help you," Redvyr told them before pulling me to him. "Stay close to Wolf while we build the pyre."

"Of course."

His gaze lingered, his brow pinched with concern before he did something unexpected in front of not only his men, but these strangers. He cupped my face and pressed a tender kiss to my mouth. I could do nothing but stare when he drew back, clenching his jaw with a grunt before he turned to join the other males, all of whom had watched—the beast fae with amusement, the shadow fae with surprise and curiosity.

When they marched off into the woods, leaving Tessa and I surrounded and protected by the wolves, my gaze followed the beast fae lord.

"Tessa."

"Hmm?"

"How often has a beast fae king bound himself to a light fae female?"

A whoosh of wind gusted across the open plain. Hallizel tittered and burrowed herself into the folds of the blanket where Saralyn slept in her mother's arms.

"Never," Tessa whispered.

My heart sank. That was what I'd thought.

CHAPTER 18

Redvyr

Vallon stepped up to the pyre we'd built, having set Tylok—all of him—upon the burial bed. Vaygar had placed Tylok's hands gripping the hilt of his blade upon his chest. Vallon had found a bonnet of his daughter's, a wooden sword of his son's, and the apron his wife wore. An old dark fae custom in burial—to take a token of your loved ones into the afterlife.

The priest, holding a lit torch, then said the shadow fae prayer for the dead.

"May Solzkin warm you on your journey. May your ancestors greet you at the gate. May your pain be gone into the afterworld. May your soul rest in this final fate."

He lit the kindling along the bottom of the pyre then tossed the torch on top, stepping back to where we all stood and watched in silence. In reverence to the dead.

Tylok had fought hard to save his family. He'd died for them, as would any male who loved his family. It grieved me that he'd given his life, and yet, his wife and children had still been taken by these creatures. And for what purpose?

Once the flames had devoured Tylok, the fire beginning to die, I turned to Prince Torvyn.

"We must be on our way to meet our clan. Especially with this news of the grimlocks, I want to be sure our camp is fortified and protected for the winter."

"In Ghasta Vale, correct?" he asked.

Though the shadow fae kept to their city in the Solgavia Mountains, their priests monitored the surrounding territories. I'd seen Vallon on more than one occasion. They would know our routine of wintering in Ghasta Vale.

"Yes."

He gave a stiff nod. "It is a good place for your clan. Easy to defend. Just keep your warriors on guard at all times."

"No need to remind me. I will watch over my people, though it will be a long winter."

"For us all, Lord Redvyr." He gave me a respectful nod, as one fae lord to another, then he turned and marched away.

Vaygar followed right behind. Vallon said to Tessa, "I will give Murgha your love."

"Thank you. Please watch over her."

"Always," he assured her before turning to follow the prince and Vaygar.

The prince took flight first, his great wings spreading wide. The other two beat their wings and lifted off after him, the three of them disappearing quickly into the gray skies.

"There will be more snow today," said Bezaliel.

"Heavy snow." I whistled to Wolf, who trotted over. "Come, Jessamine. You and Tessa must ride. We are running the rest of the way."

Rather than question me, she joined me at Wolf's side. I took great pleasure in wrapping my hands around her waist and pulling her close before I lifted her onto Wolf's back. He still carried a heavy load of grain, but he was strong. Even more so, he was devoted to Jessamine. He would welcome her slight weight, glad to carry her the rest of our journey.

I simply needed us to be there, among my clansmen and my warriors. The need to warn them and ensure we were protected and on guard for these grimlocks drove me to act quickly.

Within minutes, the women were secure on Wolf and Mishka, wrapped well in their cloaks. I headed out first, setting the pace. It was fortunate that Tylok's home in the old oak wasn't far from Ghasta Vale. I skirted the woodlands, choosing the open valley floor instead, not wanting any more surprises. The gray skies grew heavier. I was determined to reach the camp before the snow began to fall.

We entered the communal cave to find most of the clan there. For our winter camp, we set up tents for sleeping between the two mountains called The Sisters, which flanked Ghasta Vale and blocked the harsher winds. But this cave had always served as our gathering place for meals and fellowship, and even for shelter if a blizzard hit.

This cave was a wide, hollow opening at the base of one of the two mountains called The Sisters, which flanked Ghasta Vale. The smoke filtered through a tight channel carved by snow melting over centuries, and eventually escaped outside.

The fire pit was a long oval encircled by stones, large enough for cooking on one side and to heat the cave entirely for communal gatherings. We draped hides along the cave entrance to keep the winds out and the cave warm.

Some of my warriors were unloading the saddlebags of grain from the wolves outside and bringing them inside to store. I'd told them to gather all of the males except those currently on watch to meet me here when they were done.

"Thank the gods," said Lorelyn, the first to greet us when we entered the cave. "I saw a dark omen this morning in the skies, and I feared the worst."

"What did you see?" I asked, shaking the snow from my head and horns as we joined her and others around the fire.

"An injured raven," said Lorelyn solemnly. "He'd broken a wing and fallen into the woods. When I looked, I couldn't find him. I realized it must've been a vision. Sometimes I can't tell which is real and which is from the gods."

Lorelyn was a young seer, but she had always been right.

"Do not go into the woods alone anymore. For I can tell you what the bad omen was warning you about."

I stared around the cave, noting that council members Wyzel, Melgar, and Bowden were present, currently sitting along the wooden benches we'd built for this space. Good.

Everyone had already gathered closer, greeting us after our travels, glad to see we'd accomplished our mission in getting provisions to last the winter. But the smiling faces dimmed in hearing my voice, everyone silent and waiting for me to speak. Jessamine had remained close to the flap at the entrance, which I didn't like. I wanted her near me, but I'd have to remedy that later.

"On our journey, we met with Prince Torvyn of the shadow fae and two priests with him." I didn't want to upset them more by telling them Tylok had been killed, and his family was missing. Many of my men had met and admired Tylok. "There has been a sighting of dangerous creatures called grimlocks. They are killing our kind. They are abducting others."

"Grimlocks?" Wyzel stood, using her cane, sidling toward the fire. "The evil monsters from fairy tales? The shadow fae prince must be mistaken."

"He is not. We saw proof of their existence, I assure you. We will double our guards on watch. Though we are in a place more easily defended, we are still vulnerable to attack. Keep the children close to the center of camp at all times. All trips into the woods for kindling and other supplies must be with a minimum of four guards. I will speak to the warriors about watch detail."

"Are we safe here?" asked Bowden, standing near his wife who was delicate and small for a beast fae female.

"We are just as safe here as we would be in Vanglosa. The creatures have come south out of the mountains. Perhaps this is even safer with mountains surrounding us."

Bowden nodded, the others murmuring to one another as my warriors returned from storing the grain. I pointed to the benches lining the inner curve of the back wall. It was where we could have a bit of privacy to speak.

Leifkyn murmured something to them and they followed him to the back of the cave, while I walked to Jessamine still standing there looking exhausted, bewildered, and anxious.

"Dayn," I called out—he had entered through the flap last. "Take Jessamine to my tent and start a fire for her."

"Yes, my lord."

"You're sending me away?" Her cheeks flared pink with anger.

I slid my hands to cradle her face, pressing my body close to hers. "No. I'm sending you to my tent where you can rest and get warm and wait for me." I pressed my forehead to hers for a brief moment. "You're exhausted. Go with Dayn. Don't argue."

Her fingers curled around my wrists, squeezing gently, her anger fading. She pulled away, glancing over my shoulder. I didn't have to look to know that we had an audience for that small embrace. There would be questions, and yes, likely some protests. I'd deal with that later. Right now, I simply wanted my woman safe and warm. And ready for me when I returned to her.

"Dayn," I called. "Keep watch over her until I come."

"Of course, my lord."

Once they'd left, I turned toward the fire. Yes, there were many eyes on me now, most of them confused and some of them angry. Wyzel and Sorka were among the confused, Velga among the angry. I stared them all down until they lowered their gazes. There was only one lord here. And they must remember that. When I felt sufficiently satisfied that they'd keep their opinions to themselves, at least until I left the cave, I joined my warriors to prepare them for the defense of our camp so that I could quickly return to Jessamine.

CHAPTER 19

Jessamine

"Thank you, Dayn."

The handsome beast fae male stood awkwardly after building a fire in a black disk set on a tripod at the center of Redvyr's tent. The smoke swirled in a plume straight out of an opening at the top. There was a giant bed of furs to one side, baskets of what looked to be his clothes and other items, and an oval wooden tub to the other side currently full of cold water.

"Um, there is water there to wash." He scratched the back of his neck nervously.

"Do you all bathe in freezing cold water?"

"The women sometimes heat it in buckets for the children. But we're a hardy people. The cold doesn't bother beast fae very much."

"Yes, I've noticed," I laughed, noting he was still wearing short sleeves although the snow had begun to fall in heavy flakes before we arrived.

"I'll be right outside if you need anything." He hurried through the tent flap, leaving me alone.

There was a thick, round candle on a stand at Redvy's bedside. I lit it on the fire and set it back on the stand, staring at the tub.

Glancing at the door, I began to undress, the weight of this journey and all that we'd seen and done lifting with each layer of clothes. With my cloak, dress, and chemise in a pile, I slid out of my boots and stepped over to the tub.

The beast fae may not need warm water, but I certainly did. Sliding my fingertips along the surface of the water, I summoned my magick. My skin began to glow as it always did when I called my power to the surface. My veins pumping with magick, I whispered to the water, willing it to change for me. To warm up for me.

Within a minute, the water had heated, steam rising from the surface. My skin aglow, the pattern of green and blue markings showing on my arms, legs and breasts, I stepped into the tub.

"Gods above," I whispered, moaning as I settled in until the water lapped at my chin.

My cold, stiff muscles relaxed, my mind drifting to all that I had seen. The mob in Hellamir; the moon fae witch bound for execution by burning; Lord Gael—my betrothed—calling for hatred and rebellion; Tylok's body without his head, his family missing, his funeral pyre; and lastly, the deep, profound pleasure in the woods with Redvyr, lord of the beast fae. The one male I should not want and could not have.

Tears slipped down my cheeks. I wiped at my face and slid under the surface, letting the water wash it all away. When I broke the surface and sat upright, combing my slick hair back over my head, a purring growl snapped me out of my thoughts.

Redvyr stood in front of the fire, his arms crossed, watching me. I realized my skin still glowed, and my breasts were exposed, and yet, my old inclination to hide my body didn't take hold of me. Rather, I placed my hands on the sides of the tub and sat straighter.

His golden gaze flared with inner fire. "Stand for me, Jessamine. I want to see all of you."

"I believe that will lead to danger."

"What kind of danger?" His voice was a dark, velvety caress. My nipples tightened to peaks.

"Me in your bed."

"Oh, that is undeniable." He uncrossed his arms and walked toward me, bending and gripping the edge of the tub as he leaned over me. "I'm going to make you mine tonight, Jessamine. Prepare yourself for that certainty."

I was breathing heavily, my chest rising and falling. To his credit, his feral gaze remained on mine, daring me to contradict him.

"Do you think that's wise, Lord Redvyr?" I used his title on purpose, to remind him who he was.

"I don't care."

"I'm a light fae female."

"I can see that." That was when his gaze wandered down my body, still partly concealed by the water.

"What if your clan protests?"

"I am their clan lord. They won't protest."

"Perhaps not to your face, but not all will be happy if you take me to your bed."

"I do not care."

"That's reckless," I warned him. "You may regret it."

He huffed and stood to his full height, unbuttoning his vest and tossing it aside, revealing the wide expanse of his muscular chest.

"I can promise you this, Jessamine. I will not regret this." He held out his hand. "Stand. Let me see all of you."

I'd never been nude before anyone, always hiding my body even when I was in front of my sisters and mother. I'd certainly never shown anyone my entire body glowing in syrenskyn magick. And while I hadn't intentionally kept my magick humming, it burned brighter than ever. Like a beacon for the beast fae lord.

Focusing on sheathing my claws, transforming my hands back to normal, I held out one hand and let him lift me from the tub. Water sluiced down my body, over the curves of my breasts, belly, and hips. Redvyr watched with rapture.

"By the gods, you are stunning, sweetheart."

He helped me step out then took a towel on a hook by the tub and dried me off, squeezing the water out of my wet hair, lingering between my thighs.

I whimpered when he brushed my already throbbing clit. He dropped the towel and wrapped his hands around my waist, his large hands spanning the width of my back and belly.

"Listen to me. This will hurt, since you are a maid. But there will be pleasure too."

I swallowed, gripping his biceps. "How can there be both?"

He smiled, his fangs flashing. "Let me show you. Trust me?"

"Yes."

Urging me to lay down on the furs, I did, watching him unlace his boots and then his trousers. I closed my eyes, overwhelmed by the sight of him.

"Afraid, my princess?"

I felt and heard him climbing onto the furs. I opened my eyes to find him on his knees between my legs, one hand on his cock.

"A little. But not of you."

"Pleasure first, then."

He gripped my thighs, sliding them open and stretching his huge body upon the furs. Propped on his elbows, his mouth above my sex, I knew what was coming, my body coiled and tense but ready.

He nuzzled his nose along my inner thigh and mound. "Paradise is right here," he said, stroking his tongue along my slit. "Between your thighs, Jessamine."

Moaning, I reached down and gripped one of his horns. "Show me the pleasure you promised, my lord."

His eyes heated, a growl rumbling as he lowered over me and set me on fire. His mouth and tongue teased, stroking inside me then around my clitoris.

"Yes, Redvyr. Goddess, *yes*."

He clamped his lips around my tight nub, sending me over the edge quickly. I arched my back then thrust toward his mouth, grinding against him. He licked me and sucked me until my orgasm subsided.

Climbing up my body, he lowered his head to my breast, flicking his tongue and scraping his fangs gently over the flesh and my nipple.

"Ah!" I fisted my hands in his hair.

He chuckled, sliding over to give his attention to the other breast.

"Redvyr," I whispered, "it feels so good."

He lifted, moving up until his face was close to mine. "Not as good as it's going to get." He angled his mouth over mine, stroking his tongue along mine with a humming purr.

I whimpered, my hips moving, wanting more. He moved a hand between us, took hold of his cock, then I felt the head nudging at my entrance.

"Open your legs wider," he whispered against my lips. "So wet for me." He kissed me again then raised his head, holding my gaze. "This is where it will hurt. But I'll make it good for you."

I could do nothing but nod, panting and whimpering with each nudge of his cock. He slid one hand behind my nape, gripping the back of my throat, and hooked the other hand behind my knee, flattening my thigh to the furs.

"There you go, my girl." With each thrust, he went deeper inside me. "Let me in."

I thrust up with him on the next pump of his hips, a sharp sting making me cry out as he seated himself fully inside me.

"Yes, yes," he crooned, nipping at my lips, sliding his mouth along my jaw to my throat. "Fuck, this is so good. Let the burn fade, then I'll make it good for you."

He sucked at the base of my throat, making my sex clench around his wide girth. He groaned.

"That's right, my little light fae. Your cunt is hungry for me now."

He slid out to the tip and pumped back in, the sting still there but less. I whimpered, half pain, half pleasure. Then he really started fucking me, his hips pumping hard and deep, his cock filling me up. He groaned with pleasure, wild in his thrusting.

With blinding speed, he gripped my hips and rolled to his back. I straddled him, his cock still inside me, and braced my arms on his chest.

"You set the pace now. I'm afraid I'll break you."

I wasn't going to admit that, while he was ferocious in his fucking, the pain was bringing me to ecstasy. Instead, I did what he told me to do and set the pace.

Reaching up to hold his larger two horns, I rolled my hips, my mouth falling open when his cock stroked a pleasure spot inside me. His grin made me smile as I continued to ride him, speeding up with each downward stroke.

I admired his body, even the thicker hair that lined his forearms and the line from his navel to the bed of hair at his cock. He wasn't like the fair-skinned, hairless men of the light fae. He wasn't civilized or tame or properly groomed like the males of my kind. And yet, he was the most beautiful male I'd ever seen.

He planted his feet wide, his clawed hands gripping my hips, helping me fuck him from above.

"How's that, my princess? Does that feel good?"

"Yes." I arched my back and he bent upward to suck my nipple. My sex clenched. "Gods yes."

Suddenly, he fell backward, arching his neck, his horns tearing into the furs. I braced my hands on his chest as he thrust upward, deep, and held himself there.

His groan was feral and wild as his seed emptied inside me. His cock pulsed hard. I held still, in complete wonder at the intimate sensation.

Then something began to happen. A tingle along my skin provoked my magick. My skin began to glow. Rather than diminish, his cock swelled further, especially close to the base.

"Gods, what's happening?" My voice shook with panic.

When I tried to lift off of him, his fingers curled, his claws pinching but not breaking the skin at my hips. His closed eyes opened, that fiery gaze more fierce than I'd ever seen it. With gentleness, he rolled us until I was beneath him again, and he was still seated between my open thighs, his cock deep.

The intensity of his expression almost scared me. He used one hand to slide a damp lock of my hair off my cheek.

"I did not think the gods would do such a thing." His voice was deep, serious, dangerous.

"What have they done?"

His hand slid into my hair until he cupped the back of my skull. "They have given you to me."

His cock swelled more until I felt that sting of my virgin pain again. "Ow," I cried, a tear slipping from my eyes.

"No, darling." He swept his lips where the tear had fallen, kissing my cheek, whispering against my skin. "This pain will turn into pleasure. For it is a gift to us."

"What do you mean?" I asked, crying now, for there was an overwhelming emotion sweeping through me that I didn't understand.

"What you're feeling is called knotting. It happens only between beast fae male," he lifted his head to look me in the eyes, "and his gods-given mate."

"What?" I scoffed. "That makes no sense."

"You are angry at the gods? For giving you to a monstrous beast fae?"

"No, you idiot. I've simply never heard of such a thing. Tessa even told me no beast fae lord has ever bound himself to a light fae."

"They haven't. But the gods have done this, and that means only one thing, Jessamine." His voice still verged on threatening, all while he soothed me with brushes of his lips along my jaw and throat.

"What does it mean?" I arched my throat, giving him better access.

"You are mine," he growled. "And no one is going to take you away from me."

It was a promise and a threat.

He began to slowly grind his hips against mine since the knot held his cock deep. Helpless to the ecstasy setting my body aflame, I hooked my heels at the back of his thick thighs and ground with him, chasing the pleasure that was sending me toward a second climax.

My fangs descended, the urge to sink them into his flesh an urgent compulsion. But I wasn't sure if the naiad Zella had lied to me. What if it was poison? What if I was the monster my parents always said I was? I held back from that darker desire.

"Gods, save me," I whispered, climbing higher and higher until that second orgasm ripped through me.

He rumbled a deep growl, his cock pulsing again, releasing a flood of his seed, allowing him to pump in and out again. His cock slid on a slick glide as his orgasm lasted longer than mine, a wet mess between my thighs when he was done.

I didn't know what to think or say, for this wasn't at all what I'd thought would happen. He stared down at me, holding his weight above me, sliding his cock out though I felt it heavy on the inside of my thigh.

"So," I swallowed hard, "this means you are keeping me with the clan...even beyond winter?"

His stare reached into my very soul, those beastly eyes more serious than I'd ever seen them.

"This means I'm keeping you for always, Jessamine. Until death." He squeezed my nape gently where he still cupped it. "Even if you leave me, I'll follow. I'll be helpless to it."

Frowning, I asked, "Helpless? So the gods tell you to do something and now you're doomed with a skald fae you never wanted?"

He chuckled and reached between my thighs, placing his hand over my mound, sodden with his seed. I jumped.

"I believe this proves I wanted you before the gods told me you were mine." He gently slid the pad of one finger through the slick of my folds.

I moaned, my clit sensitive but a shiver of pleasure sliding through me anyway.

"So sensitive, is my mate." He grinned, his fangs sharp.

"Stop teasing me." I pushed his hand away.

He rolled onto his back and stood, laughing under his breath. I watched him, admiring his muscled buttocks, his tail swishing as he dipped the towel into the water and returned. He knelt beside me.

"Open your thighs, darling."

While I was still embarrassed by his teasing, I opened them, helpless but to obey.

Helpless.

What were the gods thinking binding us together? His clan wouldn't like it, even if he said he didn't care.

Then he tenderly wiped between my thighs, thawing my heart further to him. He frowned.

"What is it?"

"There's a bit of blood. More than I realized."

"That happens for virgins."

He arched a brow at me. "I'm aware." He returned his attention back, gently dabbing at my sore flesh before he closed my thighs and tossed the towel aside. "I don't like it."

"Is Lord Redvyr squeamish at the sight of blood?" I teased.

He pulled a fur over both of us, hauling me against his chest. "I simply don't like seeing your blood. It makes me angry."

I soothed a hand down his chest until I heard that pleasing purr in his chest.

"I'm fine. More than fine."

Pressing his mouth to the crown of my head, he whispered, "Truly? This doesn't frighten you?"

"Oh, no. I'm absolutely terrified." I turned my face up to his. "But as long as you're with me, I'll be fine."

He pressed a soft kiss to my lips, coaxing my mouth open to taste me gently. "I'll always be with you. That's a promise."

I settled against him, my cheek to his chest. I don't remember if he said anything else, my mind drifting as I listened to his heart beating steadily beneath me, lulling me quickly into a dreamless sleep.

CHAPTER 20

Jessamine

"Are you Shearah?" I asked, standing inside the communal cave next to the entrance flap.

There were only two people moving about. One was an older female kneading dough on a table set against the wall. I hadn't noticed last night, but there was storage there for baskets of wheat, barley, and beans. I recognized the saddle bags folded alongside the sack of grain we had carried from Hellamir.

The other female was very pretty, with long, black hair tucked behind her tall, pointed ears. She was chopping some sort of vegetable on another wooden table set high for cooking preparation, and turned to face me when I spoke.

"Yes, I am Shearah. You must be Jessamine."

"I am. I don't want to impose, but I learned quite a bit of cooking when I worked at a tavern in the Borderlands."

Her hazel-orange eyes widened. "You worked in the Borderlands?"

"Yes." I smiled. "I told my story to the council back in Vanglosa."

"I don't usually attend the kella'mir gatherings. To be honest," she ducked her head, continuing to chop the purple root vegetable known as delly root, "I don't listen to much of anything going on. I keep to myself."

She was a no-nonsense kind of female. I liked her already. I especially liked that she didn't listen to gossip.

"Well, I've heard of you. Leifkyn bragged about your stew when we were on the trail here to the camp."

She looked up with those wide eyes again, a blush coloring her perfect heart-shaped cheeks. "Leifkyn did?"

"Yes. He seems to admire you a good deal." I wasn't sure if I was overstepping, but I was certain that Leifkyn liked her. It couldn't hurt to help them along.

She smiled down at her vegetables as she chopped faster.

"Again, I hope I'm not intruding, but I would like to help in the kitchen, if I can."

"Of course, you can. It's usually just me and Gweeda." She gestured to the older female who looked up. "Gweeda, this is Jessamine. The light fae staying with us through the winter."

I wasn't about to correct her that it may be a bit longer. Quite a bit longer. That was for Redvyr to address with his clan.

Lifting my hand in a friendly wave to Gweeda, I said, "I absolutely love the bread you bake. It's all I've eaten since I've been with the group, it seems." I smiled amiably.

Gweeda stared at me a moment, grunted, then nodded and went back to her kneading.

Shearah giggled. "I think she likes you."

"How can you possibly tell?" I joined her at the high table where she worked.

"She looked up from her kneading for a whole minute. She's not very friendly but she's extremely helpful in the kitchen. She works fast and efficiently. Every now and then, one of the other women help me out, but mostly they can't abide Gweeda's rough demeanor." She shrugged, scraping the purple sliced vegetable into a bowl. "I prefer it. It's almost like working alone."

Already there was a stack of loaves in a basket next to Gweeda. Over the giant open fire in the middle of the cave, there was a tripod spit holding a cauldron, and a second one dangling a square shaped oven for the bread.

"All you've eaten is bread since you've been with the clan? It is a shame the males didn't feed you better on the trail."

"It wasn't their fault, really. I, um, I don't eat meat. And there wasn't much else besides the bread and goat cheese."

I glanced over to the left side of the cave where a wooden fence enclosed a dozen goats. "I was going to offer to make a vegetable stew that I learned to make back at the tavern. I can take out some for myself then add meat for the clan."

"Oh, not at all. We actually have quite a few who enjoy a good vegetable stew. Mostly women." She smiled at me. "We can make two today—one with meat and one without. How would that be?"

"That would be lovely." I cleared my throat. "Thank you for being so welcoming."

She frowned. "Why wouldn't I be? It is our way to be kind and courteous to those in need."

"Yes, I know. I was told of the oath of the beast fae."

"I am happy to have your assistance. I get so very little, other than Gweeda."

Gweeda made some sort of grunt but didn't look up from where she shaped her dough into loaves.

"I appreciate that. But not everyone is glad I'm here, I fear."

And I worried that there would be many more protests when Redvyr decided to announce that we were mates. My thighs clenched, my heart speeding at the memory of last night.

"Are you alright?" Shearah asked as she plucked an onion from the basket to chop. "You seem flushed and your pulse is racing.

Those damn beast fae senses! They knew everything.

"I'm fine. Excited to cook my stew. Are those jars the stores for cooking?"

The shelves seemed old and well-used, but the jars did not. They'd likely carried them from Vanglosa. They'd made this space perfect for food storage and cooking the meals for the clan, having added plenty of seating for all to join in the chamber.

"Yes, you will find everything you need there. There's another cauldron as well, and the water is in the jugs on the ground."

"Perfect. Where do you get the fresh water? I didn't see a stream or water source as we came in yesterday."

"There's a ground spring in a small cave set on a cliff on the other Sister."

"The other Sister?"

"That is what these two mountains are called on either side of Ghasta Vale. The Sisters protect us from the harsher winter winds. And they provide." She gestured around us. "The water well, as we call it, is set in a much smaller cave, too small to be used for shelter really. Plus you can sense magick there, and we beast fae don't much like magick."

She gasped and stopped chopping, looking up at me. "I apologize. I didn't mean you, of course."

"No need for an apology. I understand what you mean."

There could be some magickal creatures living there—cave sprites or naiads.

I walked over to the shelves and peeked into one of the jars, surprised at the aromatic scent that wafted out.

"This is dill weed, isn't it?"

"Yes." She smiled at my obviously shocked look. "We dry all of the herbs during summer, enough to last the winter. One thing you'll learn is that beast fae love food."

"Oh, my," I exclaimed excitedly, opening jar after jar. "Fennel seed, pepper leaves and sea salt rocks. You have so many amazing herbs and seasonings. You even have Esher Wood mushrooms?"

It was Gweeda who piped up this time. "We may be beast fae but we aren't barbarians."

"Indeed, you are not," I added. "These mushrooms are a delicacy in the Borderlands. I could only rarely get them."

"Gweeda has a special relationship with a wraith fae at the market in Belladum." Shearah added her purple vegetable and diced onions to the cauldron hanging over the fire.

"This makes me so happy. Now I can make a delicious stew. With Gweeda's wonderful bread, it will be the perfect meal."

Gweeda grunted and kept pounding at her dough. Shearah and I shared a smile before I got to work, feeling grateful to finally be of some use.

CHAPTER 21

Redvyr

I woke in a panic, finding Jessamine gone. I'd slept far later than normal, and now I feared the worst. My first thought was that I'd demanded too much of her, that I shouldn't have pushed so hard, that I'd frightened her so much she'd run away. But as soon as I'd jerked on some trousers and boots then gone in search of her, I smelled her on the wind nearby.

She was in the communal cave cooking with Shearah. I'd frozen when I stepped into the cave to see her gorgeous hair piled on her head, exposing her delicate throat, sweat on her brow and bosom. I wanted to lick her from head to toe.

Instead, I pulled her aside and chastised her for leaving without waking me. She snapped back with some smart comment that had me jerking her close and kissing her senseless. I didn't care that Gweeda and Shearah got a good look at how far gone their lord was for the light fae female that we were supposed to be sheltering only for the winter season. I knew I'd have to hold a kella'mir and announce our mating to the council soon.

Right now, I wanted to enjoy her, to seal our newly formed bond. After my overly aggressive kiss that left her panting, she sent me away so that she could finish cooking for the night's meal. Satisfied that I could smell her arousal with one kiss, I let her be.

Still, I felt itchy all day. It wasn't until after I'd done my rounds with all of the warriors on guard, checked the perimeters for any sign of danger or intruders, and I was walking back to the cave for dinner that I realized what it was.

She didn't have my bite, my mark on her skin. I hadn't wanted to overwhelm her by biting her the first time we had sex, the first time she'd ever had sex. A growl rumbled in my belly at the satisfaction of taking her for the first time. I wanted her all the time. Every minute of the day, I needed her near me, her scent to surround me.

Perhaps that's why I was so on edge when I finally opened the flap into the cave. The light laughter and chatter of the clan eased my tension, but only a little. Bowden, ever the talented musician, played his flute, some of the young females dancing while we awaited dinner.

My gaze found Jessamine at once. She was setting bowls of stew out on the high table. Sorka, Bes, and some others were helping. I strode toward my usual seat to the left of the bench where Bezaliel sat, Tessa and Saralyn beside him, along with Brohm, Leifkyn, and Dayn.

"So good to have you join us, my lord," said Dayn.

"Yes, we haven't seen you all day. What's been keeping you so busy?" Leifkyn's tone was mocking.

"I am the lord of this clan. Therefore, I spent the day ensuring the borders of our camp are well-protected."

And pining for my mate who'd made herself absent from me all day. I itched to march across the room and delve my fingers into her hair. She was mussed, a smudge of ash from the fire on her cheek, and yet, she was the most beautiful creature I'd ever laid eyes on.

"Ah, that's where you were, of course," said Leifkyn. Again, his tone was mocking.

"Looks like we have a new cook in the kitchens," said Dayn. "I didn't know the princess had such talents."

I didn't bother to remark. They were goading me, and I knew it. I crossed my arms, leaning back against the cave wall, stretching my legs out and crossing my ankles as well.

"I'll bet she's very talented in many ways," added Leifkyn.

I growled at that. "Watch it."

Bezaliel chuckled while Tessa rolled her eyes, bouncing Saralyn in her arms.

Leifkyn merely smiled wider. "Interesting fact. I noticed that Jessamine smells different today."

"Is it all the spices she's been cooking with?" asked Dayn in a forced, casual manner.

"I don't think so. She smells a bit masculine, if you ask me."

"Mmm, I know what you mean." Dayn made a show of staring at Jessamine across the room where she was carrying two bowls of stew to the council members. "She smells almost like a beast fae."

"Almost," continued Leifkyn. "Though I couldn't tell you whose scent she's wearing."

I leaned forward, elbows on my knees, and glared at Leifkyn. "If you don't shut your mouth, pup, I'm going to shut it for you."

The bloody bastard laughed. Bezaliel leaned closer and asked in a lower voice, "So I was right, wasn't I? She's your mate."

I nodded, to Leifkyn and Dayn's utter glee. Haslek, one of my younger warriors who overheard, stared wide-eyed and almost panicked. I pointed a finger at him.

"Keep this to yourself. I will tell the council when it is time. Until then, I don't want rumors circulating around camp."

"Too late for that," whispered Tessa. "They saw you kiss her last night. Unfortunately, no one thinks she is your mate. They think she is your bedmate and that alone."

The mood sobered quickly, my inner beast growling with menace in my chest. It was Bezaliel who spoke first after a tense silence.

"You should've bitten her. That's what I did the minute I knew Tessa was mine. Then there's no question from anyone else."

I wasn't going to explain to them that I didn't want to frighten her further after the knotting. Or bring her more pain. She'd bled quite a bit from her first coupling, and the knotting had only increased the pain of the experience. The thought of adding a bite mark to that turned my stomach.

Not that I didn't crave to bite her even now. To ensure everyone knew she wore my mark, that everyone knew she was my mate. Not simply a lover. And there was another thing that had kept me from marking her.

She wasn't beast fae. I hadn't lied to her when I told her I'd follow her if she left me. I could do nothing else. I'd abandon my clan to do so. Even if she rejected me, I'd follow and make sure she was safe. But once I'd given her my mark, every fae male—dark or light—would scent me on her skin. Forever. There was no taking back the mark of a beast fae. For that, I needed to make sure she wanted me...forever.

She might be enraptured at the moment. It didn't surprise me that there was attraction between us. Besides the gods intervening and fating us to be together, I had saved her from death in the woods and protected her more than once. She would be inclined to be grateful, which can transform into attraction. But I wondered if she'd still want me once the infatuation had worn off. Once she realized she wouldn't live in a castle with all the luxuries of a royal life.

If she left me for her own kind, I would ensure that Lord Gael of Mevia was dead so that he could no longer bother her. Then I'd send a clear message to her father that she would have a choice of her own for her life and her future.

But for now, I would enjoy this new sensation that had curled around my heart and filled my soul with a tentative hope. I could relax in the joy that being with Jessamine didn't defy the gods or betray my clan, as my own father had. She was meant to belong to me. Now the only question was, did she truly want to?

I sat up straight when she carried a bowl and walked directly toward me. Hypnotized, I watched her move gracefully across the cave, her gaze on mine, her smile for me. That smile had tilted into a smirk by the time she stood in front of me and handed me the bowl with a slice of crusty bread sticking up over the edge.

"I want you to try my stew and see if it's to your liking."

I stirred the spoon, observing that while it smelled heavenly, there was one thing missing. "There is no meat in this bowl."

"There is not," she agreed. "Taste it, Redvyr." She angled her head, that long neck luring my gaze. "For me."

So of course, I did, humming at the savory bite and hearty chunks of root vegetables, beans, and mushrooms.

"Do you like it?" She raised her brows, hopeful.

Sighing, I put her out of her misery. "It is delicious."

Jessamine smiled so big it made my stomach flip with excitement. She hurried back to the cooking station to deliver more bowls.

She exhaled a sigh of relief just as Sorka walked up with two bowls. "I have one vegetable stew and one venison."

"I'll take the vegetable," said Tessa.

"Shearah cooked the venison? I'll take that one," Leifkyn chimed in.

"That's a good man," said Leifkyn, "telling her it's the best even if it's not."

"Mmm," hummed Tessa. "This is actually so good. I had no idea a princess could cook like this."

"I think I'll try the vegetable," said Dayn. "Need to support our future queen, right?"

My heart jolted. Yes, if she accepted me and her role here, she would be my queen, the Lady of Vanglosa. Though far less prestigious as a royal princess in Morodon or the wife of the high lord of Mevia, I would treat her as the most precious gem in all the world. If she would consent to being mine.

I couldn't help but watch her move around the room, mingling amiably with the people of my clan. She carried two bowls to the females lining the bench on our opposite side, walking toward Lorelyn.

Suddenly, Velga stuck out her leg and tripped Jessamine, sending her sprawling to the ground, the bowls clattering and the stew splattering across the stone floor. Bowden stopped playing music just as I heard Velga mumble to the female next to her, "So clumsy."

I roared in rage.

Everyone fell deathly silent. The only sound was the fire crackling and Jessamine pushing to stand. The front of her gown, and her neck and face were splattered with the stew, her face flushed pink with humiliation. Shearah rushed over with a towel to help her clean off.

Fire burned through my veins as I stood and marched across the room. "*Stand*, Velga."

The female, head down, instantly rose to her feet, twisting her hands together. "I'm sorry, my lord. It was an accident. I didn't mean—"

"*Yes.* You did mean it. Jessamine is our guest. It was decreed by the council for all the clan to hear that she would be welcomed and protected by the clan. And you have broken that oath. You will not eat tonight."

Her face shot up, tears pooling in her dark orange eyes.

"You will not sit with us tonight, either. You will return to your tent at once."

"Redvyr," whispered Jessamine, "I don't—"

She flinched when I turned my glare to her and shook my head, before turning back to Velga.

"You will not eat tomorrow, either. You will not have one meal until you have apologized to Jessamine."

"I'm sorry," she muttered in Jessamine's direction, keeping her eyes on the ground, her voice shaky.

"Not now," I snapped, silencing her. "Only after you've had a night to contemplate your actions. Now, go."

Velga ran from the cave crying. I didn't fucking care. I turned to face the room, waiting for any other protests. There were none, though there may have been a few disagreeing looks. That, I could handle. But there was no question that Velga was out of line and should be punished.

Movement to my right drew my attention to Jessamine marching back over to the cooking table and whispering some words to Shearah, before heading for the exit. By the time I had marched the length of the cave to catch her, she was gone through the flap. Once through, I caught her quickly enough, grabbing her by the forearm.

She spun back toward me, fury painting her expression. "You were too *harsh*, Redvyr."

"No, I wasn't. I wasn't harsh enough."

She tsked. "If you think that is the way to get your clan to welcome me, you are wrong."

"I want my clan to obey our oaths and decrees. It is known that you are here with the council's approval."

"And after that, they may hold another council meeting and kick me out."

"Over my dead body."

She rolled her eyes. "Redvyr, you can't get everything by force."

"Sure I can. I am the beast lord of Vanglosa, the head of this clan."

She closed her eyes, her lips thinning in a disagreeable way. "By punishing Velga, you have only made her hate me more."

"Why? It is her fault that she was punished. She tried to humiliate you in front of the clan."

"She may not see it that way. And you're drawing even more attention to..." she sighed heavily, looking away.

"To what?"

"To *us*." She pointed back and forth between us.

"I don't care."

"Redvyr, you've put my feelings over those of a clanswoman. Many will see that as a betrayal. They won't like me more for it."

"They don't have to like it. They simply have to accept it."

She spun and marched away, turning right between two tents and heading toward our own, muttering, *ridiculous* and *idiot* and some other word I couldn't hear. I followed quickly at her heels.

"Jessamine. You must understand that I cannot allow any of the clan to disrespect you. If it goes without punishment, others may try."

"And now they all hate me because Velga was punished too greatly for her offense," she yelled over her shoulder.

"It was not too great. You do not know our ways."

She growled her frustration, sparking my arousal. "I know that when a woman is humiliated, it can grow into anger and then hatred. Velga has many more allies in the clan that she can turn against me."

I wrapped my arms around her, pinning her arms to her sides, drawing her to a stop. She struggled in frustration, but I held her tighter.

"Listen to me." I had my mouth at her ear, her sea-flower fragrance seducing my senses. "If you are to be my mate, they must respect you as they do me."

"What do you mean, if?" She turned her head to look at me. "Are you saying you were mistaken last night?"

My cock pressed against her ass. I ground my hips against her. "I was not mistaken."

She gusted out a breath, seeming to try and get away, while also pressing her ass back against my cock. I growled.

"That's what *if* means, my lord. It means that you don't know for certain. Perhaps the knotting our first time was a fluke."

"Let's find out." I lifted her the last few feet into our tent.

She twisted out of my arms and fell to the ground. But I was on her, dragging her onto her knees and shoving up her skirt.

"Redvyr! You're being an animal."

"That's what I am, darling," I told her as I spread her lips from behind and opened my mouth over her cunt, thrusting my tongue inside her.

"Ah!" she cried out, flattening her chest to the rug, giving me better access.

I licked and coaxed her higher, taking note of those familiar whimpers she made last night, knowing when she was getting closer to coming. When she moaned louder, grinding her hips back against my mouth harder, I released her and straightened.

"*No.* I was so close."

I yanked on the laces of my trousers, jerking my cock free. "You'll only come with my cock inside you tonight."

Gripping her hip, I wet the tip in her slick juices before pushing slowly inside her, knowing she would still be tender.

The slowness of entering her drew out the pleasure, spiking my need toward desperation.

"Unh," she moaned, her skin beginning to glow with her magick.

I grinned, relishing the fact. I leaned over her, reaching for her neckline and pulling down her gown so I could squeeze her bare breast. Her sex clenched around my cock, her skin gleaming white, the pattern of syrenskyn markings dotting her shoulders and arms.

"You see that, Jessamine," I whispered in her ear, nuzzling her hair aside so I could lick her neck. "I can summon your magick by fucking your sweet cunt. Your gods know you are mine, too."

She gasped as I pinched lightly at her tight nipple and pumped inside her, thrusting with long, slow glides.

"I'm going to come," she moaned.

I pumped faster, determined to get there with her. I wanted her cunt squeezing the seed out of me. Licking the slope of her neck and shoulder, my fangs itched to sink into her. I needed my mark on her, but I promised I'd give her the choice first. And right now, with my cock balls-deep inside of her, wasn't the time to have that delicate conversation.

Right now, all I wanted was release. And to prove to her that my gods weren't wrong.

"Oh, gods, I'm coming," she said on another moan, and then she was, her sex clenching tight.

I buried myself deep and let go, releasing inside her. Her thighs trembled as I ground deeper, growling as my knot formed and tied her to me yet again.

"There now," I whispered in her ear. "You feel that, darling. There's no mistake."

"It feels so good. So intense."

Brushing my lips along her jaw, I angled my head and pressed her chin toward me so I could graze my mouth along hers.

"This is how it's supposed to be."

After the knot loosened, my seed deep inside her, I pulled out and lifted her off the floor, taking her to our bed. We didn't speak as we undressed completely and curled up in the furs together.

I felt restless, knowing I had been harsh with Velga and that some might not agree with my punishment. But I knew I was right, even if I had grumbling council members to deal with tomorrow.

Apparently, Jessamine's mind wandered as well, but not on the same issue.

"That dryad stag."

"Yes?"

She traced a finger through the hair on my chest. "He said that I was more than a mouthful. I was sure he planned to eat me. Until you came, of course."

"What made you think on this?"

"I was thinking of Tylok's family. The dryad seemed to be infected with this dark illness the shadow fae spoke of. I think the grimlocks are taking the females and the children for food."

I pondered this for a moment, wondering how I didn't make this connection earlier. "Grimlocks are an abomination. They are not born, but created. A mesh of creatures brought to life with black magick. They serve a master."

"But who?"

I breathed out a sigh. "That, I don't know. I'm wondering if the shadow fae know but just aren't saying."

"Why wouldn't they tell you? Aren't you working together?"

I chuckled. "One thing you must know about the three dark fae races. None of us work together—unless we have to. We prefer to stick to our own. Even so, I'd say the wraith and beast fae are more allied than we are with the shadow fae."

"Why is that?" She propped her chin on both her hands atop my chest, gazing up at me.

"There is no reason why. The shadow fae live farther apart from the rest of us, high in their city of Gadlizel in the mountains. They are very secretive, but there have been rumors that their king is dying."

"The prince's father?"

"Yes."

"It's surprising, then, that Prince Torvyn was down here chasing grimlocks. I would expect him to leave that to his warriors."

"He may be a cold bastard, but Prince Torvyn is a man of honor. When there is a problem in his lands, he prefers to take care of it directly himself."

"Hmph." She turned her head to lay her cheek on my chest and wrap an arm at my waist. "That makes sense. I was thinking of how my father handled his problems. He never risked himself to do what needed to be done."

I coasted a hand up and down her spine, the length of her pale back a lovely sight, an unsettling thought now surfacing that had been pricking my conscience for some time. I decided to ask her, though I truly didn't want to know the answer.

"Did your father ever force you to use your syrenskyn magick on someone for him?"

She was quiet for a moment, and I knew he had. I buried my rage and kept soothing my hand up and down her back.

"There was a merchant," she began softly. "He's stolen from my father more than once, skimming from the coin he was supposed to tithe to the king. So Father told me I was to prove that I was a worthy daughter and kill the man for him. His own guards could've killed him just as easily, but I didn't think about that. I knew that I had to prove my worth."

I tightened a hand on her hip, willing myself not to interrupt her story with the curses I wanted to throw at her abysmal excuse for a father.

"I was sent into the chamber where the merchant was waiting. I'd been forced to go in nothing but my chemise so that my glowing skin could be seen, could bewitch the merchant." She sighed. "It did. He was frozen and in a trance, just waiting for me to swipe my claws and kill him…but I couldn't do it."

I held her close as she finished her terrible story.

"Father was both furious. He scorned me on my knees in front of his guards for not finishing the job, then he warned that I'd better do as I was told next time, when the lord who won my hand came calling. The next thing I knew, I was betrothed to Lord Gael and preparing for his arrival at court."

We were both quiet for a moment, me trying to wrangle my fury under control and her trying to come to terms with the fact that her father used her abominably.

"Your father misused his power. And he betrayed you in betrothing you to that noble from Mevia. But worse, he didn't protect you or cherish you the way a father should."

She remained silent for a time, then finally squeezed her arm tighter around me. "Thank you," she murmured softly.

"There is no reason to thank me for speaking the truth." I pressed a kiss to the crown of her head, inhaling deep. "You are a treasure, Jessamine. You should be treated as such."

Her heart sped faster, beating swiftly against my abdomen where she lay across me. But she didn't say another word before sleep took us both.

CHAPTER 22

Jessamine

"There was absolutely none of your stew left," Shearah admitted as we cooked breakfast. "And nearly half of mine went untouched."

"You are lying to make me feel good."

"No, she's not," snapped Gweeda, punching at her biscuit dough in the bowl.

"Truly," smiled Shearah, "I am not. And I do not take offense. While I know I am good in the kitchen, I would love to learn some of your recipes."

"I'd be delighted to share," I told her.

We were both laughing when the flap to the cave opened and in stepped Velga. She looked awful with dark circles rimming her eyes as if she had not slept. She looked a little pale and winced when she saw me. Then with a deep breath, she marched straight to the high counter.

I stepped away so she wouldn't have to speak to me directly in front of Shearah, though everyone knew how well the beast fae could hear.

"Lady Jessamine," she started formally. "I want to apologize for tripping you last night." Her voice quivered but she didn't cry. "I did mean to embarrass you, and it was wrong."

"Thank you, Velga," I said softly. "I accept your apology. Can I ask, why did you want to embarrass me?"

"Because you do not belong." She held my gaze, a hint of anger or perhaps fear behind her intense stare. "I know that you are our guest through winter, so I was wrong. But you hold the king's attention too much for an outsider. I mean, a visiting guest."

I didn't have to ask to know that Velga likely thought Lord Redvyr should be giving her attention, or any beast fae female other than me. I certainly wasn't going to tell her that apparently, her gods had chosen me—the outsider—to be her king's mate.

"I see," I said sincerely. "Well, why don't you come and enjoy some breakfast. Gweeda will have biscuits shortly. I have some hot oats and cream with honey while you wait."

She frowned but said, "Thank you."

She sat on the bench stiffly near Gweeda, scowling at me. This time, her look didn't seem menacing or petty, but simply confused. I'm sure she expected venom from me, not kindness. But I was aware that if I was to ever get into the good graces of Redvyr's clan, it wouldn't be through force or command.

I spooned her a bowl, Shearah giving me the side eye as I poured extra honey into it. I whispered, "Maybe it will make her sweeter."

Shearah chuckled, then I gave Velga the bowl.

"Thank you," she said more nicely this time, diving into it.

Suddenly, Bes, Sorka's daughter, smiled brightly as she entered and saw me. She ran over, waving something white in her hands.

"Your gloves! I have them." She met me, panting, and held out the pair of beautifully sewn gloves. There was a delicate row of roses stitched along the hem of each cuff.

"Oh, my," said Shearah, stopping her slicing of a roasted venison shoulder to peer closer. "Is that elkmine otter?"

"It is," I told her, taking the gloves. "A trader gave me the fur when I worked in the Borderlands. These are beautiful, Bes. How ever can I thank you?"

"There is no need. Although! Mother says it would be wonderful if I learned to cook like you. Some of those delicious stews. Then I could help Shearah after you're gone."

I tucked the gloves into my pocket to wear later, swallowing hard at the realization that no one expected me to stay beyond winter. Was that why they were so accepting of me, an outsider? Because I wasn't meant to stay? Welcomed only because it was temporary?

"That reminds me," I turned to Shearah, turning my thoughts to cooking again. "I didn't see any more delly root that you were cooking last night. Was that the last of your stock?"

"There's lots more!" exclaimed Bes excitedly. "It grows even up here in Ghasta Vale. We keep a garden all winter."

"Truly? I cooked with the starchy vegetable when I lived in the Borderlands. An older wraith fae who lived not far from the tavern taught me a delicious recipe. Actually, she was the one who taught me to cook, not Haldek. He was the owner of the tavern where I worked."

"You were friends with wraith fae?" Velga asked curiously from behind us.

"I was," I told her proudly. "I made many friends among the dark fae while I lived there."

A silence stretched on, and I knew that Velga was surprised. Surely, she thought me a spoiled princess who would only lower myself to commune with the dark fae because I was forced to, since I was stranded in the cold after my betrothed's henchmen chased me into the frozen woods.

"What was this recipe she taught you with delly root?" asked Shearah.

"So you slice them into thin, round slices, fry them in butter then crumble goat cheese on top and drizzle them in honey."

"That sounds so delicious."

"It is," I assured her with a smile. "I saw that you do have honey, though I wouldn't want to use the small store you have for my dish."

"I believe the clan would be glad to use it to try this recipe of yours."

"We'll need more delly root."

"That's right. My stores are running low," said Shearah. "Bes, why don't you take Jessamine to the garden and she can help you harvest a basket for us?"

"Yes, of course!" She beamed from ear to ear. "Let's go, Jessamine!"

After ensuring that Shearah didn't mind me leaving, I wrapped my cloak around my shoulders and fastened it at my neck. I didn't want to get them dirty in the garden. Grabbing a basket and Bes's hand, putting a bright smile on her pretty face, we then set off.

The tents of the camp were scattered between The Sisters' closest points at their base, which best protected us from the harsher winds. In the valley, there were few trees. It wasn't until you climbed up the incline where the gap between the bases of the two mountains spread wider that the trees thickened into a woodland. Still, the treeline seemed far away from camp.

"Don't worry," said Bes. "We aren't going into Wyken Woods. The garden is right over there."

She pointed beyond the last tent where a wooden fence enclosed a rectangular space. The soil was obviously tilled and turned over there in neat rows. Greenish-brown sprouts stuck out of the ground, the tops of the delly root.

"I'm surprised the ground isn't frozen. And how do you have a garden so quickly? You've only been here a few days."

"Delly root grows wild here, actually. We replant this garden every year before we leave. When we return the following year, it's always bursting. Of course, much of it is rotten because we were not here the whole year to harvest. But as soon as we clear out the rot, new shoots grow in its place right away."

"That's amazing," I noted. "We can't grow it near the coast in Morodon. The first time I actually tasted it was when I lived in the Borderlands."

There were two guards posted not far away, closer to the treeline. One of them was Dayn, who smiled our way. I waved and he gave a nod as we approached the gate of the garden.

"Why did you run away from your home?"

I didn't remember Bes being at the kella'mir in Vanglosa when I first confessed my sad and somewhat embarrassing story to the council, but she wasn't a babe. She had likely overheard adults talking about me. Not surprising.

"My father is not a good man," I told her frankly.

I'd never admitted that aloud until this moment. I'd always known he wasn't a good father, but I realized that his selfish choices guided by his own greed made him not simply a bad king and father, but a bad man.

"I'm sorry," said Bes, handing me a trowel that hung on a hook embedded in the fencepost.

"It's alright." Though it actually wasn't. "He had betrothed me to a man who wanted to use my magick to do something evil. I refused to accept the fate chosen by my father. So I left."

Her face was serious as she knelt upon a wooden plank placed along the outside edge of the row, obviously to protect a harvester's clothes and keep off the cold ground.

"Well, I am glad that you ran away. And I'm glad that you found us."

"I am, too," I admitted freely as I knelt beside her. "I've never harvested delly root, so you'll have to show me what to do."

She blushed. "Oh, it's easy. See these sprouts here that are dark green? Those aren't ripe yet. This one here where the top has turned brown, that means it's ready."

"I see."

We began to work our way down the row, moving the basket between us. After a few minutes of us digging out the ripe vegetables, Bes glanced over her shoulder then scooted closer to me.

"What kind of magick do you have?" she whispered, as if she sought a well-guarded secret.

Smiling, I whispered back. "I'm a willoden for one."

"What is that?" she asked, blinking her long-lashed eyes up at me curiously.

I pulled up a rather large delly root from the soil and dropped it into our basket, glancing around.

"I can do special magick with water. Let me show you."

Standing, I walked to the fence surrounding the garden. The snow had been shoveled and piled along the fence line. I scooped a coin-sized amount into the palm of my hand and met Bes near the row where she stood waiting for me.

"Watch," I told her.

She stood close to me, her shoulder pressing into my arm as she stared down into my palm. Calling my magick to the surface, my hands beamed a faint glow.

"*Keskavalla,*" I whispered down to the ball of snow at the center of my palm.

Instantly, a luminous dome of light formed over the snow, stretching from my fingertips to the fleshy part of my palm.

"Oh, my goodness." Bes stared in awe.

"I'm not done yet," I told her.

The ball of snow melted and transformed into steamy mist within the magickal dome I'd created.

"Put your hand inside the dome," I told her.

She glanced up, wide-eyed and unsure, but then reached her dainty fingers toward the tiny oasis of warmth I'd created.

"It's alright," I urged her. "Slip your fingers inside."

Tentatively, she touched the edge of the dome then pushed her hand inside. She gasped.

"It's wonderful," she giggled. "It feels like a steamy bath."

I laughed. "Yes. A willoden can change water, both in form and temperature."

"Amazing," she whispered in awe, turning her hand around inside the dome.

"What are you two being so secretive about over here?"

We both jumped back, my magick fading as I dropped my hand, wiping my damp palm on my cloak. Tessa grinned like she'd caught us committing a crime.

"Hallizel!" Bes squealed with excitement.

The sprite fluttered over to Bes and zipped around her head, chittering excitedly. Bes danced in a circle, trying to chase the sprite. Saralyn giggled, watching the display.

"Bes, why don't you take Saralyn off my hands while I help Jessamine? I could use a break."

"Yay! Come see, Saralyn." Bes clapped her hands then held them out to the babe, who raised her chubby arms with a giggle.

Bes took Saralyn outside the gate where they had more room to dance around with Hallizel.

"Saralyn is getting bigger by the day," I noted, realizing the infant had more dark hair curling out of her head than the first day I met her.

"She is. And her first teeth, her fangs, are coming in. I actually came here to find a frozen delly root for her to teethe on."

"That's a good idea. You can take one of those, you don't have to dig your own or help me. I'm sure you're exhausted."

But she settled onto the wooden plank and lifted Bes's trowel anyway. "Jessa, I am actually happy to do something besides breastfeed and comfort my crying baby."

"She seems happy now." I watched Bes twirl in the snow with a giggling Saralyn, Hallizel zipping and chirping around them.

"Bes can always make her laugh. I was happy to find you both here."

I settled next to her and set to work, feeling a sense of contentment wash over me.

"It's nice to have you here."

She plopped a delly root in the basket. "I would've joined you sooner if I'd known."

"That's not what I mean." I sighed. "It's nice to be here with another light fae."

She flashed a smile and nodded. "I know what you mean. I felt so out of place when I first came here with Bezaliel. He was the only one who I felt *at home* with, if that makes sense."

"It makes perfect sense." I remembered the way I had felt so right, a sense of belonging as I drifted off to sleep in Redvyr's arms.

"But I am very glad you are here too." She sat back on her heels. So did I. "It will be nice to have another light fae sister among the clan."

"Oh." Frowning, I glanced over at Dayn who had wandered closer to chat with Bes and tease the baby. "So you know."

"Of course, I do. Bezaliel suspected before even Redvyr knew. Being mated to a beast fae is a wonderful thing. The bond is beautiful."

"I'm not so sure the clan will think so."

"Hmph. They weren't sure about me either at first. But once they realized I was truly Bezaliel's mate, and that I didn't think myself above them, that I could contribute to the clan, they did finally accept me."

"I hope they accept me too," I admitted.

She stared at my neck for a moment. "Has he marked you yet?"

I frowned. "How do you mean?"

She tapped her own shoulder. "Did he bite you?"

I winced. "Why in the heavens would he do that?"

Tessa laughed. "It doesn't hurt very much. It's a superficial bite that embeds his scent on your skin. A beast fae always marks his mate to warn off others and make the bond permanent." Her brow furrowed. "Redvyr hasn't bitten you yet?"

Wondering at this strange ritual I had never heard of, I simply shook my head. Her expression softened to embarrassment as she turned back to the vegetables.

"He will, of course. I suppose he wants to speak to you about it before he does it. With you being a light fae, after all."

"Did Bezaliel ask before he bit you?"

She paused before answering. "No." Then she added lightly, "They believe they have no magick, other than their strength and heightened senses. But I felt it when the bond was made."

"How do you mean?" I asked anxiously.

"When the bond is made with the bite, there is a distinct sensation of magick pouring through you. As if the gods are pleased we have honored the union."

"Interesting," I noted, digging more fiercely into the hard ground.

I couldn't even pretend not to be frustrated that Redvyr hadn't mentioned this to me. I'd given myself to him, and yet, he hadn't chosen to seal our bond. Perhaps he was regretting it. I'd ask him at dinner.

He woke me this morning with his head between my thighs, licking me to an orgasm. He then stroked to his own release, coming on my belly and pussy. When I asked why, he said he knew I was sore from our rougher coupling the past two days.

I thought it kind, that he was being gentle with me. Now, I was angry that he was. Perhaps he thought I was too soft to take his bite, that I wouldn't be able to handle the pain that came with sealing our bond.

"Jessa. It's customary to chop the delly root just before you cook it, not when you're trying to pull it out of the ground."

I sighed, pulling up the poor vegetable hacked into thirds. "I'm just frustrated."

"Redvyr is a frustrating male. Obstinate and headstrong."

"Ha! You're telling me."

She laughed. "But you are his mate, Jessamine. Just tell him what you want."

"I certainly will. Tonight, I'll—"

A shrieking scream pierced the valley. We both jumped to our feet. My skin burned with the magick of the syrenskyn, suddenly flaring bright.

Dayn and the other guard on duty faced the woodlands, swords drawn when a second harrowing shriek echoed closer.

"Run!" Dayn shouted.

Hallizel zipped in quick circles around Bes's head. "It's them! It's the grimlocks! Run, Bessie, Run!"

"Saralyn!" yelled Tessa.

We both ran for the gate, pushing it open right as six or seven grimlocks, no, more, darted in flight from the woodlands.

"Gods above," I mumbled as three attacked Dayn.

Four attacked the other guard. He roared and sliced with his claws and sword, slaying one while three more gouged his face and throat with their dagger-like claws. I was nearly to Bes when I saw him fall.

"Hurry!"

I didn't have time to look behind me as I grabbed Bes's hand, Tessa scooping Saralyn into her arms, and we all ran for our lives. Beast fae warriors sprinted toward us from the camp, but the garden was too far away. We wouldn't make it, and I knew it.

Running like wildfire, I heard them drawing closer. My syren claws descended.

"Keep going!" I screamed at Bes, letting her hand go as I whirled around at the grimlock nearly on top of us. More of them flew past me.

Swiping out at its throat, I gagged at the putrid stench of the creature. Its eyes gleamed red from within a horrifying face. It hissed through two rows of pointed, black teeth, and dodged my claws when I went for his throat again. The creature beat his wings—shaped like a sprite's wings with a green sheen—lifting above and then behind me. Then he had his arms around my waist and my feet left the ground.

I screamed. Then an ungodly roar bellowed across the field. Redvyr was coming.

CHAPTER 23

Redvyr

I charged on all fours, Bezaliel and our wolves right beside me. Enraged that these creatures dared to come into our camp, my fury turned into raw fear when I saw Jessamine being lifted off the ground by one of the grimlocks.

My roar shook the loose rocks from the mountains. The grimlocks screeched but didn't deter from their targets. Using all of my strength, I burst into full speed and launched myself into the air right as Jessamine reached back and grabbed one of the creature's pointed horns.

Colliding with them, I pulled us all to the ground, one arm around Jessamine's waist, my other hand wrapped around the grimlock's throat. When we tumbled to the snow, I embedded my claws into its green-gray skin and ripped out its throat, its crimson eyes rounding wide as it died. Foul blood spilled into the snow, the grimlock dead before I stood to my full height.

Lifting Jessamine to her feet, I gave her an urgent shove toward Wolf. "Take her to safety!" Then to her, "Go, Jessamine!"

She didn't hesitate, climbing onto Wolf who then launched into a gallop back toward the camp, while my clansmen and their wolves charged out into the field toward us.

Tessa screamed, she and her baby being carried off by two grimlocks. Bezaliel launched into the air, high enough to grab hold of Tessa's ankles. He roared and pulled. Tessa fell free as Mishka snarled and leaped, clamping her jaws over the grimlocks head, but the other creature snatched the babe, making a delighted screech before speeding off in flight toward the woods.

"Noooo!" Bezaliel bellowed as I ran after the creature with him, charging across the snowy field.

A shrill squeal rent the air and a zip of blue light darted toward the grimlock carrying Saralyn. It was Hallizel, circling and pecking the creature. It did not slow him as he reached out with a clawed hand and batted her to the ground.

"Bes!" Sorka screamed, running across the clearing toward the woods on our right.

Two more grimlocks carried Bes—kicking and screaming—too high for us to reach her, too fast for us to follow.

"After them!" I called, tearing off toward Wyken Woods.

Bezaliel fell in beside me as did the rest of my warriors, all of us charging at full speed after the monsters who'd stolen two of our children. One of them was the sweet infant of my dearest friend.

The air in Wyken Woods was oppressive, the bare trees with bony, craggy branches standing like sentinels to the underworld. This forest wasn't dead, for the trees were tall and strong, even if they bore no leaves. But never had we caught game here for our winter meals. As if woodland creatures sensed there was something wrong in the atmosphere, something unwelcoming.

"This way!" yelled Brohm, bending close to the ground, examining a knotty root jutting across the path.

As I passed, I noticed a drop of bright blue blood on the bark, the smell of Bes on the wind. She had been injured when they took her. My gut clenched. Two of the most vulnerable members of the clan had been taken, one of them wounded.

We hurdled on, the woods darkening the farther we went. We only ever came here for kindling, and we never ventured too deep into these woods. The trees' spindly, naked branches reached up, tangling with their brethren overhead, creating a lattice of interlaced fingers. I never sensed dryads or naiads or sprites, not any of faekind, living here. It was a barren place that we avoided.

A baby's cry echoed in the distance.

"Saralyn," groaned Bezaliel, chasing in the direction of the sound.

We followed, helplessly. The next time we heard her cry, it was much farther away. Still, we ran on, going deeper into Wyken Woods than we had ever been, the coldness of this place seeping into my bones.

We ran until the gray sky peeking through the trees turned dark. Until we were all exhausted from our fruitless chase, the moon beaming through the branches above us.

Fungus grew along the base of some of the trees this deep in the forest, the snow piled in sparse patches against the knotted roots. We came to a clearing and Bezaliel stopped, as did I. The others circled around us. We all stopped and listened. I inhaled deep, seeking our enemy. The grimlock scent was faint. A hard gust of wind rattled the branches above us like bones in a mass grave.

"She's gone." Bezaliel's voice broke with agony. "My child." He thrust his hands into his hair and roared up at the half-moon peeking through the canopy of bare branches, as if it was watching our helpless despair.

I remained still, smelling the air, trying to find a trace of them. This time, even the scent of the grimlocks was gone. There was no sound of a baby's cry or Bes's whimpers on the wind.

Meeting my friend at the center of the clearing, I put a hand on his shoulder. "We must go back."

"No! We can find her. We *must* find her." He shook his head, agony in his eyes. "I can't go back to Tessa without her."

I hauled him to face me, both my hands on his shoulders, holding his terrified gaze which made my gut clench. "This is *black* magick. We need help. We are no match for this without those who wield magick also."

It galled me to admit it, but there was one thing we could not fight alone. And that was this sorcerer who wielded the grimlocks with his magick.

"I can't leave her," he choked out, swallowing hard against the pain building inside him.

My heart ached at the grief and anger tearing him apart.

"We aren't leaving her," I assured him, mustering all the confidence that I could. "We will find someone to help us bring her back." I shook him to make him look at me again, his gaze wandering toward the darkness beyond my shoulder. "Then we will kill them all."

"Tessa," he murmured, clearing his throat. "She won't survive this."

"She is a strong woman. You know this." I squeezed his shoulders to get his attention, despair engulfing him. "Let's return to them. We'll get the help we need and hunt them down when we have it."

He wrenched free of me and roared to the skies. "I will find you!" His voice was malevolent. "I will kill you all!"

His rage echoed through the woods. But no answer echoed back to us. Nothing but silence and the wind.

He fell to his knees, finally giving into his fear and grief. When his shoulders shook, I strode to him and pulled my chief to his feet.

"Do *not* despair," I commanded him in my kingly voice. "This isn't the end. We must go to Tessa. It's time for action."

He swiped his arm over his eyes, his face set in tight, grim lines. "You're right. We need a plan."

The other warriors remained silent, knowing there was nothing they could say to ease Bezaliel's pain. They simply corralled closer in silent support.

Finally, we raced back home—empty-handed.

As we always did when there was danger—like that year a blizzard had broken through the Sisters and dumped six feet of snow in Ghasta Vale—the entire clan gathered in the communal cave. Instantly, I found Jessamine kneeling at Dayn's side, wiping his brow.

I strode straight to them as Bezaliel charged toward Tessa and hauled her, crying, into his arms. Lorelyn had her arms around Sorka who sat on a bench near Dayn, whispering words of comfort in her ear. Sorka held Hallizel in her cupped hands. Though it was dim, she still illuminated a pale blue light. Thank the gods, she had survived.

Jessamine stood when I came to her, her gaze sweeping over me to look for injury. She pressed a hand to my chest and closed her eyes, sighing in relief. Taking her hand in mine, I kissed her palm.

"How is Dayn?"

"The injury is bad. But he is strong. He'll make it, Tessa says."

His vest had been removed, revealing two deep claw marks over his heart and the reddened sutures that Tessa must've stitched. Even in her worry and grief for her daughter and mate, our healer had taken care of our own.

Dayn lay unconscious, which concerned me. We weren't the fainting sort due to pain or injury.

"Shearah made him a sleeping draught of tea." Jessamine seemed to read my mind. "He kept trying to stand and go after all of you into the woods. But I made him drink it all so that we could tend his wounds. He bled quite a lot."

"Good. Smart thinking."

My gaze fell to the back of the cave where a white cloth covered one of my warriors.

"Breygar didn't make it."

"No, he did not," said Lorelyn, standing beside us now. "Lord Redvyr, you must speak to the council and the clan. They are afraid. We must all know what is to be done."

Giving Jessamine's hand a squeeze, I left her to march over to the fire, then turned to face the clan spread about the cave. The benches were completely full and many stood, with some clansmen huddled on furs spread on the floor for sleeping. No one would leave this cave tonight.

"Tell us," said Wyzel, her somber eyes already grieving the news I brought.

"We did not recover Bes and Saralyn."

Sorka sobbed while Tessa stared, her face grim, her eyes haunted.

"Why have these creatures come to us?" Melgar, one of the elderly council members, stood from the bench. "The shadow fae said they've not been this far south before, did they not?"

"They did." I paused. "We don't know why they've come, only that we must find them to get our loved ones back."

"Perhaps the gods are angry with us." It was Pavlok, Velga's father. "Because our king has taken an outsider to his bed."

He was lashing out at me for humiliating his daughter in front of the clan. So he thought to bring the rumor out into the open, to challenge where I stood, and try to humiliate me.

"Have the sins of the father been passed onto the son?" Melgar asked, the accusation that I had taken a woman who wasn't meant to be mine clear in his voice. That I might shame our clan by forcing them to take a queen who did not belong, who the gods had not chosen.

Now was not the time, but Pavlok and Melgar had forced my hand. So be it.

The room was silent, all eyes riveted on me, except those who were glaring at Jessamine. And though her cheeks were flushed with embarrassment, my mate stood with her head held high and proud. As she should.

I held out my hand to her. "Come to me, Jessamine."

A few fae gasped and whispered as she walked across the room and took my hand, standing by my side. I met their accusing stares.

"My father took what did not belong to him. My mother. He paid the price, as did she. And as did I, being raised to a full-grown beast fae without parents of my own. The clan raised me. And they raised me well." I swept my gaze across the room. "I would never repeat my father's sins. Jessamine," I tugged her closer, "is my gods-given mate."

"She can't be," said Melgar, his expression contorted in confusion.

"Are you calling me a liar?" I asked.

Melgar's eyes widened. He looked at Jessamine then shook his head. "No, my lord."

"Where is her mark?" someone asked.

Jessamine wore a dress with a scooped neck, revealing the fair, unbroken skin at her shoulder. "That will come," I assured them. "For now, you must all know and *accept* that, yes, I have taken her to my bed. And every time we've coupled, it has been proven that she belongs to me. And I to her."

There was no need to be any more frank than that. I'd had plenty of lovers outside of this clan, choosing never to take one among my own for the troubles it could cause. Many beast fae took lovers for pleasure, but they rarely took them for long, always seeking the mate the gods intended for them. It was wrong to procreate with any but your mate. And I'd never found my mate among the beast fae females I'd bedded elsewhere.

Melgar and Pavlok were angry because they thought I was simply sating my appetite with the pretty foreigner in camp, that there was no way the gods would bind us together as mates. They were wrong. And though I'd thought the same before, I was wrong too. Happily mistaken.

And there she was—this light fae female, with her pale skin and blood-red hair, her defiant chin in the air. She was my mate, and I couldn't be prouder or more grateful.

I turned to face my clan, finding expressions of surprise and wonder, disappointment, and a few smiles.

"Now that that's settled, Leifkyn, gather ten warriors and meet me in my tent. The rest of you stay here," I commanded, roughening my voice with the dominant beast that lived inside me. "The clan sleeps together in this cave tonight."

I wasn't going to speak of our plan of action in front of the council or anyone else who thought they knew better than the king of this clan. My command for them to stay put was to keep them safe.

"Come with me," I told Jessamine. "Let Shearah tend to Dayn. Lorelyn," I called. "Follow us."

I marched out first, sniffing the air for any signs that the grimlocks might have returned. But I knew they wouldn't. They'd caught their prey and were far away by now.

We moved silently through the darkened camp to my tent. Leifkyn carried a torch inside and lit the fire pit on the tripod.

With the ten warriors Leifkyn pulled from the crowd—I noted they were all unmated males, which was wise—we gathered around the fire and sat upon the rug. Jessamine settled next to me, Lorelyn on the opposite side of the circle. Bezaliel and Tessa burst in.

"You're a fucking madman if you think you're planning anything without me," Bezaliel barked.

"Sit down, Bezaliel. I would not cut you out of the plan. I merely thought you might need more time with Tessa."

"No," said Tessa. "We are not grieving or in mourning. Our child is alive." She thumped her breast. "I can feel it *here*. She is *alive*, and we will help find her."

I gave her a grim smile, buoyed by the fact that Bezaliel had mated a fierce woman.

"Good. Then we will find her." I turned my attention to Lorelyn. "When we chased the grimlocks, they vanished deep into Wyken Woods. There is no way they simply outflew us that fast. One minute we heard Saralyn, the next we couldn't hear her anymore."

"By all the hells, I'll tear them to pieces," cursed Tessa.

Bezaliel took her hand in his lap. "It is true. There is no way they outflew us so fast."

"You think it's black magick," said Lorelyn.

"Yes," I assured her. "So we need magick of our own to find them."

Lorelyn shook her head. "I can cast the runes or scry. But it would be better if we had some of their blood."

"I don't have their blood," said Jessamine, "but I have some strands of hair."

She reached into her pocket and pulled out a clump of coarse, green hair. "I pulled some loose when I was fighting one of them. I don't know why I kept it."

I did, but I didn't voice it. Jessamine was full of magick, likely had some seer powers of her own. She somehow knew we might need it.

"Leifkyn, fetch some of their blood as well. I left a corpse out in the field. Balko, go with him."

The two left while Jessamine stood and went to our washing bowl. She emptied it outside then filled it with my water satchel hanging on a hook near the tent entrance. I liked watching her move about our tent, like she belonged here.

Before long, Leifkyn returned and we gathered back around the fire, Lorelyn sitting before the bowl. She squeezed the blood from Leifkyn's handkerchief into the water then sprinkled the hair onto the surface.

We all sat quietly, waiting in anticipation. Lorelyn was our only beast fae with magick, and we depended on her time and time again. I was afraid to wish for too much, for her to discover where they were by simply scrying.

Lorelyn murmured in a whisper as she used her forefinger to swirl the blood and hair into the bowl. Magick sizzled along my skin as her power filled the room. Jessamine had taken a seat beside me, resting on her heels.

A subtle red glow radiated from the scrying bowl. Lorelyn continued to chant inaudibly, faster and faster as she stared down. Her dark hair hung loosely, blowing in an ethereal breeze. The water stopped rippling, flattening into a sheet like glass. Lorelyn gasped and clenched her fists, her gaze fixed on the bowl.

After another moment, the red glow faded, mist hissing up from the surface. Lorelyn's shoulders relaxed and she straightened as the scrying magick slowly disappeared.

"What did you see?" I asked instantly.

"It doesn't make sense." She shook her head.

"Whatever you saw," said Bezaliel, "please tell us. Anything at all could help."

She blew out a breath, her brow beaded with sweat. "Scrying doesn't always give me a clear picture. Since we used the blood and hair of one of the grimlocks, my vision was from his point of view."

"And?" pleaded Tessa.

"He lives in a cesspool of malice. There are two voices in his head."

"Two?" I asked. "How do you mean?"

She shook her head, tucking a lock of her hair behind her pointed ear. "I can't say exactly. One is strong, one is weak. The stronger voice is not his own, but it lives there inside his mind, guiding him."

"And what is it guiding him to do?" I asked.

She swallowed hard, her throat working as she glanced piteously at Tessa. "To gather food."

"Goddess, help me," Tessa cried, burying her face in her hands.

"But this dark master does not simply eat for sustenance. It is the power he gains, that he craves."

Bezaliel wrapped his arm around Tessa's shoulder and pulled her against him. "What else did you see, Lorelyn?"

Nodding, she added, "This is the part I believe might be helpful, though I'm not sure how. When I blocked out the voices and focused on my visual senses, it was hazy. But I did see something. There was complete darkness, but inside a small hole or pit of some kind there were balls of light. They were different sizes—all bright white. One was very small, but the brightest of them all. Before the vision ended, I heard the cry of a baby. Of Saralyn."

Tessa wiped her eyes and took Bezaliel's hand. "It was her? You're *sure*?"

"I'm sure." She gave Tessa a sympathetic smile.

"What else did you see?" I asked.

"Nothing. But I smelled earth. Musty soil and mildew. It was odd. They're somewhere dark and enclosed, but it was not a cave."

"But where?" demanded Bezaliel, his patience gone.

"I don't know." Lorelyn exhaled a sorrowful sigh. "I wish I did."

"What good is your magick if it can't help us get them back?" snapped Bezaliel.

"*Hush.*" Tessa squeezed his hand, gentling her voice while still being firm. "Lorelyn has given us the knowledge that our child is alive. That is more than we knew before."

Bezaliel stood, his expression grim, his face flushed, still riding his anger. "I apologize, Lorelyn. But this isn't enough." He moved his gaze to mine. "This won't help us get my daughter back."

He stormed from the tent, knocking the flap back with a hard *thwack*. Tessa hurried after him.

"Do not listen to him," I told Lorelyn. "We appreciate your gifts, and what they can offer us."

"But he's right," she admitted sadly. "It's not enough. We need someone with more powerful magick."

Another silence fell between all of us. Then Jessamine cleared her throat, sitting up straighter beside me.

"I think I know a way."

All our attention was on Jessamine, her emerald eyes wide with apprehension but also determination.

"Or at least I can try."

"Tell us, my lady," said Leifkyn.

"The water well." She looked at me hopefully. "I've sensed a naiad lives there. Though I've never seen it, I felt them when I fetched water there."

"How could they help?" Haslek asked, one of the ten warriors Leifkyn selected.

"Naiads know things," she said simply.

Then Lorelyn chimed in. "That is true. Can you summon the naiad and speak to her?"

Jessamine's mouth quirked into a rueful smile. "Like I said, I can try. They are not biddable creatures."

Indeed, she was my fated mate. The gods sent me a beautiful and powerful woman, to aid me and our clan when we could not help ourselves. We took her in to offer her help and protect her, but it was she who may be our saving grace.

I reached over and took her hand in mine. "Then by all the gods, my heart, please try."

CHAPTER 24

Jessamine

Water dripped from stalactites hanging from the ceiling, forming crystalline stalagmites around the cave floor. It was the only sound other than my voice speaking the old naiad tongue. The chamber was bathed in blue light from the piece of blue coal Redvyr burned in a lantern beside him. I'd told him I thought bright torchlight might frighten a naiad from answering my call.

I'd been reaching out to the naiad I believed lived here in the cold of this entombed cave since before dawn. Redvyr had settled himself against the wall near the entrance. While the ethereal energy of a naiad resonated in this chamber, she did not heed my call.

"Perhaps it's your presence," I told him. "Sometimes, they're shy. If it's a female who lives here, she may not be answering me because you're here. Many of them don't care for males."

With his arms crossed over his chest, his long legs stretched out in front of him, also crossed at the ankles, he heaved out a breath. "What if she gets violent? I've heard these creatures can be vicious sometimes."

"They can," I agreed. "But none has ever hurt me before."

I didn't tell him that one had threatened me back on the isle near my home in Morodon.

"I don't like leaving you here alone," he growled.

His rumble echoed in the small chamber. The well was a circular pool as wide as I was tall. The water was as blue as a midnight sky, no telling how deep it went. There appeared to be no bottom.

"Please, Redvyr. Let me try on my own. I'll be fine."

Confidence filled my voice, but it didn't fill my heart. Naiads were independent fae creatures with a will of their own.

He pushed to a stand and strode over to me. Crouching next to the pool where I knelt, he cupped my face in his hands.

"I will be right outside. If you sense any danger, call out to me."

"I will," I promised him.

Then he brushed his lips across mine, purring against my mouth as he swept his tongue inside. When he pulled back, his hold on my face tightened.

"Call me if you need me."

When he stood and turned to leave, a tinkling laugh, then another, filled the chamber, raising gooseflesh on my skin.

"No, no, no, beasty. Don't leave so soon."

My skin glowed, responding to the presence of magickal fae. On the far side of the water well, two naiads stared at us. Their skin was as deep blue as the water, their hair only a shade lighter, and their eyes pinpoints of silvery-white light.

"Hello," I spoke to them in the demon tongue rather than their own language I had been using the past several hours, since they spoke it themselves.

"Greetings, water fae," said the one on the right. "I have never seen one of them, sister, have you?"

"Never. She beams too brightly. You must douse your lights, girl, or you will hurt our eyes."

"He does not hurt our eyes," said the first, her tone dripping with seduction. She was identical to her sister. "Beasty is a feasty for my eyes."

Their voices were sibilant and otherworldly. I didn't simply hear them, I felt their words skating across my skin. They were old naiads. Very old.

"I apologize," I told them with Redvyr kneeling beside me, who stared with both fascination and wariness. "My magick responds to the power you hold. I am a willoden."

"Tsss," the one on the left hissed. "We know what you are. You've been babbling—"

"Begging us," chimed in the other.

"To come out and speak to you."

"But you are more than that," said the one on the right, gliding to the middle of the pool, her eerie silver-white eyes searching me up and down. "A syrenskyn, sister. That is what she is."

"My, oh my." The other slithered across the water without making a ripple, both of them coming closer. "Rare water fae, aren't you, little girl?"

"My name is Jessamine," I said politely, not bothering to correct their insult in calling me a girl. To them, I likely was one. But naiads, especially old ones, were moody creatures that could decide I wasn't worth talking to and vanish before I ever got around to seeking the answers I needed. "I come from Morodon."

"And yet, here you are in our mountain home in Ghastagar Valley."

I looked at Redvyr, confused.

"That is an old name," he said. "We call it Ghasta Vale now, my ladies."

They both giggled, sounding much younger than the centuries old beings I knew they must be. "He calls us ladies, sister."

"A long time since we've been called that." They tittered again.

He crouched closer. They obviously liked him more than me. "I am Redvyr, Lord of the beast fae of Vanglosa."

The naiad on the left glided toward our side of the pool, still not touching the rim of the well. "I am Bethevier. This is my sister Lethemier. We are pleased to meet the beasty lord who brings his people to sip at our well each winter."

"I thank you for your kindness in allowing us to drink your cool waters." He smiled and flirted back. "It keeps my clan healthy and strong."

They laughed again, batting their long blue lashes. They were obviously infatuated with him. I couldn't blame them, but it was irritating. We needed answers, not to engage in this ridiculous flirtation.

I rolled my eyes then nodded toward the sisters, meaning for him to ask the questions we needed the answers to. He understood.

"My ladies, our clan has had some trouble, and I'm wondering if you might be able to help us."

"Speak, beasty," said Bethevier. "We may answer."

"And we may not," said Lethemier, narrowing her gaze.

"I understand," he said, though he honestly didn't.

Naiads were fickle and moody and, yes, they could be quite vicious. These two might seem receptive and even benevolent, but they radiated with power and their ancient lineage. I could sense it so easily.

"Trouble has come to our clan here in Ghasta Vale," he told them. "Fae monsters called grimlocks have come out of Wyken Woods and attacked our clan."

Lethemier grimaced and hissed again, revealing a row of serrated teeth. "The grimlocks do not come from Wyken Woods, beasty lord."

"They were born far beneath Mount Gudrun." Bethevier twirled in a circle, ending up directly below Redvyr.

I knew my geography well enough to know that Mount Gudrun was the tallest mountain in the Solgavia Mountains, where the shadow fae lived.

Bethevier gripped the sides of the pool, her pearly white claws long and sharp. "The mountain wights have come to bother you, sweet beasty?"

"They have taken two of our youngest clan members, mere children. Why do you call them mountain wights? They do not look like those controlled by the wraith fae."

The wights, which were created by wraith fae that held this power, like the former King Xakiel were nothing more than an army of the dead. Skeletons that crawled out of the ground and were bound to that evil king with a blood bond to do his bidding, to attack his enemies.

"Grimlocks are golems," said Bethevier, gazing up at my male like he was hers. If I didn't need answers so badly, I'd shove her backward.

Of course, then she might drag me into the pool and kill me.

"They are soulless creatures," added Lethemier, "a fusion of many of faekind, created only to do their father's bidding."

"Who is their father?" I asked.

Bethevier furrowed her brow at me, having forgotten I was there apparently. When she did not answer, and nor did her sister, Redvyr repeated my question.

"Tell me, sweet ladies, who is their master?"

"We do not know," Bethevier admitted, tracing the claw of her forefinger in a circle near his boot. "He is older than us and he blocks the intrusion of magick."

Older than them? By the gods, who was this sorcerer?

"Oh, ho, ho, dear sister. But he does like to pour his rotten power into the world, that is for certain. He whispers through earth and stone to those who will listen."

"Indeed, sister."

"Thank you for your knowledge," said Redvyr. "These grimlocks, or golems, have taken two of our children and hidden them somewhere in Wyken Woods. Or perhaps somewhere beyond. Do you know where they might have taken them?"

"How would we know such a thing?" asked Bethevier coyly, rising out of the water up to her waist next to Redvyr, leaning her weight on one arm. She tipped her head back, jutting her breasts outward—and while she was hundreds of years old, her body was perfect. Naiads didn't age. Not like faekind. The only hint of their age were the threads of silver in their blue hair.

"You know many things," I stated, though it was more of an accusation. "You know where this dark lord dwells. You know what he creates. Two naiads of your age and with your power would certainly have knowledge of where the golems might keep the children."

"It is not always children they catch," said Lethemier. "Any light fae will do." She looked me up and down, my skin still glowing. "You would be a tasty morsel for their father."

Redvyr's expression darkened, but he kept his voice genial when he spoke. "If you know something, I would be most grateful."

"What will you give me if I tell you?" Bethevier tilted her head coquettishly.

"What do you require?"

"A taste of your blood."

"No!" I snapped, my skin pulsing with white light.

The sisters hissed and guarded their eyes from the glare.

"You cannot have his blood," I told them. I shook my head emphatically at Redvyr.

Giving your blood to any magickal creature was a dangerous risk. They could use it to control or curse or spy upon the one whose blood they tasted.

"Douse your light, fae girl!" shouted Lethemier.

I focused on calming my breathing, which did dim my skin's brilliance.

"No blood, then." Bethevier swished in the water and pushed up with both hands on the stone lip of the pool beneath Redvyr, bringing her face closer to his. "Give me a kiss."

Redvyr instantly shot me a look. My belly soured with the thought of his lips on hers, but a kiss couldn't hurt him. And it could give us what we want.

"Alright. Give me your hand."

Bethevier's silver eyes glittered, her mouth dropping open as she lowered back into the water and held out her hand. I wondered why Redvyr needed to lift her out of the water to kiss the stupid naiad. But rather than pull her from the water, he lifted her hand to his mouth and pressed a kiss to the back of it before releasing her.

She bared her serrated teeth and made a sibilant growl. "Not a kiss on my hand! On my lips, beasty!"

"You did not specify." Lethemier laughed with glee, spinning in a circle in the water. "You know the rules."

"I want a second kiss!" cried Bethevier.

"Sweet lady," he said in that crooning voice that always made me feel warm and tingly. "I cannot give you what I can only give to my gods-given mate. But I will cherish the memory of my lips on your elegant, soft hand."

"Ooooooh, beasty talks so sweetly, sister. You must give him what he bargained for. He gave you the kiss. Now it is your turn to give him what he wants."

Bethevier seemed mollified, twirling back to the center of the pool beside her sister. "The golems lock their captured in a cell made of magick. It is within the trunk of the Ancient One. When they are done hunting these woods, they will carry them back to their father."

"The Ancient One?" he pressed.

"The oldest oak in Wyken Woods. He stands at the center where the trees grow thin. No other will grow too close to him, giving him space, for he rules as their king. You cannot get into the hidden chamber by cutting down the tree. In fact, if you try, you will kill them. The black magick that holds them will crush them if it feels threatened. You must use magick against magick."

Her eyes glowed pure white, the hum of power wafting over me. Her voice took on a dreamy timbre when she spoke. Her words rang with the tone of prophecy.

"The father of the golems is a hungry god. If you kill his golems, he will simply beget more of them. For he has awakened from a long slumber, and he will not go to sleep again. The Father of Night will *never* sleep again."

"We must kill him, then." Redvyr's voice was gruff and aggressive.

Bethevier blinked her blue lashes, returning from her trance-like state. She scoffed at him. "You cannot kill a demi-god." Then she vanished beneath the water.

"You cannot kill a demi-god," repeated her sister before disappearing as well.

The ripples lapped at the edge of the pool, and then it was quiet again. Only the sound of the water dripping from the stalactites on the ceiling broke the silence.

"A demi-god?" Redvyr stood, staring at the still pool. "Why would a demi-god be plaguing us?"

His mind was racing, I could tell. I stepped into his arms and forced him to look at me.

"First things first, we need to get Bes and Saralyn back. Then we will worry about the rest."

"We need magick to get inside the hidden chamber. You heard them. If we hack it down, it will only kill the ones inside."

"Don't worry. I have a plan."

CHAPTER 25

Redvyr

“No! It isn't happening.”

"By the gods," Jessamine fumed angrily, pacing in our tent where Bezaliel and Tessa had joined us. "You are a *stubborn* male."

"Call me whatever you like, but you are not sacrificing yourself."

"Please explain to me exactly what you intend to do." Bezaliel broke through our argument, which had been going on ever since they walked in and Jessamine explained her plan. "I don't understand what you're talking about."

"She's going to use herself as bait," I bit out angrily. "And one of those fucking creatures could kill her or carry her off or seal her into an earthly tomb like they've done to Bes and Saralyn."

Jessamine stopped her pacing and faced Bezaliel, ignoring me entirely. "I have the gift of a syrenskyn. It's hard to explain, but I have the ability to lure others to me with magick. A seduction of sorts. It's possible that I could seduce one of them and make them open the cell. When I'm wielding my syrenskyn magick, my claws can inject a deadly poison, so I *can* defend myself. Contrary to what others may believe."

"Or," I snapped, striding to loom over her, "he will see that you are a juicy morsel for his master and abduct you."

"And if he does," she snapped back, her face heating, "he will open the chamber and allow you all to attack, kill them, and set us free."

"Infuriating woman." I shook my head. "It's *too* fucking *risky.*"

"What other choice do we have?" she asked, throwing her hands in the air.

I turned away, fuming with anger, unable to even look at her. But then I caught the hopeful and desperate gazes of my closest friend, my chief, and his dear mate, our healer who had already done so much for our clan. An oppressive silence fell between us, my jaw clenching so hard I thought I might crack it.

"Let us give them some time to talk, Tessa." Bezaliel didn't look at me with those pleading eyes a moment longer, knowing exactly what I was risking and unable to ask it of me. Even though Jessamine was right.

The pair left quietly while I remained still as stone, arms crossed, tail lashing angrily. I felt her draw near. When she slid her arms around my waist from behind and pressed her cheek to my back, I wrapped my tail around her ankle. Even while furious with her, I wanted to draw her close and touch her and keep her near me. Safe.

And just like that first time my temper flared when I killed the dryad stag, she soothed my spirit, calming my soul with her soft touch. How could the gods bless me with such a perfect female and then ask me to risk losing her?

"We must try," she whispered.

"And how exactly do you plan to do this? You're going to strip naked in the woods and summon your magick and then seduce one of these foul monsters when they show up? *If* they show up?"

"They will return for the children. Of that, at least we can be sure."

"You didn't answer my other questions."

She paused, still holding me from behind. "Yes. That's exactly what I plan to do."

Pulling her arms from me, I whirled around. "Are you *mad?* They may descend upon you then and there and mount you like the monsters they are rather than save you for their master."

"I am a powerful syrenskyn. I have used this magick before."

"It may not even work on these golems. They're monsters, abominations. Not men."

"They're made of flesh and bone." She smoothed her hands up my chest. "We must try, Red."

Her imploring gaze broke me. I knew she was right. I hauled her into my arms and pressed my mouth to her soft hair.

"I can't lose you, Jessa. You're my whole heart, my entire soul."

"You won't. You'll all be hiding and waiting. Ready to attack."

"How? They'll scent us on the wind."

"We'll come up with something to disguise your scent, but it's probably better if it's not all of you. Only your best warriors. Too many will be too risky."

Pulling back, I cupped her beautiful face in my palms. "How did you become such an expert tactician?"

She shrugged. "It's common sense."

"I don't like it," I told her.

"I know."

"I *hate* it. It makes me want to claw and bite something."

She bent her head to the side, revealing the slope of her elegant throat. "You can bite me."

Staring at her perfect pale skin, my mouth salivated. I wanted to sink my teeth there, to ensure she could never have anyone else but me. That no man would ever touch her with my scent on her skin. But I couldn't be that selfish. The gods gave her to me, but *she* hadn't given herself to me. Not permanently.

"Sit with me." I took her hand and guided her to the bed of furs.

When I paused for too long, trying to find the words, she said the most ridiculous thing in the world.

"You don't want to give me your mark. Is that it?"

I laughed. "Jessamine. I have wanted that from the first time I watched over you, when you were laying in my tent at my hunting camp."

"You have not. You hated me then."

I snorted. "Female, that is an unholy falsehood."

"Then why haven't you given me your mark?" she asked softly. "We're mates. You said so."

I nodded, holding one of her hands in both of mine, my body angled so that I could look at her.

"Once I bite you, my scent will remain on you forever. If you change your mind and decide in a year or two, or ten, that clan life isn't what you want for yourself, that you'd prefer someone of your own kind, a more comfortable life in Morodon, you will never have another male. They will never want a female with the smell of another embedded in their skin. Especially a beast fae."

"I thought that beast fae mated for life."

"They do," I assured her. "That's what I'm telling you. I will have no other. And no other will have you once my mark is on you. It will spoil any chance you have of seeking another life elsewhere."

"But I want my life with you. Here. I don't want a life elsewhere."

My heart lifted at her confidence, but she was a skald fae. And a princess at that. I knew that she'd been raised with comforts and riches that we did not have. While she enjoyed clan life for the brief time we had been together, a lifetime was an entirely different thing.

"I simply want to give you time, to give you the choice to choose me. To choose the clan of Vanglosa. Once it's done, there's no going back."

She frowned as she stared down at our entwined fingers. "How long do you think I need to make this decision?"

I had already thought about this a great deal. It pained me to give her time. The beast inside me wanted to push her down and embed his fangs in her right now, this very instant. But I would not be a tyrant and take without a thought or care like my father had done to my mother. I would not become a male like him, a beast fae with no honor.

"When we return to Vanglosa, you will give me your answer. If," I hesitated, taking a breath, "if your answer is what I hope for, then we will be bound at the kella'mir under the sacred tree of our clan."

She nodded, staring down where I held her hand. "I wish winter was over now."

Pressing the back of her hand to my mouth, I whispered, "It pleases my heart to hear you say so. I want to be sure you feel just as certain at the end of winter."

"I had no idea you were such a patient male," she teased, smiling up at me.

I laughed. "I am not. Not at all." My smile slipped. "But I will not become my father and force my female into a life she does not want."

Her brows knit together. "What happened with your father?"

For the first time in my entire life, I wanted to tell someone. No, I wanted to tell *her*. If she knew my harrowing past and still accepted me, it might absolve me of this guilt that weighed on me so heavily, this wrongdoing of my father's that followed me like a ghostly shadow.

"My father made the greatest mistake a beast fae, especially a beast fae lord, can make." I met her gaze, owning my father's sin before it left my lips. "He met my mother at the end-of-winter gathering of the clans at Jôhl Tundra. She was the daughter of the lord of the Bolgar Clan. She was beautiful and coveted by many males. My father believed she was meant for him."

I paused, my throat thickening the closer I got to mentioning the damning offense he committed.

"My mother was in love with another, a warrior named Gunlyn of her own clan. Father knew this. Gunlyn and my mother planned to consummate their bond at the winter gathering. It is a custom, with many choosing that celebratory moment to couple and discover if the gods have blessed them as mates."

My memory drifted, remembering my own mother telling me this story. I'd found her crying more than once over the years as a boy. She would then hide her tears and tell me it was nothing.

But one day, when I'd reached my final teen year and was to become a warrior of our clan, she told me the truth.

"But before Gunlyn and my mother could do so, Father took her into the woods and mounted her, against her will. She was not his mate, but his lust and desire for her to be his queen was too great." I cleared my throat and turned to look away, watching the flames lick up in the pit next to the bed. "He threatened her, saying that if she didn't keep quiet about the fact that knotting hadn't occurred in their coupling, he would kill her beloved."

"Oh, Redvyr." Jessamine's pained whisper was awful. I couldn't bear to look her in the eyes. Especially since I wasn't done yet.

"My mother protected her love, Gunlyn, and bound herself to my father. It took her many years to conceive me, and I was their only child. But on the day of the kella'mir that made me an official warrior of the Vanglosa clan, she pulled me aside from the celebration. She hugged me and gave me her blessings, told me she knew I would one day be a lord that everyone would respect and love, and then she left."

I closed my eyes, wishing I could change history, go back and stop her.

"We found my mother floating in Lake Moreen the next day."

She gasped, clenching one of my hands in both of hers. Before she could tell me how awful it was, I quickly finished the story.

"We burned her on a pyre that night. Then my father wandered into the woods and shoved his blade into his heart."

I waited for her to say something, to tell me how awful my father was, how sad of a story I had just shared, or how sorry she was for me. She did none of those things.

She stood from the bed and unlaced the corseted bodice of her gown, slipping it off her shoulders and letting it fall to the floor. This wasn't the reaction I had expected. I remained still as she shuffled off her boots and stockings then stepped closer and settled onto my lap, straddling my thighs.

Without hesitation, she slid her small fingers along my jaw and angled her mouth over mine. I didn't hesitate either. I fisted a hand in her hair and held her firm, licking into her mouth on a groan. The scent of her arousal spurred me on.

Her fingers were unlacing my vest, but I made quicker work of it, tossing it aside. She whimpered, clawing her blunt nails down my chest, grinding her cunt against me and soaking my pants. I didn't care. I loved it. I just told her a sad story and she was unhinged with desire. I didn't understand it, but I was no fool either.

Gripping her waist, I lifted her higher and suckled her pink nipple, teasing the tip until she cried out, squirming in my arms. I tortured her more, sliding my forked tongue across the valley of her breasts to the other, scraping my fangs lightly over the swollen peak.

"Ahh! *Yes.*"

Falling back to the furs, I went for the laces of my trousers. "Stay on top of me. I'm going to fuck you like this. I want to watch you come undone."

Her green eyes were swallowed by black, half-lidded, her cheeks pink with the heat of desire. She remained above me, panting, waiting, her hands sliding restlessly over her hips and belly. When I opened the flap and freed my cock, holding it hard at the base, her mouth fell open, one of her hands sliding to cup her breast. She instantly jerked it away, shame washing her face now.

"No, baby." I gripped her hip with my free hand, guiding her down. "I want to see you touch yourself. Squeeze those perfect tits for me."

The head of my cock nudged her entrance as she began to slowly sink down. Tentatively, she cupped her own breasts, squeezing gently, letting her thumbs roll over the peaks of her nipples, and she began mewling a soft repetitive moan.

Gripping her hips, I thrust up gently. Her cunt was so drenched, I slid in easily.

"You're soaking me," I said on a grunt, pumping up all the way, her breasts bouncing in her own hands. "Fuck yes."

I couldn't take it anymore. She was the most beautiful, sexy female I'd ever beheld. And she was mine.

"Hold on, my sweet."

She leaned closer, pressing her palms on my chest for balance. Then I fucked up inside her in a fierce rhythm. Her tits bounced with each thrust, pulling a feral growl from my throat. Her mouth dropped open wide when I felt her climax coming, her cunt squeezing my cock hard.

"Ahh!" she cried out her pleasure, making me only want to fuck her harder.

In a flash, I had her under me, cradling her skull, her red hair spilling across my arms, my furs, my bed, my world, as I thrusted inside her like a madman, slamming home with ferocious need.

The whole time she moaned, her cunt pulsing with a long orgasm, or perhaps a second one as her skin began to glow white, the markings of her magick dotting her forehead, arms and breasts.

Suddenly, a look of intense determination swept over her face. She reached up and gripped my horns, even as I continued to fuck her fast and hard, my desire spinning me into a maddening frenzy.

She grabbed my two larger horns the way she liked to do, taking possession of her beast.

"You may not be ready to give me your bite, but I will give you mine."

She opened her mouth wide, her slender, pointed fangs curving, as she pulled me down to her. I went without a thought. Then she pierced the skin at the base of my throat, and I bellowed a groan, my cock jerking, my seed spilling inside her.

Euphoric pleasure washed through me as I clutched her to me, pulling her with me as I sat back on my heels, my cock speared deep, still pulsing, my knot locking tight.

She moaned as she suckled my blood, a pleasure-inducing elixir from her fangs filling me with such ecstasy I thought I'd die from it. Indeed, I wished I could die just like this, her fangs in my throat, my cock in her cunt, awash with pleasure and drowning in her scent. Drowning in her. My Jessamine.

My love.

I gasped at the realization, quivering with the new knowledge, worried that it would crush me entirely, break me into a thousand shards if she left me.

And yet, I still had to give her the choice.

She lifted away, sliding her fangs from my throat, a drop of my blood on her bottom lip as she looked down on me. Though I still had my hand at her nape, the other arm wrapped around her waist, it was my knot that held her closest to me.

She cupped my face gently, like she had the moment I told her what my father had done. Her eyes softened.

"You are not your father." She licked her lips and pressed a tender kiss to my mouth. "You are not responsible for his shame. Or your mother's death. Those were his choices."

I knew these facts. I'd been told the same by Bezaliel. By myself. But it was different, coming from Jessamine.

"You are a good leader, a wonderful protector of your clan. Of your friends." Another kiss, this time to my cheek, then my jaw. "Of me."

My heart expanded. I buried my face in her hair, inhaling her deep into my lungs. "Maybe I should mark you now. Not let you go."

She pulled away. "Ah-ah." She shook her head with a teasing smile. "You're going to wait. You want me with no lingering doubts, isn't that so?"

"It is."

"Then we wait until winter's end, when we return to Vanglosa."

We said nothing more, curling up together beneath the furs a short time later. I felt her body ease, her breaths slowing when she fell asleep. But I stayed awake a long time after, worrying over tomorrow.

Her plan might be the only one we had, but it was also a good one. The grimlocks would be drawn to the magick. They were conjured and formed by magick themselves, even if it was from some dark master hiding somewhere. So it was likely they would be easily summoned by her syrenskyn powers.

That was why I couldn't sleep. I had to ensure there was no way this could go wrong. The problem was, no matter how well we planned it, there were a million ways that it could.

CHAPTER 26

Jessamine

I wore only a blue cloak with a fur collar and soft hide slippers. The cloak draped to my ankles. While Redvyr wanted to protest the fact that I would be traipsing through the woods naked beneath the cloak, it was decided—by me and Tessa—that I was right. This would be the easiest way to use my powers quickly if and when one of the golems showed themselves.

Of course, when Leifkyn smirked and opened his mouth to make a comment about my attire, Redvyr shot him such a murderous death glare that he snapped his mouth shut instantly without a word.

Tessa, Lorelyn, and Shearah had taken every item of clothing and weapon that Redvyr and his warriors planned to wear and use and smudged them in magwort weed before also burning the weed in a tent with all of the items, to ensure the scent of beast fae was fully covered. Apparently, magwort weed grew in abundance in Wyken Woods and the surrounding woodlands. The only useful property of the weed was that its dark purple leaves could be boiled and used to dye clothing. It was more useful to us now because its pungent scent would camouflage the beast fae who had entered the woodland an hour before me.

The plan was for them to go in one at a time well ahead of me. Stealthily, they would take a position surrounding the old oak at the center of the woods. Redvyr had given me explicit instructions—thrice—on how to get there. He was beyond anxious. I soothed him, even though I didn't feel it. Especially now as I stood facing the woods with Shearah, Sorka, Lorelyn, and Tessa beside me, staring into the bleak semi-darkness.

It was midday and yet the sky loomed heavy with a thick, gray pall, promising snow soon. Wolf stood sulkily, his head hanging as I prepared to go without him. We knew none of the wolves could go on this quest. The grimlocks would certainly scent them and know that beast fae were nearby.

I exhaled an unsteady breath. "Well, it is time." I rubbed my palm down Wolf's neck. "I'll be back soon," I told him, hoping it was true.

Tessa reached out and took my hand as I stepped forward. She pulled me into a tight hug. "I know it is selfish to ask this of you, but by the Goddess Elska, I pray you bring my Saralyn back to me and that you return safely as well."

I hugged her back, feeling her sob against my chest more than hearing it. When we parted, Sorka pulled me into a tight embrace, whispering only a nearly inaudible, "thank you."

When I reached out a hand to Shearah and to Lorelyn as a goodbye, in case this was indeed a goodbye, they embraced me together.

"I scried with the snow upon the eastern Sister where the first light of dawn kissed its stone face. I melted it in the cup you used at dinner last night." She lowered her voice into my ear. "There is danger. There is certain death. But I see bright lights returning from the woods. May Elska be with you."

I stepped back and looked at the four of them—concern, hope, and fear etched into their solemn faces.

While many of the clan females still snubbed me or gave me a wide berth, these four women had given me something beyond hospitality and kindness. They had given me a sense of belonging. I rallied my courage, but it was more of a pretense than an actuality.

"I will use all the powers the gods have given me to bring the children home safely."

"May Elska be with you," Tessa repeated Lorelyn's blessing.

I smiled with all the confidence I could muster and gave a sharp nod of my head. "She will be."

Without another moment of hesitation, I turned and marched into Wyken Woods. When I rounded the first corner of the path, my friends no longer in sight behind me, I felt the oppressive air of this place.

It wasn't simply because it was winter and the trees' branches reached outward and upward like deformed limbs, rattling in a gust of wind with an eerie sound. Nor was it that the thick snaking of the branches overhead from tree to bare tree blocked out what little light there was in the sky above. There was magick here—dark magick.

I'd met a number of dark fae with magickal powers over the many months I lived in the Borderlands. Their birth didn't make their magick evil. It was the nature of the individual fae that determined whether their powers were used for good, the way the gods intended, or for more sinister, unholy pursuits.

I realized quickly that my father had been wrong about the dark fae. He preached and taught to not only his children, but his courtiers, his guardsmen, and his people that all dark fae were the enemy. A vile race who must be treated as the villains that they were.

I realized quickly that my father had been wrong. The gods didn't create a blessed fae race and a cursed one. They simply were borne of different gods—some had gifts of light and healing, while others had the gifts of power, to destroy and control.

Vix, an ancient god of the earth and his Mizrah—his blessed mate who was mortal—bore the children who would become the forefathers of the dark fae. The scholars' texts of Morodon stated that these children were the demons of fire, earth, shadow, and beast. Those of fire were the wraith fae, many of whom were fire wielders like King Gollaya. The shadow and beast demons were of course the fae with the same name. The earth fae were cursed by Vix's son Dagdal and banished from the world of the living.

As I continued deeper along the path, stepping over a particularly knotted root that jutted out of the dirt, I wondered at my own gift as a syrenskyn. It gave me the power to seduce and destroy an enemy. By all rights, I should be a dark fae, then. But I was not. I was kissed with a rare magick—so rare that no one among my people contained this power. Its existence was only known about because of the scholars' texts. And even they had been wrong. My power wasn't only for killing—it was for giving pleasure as well. I wondered about the goddess Nemia, patron of the sea, who had given me such a gift.

Why would she do so? What was my purpose?

Just as I wondered about these questions, a pulse of magick warmed my blood. It was as if Nemia herself were speaking to me, willing me to summon my power so she could show me what I was meant for.

The forest darkened as I grew closer to the center of the Wyken Woods. No animal made a sound as if all living creatures had fled this foul place. I realized why the naiads and dryads had forsaken it. This was a cursed woodland, and I didn't have to guess why. The grimlocks' presence would have tainted the air. I had not seen or heard any sign of them, but I could *feel* their vileness on every gust of the wind. If they weren't here now, they were close.

On instinct, I began to hum an old ballad. One I'd heard my grandmother sing when we sunbathing by the Nemian Sea. She was the one light in my life next to Draydyn, but she died when I was very young. I don't remember much beyond her tender smile, her loving touch, and this song she would sing to me and my sisters on those days at the white sand beach, though I always felt she sang it for me alone.

"Deep fathoms of the sea, whisper a beckoning to me, a longing to return to Nemia, our sweet mistress and queen."

A gale rattled the bare branches as I came into a clearing. Redvyr had told me that once I reached the clearing, I was nearly there. I simply had to continue on the worn path—a game trail that had been abandoned when all the animals left these loathsome woods. It would take me to the old oak.

I continued singing, noting that my skin had already begun to glow white, my syrenskyn powers awakening to the melody and perhaps the nearness of danger.

"The waves call us home, from this land not our own, singing a sad, sad lament, for her children who roam."

I walked along the path, thickened with the brush of magwort, its purple leaves darkening the ground. Turning the corner, I stepped out into another clearing, this one wider than the one I'd left. I gasped.

The old black oak was a monstrosity. His thick branches—wider than three beast fae—curved outward and dipped down toward the ground like spider's legs. Some of the branches were so thick and heavy that they grew into the earth before reaching back out of the soil toward the sky. The trunk was massive and knotty, thicker than the one Tylok had built with his family.

No trees grew anywhere near the old oak. That's why there was a clearing. He had forced the others to back away, likely because his roots extending above the ground and deep underneath devoured all the nutrients in a wide perimeter.

But that wasn't what sent a frightening chill down my spine. It was the unnatural, black viscous threads that spread out web-like from the middle of the trunk, oozing from a circular mass. The webbing wrapped in tendrils around every branch, as if it were strangling the old tree, slowly suffocating it.

What was more, when I approached its center where the mass was thickest, it pulsed with dark magick. I shivered.

I didn't see any sign of Redvyr or the four others who were somewhere nearby surrounding the great old tree, though I knew they were there. It was a different presence that prickled along my skin, raising gooseflesh.

Forcing myself to remain calm, I strolled in a semicircle in front of the old oak, continuing my song as if I hadn't a care in the world.

"The sea goddess of the deep, tells the skald fae they must keep, all their promises and vows, or her wrath they will reap."

Movement out of the corner of my eye drew my attention to the right. I watched the darkened brush, two red eyes glistening, intent upon me. My pulse raced, but I kept my casual pace, wandering back and forth before the tree. All the while, I summoned my syrenskyn magick, now beaming bright. I didn't have to look to see that my syren markings illuminated my skin with vibrant patterns of the palest white. The hum of power warmed me from the inside out. I kept singing, coming to the last verses which my grandmother had only ever sang to me, when my sisters and brother had wandered away, bored with her silly songs.

"There is one treasure of your kind. Centuries, you look but never find. When she comes to your shores, know she is light and dark entwined."

I stopped pacing as the grimlock crept farther into the clearing, his appearance more arresting than the others I'd seen when they attacked us. More than that, an oppressive heaviness radiated from the creature, making my breath falter.

"For her gift of syrenskyn, can save all of your kin. Lest you abuse her with foul lies." My voice vibrated with syren magick. *"Then your dark ages will begin."*

My grandmother had cried when she sang the last verse, and now I knew that she bore the sight. She wasn't simply entertaining the lonely granddaughter who didn't fit in with her siblings. She was telling me that one day I would turn my back on my own kind, because they'd forced me to, that I would fight for the fae that were truly my own.

Focusing on breathing in and out, I watched the repulsive creature stalk into the clearing. That aura of gloom came with him, filling up the space between and around us.

He was much taller than the others, his red eyes gleaming with cunning and calculation. He was an amalgamation of faekind, like the others. His ears were pointed long like those of a dryad, his hair a mass of sticks and fungus sprouting in disarray. He had six black horns curling out of his skull. His grayish-green skin, more green than the other grimlocks, was scaled like a serpent's. His fingers were twice as long as a normal fae, all spindly and bony, tipped with needle-long black claws.

He wore no clothing at all. The others hadn't either, but I hadn't noted it when they attacked us. I'd only seen their claws and wings and teeth diving at us, snatching away the children.

Now, I noted that this grimlock was easily as tall as Redvyr, though much thinner. Redvyr had thought they may not be equipped like other faekind, being more monster than male. But he was wrong. His chest was broad, his wings closer to that of a moon fae male—tall and wide, iridescent black. And between his legs hung a long cock.

"What are you doing here, she-fae?" His voice resonated more melodiously than the screeching cries of his minions. And still, a dark power emanated from him.

Was this the master who ate the light fae for power?

My heart beat faster, pulsing in my throat. I hadn't thought I would be using my magick on their lord.

"I have come seeking friends," I answered ambiguously, knowing it wasn't time to demand what I wanted. He was enthralled, that was certain, but I wasn't sure he was completely under my syren spell.

"I will be your friend." His red eyes glittered brighter as he took another step closer, the scent of soil and fungus and some earthy darkness I couldn't identify upon him.

"I am a princess," I confessed boldly, noting the excitement in his expression at this news. "I only have friends with great magick and power."

"I am my father's first born." He tilted his pointed chin higher, looking down at me with wariness as well as condescension, as if I were beneath him. "I am a powerful earth fae."

His father's first-born? So he was not the sorcerer, but likely the strongest of his father's grimlocks. He'd have the full potency of his father's blood running through his veins.

"First born? There are more like you?"

"My brothers are not as superior as I am," was his cold response.

"Only brothers? No sisters?"

"Females have no use."

"None at all?" I asked teasingly, letting my voice drip with suggestion.

"Perhaps one." He stepped closer, sniffing the air. "Your scent is of the sea."

"I am a skald fae."

"Far from home." His mouth slid wide as he grinned, revealing two rows of razor-sharp teeth.

"I am." My skin crawled. "My name is Jessamine."

"Jessamine," he hissed on a sibilant whisper, the wind echoing his voice amongst the branches above us. "I am Selestos."

"It is a pleasure to meet a powerful dark fae like yourself, Selestos."

The lies came so easily, falling so prettily from my lips.

"I've never heard a name like yours."

"That is because I am one and only. Selestos was the name of a fallen god. Like my father."

My heart tripped faster. "Your father is a god?"

That couldn't be. No god would create an abomination like this creature before me. Rather than answer my question, he eased forward with that devious gleam in his watchful gaze.

"You are deep in dark fae territory, singing a song of your goddess. While intrigued by these lovely markings upon your," he paused, perusing my exposed arms outside my cloak before dragging his baleful eyes down my lower legs to my ankles, then skimming back to my face and neck, "soft, soft skin, I cannot help but suspect you are intruding here for a purpose. I demand that you tell me, for you are a trespasser, most likely with ill intent in my woods."

He stepped boldly in front of the tree. It was a move to block me, to protect what he was hiding inside. It was now or never.

"You are unlike any creature I have ever known," I gushed, pouring my magick into my voice as I unclasped the hook at the throat of my cloak. "You appear so powerful and yet, so different than the other dark fae I've met."

With a swift flick, I dropped my cloak from my body, my glow illuminating the clearing. His red eyes widened, the luminescence from my skin shining on his scaly, green body. His cock hardened as he took hold of it, still staring at me in complete fascination. His member was a brighter green than the rest of his skin, which only turned my stomach. He was not of this world, his body an unnatural abomination.

"You are such a bright treasure, aren't you?" He crooned, his eyes glazing over. "You've come to give yourself to me." He stated the last words, rather than ask them as a question, all while he began to slowly stroke his hardening cock.

He'd already fallen into the stage where he believed I wanted him. That was part of a syrenskyn's power. Simply by revealing my body with luminescent markings, the victim falls into a delusion that I want them. It seems Selestos was already there.

The last time I'd used my magick, my father's target wasn't so obviously aroused. He'd kept his clothes on. But this creature was…other. He was not born into a world of civilities and proper etiquette. He was a monster made of raw, dark materials. He did not hide his obvious lust. I suppose that was an advantage, since I knew without a doubt that my magick was working.

My claws and fangs had already descended, but my goal wasn't to kill the creature. It was to persuade him with my magick to do my bidding. I'd never used it in this way. The last time I'd tried with the dryad stag, I'd failed. I had to test my strength of power over this grimlock.

"That is not my purpose here," I finally answered, "to give myself to you." I slid my hands up my thighs and along my hips, dragging his heated gaze to the movement.

He grunted, stroking his cock harder. "But you will."

"I might," I said coquettishly, combing my fingers through my unbound hair and covering my breasts in the appearance of being shy.

He frowned, sucking air between his serrated teeth, walking closer, still holding his cock firmly, idly stroking.

"You will, skald fae princess. Or I will make you."

He was nearly upon me already.

"Stop!" I shouted, thrusting my arm forward, palm out. He was so close, I could feel the heat of his chest against my palm.

But he had stopped, confusion contorting his expression. He wasn't sure why he'd obeyed. He didn't need to know. It was a type of magick he didn't understand.

Suddenly, I noticed several other pairs of red eyes appearing from around the trunks of the trees farther away from the giant oak. A chittering noise, a flap of wings. The other grimlocks were venturing into the clearing, very slowly.

I had to move quickly.

"I *will* give myself to you," I cooed, flicking my hair over my right shoulder so that he could gawk at my breast, the pattern of markings rounding the top in an elegant swirl. "But only after you give me a gift first."

"*Tell* me," he growled, his body trembling with obvious lust and frustration. "Tell me *now*."

I didn't hesitate.

"That tree holds a secret." I pointed over his shoulder. "I want to see what's hidden inside." My voice vibrated with power, whirling in the air like a whipping chain.

"Why?" he snapped harshly, even while he was panting, slowly stroking his cock which had swollen even bigger.

The chittering and sibilant whisper of his brothers speaking to each other grew louder as they appeared out of the shadows, mesmerized by the scene.

"I love secrets," I whispered, injecting my magick into my voice with more force, holding his eerie gaze.

My voice echoed through the boughs of the ancient tree.

Secrets, secrets, secrets.

There was a sudden pulse of vibration coming from the tree itself rather than me, as if he were responding with his own power, trying to join me in this fight.

The other grimlocks squealed, certainly feeling the vibration of my magick, keeping themselves at a distance.

My power hummed hotter than ever before, amplifying me with confidence. I'd never felt this level of magick blazing through my limbs, through my flesh down to my bones. An eerie wind blew through the clearing, lifting locks of my hair in the electric air.

"Show me your secret, Selestos," I whispered, my voice nothing but sex and seduction, "then I will lower to my hands and knees and let you mount me." I tilted my head to the other side, my hair cascading away to reveal my other breast. "That is what you want, isn't it?"

He blinked, bewildered, panting in frustration. "I can have you now," he snarled, but his voice was filled with uncertainty. "I am my father's son. I can *take* what I want."

"No, Selestos. You cannot. I am a special treasure. You cannot breach my magick. Why don't you try?"

I swore I heard movement in the woods beyond the clearing and the grimlocks squatting on or peeking from the perimeter of trees. My clansmen. But I didn't look, keeping my focus on Selestos.

He let go of his cock, which stood obscenely erect, as he thrust out his arms toward me, freezing with his hands halfway to my throat. I summoned from the well where my magick sprung, pulsing out a white light that vibrated from my body.

He grunted in distress, taking a step back, his hands shaking, still frozen in midair.

"You cannot take from me what I will not give." I slid my hands up over my hips and waist, over my breasts and down my belly. "If you want me, you must give me the gift I ask for."

Trembling, sweating, he looked over his shoulder at the oak. "You want only to see what is inside."

"You will open the door," my voice trailed with the essence of magickal persuasion, "and let me see what secrets are there. You will do this now."

"Then, come!" he bellowed, stalking across the clearing, over the knobby roots to stand in front of the black, viscous mass. "Watch what power I hold, skald fae," he hissed. "Then you will get on your knees for me."

He held both palms up toward the otherworldly mass feeding on the oak tree and whispered in a tongue I did not know.

The black mass shimmered and dripped faster, oozing with a grotesque noise of slime slicking away as it slid outward from the trunk's center.

Goddess above!

As the black film thinned and washed away, there in the darkness of the hollowed-out trunk, several pairs of frightened eyes and pale faces turned up to look at me. The first I recognized was Bes.

CHAPTER 27

Redvyr

All the fucking hells in the underworld.

I was going to slit that piece of shit from throat to cock and then rip out his entrails.

I'd nearly charged out of hiding, but Bezaliel caught my arm. It was his smart decision to stay by my side for exactly this reason. Leifkyn, Haslek, and Brohm were in the boughs of the surrounding trees, waiting for my command.

My body was poised to leap, watching Jessamine stand right behind that fucker Selestos, while he weaved his magick upon the tree. I kept perfectly still, waiting to see if the naiad sisters in the well had been right.

Suddenly, Jessamine gasped, staring into the gargantuan hole in the trunk, now void of that black mucous.

"Bes!" she screamed.

With a deafening roar, I leaped out alongside Bezaliel. My other warriors did the same, a cacophony of snarls and roars descending upon the grimlocks.

Lunging between Jessamine and Selestos, I slashed my blade toward his throat. He was wily, leaping and flying over and behind me. I spun. He landed with a hiss, facing me.

A banshee scream filled the woods as Leifkyn stabbed one of the golems through the chest. There was nothing but grunts and growls, blades and claws swinging.

I launched myself at Selestos. This time, he didn't move fast enough. My claws caught his shoulder. He growled and swiped back but I ducked in time.

He scrambled to his feet, crouched in a defensive stance. I shook my head.

"That won't help you," I told him with deadly intent. "I'm going to gut you and watch you bleed out with such great pleasure."

He narrowed his eyes, his needle-like claws poised to gouge me. With a deft move, I charged and ducked at the same time, slicing across the top of his thigh as he stabbed my left shoulder with three claws.

He shrieked, sounding more like his weakling brethren. With a swift glance around, I saw that most of them were already dead on the ground, Leifkyn and Brohm corralling one of the last two between them.

Selestos pressed a palm to the deep gash I'd sliced across his thigh, black blood dripping down his leg. "You cut me!" he bellowed, as if in disbelief.

"Don't fret, little golem. I actually missed." I spun my blade by the hilt, crouching, ready to go again. "I was trying to cut off your cock."

I wasn't sure if it was the *little golem* comment or the fact I meant to cut him where it would really hurt that had him launching and flying at me, his claws reaching for my face.

"Good," I growled, dropping my blades, ready for him.

Before he could gouge out my eyes, I grabbed his wrists and tumbled to the ground with him beneath me. I couldn't let go of his wrists or he'd have those knife-like claws in my throat, so I bashed him with the only thing I could. My head.

I pounded him once, twice, a third time and was rearing back for a fourth, grinning at the blood pouring from his nostrils and forehead, his dazed expression, the red eyes rolling in the back of his head, when suddenly Jessamine screamed.

Across the clearing, she held Saralyn in her arms, Bes clinging to her waist. There were three other children and Tylok's wife, Farla. For a moment, I was stunned to see her alive as she held the hands of her children.

Four more golems had flown in out of nowhere, another running in on foot and attacking Haslek before he could reach the women. One of the grimlocks shrieked and dove for Tylok's son, his shadow fae wings obviously broken, then Farla screamed and jumped in front of him, hauling back and hitting the golem.

"No!"

The golem spun with his claws, raking her across the neck.

"Momma!" yelled her daughter, falling on top of her.

Leifkyn and Brohm sprinted across the clearing as two more descended out of the skies. I had to help them, leaving the half conscious Selestos to launch over the dead golems to get to them. Another one dropped from the skies, shrieking like a ghost from the underworld.

"Where the fuck are they coming from!" yelled Leifkyn as he decapitated one and spun toward another.

Glancing to see that Jessamine was safely off to the side with the children, having pulled Tylok's daughter away from her mother sprawled across the tree roots, I spun to kill the enemies that were descending on us like insects. It was like they knew their brothers were in need and flocked to us, like a hive mind.

Lorelyn's words returned to me. *There are two voices.* They must hear their master, guiding them where to go.

If we killed them all, there would only be one left to deal with—the master who made them. And that fucker needed to die.

We assembled as one as we did in battle, corralling our enemies toward the center, giving them no way out. I leaped into the air toward one of them, clawing out his throat before we fell to the ground. We were making quick work of them when the children began to scream and cry, Jessamine yelling, "No! No!"

When I turned, all I saw was a fleeting glimpse of Jessamine, Saralyn held tightly against her chest, being grabbed around the waist by Selestos. He faced me and grinned right before he took a step back and disappeared into the earth with them.

Jessamine

Selestos spoke an ancient word as he gripped me from behind. Suddenly, a giant hole opened in the earth, filled with unnaturally dark water sluicing over the edges as if it was alive. Then Selestos leaped inside of it with me and Saralyn in his grasp. Icy water swallowed us whole as he held me around the waist with one arm and swam deeper into the abyss with the other.

By the gods, we were descending into hell.

I had always been able to hold my breath longer as a skald fae, but Saralyn was a babe. I covered her mouth and nose lightly, hoping with all that was in me that this underground channel he'd created with old magick opened up into a chamber of air. She kicked her tiny legs, her eyes wide and frightened, and that was the last thing I saw clearly as we descended deeper into this subterranean channel of dark water. And where was he leading us? Down into the chamber of hells of the afterworld?

The dim light above us grew distant.

I had not prayed to our goddess for many years, not since my parents had told me that the goddess had given me the gift of destroying and killing. I had been furious with Nemia for bestowing on me this body that my family and the courtiers thought vulgar and good for only one purpose—to seduce others as a whore, to murder and kill.

I abandoned Nemia, but now, in this abyss leading farther into darkness, knowing Saralyn would die soon, I opened my heart and I prayed to her.

Nemia, I beg you, help us survive. Help me find a way.

As the light faded from above, I heard a regal, powerful voice clear as the bright light of day ricochet inside my head.

I've given you all that you need. Use it! Do not be a quivering coward. Use your gift. Save the child. Save yourself!

Saralyn bucked in my arms, then went limp.

No! She couldn't die. I couldn't allow it!

Selestos had a grip around my waist as he let our bodies fall into this watery pit in the earth he had opened with dark magick. My upper body began to drift to the side of him then he gripped me tight by the arm as we descended further into darkness.

I pressed my forehead to the babe and thought, 'Please don't die, Saralyn.'

Then I removed my hand from her nose and mouth, reached down with my claws and scraped a deep gash across Selestos' cheek. A gargling scream bubbled up as he let go of my arm.

That brief instant was all I needed. Using my strength as a skald fae, I shoved him in the head with my foot, propelling myself upward, kicking my webbed feet and scooping the water with my free webbed hand. My lungs squeezed, beginning to fail, the babe still and unmoving in my arm as I rocketed toward the surface with all my might.

Don't die, Saralyn, sweetheart. Please, little love, don't die.

I swam faster than I ever had, the gray light of the forest coming closer and closer, someone leaning over the ledge and reaching into the dark waters frantically. There was muffled shouting, one of the voices was Redvyr for certain. Two muscular arms and hands I recognized reached down. He pulled me out before I breached the surface of water and laid me across his lap.

"Saralyn," I croaked, spluttering out water.

Her tiny body was pale blue, her lips purple.

"Please," I sobbed as Bezaliel jerked her from my trembling arms.

He wrapped her quickly in my cloak, which was already in his hands, whispering, "Hold on, my sweet girl."

Then he was on his feet and sprinting off with Haslek and Leifkyn behind him, both with a child in their arms. Brohm held Bes and another child in his arms and hurried after the others.

Redvyr hauled me close, my naked body still trembling from the icy depths and the terrifying plunge toward death. Wrapping my arms around his neck, I buried my face in the crook beneath his chin as he lifted me and bounded out of the clearing. All I heard was the pounding of beast fae boots, the crunch of snow and the swiftly beating heart of my love as he carried me back to the clan.

CHAPTER 28

Redvyr

"**S**till asleep?"

Bezaliel had stepped into my tent, but I hadn't even turned to see who it was. My sole focus was on Jessamine, who was sleeping after taking a healing draught from Shearah. Wolf remained at her side, reminding of when he'd first brought her into my hunting camp.

When we'd returned, she was trembling so much, her skin as white as snow, her lips turning blue like Saralyn. Even after I'd covered her in the furs in my fire-heated tent, she still quivered, her eyes listless like she was on the edge of death. It wasn't until Shearah rushed in with the draught Lorelyn had made that her tremors eased and she slipped into sleep.

Lorelyn had rushed to Sarlayn's aid to assist, and as of yet, I hadn't heard a word of whether the babe had survived.

Upon hearing Bezaliel's voice, I rose instantly and faced him, preparing for the worst. But the wet sheen in his eyes coupled with his smile told me what I longed to hear.

"She made it."

We met each other halfway and clasped one another as brothers. He thumped me on the back as I did him.

"Thank the gods," breathed Bezaliel. "Thanks to your female." He pulled away to look me in the eye, his gaze intense and powerfully vulnerable. "If it had not been for Jessamine, my baby girl would be dead. The wintry cold of the waters slowed her blood and her heart rate, even her need for air." His eyes widened in wonder. "Lorelyn said this can sometimes save those who might otherwise drown."

"By Vix." I gripped his nape. "We are blessed."

"Indeed."

On a heavy breath, he broke the embrace and turned to Jessamine, concern pinching his brow. "Is she alright? I'm afraid I was consumed with my own worries…I did not know she was—"

"She is well," I assured him, returning to Jessamine's side and sitting on the stool beside our bed.

Our bed. She was right where she belonged, her fiery red hair spilling across the pillow, her cheeks pink, her breathing steady and even. Safe and warm.

"I cannot begin to thank her enough for saving Saralyn. For saving all of them."

"Did they retrieve Farla's body?"

Bezaliel remained standing, crossing his arms. "Yes. Brohm returned to the battlefield as soon as he delivered the children. The clan females have wrapped her in a shroud."

I grunted my approval. "How are the other children?"

"Lorelyn told me they are all well when Saralyn recovered. Bes has been chatting away ever since she returned."

"Does she know who the other wraith child is?"

Finding both our clan's children, as well as Tylok's family and another wraith fae child, in the hidden chasm of the old oak was surprising to us all.

"His name is Gershal. He is from Belladum, but that is all she knows. Bes says he barely speaks at all. Apparently, he'd been in that tree all alone in the dark for longer than anyone else. The grimlocks would bring them insects and raw rodents to eat. They were starving, since they refused most of it." He grunted in disgust.

"They were trying to keep them alive for their master. Whoever he is." I clenched the fist on my knee, wishing I knew more. "These grimlocks aren't just after light fae or simply children either, but women as well. Perhaps, they are only taking them because they are weaker and can be overcome easier to drag back to their master."

I was frustrated that we now more questions than answers from when we'd begun. And while we'd defeated a horde of grimlocks, that foul fucker Selestos had gotten away. The frightening part was that Jessamine had clawed him she'd told me on our way back from Wyken Woods and that would've killed any fae, but Selestos was still alive.

What kind of black magick were we dealing with? And we still didn't know the identity of this lord of evil who was feeding on innocents.

"How is Hallizel?" I asked.

He chuckled. "Healthy as ever. She hasn't stopped fussing at me for not letting her go into the woods with Jessamine."

"I imagine she is." I smiled before adding, "She is well enough for a long flight, is she not?"

He nodded, sobering. "We need to speak with Prince Torvyn."

Bezaliel knew exactly what I was thinking. "We do. And soon. The naiad sisters I spoke to at the well declared that the monster causing all of this lives deep under Mount Gudrun. If we are now seeing the spread of his evil here, then they have certainly already seen more."

"King Halvar. The rumors have been spreading for ages that he is mad. If it's this madness that we know infected one of King Goll's warriors and those Meer-wolves who attacked their camp months ago, then it is this dark sorcerer whose caused it."

I nodded. Goll had confided in me that one of his own had been infected, but not with a regular sickness. It was like he was possessed by a dark demon, by black magick. I was sure this sorcerer who created the grimlocks was the cause.

"I never like to listen to gossip. But I would bet there is much truth to this one about the shadow fae king. That means Tor, Vallon, and the rest of them know more about this lord wielding black magick and abducting our kin than they have admitted."

I couldn't stifle the growl that rumbled in my belly. The mere fact that the prince and Vallon had more information and they didn't share it with us provoked the beast within me. They might have known something that we could have used to protect ourselves from Selestos and his fucking golems. I had a word or two to say to the shadow fae prince.

"I will send Hallizel to Gadlizel at once and demand a meeting."

"Good."

There was no need to tell them why or where to meet us. We'd seen shadow fae cross over Ghasta Vale every winter, high above us. They knew where we camped. And I had no doubt that all Hallizel had to tell them was that we killed the grimlocks they were hunting. They would swiftly be on our doorstep.

Movement pulled my attention to Jessamine. She turned her head in my direction, blinking her eyes open.

"Why are you growling?" Her voice was craggy from disuse.

Wolf whined as he stood beside the bed and licked her hand. She wiggled her fingers and patted him limply.

Instantly, I moved to sit on the furs next to her, coasting a hand to cup her cheek. "How do you feel?"

"Better." She smiled. "Why are you angry? Your growling woke me."

I chuckled. "Now I know how to get your attention when I want it."

Her sweet mouth tipped up on one side. "You always have my attention, Red."

I leaned forward and pressed my forehead to hers, gazing into the lovely depths of her eyes, relishing this precious moment, knowing she was alive.

Bezaliel cleared his throat. "My lord, may I speak to Jessamine?"

Having nearly forgotten he was there, I broke away reluctantly and stood, allowing him to come forward. He knelt on one knee at the side of the bed and bowed to her.

"My lady, I owe you my life for saving my daughter. For risking your own."

"No, Bezaliel." She smiled faintly, her body still frail. "I only did what my heart commanded me to do."

My lungs seized, and my love expanded for her even more. Her heart bade her save the children of my clan. That was because her heart belonged to us. She was mine, and I was hers. As was our clan.

I didn't have to nudge Bezaliel to get rid of him. He sensed my need to be alone with her.

"Get some rest, my lady. My mate would like to thank you as well. When you're better." He stood and smiled at me before ducking his head and leaving our tent.

I removed my loose shirt while shoving off my boots, her gaze following my movements with that tilted smile on her beautiful face. Heat flared within me as she trailed her eyes down my body when I shoved off my trousers.

"Don't even think about it." I lifted the covers and climbed in, pulling her body gently against mine. "I merely want to feel you. And warm you."

"I know ways you can warm me." She wrapped a hand around my waist, settling her head beneath my chin.

I sighed with absolute, profound relief and joy.

"Not today, temptress."

She ran the pads of her fingers up my abdomen, tracing the pattern of runes across my chest. "How are the children?"

"Alive and recovering." I paused. "Thanks to you."

She said nothing, but I had much to say.

"You were right. Your plan worked, but I'm still furious."

"You don't sound furious."

"That's because I have you safely in my arms. But when that…" I blew out a breath, a rumbling growl rising up my throat again, "that *thing* called Selestos thought to take you with him, I was going to follow you into whatever hell he took you to and drag you back."

She smoothed her palm over my heart, trying to soothe the beast of fury inside me. As always, I eased at her gentle touch.

"Where was he taking you?" I asked, fear replacing the rage.

"I don't know. But I believe to his master." She exhaled a deep breath. "He spoke to me in demon tongue at first. But he also spoke in a language I have not heard. I always prided myself on the number of languages I could recognize, but that one—"

"Godjin is what we call it. But I have never heard it spoken like that."

"What is it? Where is it from?"

"Godjin is an ancient language, believed to have been spoken by the gods themselves."

She pushed up onto her elbow, frowning down at me. "How could you know this language?"

"We only know a few words, actually. Dark fae god seers have recorded them from visions they've had of the old ones. In their visions, they can understand the language as part of their magick. I recognized one of the words the grimlock spoke. That is how I know it is Godjin he speaks."

"Does Lorelyn know the language?"

"As far as I know, no one truly knows the language. We only have pieces of it. There are old runes on some of the ancient monuments in different parts of Northgall. Some seers believe this is Godjin writing."

"But Lorelyn may know the words that we heard Selestos speak."

I grumbled at hearing his name. "She may. We will ask her."

She pushed as if to rise out of the bed.

"Where do you think you're going?" I asked.

"To speak with Lorelyn."

I instantly hauled her back to my side. "You are going to rest."

She wiggled against me, frowning at me. "I imagine I've been resting for hours already."

"Not long enough, stubborn female. You nearly drowned yourself! And besides, it is the middle of the night still. Everyone will be sleeping from the ordeal. You must sleep and get your rest."

Heaving a frustrated sigh, she remained still, no longer trying to struggle her way out of my arms.

"That's what I like," I told her, "an obedient female."

She pinched the flesh at my hip.

"Ow!" I jerked and snatched her by the wrist.

She scowled up at me. "I am not your *obedient* female."

I grinned, knowing I'd riled her temper, relishing that she seemed truly well now. "You usually are when I have my tongue or my cock inside you."

Her cheeks darkened with a heated blush, but she arched her brow, giving me that superior look that made me want to do naughty things to her.

"When I'm in your bed, then yes, I will *comply* with your commands, if only to seek my own pleasure. But I am not your female to be ordered around."

I grinned wider, lifting her hand to press a kiss to her palm. "No, you are not, my love." Holding her gaze, I opened my mouth against her palm, touching my tongue to her skin for a brief taste of her. "You are the mistress of my heart. Order me anything, and I will do it without question."

Her expression softened, her mouth smiling again. "Oh, Redvyr." She lowered her head to my chest.

Soon, we were both sound asleep.

CHAPTER 29

Jessamine

"The word he said before the earth opened up was something like, 'Vahka-dool'," I told Lorelyn from the bench by the fire pit, which was set in black cast iron on a short tripod, the same as in our tent. Wolf sprawled at my feet, his paw resting over my slipper.

We were gathered in Bezaliel's tent where Tessa held Saralyn, who was nursing at her breast. Leifkyn and Dayn, who was now mostly healed, joined us as well. Brohm stood with his arms crossed, scowling beside Dayn. I had come to realize that while Redvyr had many strong warriors, Leifkyn, Dayn, and Brohm were those he and Bezaliel trusted the most with the more delicate information or situations in the clan.

"'Vahka-dur' is what you likely heard." She rolled her tongue on the 'r' sound.

"Yes," I added excitedly, "that's exactly what he said."

"Do you know its meaning?" asked Redvyr, sitting beside me.

"When I was young, before I came to the Vanglosa clan, my mentor was a god seer. She taught me many things. One of them was the words of the Godjin that had been recorded by others." Her expression was sober and grave as she added, "Yes, I know the meaning of 'Vahka-dur.'" She rolled the 'r' again. "The literal meaning is, 'By the god's blood.' The god seers who have heard this command in their visions believe that it is a summoning power from the god who holds command over the dark shadows of the world." She swallowed hard before saying, "The most feared and twisted god of the underworld, Somdahl."

I frowned, for there was only one god of the underworld—Mavgahr. He was depicted as cold and somber, but also benevolent.

"Is this a dark fae god?" I asked, petting Wolf's back as he snoozed. "I've never heard of him."

Redvyr was scowling. "No one worships Somdahl. He keeps his souls in the deepest pits of the hells, where he tortures them endlessly. He is the lord of the most wicked and evil of spirits. He is only known as one to fear. That is likely why you have never heard of him."

"Great," snapped Leifkyn. "So this piece of filth Selestos was commanding the power of the most evil god known to dark faekind."

I shivered at the thought of him dragging me down into that abyss, no telling where he'd been trying to take me and Saralyn. Redvyr wrapped an arm around my waist, pulling me closer on the low bench we sat upon together.

"That makes sense," I added. "When Selestos first entered the clearing with the old oak, there was a pall of heaviness that came with him. I can't quite explain it, but I know it was dark magick radiating from Selestos."

"I felt it," said Bezaliel, his voice serious and deep.

"I did as well," agreed Redvyr.

"Aye," added Brohm.

A tinkling sound and the flapping of tiny wings alerted us to Hallizel arriving. Wolf twitched his ear and lifted his head then instantly laid it back down and closed his eyes.

The sprite had been gone for a few days since the incident in the woods. She zipped across the tent directly to Tessa and Saralyn, the babe snuggled tightly to her mother's bosom.

"Hallizel," said Bezaliel, the only one besides Tessa and the baby who she listened to, "did you deliver the message?"

The blue-bodied sprite turned her wide, round black eyes to the group, her taloned-feet clutching the blanket wrapping Saralyn's legs. The sprite was obsessed with and devoted to the infant. According to Redvyr, it had taken Bezaliel quite a lot of convincing and coercion to get her to leave Saralyn to deliver the message to Prince Torvyn in the Solgavia Mountains.

"Yes," she chirped in her high trilling voice. "I delivered the message."

"Did you deliver it to Prince Torvyn? Or his priest, Vallon?"

She blinked her owlish eyes and shook her head, the blue feather-like hair at her neck puffing up. "I could not find him."

Bezaliel heaved out a sigh. "Who did you tell?"

"My lady's sister." She turned to Tessa.

"Murgha?" Tessa asked excitedly. "How is she?"

Hallizel hopped up the blanket to perch on Saralyn's middle, making a happy purring sound. "Yes, my lady," she told Tessa. "Your sister is very well. So pretty and kind. She fed me and gave me a soft pillowy bed to sleep in before I left."

Bezaliel growled, annoyed. "*Hallizel.* Why did you not tell the prince or his second as I'd asked?"

"Because Murgha said she did not think they would return anytime soon. That is what she said," Hallizel trilled, then turned her attention to Saralyn who was no longer nursing, but sleeping soundly. "The prince and his priests are hunting the grimlocks."

"Not very well," Leifkyn snorted. "If they were, they'd be right here in Wyken Woods where we killed them all."

"Perhaps," Redvyr added soberly, "we did not kill them all. There could be more than one horde. There could be far more."

Silence fell within the tent, the fire crackling. After a while, our thoughts buzzing but no one saying a word, Redvyr took my hand and pulled me to stand with him.

"There is nothing more to be done now. We have burned the carcasses in the woods. Shearah wants to try and save the old tree by giving it special nutrients to counteract the black magick spell that left a hole in its trunk. Dayn, you will lead a party with her tomorrow so that she may try."

Leifkyn grinned and nudged him with his elbow. Dayn shoved him back and scowled.

"Other than that, we will keep watch at the border of the camp that leads to Wyken Woods. Be vigilant in *all* patrols." He looked at Bezaliel. "See that the guards understand that the danger may not be gone."

"Of course, my lord." Bezaliel stood as did the others, following us to leave.

I shared a smile with Tessa. "Goodnight."

"Come and visit tomorrow," she told me.

"I will," I promised.

Tessa hadn't wanted to leave the tent, keeping Saralyn in her arms except to allow Bezaliel to hold her. She'd been relieving herself in a chamber pot in the tent, terrified that if she left even for an instant, her precious babe would be snatched from her arms.

Tessa was the clan healer, but Lorelyn and Shearah had stepped in and taken over. But Tessa's injury wasn't a wound to be cured with a salve or a suture. It would take time, compassion and love to heal this heart-wound.

As we stepped out, I walked toward the open area beyond their tent which was close to mine and Redvyr's on the southern edge of the camp. The others waved and ventured off in different directions.

I faced the setting sun and the hills beyond Ghasta Vale. The fading light cast a pink and golden blanket over the snow and rolling landscape in the distance. Redvyr stepped up behind me and wrapped both arms across my upper chest, pulling me against him.

"What troubles you?"

I clasped his thick wrists, wanting to hold onto him. Needing to feel his hold on me, his strength at my back. There was something terrible going on in the world, an intangible menace that was growing and spreading. My heart felt bruised and hollow from what we'd seen. What we'd survived. And it wasn't over.

"Tessa," was all I answered, watching the fading light paint the far-off hills, wishing the winter was over so that we could return to Vanglosa.

"Give her time," he murmured, squeezing me close.

"How long before your men return from the Bolgar clan?"

He had sent Haslek with two others to the Bolgar clan's winter encampment to warn them of the grimlocks. Though we'd hoped we had encountered and killed the only horde, Selestos had escaped. And there was no guarantee that there weren't more of these golems roaming the wilds of Northgall.

Redvyr had instructed the clan leader of Bolgar, which was no longer his grandfather who had died a few summers earlier, to send word to the next clan. The new leader was a younger beast fae named Behrvyne. Redvyr had told me that there was a chain of communication between the clans in times of crisis. The other clans would be informed quickly to be on guard for the grimlocks.

"I'd say tomorrow or the next day."

"Will we break camp sooner and return home?"

He pressed his mouth to the crown of my head. "Home. I love that word on your lips, my heart."

Smiling, I admitted, "I do, too."

He kissed me again at my temple. "As soon as we see the first sign of the snows melting over those hills, we will leave for Jôhl Tundra. I've sent word to Behrvyne of this. The other clans will likely join us sooner as well."

"I think Tessa will fare better when we return to Vanglosa."

"Indeed. In the meantime, she will find comfort with visits from her new friend, the light fae, who is soon to officially join our clan. When we are bound beneath the sacred tree."

"Hmph." I turned in his arms and set my hands on his broad shoulders, loving the mightiness of his figure. He made me feel safe and precious. "I do not recall you officially asking me to be your wife, beast lord."

His smile was easy and mesmerizing, his fangs prominent. He wrapped his hands around my waist, spanning his fingers across my back. "Will you become my one and only mate before my clan, Jessamine?"

I smiled. "I will tell you at winter's end. That was our bargain, wasn't it?"

He slid his hands to my hips and squeezed, his golden eyes dancing with the knowledge that I would certainly say yes when the time came. "It was."

Laying my cheek against his chest, I hugged him closer. "Now what shall we do to while away the winter?"

"I can think of something." He pressed one last kiss to the crown of my head, then took my hand and led me back to our tent.

CHAPTER 30

Redvyr

The winter passed quickly. There were no more instances of danger, no sign of the golems or that fiend Selestos. The only excitement that stirred the camp was that of Dayn trying to court Shearah. He accompanied her into the woods daily to try and save the old oak tree.

I hadn't entered Wyken Woods since that dreadful encounter with the grimlocks. Since I saw Jessamine get swallowed into that hole and feared I'd lost her forever, I refused to step foot in the place. But Dayn reported that the tree was indeed healing, the black fungus-like threads that had wrapped around every branch had been killed by Shearah's tonic. They'd filled the hole in its trunk with nutrient-rich soil dug from the winter garden, and while that left less room to grow the winter vegetables, no one had minded. Actually, several clansmen had offered to help, but Shearah had taken on the task alone—with her one helper.

One thing about beast fae that perhaps other faekind didn't realize was that our connection to nature wasn't one-sided. It gave to us, so we gave back as best we could. The old tree in Wyken Woods had sheltered children from our clan and innocents of our realm. In return, we would try to save it if we could.

As planned, when Bezaliel reported the first melting of snow in the valley of Ghasta Vale, we quickly packed up camp and caravanned south toward Jôhl Tundra. I'd never thought that the golden-brown prairie grass sticking out of the patches of snow across the valley would be such a welcome sight.

Winter had finally waned. By the time we reached the tundra, there was no sign of snow at all except on distant mountain peaks. Though spring wasn't here yet, the temperatures were milder, warm enough to exchange our hide trousers for our leather skirts.

I walked beside Wolf who carried Jessamine. She returned my smile when I gazed up at her—still wrapped in her cloak—but there was tension around her eyes. It was to be expected. She would meet all of the beast fae clans at once. Even for those of our kind, it could be intimidating.

In these last months of winter, we had spent a great deal of it in our furs. While we enjoyed one another's pleasure, it was the pleasure of her company and her laugh that I cherished the most. We often ate alone in our tent, with the exception of Wolf of course, and we shared stories of our past, both good and bad.

I'd learned that I would have considered her brother Draydyn a brother of my own. He had been a fae of honor. Jessamine had asked me to retell the story of how I'd found Wolf as a pup cornered by a barga and about to become the giant bear's meal. I'd killed the barga of course and Wolf had been my companion ever since. Now, we both protected each other, though he seemed more intent on protecting her than me these days. I was grateful of course.

When I showed her which skin had been the one of the barga that had almost killed Wolf, she had made a show of spreading it on the floor on her side of the bed as her rug to stand on each morning and night. She'd even stomped on it and muttered a curse under her breath, to which Wolf had barked in agreement.

These months had been nothing less than sheer bliss. So I could see why her face showed lines of tension, that our little paradise was seemingly over. I'd make it up to her when I brought her back to Vanglosa.

The festival activities of the winter gathering often took on a raucous and uncivil bent when beast fae males did their best to impress the females. And though Jessamine wasn't beast fae, nor was she unspoken for, I could already imagine some of the males doing their best to garner her attention.

She had no tail or horns, but she was fair beyond comparison. Her hair, the color of spring red-berries, drew the eye, especially when she wore it loose and blowing in the wind as she did now. I was ready to proclaim to the other clans that she was my mate. Whether she had taken my bite or not did not change the fact that she was my gods-given mate. And that, I would make clear to anyone who questioned it.

As we descended the hill leading into the tundra, it was to see several clans already encamped and milling about the annual gathering place. We always camped close to the backside of the largest butte on the tundra. There was a small stream running between it and another cavernous rock on our western side, which gave us protection from the winds that gusted across the tundra. Especially at night, when the temperatures dropped.

As we approached our desired camping spot, some called out and waved, gathering closer as our long line—the largest clan of all—meandered into the shadow of the butte.

The tall figure of Behrvyne stalked closer to meet us, a throng of his young warriors at each side. His russet hair streamed down to his waist, his four black horns curling higher than most beast fae, and his dark brown tail lashing in the breeze as we neared him. Those who didn't know him might think his demeanor aggressive and hostile, but I'd known him since he'd first begun to train as a warrior for the Bolgar clan. He was a serious male, that was all.

"Do not be afraid," I whispered up to Jessamine as we came to a halt before they reached us. I helped her down off Wolf's back. "He looks mean, but he always looks that way."

She blew out a breath, holding onto my arms as I gripped her waist. "Good to know. I was about to ask if we could return to Ghasta Vale."

I flashed her a smile. "No, my heart. This is our last stop before Vanglosa. And you know what that means."

Her gaze lingered on my fangs, which somehow made my cock hard. "I know what it means," she said softly. And though she smiled, it was small and less confident than usual.

Taking her hand to assure her all was well, I guided her toward our greeting party. Bezaliel, Leifkyn, Dayn, and Brohm flanked us as we approached them.

Among the clans of beast fae, the Vanglosa was the oldest and considered the most superior in rank, if indeed there was a rank. But the Bolgar clan was second, and Behrvyne might be young, but he was a fierce leader who was respected by all who knew him. Whenever there was trouble in our lands, the rest of the clans turned to the two of us for guidance and answers. I knew that Behrvyne would want to speak privately about the golems while we were here.

He strode in the center of his warriors, his gaze fixed entirely on Jessamine, his scowl intense before transforming into wonder when he saw that her hand was clasped in mine. Beast fae lords didn't often show public affection to the females they claimed, or their mates. But I wanted it to be clear to all that she was mine. No one was to treat her as anything other than a female who deserved respect among the clans. So it was intentional that I kept her hand in mine when we reached them.

"Greetings, Lord Redvyr," said Behrvyne, arching a brow in question.

"And you. Your clan faired well for the winter?"

"We did. I was concerned to hear yours did not."

Bezaliel shifted next to me. Tessa and the babe weren't far behind us, well within earshot, and I was still aware of her tender state. Though she had improved greatly, especially when we began packing to leave, she was still emotionally fragile from the abduction of Saralyn.

"We are all well now," I assured him.

His gaze flicked to my right again, his gaze slipping over my mate. "I heard that you have a new member of your clan." He paused. "Won't you introduce us?"

He must've heard some rumors somewhere. Good. That would make it easier to establish the truth of it.

"This is my mate, Jessamine Glenmyr, daughter of King Darian of Morodon."

His red eyes widened, one of his warriors glancing in surprise at another. They knew I had a light fae female among my clan, and had likely heard that she warmed my bed, but they did not know her origin or that I had claimed her as my mate. Well, I would claim her officially soon enough, but I wanted everyone here to understand that I perceived her as my own already. It was the only way to ensure that no one treated her poorly.

When he spoke, his words were cautiously presented. "I had not known we sought an alliance with the kingdom on the Nemian Sea."

"We do not," I assured him. "Her father doesn't know where she is."

"Nor do I want him to," she said quickly.

Behrvyne's red eyes narrowed only slightly. "You don't want your father to know you're consorting with the beast fae, my lady?"

At least he called her 'lady', but a low growl rumbled in my belly. I was ready to punch the young lord in his pretty face.

"I will gladly inform my father that my *consort* is Lord Redvyr of Vanglosa when I'm ready," she answered haughtily, her chin jutting in the air. "But I will not do so until we've returned safely to Vanglosa, and our clan is settled back at our home in Meerland. My father can be violent when he hears news that displeases him."

"You admit," interjected Behrvyne, speaking without aggression but certainly determination, "that it is not a welcome union to your people."

My own ire vanished when I saw that her anger had sparked, her cheeks pink with passion. "The people of my birthplace abandoned me, in a way."

Every warrior's gaze was riveted to her. I simply kept her hand in mine, reassuring her with a soft squeeze that I approved of her anger.

"They threatened me, tried to force me to do harm to others. To use my magick for foul deeds and crimes. They did not treat me as one should treat their own child, like a blessing from the gods. So what they welcome or reject is no longer my concern." Her voice was steady even while I felt her anger simmering. "I have chosen my own people." She met my gaze, her green eyes blazing bright. "And the gods have sent me a mate far superior than any my father would've chosen for me. I do not care what my family or the people of Morodon think. My home is no longer with them."

By the gods, I wanted to drag her to the nearest tent and fuck her hard and true. She was so fierce, my Jessamine. By the slight curve of Behrvyne's lips, I realized he had accepted her, though I was sure many here would not. I didn't plan on staying overlong here at our solstice gathering. My clan had been through a hard and harrowing winter. As soon as it was permissible, we would pack and move on home.

"You are welcome to join the clans' feast at our solstice celebration, Lady Jessamine."

He reached out and took her free hand in both of his, pulling her gently forward, forcing her to release me. He bowed over her hand, a gesture of honorable respect. The others would accept her now as well, even if they disagreed with my choice in mate. Of course, if they believed me, they would know I had little choice at all. The gods had made her mine. One bedding had proven that without a doubt.

"Thank you, Lord Behrvyne." She appeared very much the royal light fae that she was in that moment. And I couldn't have been prouder.

"We have much to speak of," I told him, "but for now we will settle in."

"Of course. And the Skel Clan has brought many barrels of ale. We will celebrate tonight."

Laughter and excited chatter lifted from behind me where my clan waited.

"Tonight," I agreed, then called over my shoulder, "Let's make camp!"

CHAPTER 31

Jessamine

"Are you ready?" Shearah asked, peeking her head inside the tent.

I was dressed, but I wasn't ready. I was rather terrified. I might've been brave when meeting the clan lord of Bolgar, but that was only because he seemed to accuse me of being ashamed of Redvyr and wanting to protect my family from such a shame. My anger had given me the courage to lash out with brave words.

Now, standing in the new dress Sorka had sewn for me, preparing to face all of the beast fae lords, their wives, and the clans, I shrank from it. Redvyr had been asked to meet with the clan lords before the festivities tonight. They were too eager to discover the details of our attack by the grimlocks to wait until after the festivities tonight. I couldn't have asked him to stay behind just because I was frightened to walk into the gathering alone.

"Oh, Shearah, thank the gods." I rushed to her and pulled her fully into our tent.

She looked lovely in a short dress made of red deer hide that hadn't been dyed, with detailed stitching of vines and flowers around the hem at her knees and on the sleeves.

She laughed when I hauled her into the tent, stopping with wide eyes when she took in my attire.

"Blessed goddess." She stepped back to look me up and down. "You look so lovely."

"As do you."

I glanced down at the cream-colored hide, smoothed to a soft leather, that was detailed with delicate red flowers along the scooped bodice. It was tailored perfectly to cinch at my waist and curve over my hips, stopping just above the knee. I wore the long boots Sorka had made for me before we left Vanglosa.

"That dress is like nothing I've ever seen Sorka create. She put her whole heart into it, didn't she?"

Blushing, I nodded. "She told me she wanted to do something special for me for bringing Bes back." I shrugged. "I told her it wasn't just me that got her back, but she insisted."

Shearah smiled, her tail swishing happily behind her. "You did more than you think. And now, I know you're absolutely terrified of this first night's feast, so we decided to come and fetch you."

"We?"

She grabbed my hand and tugged me outside. Dayn was waiting there, staring off into the distance where the drums were already being played at the campfires.

"Are we ready, ladies?" he asked, turning to us.

"No, but we might as well go," I admitted.

They both laughed, and the three of us set off together. The rest of the camp was quiet since everyone had already gathered close to the base of the rust-red butte that protected the camp from the fierce gales that crossed the tundra.

A piercing howl echoed into the night, then others answered the call. Redvyr had told me that it wasn't only the clan members that enjoyed this reunion each year. The wolves ran together across the tundra at night, a joyful pack howling at the moon. There was only a sliver of a crescent moon tonight peeking between the low, gray clouds.

As we neared the celebration, I counted six campfires spread out in perfect symmetry. There was a long stone platform raised higher than the others where the clan lords and their mates and warriors sat. The stone platforms must have been erected years ago since this was their annual meeting place. The edges and surface looked smooth from long use.

There were long tables upon the platform and surrounding the campfires as well as benches for those not participating in the dancing. That was what drew my eye as we entered the celebration. Two straight lines of beast fae females performed some sort of dance in unison. They wore extremely short skirts that barely reached the bottom of their thighs, and corset-like tops that covered their breasts and the top of their torso, leaving their bellies bare. Their hair was unbound except for a single braid on top of their heads that wrapped around their horns.

The dance that they performed to the beat of the drums and the lively flutes that Bowden and a few men from other clans played was a joyful, seductive romp. They swayed their hips in sinuous curves in opposite rhythm to their shoulders, their bare feet moving in tiny circles until they faced away from the dais. The dancers trilled in unison, some kind of female war cry it seemed to me, swaying their backsides, their tails also swinging in unison.

"What is this?" I asked Shearah in a whisper.

"The first of many dances by the bathka."

"I don't know that word. Bathka." Which bothered me, since I prided myself on my knowledge of the dark fae language.

"Hmm. It doesn't have an exact translation. It means free, unbound women. They are all single and seeking their mates."

Something soured in my belly as I watched the dance of seduction, the beautiful beast fae females showing off their bodies. It wasn't simply envy that burned in my chest, but admiration for the fact that the beast fae were open with their beauty, specifically feminine beauty. It was cherished and celebrated, while my own family had made me feel vulgar and obscene for simply being born the way I was.

"Yes," added Dayn, leaning down to whisper, "but they aren't all seeking mates. Some are simply seeking a partner to warm their furs for the solstice."

Shearah slapped him on the arm. "Stop looking so closely, Dayn. Or should I be seeking someone else to share my furs?"

His growl was instant. "I'll blind myself, female, if it makes you happy. But I'll gut anyone who dares to touch you at this solstice, or any other."

He dragged her off to the side for a kiss, which urged me onward on my own. While the dancers held most everyone's attention, I noticed that Redvyr's was solely on me as I walked up the stone steps to the platform. He sat at the very end, which I realized was one head of the table, with an empty seat beside him, and Behrvyne sat on the opposite end.

While Behrvyne had been polite and civil, Tessa had warned me not to expect a grand welcome at the solstice gathering. She confessed to me that she had been shunned by most beast fae her first time here. It wasn't much better her second time, either. This was the third year since she had joined the Vanglosa clan, and while she had borne a child to add to their clan numbers—something that was still rare among beast faekind—she didn't much care to join in the celebrations.

She had told Bezaliel she wanted to stay in their tent and rest from the long journey. Bezaliel was encouraging her to come at least for a little while as they walked away to their own tent. I'd wanted to beg off and stay with her, but I thought it would make me appear cowardly. That wasn't how I wanted to present myself as the future wife of the beast lord of Vanglosa.

So I mustered my courage and sauntered across the platform. I felt eyes on me, which I expected. Redvyr had already announced clearly to Behrvyne and a group of his warriors that I was his mate, and I was an outsider. Not only was I a light fae, but I was skald fae—the race who lived farthest from them. I imagined that most of those here had never seen a skald fae, much less have one join them at their table.

Redvyr stood as I approached, my heart pounding fiercely by the time I reached him. Bezaliel was in the seat on my other side, thank the gods. He stood as well to greet me. I exhaled a sigh of relief as I settled, smiling at Tessa with Saralyn sleeping in the sling crossing her chest. It seemed Bezaliel had convinced her to come to the feast anyway.

The beast fae male across from me drank from a giant goblet that appeared to be made of black glass, a flower carved at its center. He stared at me keenly.

"Won't you introduce us, Redvyr?"

"Aye." He reached under the table and squeezed my hand, offering some comfort. "This is my mate, Jessamine Glenmyr."

He gestured with his free hand to the lord staring me down. "Jessamine, this is Walgar. Lord of the Stol clan. They keep along the Bluevale River to the east."

"Hello, Lord Walgar."

If he was surprised that I addressed him as lord, he didn't show it. While this lord was equal in size to the biggest of their kind, only two horns curled out of his head rather than four. They also curled lower over his skull. Gray streaked his hair, hanging loose to his shoulders, except for several thin braids at the front that fell along his temples. His eyes were a piercing orange, runes cascading from his forehead down along his jaw and the sides of his throat.

He may have only two horns, but he obviously had proven himself to the gods with so much rune-sign.

"You are the daughter of a king of your kind, are you not?" he asked brusquely.

"I am," I answered evenly, noting the woman at his side, her hair silky black and also streaked with white, though her bronze-brown face showed little signs of aging. She was strikingly beautiful, her pale, gold eyes watchful.

"I find it strange you are so far from home. So far from your kind."

A low growl resonated from Redvyr, but I squeezed his hand. He didn't say anything, thankfully. I didn't want him fighting anyone and everyone who seemed to disapprove of my presence here. I had to do some of my fighting on my own.

"I can imagine you do."

I glanced out at the clan members milling around the other campfires with cups of ale and hearty laughter, the bathka having ended their dance. I could see the subtle differences in the clans, mostly by their clothes and how they chose to wear their hair. Sorka and her guild had a particular style of stitching and tailoring that I could spot easily in a crowd, and the other clans had their own unique way of tailoring and decorating their gowns with beads and metal. The Vanglosa clan mingled with all of the others, an easy camaraderie that I would never witness at my father's court.

"Tell me, Lord Walgar. What do you see when you look out there?"

He frowned, his back to the crowd and campfires. The woman who must be his mate turned to look behind her. Reluctantly, he did the same.

When he turned back to face me, he said, "Beast fae. Drinking and talking."

My gaze caught on Bes dancing with a young beast fae male, obviously in his teen years like her, his body tall but still very lean, his horns not as thick and long as the adult males. He held her hands and guided her in a circle, bending their knees to the beat of the drums. Their movements were awkward next to the adults dancing with their partners in a similar fashion, but there was joy on their young faces. Sorka watched from nearby, smiling.

Not far behind them, sitting on a thick log near one of the campfires were Tylok's children and the wraith fae boy, Gershal. Leifkyn knelt next to them, a rough wooden game board in front of them, pointing to parts of the board as he talked. He was teaching them to play kings and bones, a game I'd seen many regulars play in the corner booth at Haldek's tavern.

Walgar's woman at his side, most likely his wife, then added in a soft, serene voice, "I see many clans celebrating together. Old friends greeting one another. New ones being made. Lovers finding partners."

I couldn't help but smile. "Yes, my lady. All of those things at once. What I see-"

I stared past them where Brohm was throwing his head back in laughter, two other males I'd never met before gesticulating wildly as they both seemed to tell a story at once.

"What I see," I said again, "is an interconnected people who not only support one another to survive, but they come together in fellowship and celebration so they might thrive." I met Walgar's gaze, his expression pensive. "That is not something I have ever seen before. Not in my father's court, and not in the nearby townships that we visited a few times. It is a treasure I recognize as valuable."

His wife smiled, her eyes crinkling in the corners.

"I am far from the place of my birth, Lord Walgar, but that was never a home for me." I looked at Redvyr, my belly flipping at the intense admiration in his gaze. "I have found my home with Lord Redvyr, and the Vanglosa clan of Meerland."

I felt the eyes of a few others on me from farther down the table. The beast fae's heightened senses helped them not simply for hunting or sensing danger but also in eavesdropping. Not that I minded. I wanted the other clans to know what I said, how I felt. Until I heard one of them say, "She doesn't wear his mark."

When I glanced toward the couple on the other side of Walgar's wife, they both averted their gazes, the female with a sneer. I'd experienced worse in my father's court. Still, I had to admit the idea stung. That Redvyr's people might find me lacking as his partner.

"And what of the wraith king?" Walgar asked Redvyr, switching the subject. Whether it was to avoid the tense awkwardness at the table or simply to be polite, I was relieved.

Redvyr glared daggers at those down the table whispering far too loud and making a show of ignoring us at this end of the table.

"What do you mean?" Redvyr asked, forking slices of roast meat from a platter onto his plate.

"Word is that he rules all of Lumeria as well as Northgall now. That he kills his own men."

"He kills his men when they commit treason," Redvyr stated coldly.

Those who had been ignoring us before now tuned into the discussion.

"You know this for certain?" asked the male sitting next to Walgar's wife.

"Aye," Redvyr answered, anger still lacing his tone.

"We were told he slaughtered his own brother," said another farther down. "That he tore him to pieces with his bare hands then lit him on fire with his magick."

"Half-brother," Redvyr corrected, forking a bite of roast meat into his mouth. "And yes, he ended him in such a way."

When he said no more, the same male asked, "What had he done to betray Gollaya? To deserve such a death?"

It was Bezaliel who spoke up. "He kidnapped Goll's mate, his queen, with foul intent. So yes," he said, his voice now dipping with irritation, "he slayed the man that was supposed to protect his mate rather than cause her harm. Then he burned him to ash."

"I'd do the same," growled Redvyr, sitting back in his chair and drinking ale from his cup, glaring over the rim down the table.

I didn't think the other clansmen disliked me enough to cause me harm, but Redvyr's warning sent a shiver down my spine all the same. The good kind.

I hadn't known this about King Goll and his queen, but it didn't surprise me after meeting him. He wasn't a fae to be trifled with. Neither was Redvyr.

"I think I'll go to bed now," said Tessa, looking at Bezaliel. "Saralyn is tired."

"I'll go with you," I offered.

Even though I hadn't eaten a thing, I was more than ready to escape the feast table. My presence was causing tension which was upsetting Redvyr. He needed time with the other clan lords. I understood from other's stories about this feast gathering that it was only once a year, and it was a time for bonding to keep the camaraderie and peace between the clans.

I stood but Redvyr grabbed my hand. "You don't have to go," he said in a low voice, wrapping his tail around my ankle like he so often did.

Smiling, I squeezed his hand. "I'm tired from the journey as well. I'll walk Tessa back and get some rest." I stepped closer and whispered, "I'll be waiting for you when you come to bed."

He lifted my hand, holding my gaze, and pressed a kiss to the inside of my wrist. "I'll wake you when I return."

With that, I bowed my head politely to Walgar and his wife. I even smiled at the others down the table, their expressions mixed—some irritated, some welcoming, some bewildered, and some altogether unreadable.

I followed Tessa, who was already down the stairs and halfway across the feasting area when I caught up to her.

"Thank you," I told her. "You gave me an excuse to leave early."

"To be honest, they were quite civil with you."

I laughed as we passed the last campfire and turned between two tents and headed toward our clan's side of the encampment.

"That was civil? I hate to see rude."

She laughed too, the first time I'd heard her do so since we'd recovered Saralyn and Bes. "I didn't receive one welcoming word from anyone in the other clans my first time here. I'd proven myself as a competent healer among our own clan, so they stood by me. By the time I returned my second year, I received more kindness. They aren't quite so openly rude to you because you are Redvyr's mate. He is a well-respected lord among the clans."

"I am sorry to hear they treated you poorly. But I can take a few hard looks and harsh words. My father's court was far more vicious. Of course, that was because my own parents were the ones who often spoke ill of me in front of others. The courtiers were only following their lead."

Tessa frowned at me, Saralyn asleep in her arms. "Your own parents did that?"

I shrugged, the pain a dim memory now. The leagues of land between us seemed to dull the hurt they caused me.

Even though it had been less than one year since I'd left, it seemed like forever ago that I stood in my father's study like a mare up for auction, his ambassadors openly ogling me. My brother had only been buried a month when my father summoned me and his ambassadors to him. He'd had me wear my finest dress and even had me turn in a circle so they got a good look at me. His awful words still rung in my ears: *She will fetch a high price. Her magick is worth her weight in gold. And her body is made for breeding. Any husband could get several heirs from her. I want only the highest offers brought to me.*

Not long after, the highest bidder, Lord Gael of Mevia, appeared at the palace gates, and I was sold before I'd even met him.

"It doesn't matter now," I told Tessa as the laughter and voices at the feast grew dimmer. "I'm where I'm supposed to be now."

Perhaps Redvyr was right and the gods do know best. If my brother hadn't been killed in battle, then my father wouldn't have been so bold to sell me to Lord Gael. And I wouldn't have run away, eventually finding myself here, with this dark fae lord that I loved.

The sudden realization punched me so hard in the heart that I gasped.

"Are you okay?" Tessa reached out a hand and grabbed my arm, thinking I might've stumbled.

"Fine," I said a little weakly as we walked along the stone edge of the butte. "I'll just be glad when we return to Vanglosa."

"You and me both." She sighed, stopping in front of her tent to face me. "It will get better, this difficulty with the other clans. I promise."

I pulled her into a hug, making sure not to crush or wake Saralyn. Or Hallizel, who hadn't left the baby's side since we left Ghasta Vale. "Yes, I know. Goodnight."

She went into her tent and I walked on, not worried about whether the clans liked me at all. That wasn't what suddenly weighed on my heart. It was that I knew for certain that I loved Redvyr.

I stopped in front of our tent, staring up at the crescent moon, the clouds billowing.

I exhaled a breath, wishing for him to return quickly. I'd tell him what seemed to be bursting inside me and demand that he give me his mark. That I didn't need to wait until we returned to Vanglosa. I was absolutely certain that the gods meant for him to be my mate, and beyond that, I knew with all my soul that he was meant to be my love.

A whimpering cry jarred me from my thoughts. It sounded like a hurt wolf off to my right. When the pained whimper came again, I walked toward the sound.

"Mishka? Is that you?"

Though I'd seen Wolf run off with the pack, I'd noticed Mishka still close to camp earlier this afternoon.

The cry came again as I neared a shadowed indention of the butte wall. The clouds overhead cleared, revealing Mishka on her side.

"*Mishka,*" I rushed forward and knelt beside her, feeling along her fur for the injury. "What happened, girl?"

Her eyes were half-lidded. Though there was little light, I could see and feel that she was breathing quickly. Running my hand along her side, I felt something long and thin sticking out of her haunch. Instantly, I pulled it free and held it up to the moonlight. A dart with blue feathers on the head, the length made of a silvery metal. I'd never seen any beast fae with such a weapon. It looked more like—

Someone grabbed me around my chest, pinning my arms to my sides and knocking the dart from my hand while at the same time covering my mouth and nose with a damp handkerchief, a strong medicinal scent on it.

I struggled while the person held me hard, breathing deep from the handkerchief, my limbs suddenly going weak.

"Watch her hands," a male voice I didn't recognize said somewhere in front of me. "Her claws are poisonous."

"She's going out." That was the hard voice of the male who had me in his tight grip. "Almost there."

I kicked and struggled, but the male was far too strong to overpower, and my body was drifting, my arms and legs feeling light, unresponsive.

"There she goes," said the gruff voice next to my ear in high fae, the common tongue of all light fae.

Before I fell unconscious, I heard the flapping of wings—moon fae wings—as I was lifted and carried up into the sky.

CHAPTER 32
Redvyr

After the meal, Walgar and I had turned our chairs to face the celebration while his wife had gone to socialize with the other wives. Behrvyne had also joined us. The other clan lords had kept to the table, drinking and carrying on about their hunting exploits and trying to impress one another.

It was good to see our clans enjoying the feast, but my mind was elsewhere. On Jessamine. It had taken everything in me not to follow her back to our tent, to make sure she was alright. While those rude fuckers at the table had made me want to crack a few jaws, she had smiled like it was nothing. Unbothered. Or so it seemed. I wanted to be certain, wanted to hold her close and assure her she was meant to be by my side no matter what others said.

I'd expected some unwelcome comments, but I hadn't been prepared for how it would burn me up inside.

"Do you believe the golems are gone for good?" asked Behrvyne.

This was why I hadn't left the feast so soon. I knew he and Walgar, the most insightful clan lords, would want more information. And they deserved it.

"No," I answered honestly. "One of them got away."

I wasn't going to recount the horror of that fucking grimlock Selestos opening up a chasm of water in the earth with a word in Godjin and vanishing into the watery pit with Jessamine and the babe.

"And I believe," I continued, "that his master, whoever he is, will make more of his grimlock minions."

"Who is this master?" asked Walgar, violence in his voice.

"We don't know. The grimlock who got away called him a god."

"Fucking hells." Behrvyne drank a gulp of ale. "If a god has sent these creatures to kill us then we will all die."

"Don't be so dramatic, beastling."

He growled at me, for the insult. But he was talking like a child.

"If our enemy was a god, then we wouldn't have been able to kill his minions. Gods have divine familiars and helpers. I can promise you these creatures were made of flesh and blood. Even if their blood was black."

"Black," muttered Walgar. "Then black magick is at play."

"Aye," I agreed. "I believe this master of golems lives deep in the Solgavia Mountains." At Mount Gudrun, was what the naiad sisters had said. But I wouldn't share all of my information, lest Behrvyne decided to take a war party and head up there himself.

"Shadow fae territory," said Behryvne. "What are they doing about it?"

"They're hunting them just as we are. I've been in contact with them."

"And does their king know they've got a monster living in their midst, using black magick to kill our innocents?" growled Walgar.

"Prince Torvyn knows. I've spoken to him myself."

Walgar grunted with satisfaction. "They'd better hunt faster."

"What we need to worry about right now is protecting our own," I told them both. "I've sent word using our sprite, Hallizel, that the prince and his priests need to come to me as soon as possible. Hallizel left a message with the wife of their chief priest, Vallon. Bezaliel's mate is her sister. I can promise you they will come as soon as they get the message."

"Good." Behrvyne emptied his ale down his throat. "If you need warriors to go after more of them, let me know."

We were quiet for a while, watching our people dance and make merry. There was laughter and dancing, some of the couples venturing off to their tents. Again, I longed to return to my tent and crawl into the furs with Jessamine. But my duty to my clan came first tonight, so I remained. There was more that I felt compelled to tell.

"Tell your people to be careful of other fae creatures as well."

Walgar turned to look at me. "What do you mean?"

"Wolf brought Jessamine to me at my hunting camp near Vanglosa. She was freezing to death in the woods."

"Why was she there?" asked Behrvyne, interjecting before I could explain the point of the story.

"She was running from her own kind. Moon fae males, sent by the man her father betrothed her to, were hunting her."

Both Behrvyne and Walgar rumbled growls. While many thought beast fae were the most monstrous of the dark fae, we adhered to strict rules about protecting our females. No matter what crime she might have committed, we would never treat them ill or hunt them down like dogs.

"She had done nothing wrong," I informed them. "Except to go against her father's wishes of marrying a bastard who wanted to use her for her magick." I turned to face them. "That's all beside the point. I tell you this only to explain how I came to travel alone with her through the woods back to Vanglosa. I'd traveled this same path countless times over the years and stayed in a cave I was familiar with. Jessamine stepped away to relieve herself and a dryad stag attacked her."

"What did she do to him?"

"Nothing. He was infected somehow. When we encountered the grimlocks, I smelled the same foulness on them as I did the dryad. This sorcerer who created the golems has the power to infect other fae creatures. So be forewarned."

We were silent again for some time. Then Behrvyne said something unexpected.

"Word has it that your skald fae female used her magick and saved the children from the golems."

Grinning, I took a sip of ale. "She did. Without her, they'd all be dead by now."

"Hmm. She is different than what I expected of a light fae royal," said Walgar.

"In what way?"

"She is…genuine, but also seems fierce in a way."

"She is both," I agreed proudly. "And more."

"She also seems to be smitten with your ugly face," said Behrvyne.

I grinned. "She is."

"More than his face," added Walgar suggestively.

Growling, I shot them both a warning glare which made them laugh.

"Walgar!" shouted one of the other clan lords from the table behind us. "Come tell us about that barga you killed last summer."

"I suppose we should rejoin the others and be sociable." Behrvyne stood with his goblet. "I'm out of ale anyway."

The three of us sighed almost in unison as we rejoined the table, regaling stories we'd told more than once before. It was difficult to force myself to stay, but I was glad I did.

There were many smiling faces by the night's end. And when one of the chief's mates asked about the wraith fae boy and the two shadow fae children at the feast, Behrvyne explained before I could that they had also been captured with Bes and Saralyn by the golems. He added that it was Jessamine who had saved them. When many turned surprising looks at me before the conversation changed, I subtly raised my cup to Behrvyne.

When the fires finally began to burn down and nearly all had gone to bed, I said goodnight, Behrvyne and I walking away from those who still lingered. A thin line of gold on the eastern horizon lightened the early morning sky.

"It ended better than it started," I told him as we weaved between tents and onto the path near the rockface. "Though I'd hoped to have Jessamine at my side for longer."

"They'll come around."

"I'm surprised you so easily welcomed her," I admitted.

"That's the beauty of being a young chief. I don't carry the old ideas around in my head like the rest of you."

I chuckled. "Are you calling me old?"

"You're lucky you already discovered Jessamine is your mate, old man, or I'd fight you for her." He shot a teasing smile at me, but it made me growl all the same.

Then the sound of a wolf whimpering caught my attention. A second later, Wolf bounded toward us.

"What's the matter, boy?"

He whined and yipped, stomping his forelegs in front of me before hurrying back the way he'd come. Behrvyne and I glanced at each other then ran after him, halting suddenly when we saw Mishka still as stone on the ground in a small niche of the rockface.

Falling to my knees beside her, I felt for a pulse and put my palm in front of her nose. "She's alive."

"What happened?" Behrvyne studied her, as did I, searching for injury.

"No fucking idea."

Then he leaned across and behind me, snatching something off the ground. A silver dart with blue feathers. He smelled it, his expression hardening as I took it from him.

The scent was both unfamiliar and familiar. It was of a foreign fae who didn't belong here. The dart was made of a metal the light fae used.

"Why would they come here and poison Mishka?" Behrvyne asked.

My gut clenched. I stood and ran to my tent, because I knew why they'd come here, why they'd silence any wolf nearby.

"Jessamine!" I called as I reached our tent, flinging the flap open. My entire soul left my body.

The fire pit was cold, our furs untouched and the bed empty. A furious roar left my throat before I moved, suddenly at my weaponry, stripping my vest and then buckling my belt with a sword and scabbard at my waist.

"What is it!" Bezaliel was suddenly in my tent, Behrvyne beside him. Then Leifkyn and Dayn appeared right behind them.

"They've taken Jessamine." My voice was more beast than fae.

"Who?"

"Where?"

"That fucker in Mevia."

I strapped another scabbard across my chest.

"Wait," said Behrvyne. "You need a plan. You can't simply stroll into Mevia and expect to get to past all of his guards to find her."

"Watch me. That fucking bastard took my mate." I turned, finally fully armed, my claws itching to gouge flesh. "Today, he dies."

CHAPTER 33
Jessamine

I wasn't sure how long I'd been unconscious when I finally came to, but I certainly didn't have to wonder who had abducted me. I was sitting down, my hands and legs bound to a chair.

Finding Lord Gael sitting on a silken gold chaise in front of me, smiling while sipping his wine, sent a wave of nausea over me. I bent my knees toward each other to close my legs as best I could.

"Good to see you again, my lady," he said in that syrupy sweet voice that grated my nerves.

It was that obsequious sort of tone that my father's ambassadors always used.

We were in some sort of parlor with no windows. A wall of books was on one side, paintings of stern-looking moon fae on the other, all depicted wearing the blue and silver colors of Lord Gael's family. My gaze went to his two guards standing at attention near the door, both of them bearing the same color of blue wings.

"You've truly gone native with your beast fae, haven't you?" His gaze wandered down my dress and boots, his lip curling in disgust.

He looked every inch the light fae lord in tailored silk and brocade with shining silver buttons. His dark hair was combed to satin perfection. He looked elegant and sophisticated, yet there was nothing noble about him other than his name. My stomach curdled.

"I thought I was getting a compliant, noble lady of Morodon." He swirled his goblet of wine. "Instead, your father sold me a disobedient whore who'd rather spread her legs for demon fae than be the Lady of Mevia."

"Yes." I finally found my voice, though it trembled. "I am Lord Redvyr's woman. It is my privilege to stand at his side. I will never stand at yours."

"Glad to know you haven't lost your voice. I was afraid Selwyn had used too much of the sedative. An overdose would've killed you. But you're a healthy girl, aren't you?" His sinister gaze slithered over me again. "Now, we are going to renegotiate our betrothal terms."

"Did you not hear what I just said? There will be no wedding," I hissed.

"Oh, that is for certain. I would not sully myself by parading you in front of my people as the Lady of Mevia. You've ruined any chance of remaining a part of the nobility, or of having a place in good society. But you can still be of use to me."

"No." He wanted me to use my magick. That was all he ever wanted of me.

"There will be a binding ceremony, Jessamine, but not a wedding." His voice had gone cold, losing all civility. "It will include a contract that has new terms in place to bind you to me."

"I will not do it."

"I've already bought you from your father. And since he's washed his hands of you after you fled from the palace, disobeying his wishes, I have the authority to do whatever I want with you."

He picked up a piece of parchment and waved it casually.

"This right here says you're legally mine."

Though I wasn't surprised, tears pricked my eyes to hear that my parents had officially abandoned me. That my own father had given me to this malevolent monster.

"And this," he picked up another piece of parchment with his good hand and waved it in the air, "is a list of the fae you will kill for me."

He wore a steel prosthetic and glove on the hand where his three fingers had been cut off by King Gollaya. Everyone had heard the story. I had once felt sorry for him for being humiliated and hurt in such a way, until I'd met him and he'd whispered all the wicked things he wanted to do with me. He'd believed our children, his heirs, would have my powers. And that I would have been his weapon to help him regain the kingdom of Lumeria for the light fae.

"No," I grated through my teeth, trembling with both fear and fury. "I will not kill for you."

"You know, I'd thought to let my guards have their way with you, to take turns until you softened your resolve." His lusty gaze roamed over me. "But they won't even touch you." He laughed. "I had to pay Selwyn a bonus bag of coin to be the one to capture you and carry you back. They're all afraid you'll kill them with your magick."

I said nothing, glaring at him with the hatred burning up my soul.

"I have no patience left for you. Rather than waste my time with torturing you, and to be the honorable fae lord that I am, I am going to give you a choice between two options. The first option, you live here in my palace in comfort with all the luxuries I can afford. In exchange, you will obey my every command without question." He leaned forward, his icy blue eyes menacing. "Or, you will burn at the stake."

My voice quivered as I said clearly again, "I will *never* kill for you."

"Then you will die. I have no use for a poisonous witch who won't do my bidding. Especially one soiled from fucking a dark fae." He snorted with disgust. "A beast fae, at that."

He stood suddenly and I flinched back, thinking he meant to strike me. He laughed at my fear of him.

"They are cursing your name all over the city. The light fae whore who spread her legs for the enemy rather than marry their high lord and serve her own kind."

I gulped at that.

"Yes, that's right. It's been told far and wide that Princess Jessamine Glynmyr fled to the Borderlands rather than marry her father's choosing, running to live amongst the beast fae clans and fucking their king like the whore she is." He tugged on his silver-embroidered tunic to smooth out the brocade fabric. "Even if you escaped my palace, the townspeople would stone you to death for betraying your own kind."

"I haven't betrayed anyone but you."

He stepped close and pinched my chin between his gloved fingers, forcing my head to tilt up at an awkward and painful angle.

"And for that, you will become my witch to rule and obey. Or you will die."

His gaze narrowed as he grinned wider. For a moment, I expected to see the black striations in his cold eyes as I did in that dryad and in those of Selestos. But no, the evil that ruled this male was entirely his own.

"You made a fool of me, bitch." He pinched my chin hard. "You're lucky I'm giving you a choice at all."

"Just like King Gollaya made a fool of you, right? Is that why you want to kill him so badly?"

He backhanded me hard with his metal prosthetic. I gasped at the sharp sting on my cheek, panting through the pain.

"You have one hour to decide. My *lady*."

He stopped in front of Selwyn and the other guard at the door. "Don't leave your post for anything at all. Keep the door locked, and no one is to enter. Trust me, if you allow her to use her magick on you, you'd be dead before we found you."

"Yes, my lord," said Selwyn. I recognized his voice as the one in my ear right before I lost consciousness back in the tundra.

They exited and I heard the hard snick of the lock.

My thoughts instantly turned to Redvyr and the others at the tundra, knowing he would be beside himself with worry. I hoped he didn't think I'd left on purpose, fled from him after that little scene at dinner. He had to know what he meant to me, that I would never abandon him.

I fought with the bindings, trying to weaken them, but I realized quickly that they had wound the rope several times around each wrist before tying the knot to the legs of the chair. I wasn't getting out of this.

Focusing on my feet, I soon learned that they'd done the same to my ankles. Hanging my head, I focused on the red flowers embroidered on the neckline of my dress, the one Sorka had made especially for me. That was when the first tear slipped free.

Knowing there was nothing but death ahead for me, I hoped that Mishka was alright. And I prayed that Redvyr would know I'd never leave him without telling him, that I'd never leave him at all. For the first time, I prayed to a dark fae god, the god Vix, who the beast fae revered above all others. Perhaps Vix might hear me and save me from the witch's pyre.

Bound in a vegetable cart, I was barefoot and wearing the dress Sorka had made for me. I believe Gael wanted the people to see me wearing the garb of the dark fae people I had been living with, to prove I was a traitor. But it gave me peace that I was left with a piece of the only home I'd ever known, a gift from the only family I'd ever had.

Two work horses hauled the cart from Lord Gael's palace on a hill toward the town's center. He rode his giant Pellasian stallion, his guards riding their mounts in front and behind me. I recognized the auburn-haired guard who rode at his right side, the one who gave the speech at Hellamir. He must be giving mine today.

I noticed all of his guards were moon fae, bearing different colored wings showcasing the various bloodlines, but the townspeople yelling obscenities at me on the sides of the road were mostly wood fae. A few moon fae aristocracy watched from their carriages and horses behind the maddened throng of townspeople.

"Traitor!" yelled one man.

"Whore!" screamed another.

"Burn the witch!"

Then someone from the crowd threw a rotten vegetable, hitting me square in the chest. I whimpered when the next one hit me in the head, then another slapped me in the neck before sliding off. Pieces of the decaying vegetables clung to my skin and hair as more of the crowd threw things at me as I passed.

I kept my gaze straight ahead, even if my vision blurred from unshed tears that I blinked away, refusing to let them see my pain. Up ahead, the stone platform built at the center of the square came into view. It was eerily familiar to the one in Hellamir where we had saved the moon fae seer, Aelwyn.

The cart's wheels clattered as they rolled from the dirt road onto the cobblestone where the town square began. Mevia was a thriving town with rows upon rows of shops and bakeries and butcheries—all currently closed. The contrast of the town's civility and the screaming horde calling for my death was a sickening sight.

As we approached the platform where a pyre was ready and waiting for me, I felt a wave of calm come over me. It was as if this wasn't happening to me, but someone else. My body was relaxed, my mind tranquil, as I was taken down gently from the cart by Selwyn and guided up the stairs in a dreamlike state.

I didn't struggle or fight. I walked to my fate with my chin up, my head held high. Rather than be forced up the final step to the pyre, I pulled away from Selwyn and went of my own accord, turning to face the screaming mob. I gripped the pole at my back before Selwyn bound my already tied hands to it and stepped back, pausing to frown at me.

"I forgive you, Selwyn," I told him. "I know you're only following orders."

He flinched, his frown softening into something like guilt or remorse. Then he turned his face away and stalked to the foot of the platform where the crowd had gathered, still shouting obscenities. Gael dismounted and walked up to the platform, the crowd parting to let him through. He held up a hand, his good one, and the crowd hushed. But it wasn't he who spoke, it was the auburn-haired guard.

"Good fae folk of Mevia! We have finally captured the princess of Morodon and we brought her here to face justice." The crowd roared, then they died down when he continued. "She promised her hand in marriage to our honorable Lord of Mevia. And after the dowry was paid to her, she fled to the wilds of Northgall, absconding with the coin she'd earned through her betrayal."

More obscenities were shouted at me. He was lying, of course. My father was paid the dowry, and I received none of it. I ran for my life when I realized the kind of male I was supposed to marry, when my own mother refused to hear my pleas.

"Then she committed a worse betrayal!" He paused for dramatic effect. "She lay with one of the demon fae."

Cries of disgust and words like "harlot" and "whore" were shouted at me. I kept my gaze above the crowd, looking down the road, past the snaking Bluevale River glistening in the sunlight and to the hills beyond—the hills of the Borderlands.

"Not only did she lay with one of our enemy, but it was the lowest of their kind. A beast fae lord!"

More appalling and vicious curses were slung at me. I bit my trembling lip, the tears I'd held back falling now. Not because of what they said, but because I'd never see my Redvyr again. I'd die before I was ever able to tell him that I loved him, that I wanted to be his wife and partner till the end of our days.

"See how she cries now, regretting her crimes against our good lord."

Lord Gael then stepped forward, facing the crowd but looking back over his shoulder at me.

"Even now, after all you have done," he said, his voice ringing falsely with the so-called pain I've caused him, "even after your thievery of my coin, your betrayal with a wicked enemy, I will forgive you…if you kneel before me and the people of Mevia and swear your fealty to me, to use your magick to protect us. To rid us of the oppression we suffer under King Gollaya and Queen Una."

What he was really demanding was that I murder for him, that I become his puppet and use my magick to kill for him. But he couched it in terms so that my refusal looked as if I was refusing to protect the people of this town. They were truly fooled by their lord. There was no telling how many lies he'd told to sway them against King Gollaya and his queen.

I held Gael's gaze. "No. I will not become a murderer for you."

It was useless to try and defend myself at this point. He had them in his thrall of deception.

"Then so be it." He nodded to Selwyn.

My executioner marched to the edge of the stone platform where a torch burned, before lifting it from its holder, and then returning to stand in front of me. His gaze flicked to mine, hesitating only for a moment before he lit the kindling at the base of the pyre. Then he stepped back, the crowd erupting with more shouts for my death.

"Burn!"

The gusting wind fanned the flames, my bare feet beginning to sting with the rising heat. I had to force myself not to think of the coming pain.

Blocking out the hatred being spewed at me as the smoke rose in the billowing breeze, I looked out toward the hills again.

Movement on this side of the river caught my eye. A line of fae was storming toward the town. Beast fae. And wolves.

And at the head of the line, charging faster and faster, was the beast lord. My heart leaped at the sight of him. He was wearing a leather skirt, his chest bare, his runes a stark black against his bronzed skin. With his long legs pumping fast, a black-steel blade in both hands, and his golden eyes burning so bright, he was the incarnation of vengeance—and fierce love.

I smiled as more tears slipped from my eyes, the black smoke clouding my vision, but I kept my gaze fixed on the one who held my heart and soul.

"Redvyr."

CHAPTER34

Redvyr

My soul shook when I saw her on the scaffold, the smoke from the burning flames licking up from the bottom of the pyre. My rage renewed, burning higher than the blaze trying to devour my dear one.

By the gods, I had made it in time, but just barely.

When the crowd finally realized that we were charging up their main road toward the town square and had started screaming and running for their lives, it was too late. We were already upon them.

My command was to for my men to kill only the townsfolk who stood in our way and let the others go. But the moon fae guards of Mevia were all to die. Gael would die by my own hand.

Several moon fae guards were drawing their swords, facing us for the fight. And by all the hells, they would get one. But my first priority was Jessamine.

Charging up the stone steps, I leaped completely over the line of guards and landed at the base of the fire encircling her. Without hesitation, I leaped through the flames and blocked her body with mine.

"Redvyr," she cried, her voice cracking.

Slicing through her bonds, I swept her into my arms and launched off the back of the stone platform. I didn't have to call for him. Wolf sprinted toward us, snuffling her hair. I wanted to hold her, reassure myself that she was safe, but she wasn't. Not yet. But I would make damn fucking sure she always would be after today.

Taking a brief moment to brush my cheek against hers, I tossed her onto Wolf's back. "Go! Take her where I told you!"

Then Wolf launched into a run back toward the river, Jessamine clinging to his fur, but looking back at me.

The sound of clanging swords called my name. I rushed back onto the stone stage, where ten moon fae surrounded one fucker in fancy clothes. That had to be him.

"Gael!" I bellowed.

He instantly turned his head to face me, his eyes widening with a touch of fear. He should be afraid. I marched toward him, one of his guards leaping in front of me and slashing his sword at my chest.

With a deft movement, I clasped his wrist and snapped the bone backward.

"Ahh!" my opponent cried, dropping his sword.

With a swift plunge of my blade into the center of his throat, crimson blood spraying, he fell backward. I spun back to Gael.

He saw me coming, stared up and then leaped into the sky, his wings beating hard and taking him into the air.

"Fucking coward," I muttered, pulling the long blade from the scabbard at my hip.

With a quick aim, I let it loose, sending it flying toward my target. It hit exactly where I wanted, ripping a hole through one of his wings. He spiraled and fell.

Pushing my way through the battle, I launched off the stage and sprinted toward where he had fallen behind a building. When I rushed down the alley, he ran around a corner up ahead. I chased after him, but when I rounded the corner he was nowhere in sight.

I knew he couldn't fly, so I let my beast fae hunting senses take over. He smelled of sickly perfume and floral-scented soap, so it was an easy trail to follow, guiding me directly through the back door of an alehouse.

I stood in a storage room stacked with barrels and bags of barley. His scent led me into the main hall of the tavern. I didn't have to guess where he was, following his foul aroma to the bar.

"You can come out, Gael, or I'll drag you out."

Suddenly, he popped up and threw a dagger at me before taking off for the front door. I swatted the dagger away and dove for him, tackling him to the floor.

"This is how you want to die, my lord?" I held him down with one hand wrapped around his throat. "Running and hiding. I should've known. You parade yourself around like a great cat, but you are nothing more than a tiny mouse."

He struggled and kicked, trying to pry my hand free from his throat to no avail.

"You can have her," he choked out.

I loosened my grip. "What did you say?"

He must not have heard the warning in my voice, for he prattled stupidly on.

"You can have her. Jessamine. She means nothing to me. You want to get some pups in her, I'm sure. She's healthy for breeding. I'll even throw in some coin. Just let me go."

"She means nothing to you?" I struggled to keep from digging my claws into his throat.

"Nothing at all."

I leaned forward, bearing my fangs. His eyes went wide as I growled, low and feral, "She means everything to me." My grip tightened. His eyes bulged. "She isn't a horse to be bred, you fucking bastard. She is my gods-given mate. My heart and my soul."

A nearly silent step behind me was my only warning that someone approached. I rolled to the side, the blade of an auburn-haired guard clashed with the wooden floor of the tavern, barely missing Gael who scrambled away quickly. His broken wings dangling behind him, he limped for the door.

I picked up a table and threw it at the guard. He cried out as he tumbled to the ground with the table landing on its side on top of him. Leaping across the room, I leaned all of my weight on the table, pinning him to the floor. Using my tail, I dragged his sword on the floor to my hand and then plunged it into his stomach, straight through the wooden floor.

Wasting no time, I ran after Gael, finding him hobbling quickly back toward the fighting.

"Guards!" he cried out. "Help!"

I stalked after him. He came out of the alleyway, his breath dying in his throat as he called out again, "Guards!" He limped a few more steps and stopped, staring.

There was little sound coming from the battleground of Mevia's town center. And I knew why. When I exited the alley, it was to find the town center empty of all the fae folk. The Mevian guards were all dead on the ground, and the beast fae warriors who'd joined me to save Jessamine stood over them, bloodied and whole. Not a single warrior had fallen.

Breathing hard, spattered with the red blood of our enemies, black-steel blades in hand, they stood facing Gael. Bezaliel, Leifkyn, Dayn, Brohm, Haslek and every warrior of the Vanglosa clan, as well as Behrvyne and Walgar with a party of each of their own warriors. They all stood strong, our wolves surrounding them, staring at the last enemy to be put down.

"You see what happens, *Lord* Gael."

He spun to face me, his eyes wide with fear.

"When you take what is not yours to take from the beast fae."

He swallowed hard, glancing back at the line of beast fae warriors that stood taller than any moon fae, armed and ready should any more come barreling out from behind buildings. But I knew there would be no second assault. The people of Mevia were learning a valuable lesson. They were watching from behind closed doors and shuttered windows.

"You should not stir the beast that lives within us," I called loud enough for those hiding in their homes and shops to hear me. "If you make us your enemy, you will die."

That was all I had left to say. With two long strides, unsheathing the sword in the scabbard across my chest, I made quick work of Gael, severing his head from his body with one hard strike of my blade, my sword clinking against the stone beneath. Bezaliel met me halfway across the cobblestone courtyard, a granary sack in his hand. I dropped the still-dripping head of the moon fae lord of Mevia into the sack.

"Do we burn the bodies for them?" he asked me.

"No. This is as much their mess as it was their lord's. They followed him. They can do the work of disposing of their own dead. Maybe that will let it sink in."

"Let what sink in?" asked Behrvyne, now gathered near me with Walgar.

Behrvyne frowned as he looked at the buildings behind us. He had never been to a town in Lumeria, and he didn't know what to expect of their people.

"That when they follow an evil lord, they are complicit in the seeds he sows." I gestured to all of the fallen Mevian guards, every last one now dead. "This is as much their mess as it was their lord's." I pointed to the sack Bezaliel held in his fist.

"They won't soon cross a beast lord, that is for certain," said Behrvyne.

Pausing, I swept my gaze to all of the warriors spread across the town square. "Thank you, to all of you, for…"

My words stuck in my throat. My heart skipped a beat as I finally took a moment to think of Jessamine and how close I came to losing her.

"I am glad we were here to help," said Walgar, raising a hand to my shoulder. "We should inform King Gollaya."

I nodded.

"I will send our sprite to him," said Walgar. "You go fetch your mate."

"Thank you."

"We will meet you back at Jôhl Tundra," said Bezaliel. "I'll go with Brohm, Leifkyn, and Dayn to make your delivery." He tightened his hold on the sack.

"It may be a few days before I return."

Bezaliel smiled, as did Behrvyne who chuckled as he added, "We wouldn't expect anything less."

With that, I turned and jogged down the main road out of Mevia and toward the Borderlands. I had something to say and something to do to Jessamine that I should've done long ago.

CHAPTER 35

Jessamine

"It is good to see you again," said Haldek, standing in my old room which was connected to the stables behind the tavern. "I was afraid for you when you fled that day."

"I know you were. I'm sorry I never explained about my family."

"Doesn't matter. I knew you were on the run from someone. Just didn't know I had a royal princess cooking in my kitchen."

He chuckled, and I laughed with him. It was a good feeling being here, seeing Haldek again. This had been my safe haven for so long.

"Thank you for this." I lifted the folded nightgown, wool dress, and stockings in my arms. "And the boots."

They came from the storage trunk he kept, of course. Above the tavern, Haldek had two rooms next to his which he rented to travelers on occasion. Over the years, people have left things behind. He was never one to throw anything away, saying someone would need it one day. He was right.

I actually remembered finding this gown in one of the rooms after a wraith fae couple stayed a week with us. They never returned, so the gown was washed and thrown in the trunk of found things.

"The boots may be too big, but that was all I had."

"I'm very grateful. Even if they're too big."

"Well," said Haldek, rubbing a hand that was scarred from years of butchering and cooking over hot stoves along the back of his thick neck. "Be sure to eat. I'll have some hearty porridge for you in the morning."

"I can't thank you enough, Haldek."

He blinked nervously and glanced down at Wolf sleeping soundly next to the cast iron stove that was toasting up the room.

"You'll be safe tonight with him for company."

"I will," I assured him.

With a last nod, he ducked out the door, his horns barely clearing the low entrance before he closed it behind him. I turned the bolt in the lock. Wolf opened his sleepy eyes, checked on me, then closed them again.

I took a moment to survey the room that had once been my sanctuary. Haldek had cleaned it, leaning my metal tub against the far wall out of the way. He'd even made my bed, because I know I'd left it unmade.

I only ever made it on my off days. Haldek had us up and chopping vegetables and baking bread very early in the mornings. Other than that, he'd left everything in its place.

Setting the clothes on the bed, I stepped over to my desk, finding the notebook where I'd scribbled several recipes. I picked it up and flipped through them, smiling that I had this again, excited to show it to Shearah. As well as the stews and vegetable pies, I had several recipes for breads made with spices and herbs.

I opened the narrow closet next to my bed, finding my extra dress and winter cloak. I fingered the thick wool lapel.

"If only I'd been wearing you the day I left."

I shivered, remembering that day I ran into the woods, nearly freezing to death. Until Wolf found me. Then Redvyr.

Sighing, I turned to the tub and lifted it from against the wall, setting it near the stove. Haldek had brought me two buckets of warm water along with the clothes. That wouldn't fill the tub, but it was plenty enough to scrub myself clean.

"Oh, my lavender oil," I said aloud, turning to my desk and opening the drawer.

Yes, my soaps and oils were still there. I'd made the oils myself last summer, the soaps I had bought from a wood fae traveling along the Borderlands to sell her wares. Taking a fresh-scented bar and my oils, I stripped Sorka's dress from my body.

The water was shallow in my little tub, but it still felt divine. I managed to scrub myself clean and wash my hair before the water cooled. Toweling off, I dressed in the simple, white gown, which smelled of Haldek's cleaning soap. Everything was a reminder of safety and belonging. I'd missed this place more than I realized.

But I missed Redvyr and the clan even more. After combing my hair, I sat in front of the wood-burning stove to let it dry. Petting Wolf's head, I thought back to earlier today, to the moment I thought I would die, before seeing Redvyr racing toward Mevia from the field between the town and the river.

"He's coming to get me, isn't he?" I asked Wolf.

He didn't even open his eyes, breathing deep as I petted him from his head down his spine.

Haldek hadn't known I was coming. When I explained briefly what had happened, and that Wolf had come straight here, he'd said, "Meer-wolves aren't normal animals. They're far smarter than you think. His master told him to come here."

Then he set about finding me clothes and food.

Oh, the food.

Standing, I sat on the bed and took the tray from the nightstand. I smiled at what he'd plated for me. Two mincemeat pies, my favorite. He made them often in the winter, using the dried fruit of summer, heavily sugared, and added spices. There were also three slices of yellow cheese and a healthy scoop of red-berry jam. A small pot of tea sat next to a cup.

I settled in and filled my belly, reminding myself I needed to make these mincemeat pies for the clan. Haldek had taught me his secret of taking the pies out before they were fully baked and washing the top crust in butter, then sprinkling some extra sugar on top before popping them back in the oven to bake a little longer. They were delicious and filling, especially on cold winter nights. I glanced outside, wondering yet again where Redvyr was.

Wolf suddenly chuffed and lifted his head. I jumped, clinking my teacup against the saucer before I hopped up and walked to the window. Wolf whined at the door. As soon as I looked out, I saw the unmistakable figure of Redvyr under the moonlight walking toward the barn.

Nudging Wolf aside with my hip, I threw the door open. I didn't even have time to blink before Redvyr scooped me up into his arms, lifting my feet off the floor. He kicked the door shut and turned us, pressing my back into the door, his mouth nuzzling my throat.

"By the gods, you smell so fucking good."

"Are you hurt?" I gripped him around the shoulders, lifting a leg to wrap at his waist.

"Only my heart, love." He skated his mouth up my throat, nipping along my jaw.

His hair was damp and he smelled of river water. "Did you fall into the river?"

"I jumped." He angled his mouth over mine and delved his tongue inside, pressing his body to mine, pinning me against the door.

I moaned into his mouth, rubbing my sex against his hard cock which pressed between my legs. "Why would you do that?" I panted against his mouth. "You're going to freeze."

"Baby, I'm burning up." Something snapped, and then his hide skirt was gone.

I moaned louder, rocking against him as he reached between us and ripped my gown up the middle. I wrapped my other leg around his hip.

"Yes," I whispered, reaching down and taking hold of his thick cock.

He sucked in a breath between his teeth, clenching a fist in my hair, tugging my head back as I slid the head of his cock along my cunt, so slick for him already.

With a deep thrust, he seated himself deep, to the hilt. I gasped, my mouth falling open, my eyes half-lidded. His eyes glowed golden and fierce.

His cock thickened, tightening our connection as I writhed on him.

"I prayed to your god Vix to save me," I confessed.

"It wasn't Vix who saved you." His voice rolled deep and dangerous. "*I* saved you." He slid out halfway and then thrusted back inside me. "You are *mine*, Jessamine." Then he opened his mouth and sank his fangs into my shoulder at the base of my throat.

I came instantly, my orgasm spasming as he gripped my ass, claws pricking my skin, and lifted me higher so he could thrust into me hard and deep. He growled, his mouth and chest vibrating against my skin as he fucked me fiercely.

"Yes, my love," I cried and moaned. "Fuck me like that. Like you'll never let me go."

He groaned and growled louder, pumping hard one last time, his cock pulsing and spilling his seed while he sucked on the bite he'd made.

His knot formed quickly, locking us together as he continued to spend inside me. My brain went hazy from the intense coupling and mind-spinning orgasm. I dropped my head back to the door while he licked the bite mark, a rumbling purr vibrating in his throat. After another moment, he lifted me, still buried inside me, and turned to sit on the bed. My legs were still wrapped around his waist, so I rested them on the bed and pulled back to look at him.

His expression was still wild with passion, but sated. The ripped gown hung on me like a robe, my naked body pressed to his.

He stared into my eyes another moment, breathing heavily, then he asked, "Are you well?"

I laughed, my cunt squeezing around his cock. He jumped and clenched my hips where he held me.

"Stop that!" he ordered.

"Am I well?" I asked, still laughing. "You just fucked the life out of me. I'm very well."

His mouth tilted in that delicious smile that made me want to kiss him. "I meant to ask if you were injured before...but I couldn't stop myself."

"Nor did you ask me if I would take your mark," I added.

His brow pinched together in concern.

"I am very well." I brushed my lips against his, sliding my tongue into his mouth and flicking one of his fangs. "And I wanted your mark long ago." I kissed him on a moan, feeling the swell of his cock again, even while his knot tethered us, unable to move. "As a matter of fact, I was going to demand you give it to me last night when you returned from the feast."

He fell forward, leaning his forehead to mine. "Vix's blood, Jessamine. When I found Mishka hurt and you weren't in our tent..."

"Is she okay?" I asked quickly.

"She is. She's fine."

"A small mercy," I whispered, rocking my pelvis slowly against his, wanting to go again. "I imagine there was no mercy spared for Gael and his men."

"None." He rolled me beneath him onto the bed, holding his weight on his forearms. "I hope you didn't want any for them."

"No. Though I am sad for the Mevian people. They were led astray by him."

"We'll inform Goll, he'll need to clean up that mess. He's the king, after all." He rocked up inside me, the knot loosening slowly.

"And what of Lord Redvyr of Vanglosa? Does he still want to marry his skald fae beneath the sacred tree?"

His eyes slipped closed on a groan as he slid his cock out to the tip, spreading my legs wider with his thick thighs and gliding back inside me. It took my breath away.

"On the first full moon of spring, my heart," he whispered against my lips. "Right now, I'm going to fuck you slow and sweet, and not so rough like I just did."

"I like it when you're rough," I admitted. "I like the beast. I love him, actually."

His eyes warmed with affection. "I may be a beast, but I can be gentle." Another brush of his mouth against mine. "Let me show you."

"Show me, my lord," I teased

He cradled the back of my head, his expression serious, grave. "I love you, Jessamine."

Then he showed me.

EPILOGUE
Redvyr

"**O**ver there." Bezaliel pointed to the copse of trees, the first bright green leaves beginning to bud.

Within the shade stood Prince Torvyn and his priest Vallon, along with a petite, fair-haired wood fae female. I recognized her from the time she had visited her sister before.

"It is her," Jessamine said excitedly, Tessa standing next to us.

"Yes!" Tessa set out quickly with Saralyn strapped to her back.

Saralyn was growing fast and almost too heavy to haul in her back-carrier, but Tessa still insisted. It didn't seem to stop her from racing ahead to meet her sister.

Murgha said something to Vallon then rushed out of the shadow of the trees. I noted that Vallon's gaze was on the sky when his mate stepped into the sunlight. There was nothing above us, which told me the priest was anxious about a possible attack. The grimlocks.

"She's so big!" Murgha gushed, lifting a wriggling Saralyn out of the carrier.

"Isn't she?" Tessa beamed. "Murgha, this is Jessamine, our Lady of Vanglosa."

I couldn't help but smile, the title of my mate and wife being freely given. Bezaliel and I walked alongside the women toward the two shadow fae still standing beneath the trees up ahead.

"It's a pleasure to meet you again," Murgha said, referring to how Jessamine had served Vallon and his mate, Murgha, in Haldek's tavern several months ago. "I'm so happy my sister has a new friend in the clan."

"It is good to see you too," said Jessamine. "I feel so fortunate myself. Tessa has been such a dear helping me acclimate to clan life."

"Well, it makes my heart happy all the same," said Murgha as the women led the way over to the prince and his priest.

"You still owe me an apology," murmured Bezaliel under his breath.

"What are you talking about?"

"You swore it would never happen." He pointed between me and Jessamine. "Seeing as I presented you to the clan as lord and lady of Vanglosa a few days ago, I think it's high time you gave me that apology."

Sighing, I said, "Sorry that you're a cocky know-it-all and that you happened to be right about Jessamine."

"I suppose that'll have to do." He smirked as we finally made our way to the canopy of trees.

"It took you long enough," I told the prince as we stopped in front of them.

"We've been occupied." It was Vallon who spoke, his red eyes watchful and wary of our surroundings. "We didn't receive your message until recently. And you left your winter camp early. It took us longer to travel."

His quick side glance at Murgha was explanation enough. They'd decided to bring Murgha with them for their meeting with us. Interesting.

"We found your grimlocks," Bezaliel said gruffly, all levity gone from his voice now. "They abducted both my child and another from our clan."

Murgha, who was still holding Saralyn, went pale. "Oh, gods." She jerked her gaze to Tessa. "Did they hurt her?"

"We were fortunate that they did not," I told them. "And Jessamine used her magick to lure them out."

Prince Torvyn, his cool expression pinching with a frown, finally spoke. "How did she manage this?"

I looked at Jessamine, letting her decide what she wanted to tell them.

"I am a skald fae with a particular kind of magick," she began, then she told them briefly and without the gory details about what happened, but she did include that Farla, Tylok's wife, was murdered trying to protect her children in the end.

"How terrible for you all," said Murgha, wrapping an arm around her sister's waist.

"And Tylok's children are still with you?" asked Vallon.

"They are." I glanced back toward our camp, pointing to the field on the right where they played with the other children in the clan, the wolves on guard. Tylok's son and daughter were easy to pick out with their small wings tucked against their backs, still visible from over here. "They are welcome to stay with us, if there is no place for them in Gadlizel."

We all knew that Tylok was excommunicated for taking a wood fae female as his wife. I glanced at Murgha, wondering how the priest had managed to get the approval of their king. Or if he'd ever told them at all.

"We will bring them back to Gadlizel," said the prince.

"Your father will allow it?" I wanted to know what the state of affairs was in Gadlizel, since no one had heard from his father or his ambassadors in some time.

Prince Torvyn held my gaze, expression stoic as always. "They will be welcome in our city."

"They are orphans, after all," said Vallon.

"Aye," said Bezaliel. "You could lie about where they came from."

Vallon and Prince Torvyn shared a knowing look, which proved that was exactly what they planned to do.

"There is something more I must tell you," Jessamine interjected. "Among the grimlocks we encountered, the one who was their leader, he called himself Selestos. He said his master named him after an old god."

Prince Torvyn's blank expression hardened, his brow pinching with concern.

"You've heard this name before," I said as a fact, not a question.

He seemed to be considering something before he finally said, "Selestos is the name of one of Solzkin's many children. He was beget from a sea vyrm."

Jessamine laughed darkly. "The god Solzkin mated with a serpent monster?"

"It's an old story. She shimmered in the ocean and sang a melancholy song that captured Solzkin's heart. He followed her into the darker depths of the Nemian Sea. There, he caught her and violated her. The following year, she died giving birth to a son. Before she died, she named him Selestos, the Godjin word for menace. From that point forward, Selestos began to kill, pillage, and rape his way across the living world. Solzkin avoided his offspring, denying any claim to him. Until one day, Selestos descended on a dryad coven and fed on them. Solzkin caged his prodigy in the eleventh hell, so he could never rise again."

For a moment, no one spoke, the horror of this story almost as frightening as hearing Prince Torvyn speak more than seven words at once. It was Jessamine who broke the reverie.

"Is this a legend, or is it true?" She stepped closer to my side.

"There is always truth in legends, my lady," he answered.

I placed a hand at the small of her back. "It seems legend is becoming reality. Selestos is the leader of his master's golems. We killed all of the grimlocks in his pack, but he got away. This sorcerer who created him may also conjure more grimlocks."

"There are more." Vallon's gaze flicked to the skies through the trees again. "That is what took us so long to get here. We've found and killed three different hordes in the foothills of the Solgavia Mountains."

I tensed, a prickle of fear raising the hairs on my neck.

"These creatures," added Jessamine, "are god-touched. Though they were created with black magick, I sensed a veil of divinity around them."

I grunted, adding, "You need to find this sorcerer. And kill him."

Prince Torvyn's expression remained unreadable. "We are looking." Then he turned his gaze on Jessamine and with a softer tone added, "You are correct, my lady. They are god-touched."

"That is why we need a god seer," said Vallon.

I huffed a laugh. "If your king hadn't excommunicated all of them, you might have one in Gadlizel."

Vallon frowned. "Agreed. Nevertheless, we still need to find one who will work with us."

God seers were few and far between. They were clairvoyants who could commune with the gods and divine their will.

"You are asking the wrong fae," I told them. "We have Lorelyn, but she is a world seer."

"I know who you can ask," said Tessa, bouncing Saralyn on her hip, the babe twirling a dark lock of her mother's hair around her tiny claw-tipped fingers. Then she looked at Jessamine, "Aelwyn."

"Yes," Jessamine said excitedly. "In Hellamir, we saved a moon fae female who was about to be burned at the stake. She was a god seer."

"What?" Murgha asked in horror.

"I know. It's a long story." Tessa glanced at me, certainly noticing how tense I was at the mention of the Mevians.

Jessamine laced her fingers through mine and squeezed, instantly washing away the anger building inside me. Then Tessa went on.

"She told us she owed us a favor. Perhaps she could help us discover how to find and kill this sorcerer."

"How do we find her?" asked the prince.

"She said she was returning to Nævhail Glen. That is all we know."

Vallon looked earnestly at the prince. "We will find her then."

He returned a grim nod.

"If and when you must deal with this sorcerer, you may call on us," I assured them.

Prince Torvyn gave no sign that he would ask for help. Stubborn bastards, the shadow fae.

"Will you introduce us to Tylok's children?" Murgha asked Tessa.

"Of course," she replied. "Come this way."

While Murgha went along with her sister, Vallon close behind her, Jessamine remained at my side and the prince didn't leave.

"You are welcome here, Prince Torvyn. You are not our enemy."

He was an aloof fae, and more than a little distrustful of others.

"My priests are encamped not far away. I will return and send two more back to retrieve the children. Thank you both," he looked at Jessamine then back to me, "for saving them. Tylok," he paused, some emotion I couldn't place arresting his speech for a moment, "though my father exiled him, he has always remained a dear friend. To me."

With that, he stepped past us into the sunlight, bent his legs and opened his vast black wings before lifting off in a whoosh of wind. We watched him in silence as he banked north toward the Solgavia Mountains.

"Well," said Jessamine, "he's a strange prince."

"He is," I agreed. "There's something wrong in his father's kingdom. Though no one really knows." I shrugged. "And it's none of my concern."

"Unless they need help when they find this sorcerer or whatever he is."

"Whatever he is? What do you think this fae is, who's conjuring golems?"

Her green eyes grew distant, worried. "I don't know. But he's more than fae."

I took her hand. "Let's not worry about that now. I want to enjoy this fine spring weather with my new wife." I tugged her closer, our hands still laced.

She went up on her tiptoes, tilting her head back as I bent for a sweet kiss. When I went to coax her mouth open for more, she broke the kiss and pulled me out of the shade of trees, but not toward Vanglosa.

"Where are you taking me?"

"You'll see." She smiled over her shoulder. I couldn't fight her when she looked at me like that. So I followed helplessly.

She prattled about the red and purple wildflowers beginning to bloom, and how she wanted to start an herb garden to introduce some of her own recipes alongside Shearah. I smiled and listened, content simply to be in her company, knowing she was mine now.

I tugged her to a stop when we rounded the top of a small hill, Lake Moreen spreading out like a vivid sheet of blue glass, glistening in the sunlight. It was beautiful, and yet, my gut clenched at the sight of it.

Jessamine wrapped both of her arms around one of mine, hugging me close. "I want you to go swimming with me," she whispered soberly.

Gazing down at her, I shook my head. "I can't. You know I can't."

Her face was serene, her gem-green eyes empathetic. "Yes, my love. You can. You must face this fear and this guilt you carry. Your mother would not want you to bear it. Her pain and grief was her own. It wasn't yours."

I swallowed hard and stared out at the lake. It looked tranquil and inviting. Still, my entire soul shrank at the thought of stepping inside it.

"You have given me a home and a new life," she added in a soft tone, like the wind whirling off the lake. "And you have given me protection. Not just from my past, but from my father."

I met her gaze.

Her mouth quirked on one side. "Yes. I know that you sent my father a message, to keep me safe."

I wondered who had told her that I'd sent Bezaliel to deliver Gael's head in a sack to the *noble* King of Morodon. My message was simple: Jessamine is no longer your daughter. She is under the protection of Lord Redvyr of the beast fae. If you decide to come looking for her, you will meet your end.

"You don't think me beastly for it?" I asked her.

"I think you're wonderful. You are the male I've always wanted and needed. Someone who truly loves me." She tightened her grip on my shoulder. "You gave me a gift I never dreamed to have. Now I want to give something back."

She looked out at the lake. So did I, not understanding what kind of a gift it would be to swim in the lake that only reminded me of my past misery and tragic childhood.

"Come." She pressed a kiss to my bare bicep. "Swim with your new wife."

I let her guide me down the hill to the embankment, unsure and hesitant. But then she backed away, facing me as she unlaced the bodice of her dress, loosening it enough to slide it off her body. She shuffled off her slippers, her pale skin bright under the noonday sun.

Then her magick rippled in the air, her skin glowing white, her syrenskyn markings illuminating in their intricate and beautiful pattern.

"Come in with me, Red," she teased, backing up slowly toward the lake.

"That's not fair, witch."

She laughed, the sound capturing my very soul as she entered the lake, the water rising past her ankles then to her knees.

"You know, there is a tradition in skald fae culture," she said in that alluring voice she used when we were under the furs of our bed. She stopped when the water reached her thighs, gliding her fingertips back and forth along the surface, creating sinuous ripples.

"What is this tradition?" I asked, my cock hardening and pressing against the leather of my skirt.

"Newly married skald fae couples find a peaceful body of water and make love there. To be honest, skald fae believe they are not officially bonded in marriage until they've coupled in water. That is the only way to receive a blessing from our goddess Nemia for a fruitful and prosperous couple."

"Fruitful?" I asked, arching a brow while unbuckling the belt of my skirt and tossing it aside.

Her gaze wandered southward and my cock hardened more. I was already barefoot and bare-chested, so I walked to the edge of the lake, staring down at the lapping ripples against the bank. For a moment, my thoughts flicked back to the day I found my mother's body in the water, a shiver creeping over me.

"Yes, Redvyr. Fruitful. I want to have lots of little horned babies with you."

My attention shot up to her. She grinned and held out her hand.

"Come to me, my love. Let's start a new life together."

So I waded into the waters of Lake Moreen and made love to my wife. The sensation went beyond the simple pleasure of sex. The ecstasy was a new entity all its own—burning passion, deep love, and a new beginning. It was indeed a gift.

Yes, Jessamine, Lady of Vanglosa, was my mate, my beloved— my heart and my soul. And I couldn't imagine my world without her.

Thank you for joining me on this journey into the light and dark fae world of Northgall. I hope you will continue with the final book, The Shadow Heir, coming in 2026.